HIGHLAND PERIL

ANNE
They all used Anne, shamelessly, and she was resigned to her bitter fate as unpaid servant in a Cromwellian household. But even they could not dim her spirit, her beauty, and her passion to see the Stuart King restored.

MONLEIGH
He was Scotland's most notorious traitor, an outlawed highland chief, condemned for his fierce loyalty to the banished King—and even more for his fiendish way with women.

MARGARET
Anne's invalid mistress, who considered pleasure a sin, and sin an invitation to death.

WALTER
Margaret's wealthy brother knew of Anne's night of love on the moors with the rebellious lord, yet he proposed marriage—was it for love, or hatred?

Other Avon books by
Jan Cox Speas

BRIDE OF THE MACHUGH   36152 $1.95

MY LORD MONLEIGH

JAN COX SPEAS

AVON
PUBLISHERS OF BARD, CAMELOT AND DISCUS BOOKS

AVON BOOKS
A division of
The Hearst Corporation
959 Eighth Avenue
New York, New York 10019

Copyright © 1956 by Jan Cox Speas
Published by arrangement with the author.

Library of Congress Catalog Card Number: 56-9421
ISBN: 0-380-01847-0

First Avon Printing, February, 1978

AVON TRADEMARK REG. U.S. PAT. OFF. AND IN
OTHER COUNTRIES, MARCA REGISTRADA,
HECHO EN U.S.A.

Printed in the U.S.A.

For John

IT may be true, as some would have it, that death comes only once to each of us. A final reckoning, they deem it, to be faced by each lonely man in his turn; one last bitter obstacle to be surmounted before we are done with this world and may partake of the joyful mysteries of the next.

I do not contradict them. Surely we may believe with impunity whatever satisfies the dictates of our consciences or our creeds, for those who would enlighten us are gone far beyond the reach of our questions.

But that day I sat in Margaret Clennon's chamber, where the late afternoon sun slanted through the tall narrow windows with their velvet hangings, and the fire mulled quietly on the hearth and cast its reflection, like a wayward flame, against my wine goblet of Venetian glass, I learned that truth is not so simple a matter, and death does not always wait upon a final judgment but lies in ambush behind each turning of the road. We die a score of times, foolish humans that we are, and each time the dying is a torment and a pain which has no hope of surcease in another, kinder world beyond.

"Have you heard," asked Lady Leslie, "that Lord Monleigh was taken in Dundee and brought to Edinburgh to await his trial?"

Jemmy MacLeish caught her embroidery thread between her sharp little teeth and broke it neatly. Her needle flashed suddenly in the thin ray of sun which fell across her lap.

"I knew last evening," she said. "Robert was one of those who escorted him to the Castle."

"You said nothing all this while," Lady Leslie reproached, quite undone by Jemmy's rudeness in snatching away so precious a morsel of gossip.

"Robert warned me against unnecessary talk," said Jemmy. " 'Tis hardly a matter for women to discuss."

Lady Leslie sniffed. "What had Robert to do with it?"

Jemmy made no attempt to conceal her pride in her husband. "The ministers feared the English might allow Monleigh to escape," she said, somewhat smugly. "Robert's orders were to bring him from Dundee and never leave him till the door of his cell in the Castle was securely locked."

"It is said he will hang. Do you think it likely?"

"No question of it. The trial is a great mummery, he deserves none." Jemmy added, with the proper tinge of distaste in her voice, forgetting that it was no matter for women to discuss, "Robert says the sentence has already been determined. He will be hung, then drawn and quartered as any common scoundrel."

"But he is a peer, Jemmy," Lady Leslie protested, horrified.

"As was Montrose," Jemmy said sharply, "another traitor."

I pushed my needle through the linen coif I was mending, then pulled it free. In and out, back and forth, a familiar task I might skilfully perform were I struck blind; and gradually my heart resumed a slow and painful surge of blood through my veins.

Margaret spoke for the first time, and though I did not raise my eyes, I knew that she looked at me.

"I thought Monleigh on the Continent, Jemmy. Why was he in Dundee?"

Lady Leslie answered, her voice grown sly and lowered. "Rumour has it he kept a woman there and she bore him a child a few years past."

" 'Tis no rumour," said Jemmy. "When Monleigh was reported in Dundee, a minister of the kirk there had the woman placed in gaol. I fear he used her roughly; Robert says she was insolent and refused to answer the questions put to her. At all events, Monleigh came to her aid and was neatly trapped by the ruse. The woman died, I hear, but the child disappeared."

The coif was growing damp and rumpled beneath my

hands. The child in Dundee had blue eyes the colour of Tay Firth beneath a summer sky, and her mother the same. She was a small lass, reaching scarce higher than her mother's hand, and she laughed often, as happy children are wont to do, and begged for a gay tune on the lute to set her feet to dancing.

"It is unseemly to speak of such matters," Margaret chided. Then, "Which crime led to his imprisonment?"

"He has been scheming with Charles Stuart in France," Jemmy said. "The English suspect them of hatching another plot to murder the Lord Protector." Then she evidently bethought herself of Robert's part in the capture. "The Kirk believes him guilty of far more than treason against Cromwell. For once the English and the Commissioners will be on the same side of an issue."

"He is guilty of many crimes," Margaret said, "but never before have they found proof enough to hang him. I despise the English no less than I do Monleigh, but if you speak the truth about his hanging, Jemmy, we shall have reason to be grateful to Cromwell's judges."

"This time he will hang," Jemmy said positively. "He is an evil man, and God Himself will see to his punishment."

I spoke at last because I could not contain myself.

"Are you so sure that He believes in hanging?"

For a moment no one spoke. I did not raise my head, but I felt three pairs of eyes turn toward me in astonished disbelief.

"Anne is so retiring that she turns her face away when she must pass by a pillory," Margaret said into the silence. "I fear no one in Scotland would be punished for his sins if Anne were to pass judgment."

Margaret's sarcasm, veiled as always when guests were present, seemed no more than a rueful acceptance of my eccentricities, and so served its purpose of mollifying Jemmy MacLeish.

"I would not presume to speak for Him," she said tartly, "but certainly we all believe in the wisdom of the Kirk. Come the Sabbath, Anne, you will hear the terrible charges against Monleigh, and 'tis the Kirk will decide his punishment."

Aye, they would thunder their charges from the pulpits, I thought numbly, and preach with righteous wrath of the virtue of hanging a man by the neck until he was dead for no more reason than his open courage in not believing as they did; and they would think to justify themselves before the world as they had once tried to justify the murder of women and the stabbing of innocent bairns in the name of their vengeful God.

Lady Leslie leaned forward eagerly. From the corner of my eye I could see her hands, thin and knobby with age, clasped together like the sharp claws of a bird of prey.

"I once heard it whispered that he murdered his wife," she said, "else she went mad from living with him. She was only a lass, a lovely young thing, and she died within a year of being wed. D'you remember?"

As I waited for Margaret to speak, for speak she surely would, I wondered if this fateful moment of revenge tasted as sweet to her as she had anticipated, or if the lengthy years of waiting had in reality dulled the edge of her triumph.

But to my surprise, she said no more than, "Aye, I remember."

"She must have been a light-minded little fool," Jemmy said briskly, "to be so taken in by the man."

"Mayhap she was bewitched," Lady Leslie said, putting aside her sewing to better relish the conversation. "He is said to deal in witchcraft, Jemmy." The wicked word, so malevolent in itself and bespeaking such dark and evil deeds, almost silenced Lady Leslie before she had well begun, but she recovered in a moment and added bravely, "Only a few months past they tried and burned a woman of his clan for a witch. It is said she swore before she died that Monleigh had consorted with her."

Jemmy was not intimidated by any mere word, however evil. "Aye, and did you know that Robert was the one who found her out?" she said proudly. "She lived in a rude bothy on Monleigh's land, and Robert had long suspected her."

The pale sun still slanted across the floor, the fire made small comfortable sounds, the tear in my linen coif was rapidly diminishing with the industry of my needle. But I sat stunned and silent, biting my lip until the scream choking in my throat subsided and no longer threatened to escape.

I thought of the bothy as I had last seen it, a small stone hut hidden from the eyes of the world in a lost glen among the hills. The woman there had worn a plain dress of saffron color, smelling of the clean wind and sun and pinned with a cairngorm brooch, and she had smiled at me with a compassion so strong and kind that it brought swift tears to my eyes. Before I left her that day she unpinned the brooch, surely the only pretty trinket she had ever possessed, and insisted that I take it. It now lay in a small leather casket in my chamber, a bit of silver with a golden stone to remind me of a few cherished hours and a moonlit night which would never be mine again, and the clear-eyed woman who gave it to me had been burned at the stake for a witch.

Lady Leslie was growing weary of Robert's accomplishments. She turned her shoulder to Jemmy and leaned toward Margaret again.

"Did you ever know him, Margaret?"

"Oh, 'tis Anne who must claim acquaintance with Monleigh," Margaret said softly. "Is it not so, Anne?"

I was forced to raise my head at last and meet her pale eyes.

"Yes, I knew him," I said.

Lady Leslie's curiosity was insatiable. "Is he quite ill-favoured? Did it give you a fright to look on such depravity in a man?"

Jemmy laughed shortly. "He has pandered his way through all the courts of Europe, and I doubt the brazen women he keeps about him would call him ill-favoured. Depraved, surely, but it would seem that royalty dotes on the godless and corrupt."

"Jemmy," Margaret reproached, "I find such gossip distasteful." Then she calmly fed another tidbit to Lady Leslie. "Anne was not frightened at all. Indeed, she seemed to find him a charming companion."

Lady Leslie turned to stare at me, her face bemused, her busy mind obviously sorting and sifting all she knew of me since I had come to live with Margaret. Jemmy also stared, but her mind and tongue were quicker than Lady Leslie's.

"I remember Robert mentioning something of the sort," she said thoughtfully. "Was it not at Clennon House that you knew Monleigh, Anne, just before he fled Scotland?"

I took a deep breath to quiet my trembling, only to find that it began deep inside me and would not be stilled.

"Clennon House is only a few miles from Monleigh's stronghold of Torra," I said. "It would be difficult to avoid the Stewarts, even if one chose to do so."

"He has discredited the name of Stewart," Lady Leslie said. " 'Tis fortunate he has no sons to inherit his earldom. But then, I imagine his estates will be forfeited, as well as his title. He is of distant kin to the King, you know; Cromwell would like nothing better than to confiscate all Royalist holdings."

"Charles Stuart is no longer a king," Jemmy reminded Lady Leslie. "Indeed, he was never a proper one in England. They showed him fairly enough what they thought of kings and the like when they cut off his father's head and tossed his crown on the rubbish heap."

"The young Charles still thinks to retrieve it, I imagine," Lady Leslie said tartly. "The man is a rascal, like his father before him, but the English cannot abolish all kings by pretending they do not exist."

Jemmy smiled. "They've a simpler way. They behead their kings, and if he would keep his own head intact, the young Charles had best stay out of their clutches."

"Mayhap he will be wiser than his father," said Lady Leslie. Then, for the sake of the argument, "He will be Charles the Second, of Scotland and England, till the day he dies. Not all Cromwell's proclamations will serve to change the bare truth."

"I've no love for Cromwell," Jemmy protested. "But I'm inclined to agree with him on the subject of Malignants. He once said that he hoped to live to see never a nobleman in England. And in London, people can scarce endure the sight of a gentleman on the streets; the nobility are pelted with rocks whenever they appear."

Lady Leslie, who had gained her title with her marriage and valued it above all things, was offended that Jemmy should openly belittle it. "The more shame to them," she said. " 'Tis only envy that they've no pretensions to nobility themselves. Give them all titles and they'd fight to the death to retain them."

Jemmy shrugged. "I've little use for Cromwell's London rabble."

"Cromwell," Lady Leslie said slightingly. "Only a farmer from Huntingdon. And his Ironsides are but apprentices and tradesmen and scullion lads."

"That's as may be," said Jemmy, "but you must agree that we'd not have suffered so greatly in Scotland had we fewer gentlemen and more Covenanters."

Margaret spoke with a certain amount of coolness in her voice. "Because one is a Covenanter," she said, "it does not necessarily follow that he is not a gentleman."

"You know I didn't mean that," Jemmy said. "I'm speaking of men like Monleigh. 'Tis incredible that so few men could do so much mischief."

"Aye," said Margaret, sighing, "I fear it will not solve our troubles to be quit of Monleigh. There are too many godless ones to take his place."

"But none in his own family," I said clearly. "The young men of his family were slaughtered at Philiphaugh, as well as their wives and children."

The mention of Philiphaugh silenced them momentarily, as well it might. Staunch and devout Covenanters they might be, the three of them, but surely no woman lived who did not shrink from the heartbreaking memory of the massacre at Philiphaugh. There the Covenanting soldiers, urged on by a frenzied clergy, had put Montrose's defeated army to the sword and slaughtered the innocent children and women as well. Scot against Scot it had been that day, the cruel reality of any civil war, and doubtless each army could be held to blame for its share of bloody deeds; but whatever their sympathies, those whose consciences did not writhe at the thought of Philiphaugh were surely beyond hope of redemption.

"They were traitors," Jemmy said defensively. "They deserved to die, one and all."

"They were Scots," I said, "fighting for their King. Do you deem the Covenanters traitors by the same token, when they later found it expedient to change their allegiance and fight for the same king?"

I looked Jemmy in the eye, careless of the danger of uttering such heresies before the wife of Robert MacLeish. The Kirk ever had a long arm, and Robert served as one of its sharpest claws; but I had never feared him and did not intend to begin.

"Have you been a Royalist all these years, Anne?" Lady Leslie asked, with a foolish simper. "I never suspected you of it."

"A Malignant, Lady Leslie?" I said. "I wonder you should ask such a foolish question. I was bred in a minister's home, if you remember, and have lived these past years with Margaret. Would you think it likely I'd have Royalist sympathies?"

"Anne's father fought for the King," Margaret said with a thin smile. "But we cannot hold her to blame for his misdeeds. I have often told her that she must feel no shame for her parents' defection."

I had never felt anything of the sort, although I had often wished that I might claim my father's loyalty for my own instead of continually playing the hypocrite and finding myself forced to dissemble before the likes of Lady Leslie and Jemmy MacLeish.

Surely there was never a war in history so bewildering in its issues, so divided in its loyalties, so utterly confusing in its course of action, as the late civil war which raged over all Scotland and England. The first Charles Stuart had quarreled with his English Parliament and Scots Covenanters alike, had fought them separately and together; and he had met a final defeat at the hands of Cromwell on a snowy morning in Whitehall. He had lost both his war and his head, and men had imagined the bitter civil strife to be ended as neatly and swiftly as the fall of the silver axe. But it had not been ended; young Charles, the bonny Prince, had come into Scotland to claim his father's crown, and the bitterness was fired again, and men took up their swords wearily and set themselves to fight an old war kindled back to life.

The young Charles made peace with his father's enemies, with the Covenanters who had betrayed his father to the English and executed his father's brave general, the gallant Montrose; and so the armies switched allegiance, the Scots Covenanters and the Scots Royalists fighting side by side against Cromwell's English. But in the end, there had been only one victor, one man who went by the title of His Highness and yet openly despised all kings, the conqueror of all England and Scotland, the Lord Protector Oliver Cromwell.

And still the Covenanters and Royalists fought amongst themselves, and turned bitter disgruntled eyes each upon the other, and the object of a man's loyalty was as hotly questioned as if the war had never ended, as if no English army had been mustered on a defeated Scotland to insure the peace. The King's men blamed the clergy for the defeat; the clergy blamed the sins of the Royalists; and only Oliver Cromwell kept his silence and blamed no one for his victory but himself.

"Was your father Sir Bruce Lindsay," asked Lady Leslie, "and did he reside north of Dundee?"

I nodded. If she had ever known my father, she would also know of his fiery loyalty to the King's cause. But what did it matter, he was long since dead, and the wars were finished, and I was old enough to defend myself.

"I seem to recall him," she said vaguely. "But it has been so long ago. The name is quite familiar, however; mayhap he was one of Lord Leslie's friends."

"I think not," Margaret said. "Lord Leslie was one of our most devout Covenanters; we all stand indebted to his memory."

Both Margaret and Lady Leslie bowed their heads briefly to honour the late Lord Leslie, he who had died in the Kirk's cause.

"I remember very little of my father," I said, plying my needle with even greater care than before. "And my mother died shortly after his death."

I closed my mouth abruptly. I had no need to defend either of them in this company. The trembling inside me had ceased, numbed to passivity, and the strange calm which replaced it gave me the sensation of being frozen, encased in an icy wall, impervious to any further pain or torment.

I was a child of twelve when my father, riding behind Prince Rupert's great red banner, fell in the first cavalry charge at Marston Moor, and my mother died of grief a few shorts months later. My memories of them, in the intervening years, had become fewer in number; but they were sharp and clear, like well-cut gems, like those small treasures a child will cherish and hoard, in secrecy and stealth, against the fear of loss or disillusionment.

I remembered a red gown that my mother had once worn,

and the faint scent about her, cool and sweet as thorn blossoms wet with rain, whenever she put her cheek against mine; and I remembered being lifted high in strong arms, and hearing my father's deep voice about the house for a few brief days, now and again, before he rode away to the wars once more. And etched against my heart, a solace to sustain me through all the lonely years after, was the sound of their laughter, amused or gay or fondly indulgent, always there to wrap me around with the generous warmth of it, drawing me into the affectionate circle of love which was theirs for the sharing.

I had stood in sore need of some solace once they had died and I was sent to live with sober Covenanting kinsmen, I who had been born to laughter and love and gaiety; and now as I looked at my companions, I wondered if the two who had died would not think themselves well quit of a world where men walked in fear and cowardice, and no one dared to laugh or love or be amused, and the smallest pleasure stood branded as the Devil's own invention.

"How exceedingly odd," murmured Lady Leslie. Her bright eyes moved from me to Margaret and back again. "Were you quite young when they died?" Not waiting for an answer, she added, "I remember your saying, Margaret, that you and Anne were related in some fashion. Wasn't that the reason she came to live with you? But mercy on us, I had no idea that you had Malignants in the family."

Margaret's smile, no more than a faint movement of her lips, disappeared completely.

"I claimed a distant kinship, by marriage, with the dear old couple who took Anne to raise as their own when her parents died," she said. "Surely you recall how Anne came to me, Lady Leslie. It was the year I fell ill with the fever, the same year Cromwell sacked and burned Dundee. I rode to Dundee, ill though I was, and found my two kinspeople murdered and Anne quite alone in that dreadful town." Margaret shook her head sadly, as if her delicate nature could hardly endure the memory. "I fear I was not so callous that I could question Anne about her past, or indeed find it in myself to care."

Lady Leslie said, "How like you, Margaret, to put your

duty above all other considerations," and I bent my head to hide the unbidden amusement I felt.

"Walter thought she would make an excellent companion for me," Margaret said stiffly, "and indeed she has proved so."

The mere mention of Walter Clennon, Margaret's beloved brother, was enough to appease Lady Leslie.

"Such a gracious man," she said wistfully. "Such a distinguished countenance, so noble a bearing. D'you know, Margaret, I have always thought Walter to be the most godly man of my acquaintance."

Margaret nodded and returned to her embroidery. She needed no one, least of all Lady Leslie, to tell her of Walter's superior qualities.

Jemmy, who knew very little of Walter Clennon, took up the cudgels at once.

"Was it at Clennon House," she persisted, "that you met Monleigh?"

"Yes," I said quietly, "I met him there. Hasn't Robert told you about it?" I thought of Clennon House, that tall stone building standing foursquare above its loch in the far western Highlands; and oddly enough, I did not care if I never saw it again. "As Margaret told you," I continued carelessly, "I found Monleigh to be a most charming gentleman."

Jemmy looked at me with disapproval. "I've not yet been married long enough to know all of Robert's past."

"It has been most exemplary, I assure you."

"A pity one cannot say the same of Monleigh," she replied shortly. "I think your sympathies lie with that evil man. Were you so taken with him then, just as the foolish lass who wed him?"

"My sympathies are my own," I said, "and I feel no need to defend them."

Both Jemmy and Lady Leslie stared at me, mouths agape.

Margaret said hastily, "Monleigh has a strange way of deluding those who meet him. Do you recall Lucy Gordon, Lady Leslie? She was my companion before Anne came to live with me."

Lady Leslie closed her mouth. "I knew you only slightly

then, Margaret. Lucy Gordon, did you say? I can't place the name."

"Lucy met Monleigh once, here in Edinburgh," Margaret said. "She was quite impressed by his charm. I would you could have seen her horror when I told her the sort of man he was."

"I can't remember her," Lady Leslie said petulantly. It was a point of honour with her that she never forgot a name, a face, or a bit of gossip. "Whatever happened to her? Does she reside in Edinburgh now?"

"She died," Margaret said flatly, and I was forced to admire her courage in taking the long risk that Lady Leslie would have forgotten the name after so many years. "It was most unexpected, and so I offered her position to Anne." Then she looked at me, unable to resist a final barb, "Such a pity, I always thought, that you never knew Lucy. You and she would have had so much in common."

Aye, I thought, Lucy Gordon and I would have had much in common. We had both been alone in the world before we fell under Margaret's sharp eye; we had both discovered, to our sorrow, that Margaret's generous offer of shelter and food in return for friendly companionship meant no more or less than that we must learn to fetch and carry for an invalid mistress, like chambermaids, and dare not complain for fear we be thought ungrateful for our good fortune. But Lucy, it would seem, had wearied of the game almost immediately, and in escaping Margaret Clennon's thin grasping hands had gone to a strange and tragic fate of her own choosing; while I, who had followed in her footsteps, still fetched and carried, and was treated like a chambermaid, and lay awake in the long watches of the night to wonder if poor Lucy had, even in death, been happier with her choice than I.

In Lady Leslie's opinion, the conversation was rapidly sinking into unpardonable boredom.

"Monleigh's hanging will be a popular affair," she said eagerly. "I dare swear it will be impossible to get within a mile of the gibbet. Where is it to be, Jemmy, do you know? At the Mercat Cross, or in the Castle yard?"

"Robert did not say."

"I do hope they will decide on the Cross," Lady Leslie said, as if she were speaking of nothing more portentous than the weather or the sermon of last Sabbath. "I have a friend with a town house on High Street. I'm certain he will invite me to share his windows."

My needle slipped in my hands and pierced a finger, and I stared at the small drop of blood staining the white linen.

"Anne, you simply must join my party of guests," she continued. "It is so seldom that anyone in my circle of acquaintances can claim to know an accused criminal. I should think you would find it vastly entertaining to view Monleigh's walk to the gallows." She added, somewhat smugly, "Windows will be jammed, you know, and the cost of a good seat prohibitive. If they erect the gallows below the Mercat Cross, we shall have the very best view."

I could only stare at her, as I had stared at the scarlet stain of blood on my coif, equally repelled by both. I wondered if she was being deliberately malicious or if her avid curiosity, devoid of any sensibility, rendered her oblivious to the sudden chill in the room; for Jemmy Mac-Leish and Margaret, despite their pious distaste for Monleigh and his ilk, were looking askance at Lady Leslie's odious and ill-bred coarseness.

I put aside my mending and stood up. "You will pardon me," I said, the surge of nausea making me oddly faint and weak, "but I have a raging headache."

"Surely," said Margaret, quite composed. "Perhaps you will feel better if you go to your room and rest, Anne. I noticed a few minutes ago that you looked quite pale."

Jemmy MacLeish looked at me sharply, but said nothing; and I took my leave of them. I could not have remained in the room another instant with their smug complacency, their righteousness, their narrow little souls. Life was ofttimes hard to endure; and when those moments arrived when it became intolerable, one could only retire to the privacy of one's chamber, and fight bitterly against the urge to scream and beat the walls and tear one's hair, and hope to gain some measure of forbearance before returning to the cynical eyes of the world.

I could not see the sprawling bulk of Edinburgh Castle from my window, hidden from sight as it was by the tall bleak houses across the way. But with my mind's eye I saw the old battle-scarred walls towering on their impregnable hill of rock above the city, and the narrow cell where he would be pacing behind locked doors, pausing to gaze through the tiny window at the city below and the freedom forever lost to him.

Or mayhap he would sit quietly, forced to listen to their frenzied cant and ugly accusations, as Montrose had once listened; and he would doubtless present in return a demeanor of grave inscrutability, as was his wont when he wished to shut the world away from his mind; and all the while he would be looking through and beyond his tormentors to the shadow of a gibbet swaying in the wind.

What did he think of there in his prison cell, I wondered; and did he give a fleeting moment's thought to Anne Lindsay?

Did he gaze at the dank stone walls closing in about him, at the long fanatical faces of the ministers who would swarm like vultures until the last instant of his life, determined to convert him to their beliefs, unable to imagine that any man might retain the courage to disagree with them even in the face of death—did he give them a slight smile of contempt for their pains, and remember another day and another hour, when his world had been walled by the wild moors and a hot blue sky, his only gaoler a lass with happy eyes and rumpled hair? Did he recall a ship's cabin, patterned with moonlight and fragrant with the sea, or a sun-warmed glen in the hills where the heather smelled sweetly and a linnet sang, or the haunting thread of melody that was a lute song played all through a quiet star-washed night?

I did not know what he thought, or what he remembered.

But I had my own memories, and mayhap they would comfort me when the slow tears fell and the wicked pain, no longer numbed by shock, twisted inside me like a sharp knife's turning.

I put my elbows on the casement, chin in my hands, and thought of that long-ago day when I had first known that no matter his crimes, no matter how evil the world regarded him, if he came riding down from Torra with his tartan blazing red in the sun and laughter on his mouth, and held out his hand to me, I would go with him to the ends of the earth and back again.

And then the day I met him, when I first came to know the meaning of witchcraft, the day he began to bewitch me, to weave his spell of enchantment over me, and in the doing gave me life and warmth and happiness I had never known before, and likely would not know again.

Aye, I remember that day at Clennon House, in the wild western Highlands of Scotland.

2

IT was a day of grace after a dreary fortnight of rain and mist, a day of bright clear skies and high wind which penetrated even the thick walls of Clennon House and made mock of the damp stale air within.

Margaret had taken to her bed with a nagging headache, and in her chamber the heavy curtains were tightly closed. I sat beside her bed, its drawn hangings giving it the look of an enormous velvet box, and plied my needle as best I could in the poor light, trying not to gag at the acrid scent of herbs which Margaret always had me sprinkle lavishly upon the floor at the first hint of her indisposition.

It was difficult to understand how she might benefit from the odour, closed away as she was in that airless velvet cubicle; but I had not ventured to say so, well aware that Margaret's headaches were cured by far more subtle means than vile-tasting potions or the scent of herbs. She was angry at Walter for bringing her to this desolate spot; her illness she laid to his sad want of sensibility, and the entire household would step warily until the siege of headaches had run its course and served Margaret's purpose.

"I would not have thought you to be so unfeeling, Walter," she had said that morning. "My head has begun to ache from the dampness, but it would seem to be of little matter to you. And Anne does not keep the fires hot enough; this miserable chill will soon settle in my lungs."

"Edinburgh is also chill and damp this summer," Walter said mildly, "and they are dying there by the thousands. Would you prefer the plague to an aching head?"

Margaret's face grew pale. Had she been any other, I would have expected to see reproachful tears; but Margaret never wept, believing it a sore weakness of character.

"You are unkind," she said, "to make mock of my infirmities."

"I meant nothing of the sort, Margaret. I have the greatest sympathy for your delicate health."

"Am I so great a burden to you, then? You might have allowed me to remain in Edinburgh while you made this ill-advised journey. There I would have had the support of my friends and the comfort of Mr. Naseby's prayers."

I knew the reason for Margaret's irritation, for I, too, had been at a loss to understand why Walter deemed it necessary to travel across Scotland into the wild and uncivilized Highlands, and to insist that Margaret and I accompany him. But Walter was a wealthy man, his affairs demanded a constant and diligent attention; and he had seen no necessity to explain to two women his purpose in acting to the best interests of his masculine world of figures and accounts and complex money matters.

"Mr. Naseby's prayers would not have availed you, Margaret, had the plague struck. Come, you needn't be in Edinburgh to say your prayers properly."

So we knelt together as Walter prayed for our sins and asked that Margaret's malady might soon, by God's grace, be improved. We then sang a hymn, not waiting for the servants to join us as was usually the case, and Walter took his leave before Margaret could say more of Edinburgh or her ill health.

But I knew what would happen and how it would end. After a few days of eating cold food while the cook struggled with custards and broth for the invalid, of going to bed between cold sheets in a cold room, of finding his boots unpolished and his clothes seldom laid out, and realizing that his cherished routine must inevitably bow to the demands of the sickroom, Walter would be exceedingly repentant. He would go to Margaret's bedside and hold her hand, and speak with great delicacy and brotherly affection; and the next morning Margaret would push back the velvet curtains and pronounce herself well enough to arise. The herbs would be swept up and discarded, the room would be aired, the servants would go back to their accustomed chores with ill-concealed relief.

And because the servants, with the uncanny ability of all such domestics to recognize the eccentricities of their masters, knew Margaret and her habits as well as I, it did not surprise me that they had already begun to anticipate the ride back to Edinburgh.

A small ray of sunlight escaped the window curtains and slipped along the floor to rest at my feet like a bright coin tossed carelessly from a heavy purse, a niggardly reminder of the forbidden wealth beyond the windows. I kept my eyes resolutely on the needlework in my lap; but a truant breath of air, bent upon mischief and lacking my docility, caught in my linen coif and touched my cheek softly, bringing with it a faint scent of wet moorland and heather. It was a west wind, surely, for I thought I could discern a bit of salt from the sea in it, blown across the wild hills and moors from the headlands reaching out into the cold Atlantic.

I stood up abruptly and went to the window to draw the curtains more snugly. But the draught was stronger there; and between the velvet folds I could see the wind-tossed loch, and above it the blue sky with its fragments of cloud racing high with the wind and bright sun. Below the window the birches swayed, silver and green, slim and supple as dancers.

Jerking the curtains together, I turned my back to them. But the room seemed darker after the glimpse of sunlight; and I felt as if I could no longer endure the smell of herbs, of clothes and bed linens and velvet curtains too long in a dark damp place, of medicinal liquids and smouldering peat fires.

I knew, of course, for I had learned the lesson well those long years in Dundee, that endurance is not the frail and tenuous thing some think it, but is in reality the measuring rod of our sanity and may be safely stretched to fill our direst need.

But as I stood quietly by the windows, the rebellion grew inside me till I felt choked with it. There was no sound from the bed. I moved slowly across the floor and held back the hangings, and saw that Margaret had fallen asleep.

She lay against the pillows, her hair covered with a nightcap, and the sharply angled planes of her face looked yellowed as old ivory against the stark white of lace cap and linen bolster. Her skin was smooth, stretched as tautly over the cheekbones as her hair was pulled tightly back into a tortured knot, the skin without a sag or wrinkle and the hair with no single curl to soften the bleakness of line.

Margaret asleep was much like Margaret awake, stiff and unyielding, the lines of her body so constrained, so chary of imprudence even in the oblivion of sleep, that I could not fancy her ever being otherwise. Had she been a baby once, I had often wondered, with a baby's swift tears and laughter, with a baby's enchanting way of curling into careless sleep; or had she, even then, disdained such an excess of indecent vulgarity?

I dropped the curtain and left her. Perhaps fled would be a more fitting word; I walked cautiously to the door of my own small apartment, but once the door was closed behind me I hurried as if demons were nipping at my heels. I grabbed my dark mulberry cloak and threw it around me, laced the hood with uneasy fingers, and as I ran down the stairs I fought an impulse to look furtively over my shoulder.

Knowing that Walter would be reading in the great hall, as was his wont in the afternoons, I took the back stairs, for the curiosity of the servants seemed easier to face than Walter's mild displeasure and almost certain refusal to allow me outside the walls alone.

I walked sedately through the myriad cupboard rooms and halls to the warm kitchen, ignoring the expressive silence I left behind me. The postern door was not latched and I managed to open it after a tug or two; but I soon saw that I was not to escape so easily after all.

Elizabeth, the dour Highland woman who had refused to wear a cap at Margaret's instructions, stood beyond the door. Her face showed no expression as she caught sight of me, but she took note of my cloak and spoke at once.

"Will ye be going out alone?"

"I would like a bit of fresh air," I said. "I'll not go far."

"I doubt the master would want ye on the moors alone."

Had I been Margaret, she would not have dared to reproach me; but I was neither servant nor lady, but one without a title or an estate to label me, and well she knew that the invalid mistress above had not given me permission to leave Clennon House.

The wind caught at my hood with robust fingers; it pushed at my coif and slapped my face, bringing quick tears to my eyes. The sun was bright, almost blinding, as I lifted my head and looked her straight in the eye. "I shall be gone an hour or more," I said quietly, for I had no wish to antagonize her, "and perhaps longer. I am accustomed to long walks and will come to no harm."

" 'Tis as safe as Edinburgh, I'll wager," the woman said, "but that's no' saying much for it. Have ye no' been told of the evil ways of the Highlanders hereabouts, and the terrible things happening to those who venture on the moors alone?" Her dark eyes glinted in the sun. "The English soldiers ride abroad only in great numbers, and they wear swords and pistols."

I would not let her frighten me back inside. "But I am a Scot," I said, "not English. And surely no one would harm a woman without due cause, even in the Highlands." I stepped forward as if to move around her, then asked casually, "Does the sea lie due west of Clennon House?"

"Aye, but the track bears south by the loch before turning toward the sea. I doubt you could walk so far."

Looking beyond her I saw the brown hills, lifting above the trees in a close half circle which enclosed Clennon House as snugly as the stone walls of a prison.

"I would like to see what lies on the other side," I said, shrugging, "but it looks to be too steep a climb."

"Aye," the woman said, and stepped out of my way. "Don't lose your way."

As I passed her I thought I saw the shadow of an austere smile in her eyes. But when I gave her a closer glance, the smile proved no more than an imagined fancy, for her face was as dour and uncommunicative as before.

It was a sore temptation to pick up my skirts and run. I had never known such a frightening urge to rid myself of everything which touched my daily life, to push far from my mind the very shape of faces and the sound of names. Margaret, Walter, the sullen servants, the odours of invalidism, the interminable prayers and hymns—I longed desperately to forget, if only for a brief hour, all the inflexible chains which bound me to the Clennons and their virtues and vices.

But I did not run. I went across the courtyard and through the gates, and so to the woods beyond. Finding a path which wound lazily in no apparent direction, I followed it until I reached a narrow stream. It must have come from somewhere in the hills, and I watched for a moment as it danced in sprightly fashion over a bed of brown pebbles and disappeared in a tangle of fern and bracken on its headlong way to the near-by loch.

I crossed the burn and wandered up the slope beyond, unaware of its gradual rise until my breath began to shorten and I suddenly found myself on the crest of the hill.

At any other time I might have been amused at the very idea of climbing a mountain, however small and unassuming, but the sight of the moors stretching before me, rising to steeper heights all about, immediately erased from my mind all thoughts of the dull and barren life waiting behind me at the foot of the hill.

Before long I found myself in a long glen between the hills where the moors narrowed below bare brown ridges and huge boulders broke the ground to form strange, almost human shapes. After I had passed a stand of stunted Scots pines and rowans, I came again to the moor, spreading downward to a track which showed barely visible against the heather.

Then I looked beyond the moor and before me lay the sea, sparkling under the sun as far as the eye could see, its brilliant blue streaked with white where the wind raced across it.

Beyond the rough track the wood began, and I held my skirts high and ran down the sloping moorland to the cool shadow of the trees. It did not once occur to me, bemused and enchanted as I was, that I might possibly lose my way in that wilderness, bereft of any road but the pony track and lacking any vestige of civilization, nor did I recall the dour Highland woman's words of warning.

When I emerged from the trees, I found myself on a wide stretch of rocky moor which ended abruptly in a sharp cliff overhanging the sea; and my disappointment was intense enough to bring tears to my eyes. I was not to reach the water, after all; the precipice of rock dropped sheer to the water's edge. The waves washed against the boulders beneath me and I felt a fine spray on my mouth, and I was suddenly weary and chilled and uncomfortably aware of my childish petulance in running away from Margaret Clennon.

The return of reason sobered me somewhat, and I noticed that the sun was lower in the west and the wind had grown cooler. But I did not turn back at once; my footsteps, by no volition of my own, slowly wandered along the edge of the cliff, avoiding the rocks breaking the heath and keeping close to the sound of the sea. The ground, covered sparsely with heather and bent grass, gradually widened, but I could see no sign of the track and reckoned that it wound above me, out of sight beyond the wood.

It was then, when I least expected it, that I caught sight of a man directly before me on the heather.

Incredulous surprise held me motionless; for a long moment, I think, I did not breathe at all. He lay on his back in the heather, hands behind his head and eyes following the exuberant antics of a pair of gulls high above the sea. He was scarcely fifty feet from me, but I would not have seen him had I not paused to look for the track; his leather clothes blended subtly into the muted colours of earth and rock and heather, and he lay so quietly at his ease that I imagined even the gulls must have been unaware of his presence.

Afterward, when I thought back to that moment when I first saw him, I wondered why I felt no fear, no premonition of danger. I stood watching him for a time; he was engrossed in this thoughts and the sea birds above him, and there was about him such a sense of stillness and quietude that the whole world began to take on an added quality of peace and utter silence, despite the surge of the sea washing against the rocks below.

A cloud moved across the sun, leaving me in shadow, then it moved imperceptibly over the moorland and the shadow went with it, and I stood in the sun again. I heard the cry of a grouse somewhere in the uplands, and as the sound faded away into silence I became aware of the quiet blue hills reaching up into a quieter sky. Nothing stirred but the cloud and the wind over the hilltops; there was no sound beyond the bird cry, the sough of the sea.

I was never to forget the enchantment of that moment, the stillness; the strange rapt peace of that high moor above the sea.

Not wishing to disturb his solitude, or mayhap intrude upon the long thoughts a man might dream as he lay in the heather and gazed at the sky, I walked to the edge of the cliff and looked for a way to descend to the beach.

At one spot the rocks were broken, affording footholds of a sort, and I lifted my skirts and began to climb carefully downward, hoping that the man had not noticed me.

I placed one foot on a seemingly sturdy boulder, which at once began to roll; thrown off balance, I grabbed for something to steady myself and found only a rounded stone, slippery with spray. It afforded no aid, and in the next instant I had begun to fall toward the jagged rocks below me.

With that instinctive sense of self-preservation which comes to us all in desperate moments, I jerked away from the face of the precipice and jumped, thinking a hard jolt on the sand preferable to splitting my head open on a rock; but too late I saw that there was no beach, and that directly beneath me the water washed to the very edge of the headland.

With the realization came the frightening shock of icy water; I stumbled and fell, and a great slap of cold salt water stunned me. For an interval of panic that seemed an eternity, I could not rise from my knees, and my wet skirts tried to pull me seaward with each receding wave.

I did not hear him descend the cliff, or indeed think of him at all; but when I felt his hands on my shoulders, lifting me to my feet, I was more gratefully relieved than surprised.

He had guided me to the narrow strip of damp sand and thence to the wider beach beyond before I managed to open my eyes. The salt stung and burned, and when I wiped my eyes childishly with my wet hands they only burned more.

"The devil take a foolish woman," he said. "Did you think to drown yourself?"

Despite the pain of salt water, my eyes widened at the anger in his voice.

"Or did you intend to spit yourself neatly on one of those ugly rocks? God's love, it would have been no better than you deserved."

I stared at him. He was a tall man, towering over me, with powerful shoulders stretched against his leather jerkin; and his hands, one resting lightly on the sheathed dirk at his waist, had a brutal strength which could easily break me in their grasp had he any such inclination. I noted those things without conscious thought, remembering them much later with no small apprehension; but at the moment my attention was caught by his face, burned to a dark bronze by wind and sun, and the astonishing cold gray of his eyes, looking down at me with so hard and angry an expression that they seemed to be fragments of the granite cliff behind me.

"You were kind to come to my rescue," I faltered. "I did not wish to drown or spit myself, but I fear I came too close to both for comfort."

"Are you hurt?" he asked curtly.

He seemed about to step toward me, and for an incredulous moment I thought he intended to take it upon himself to examine me. Hastily I moved my arms and legs and determined that I had met with no grievous injuries from my fall.

"Only my pride has suffered," I said ruefully, "and my best mulberry gown."

The latter complaint seemed not to move him, and small blame to any man if he fails to discern the tragedy of a ruined gown; but the reference to my wounded pride only spurred him to further mistreat it.

"You've no good reason to be on the cliffs, mistress, and I suggest that in the future you restrain yourself from scrambling about on the rocks. Mayhap you'd find it safer to stay away from the moors entirely."

"But I am still of a piece," I said, quite meekly indeed, "thanks to your gallantry, and I imagine the moors are safe enough if one is not foolhardy a second time."

"I admire your intrepid spirit," he said coolly. "Now take yourself home before you come to more harm."

If I had escaped injury, the sudden fall and momentary

panic had yet left me shaken and uncertain; and the force of this man's anger, directed toward me with such curtness and cold contempt, did nothing to steady my nerves.

But a portion of my mind stood apart, as so often it was wont to do, and saw the ridiculous scene as it might have appeared to another. There I stood, wet and bedraggled, a prudent spinster in a lamentable state of disarray, while an ill-tempered man who had fished me from the Atlantic reproached me roundly and then ordered me to take myself home as if this awesome wilderness were as thickly settled with houses as Edinburgh's High Street.

I put my hand against my mouth to smother the laughter, thinking as I did so that I could not remember when I had last felt an urge to laugh, and looked at him without speaking.

He returned my gaze steadily, the cold eyes never warming as he looked. I found myself unable to turn away; something about his face held my interest, something in the lean irregular features which were neither handsome nor ugly but an uncompromising blend of the two, giving him a look of ungentled ruthlessness I had never seen on a man's face before.

"Have you seen enough?" he asked abruptly. "Will you know me when you see me again?"

I did not flush, for in the years of living with Margaret Clennon I had long since grown accustomed to that sort of brusque rudeness.

"Forgive me if I stared," I said quietly. "It is only that I did not expect to meet anyone."

"Nor I," he said. His hooded eyes moved deliberately over me, repaying the favour. "What do you do, Mistress Lindsay," he asked suddenly, "so far from Clennon House?"

Astonished, I said, "How did you know my name, sir?"

"We have few presbyterians hereabouts," he answered with no little scorn in his voice, and he knew he had appraised my sober apparel and severely coiffed hair and, by all accounts, had not found me to his liking. He added carelessly. "You make yourselves as conspicuous as the English Roundheads."

He was clean-shaven and his dark hair was cropped short in the same manner as Cromwell's soldiery; yet his leather jerkin was not of plain buff but of a rich and supple stuff, and the white shirt, unlaced at his neck, had been fashioned of the finest linen. He also spoke with a faint burr which surely had not come from England.

"You are not a Roundhead, sir?" I asked, certain that he was not.

"No," he answered curtly, "I am not." Then, with a cool insistence, "I asked what you did here. Did you follow the track from Clennon House?"

I gave him as short an answer as I had received. "No, I did not follow the track."

His eyes did not leave my face, nor did they, I reckoned from their continued chill, find anything there to please them.

"Then you came by the old path through the glen. How did you find it?"

"I cannot imagine why my affairs should interest you," I said, and at once regretted the disagreeable words. It would seem that the long years spent in learning to curb my tongue and temper were to be undone by a complete stranger who, after all, had felt obligated to save me from my folly and did not deserve unmannerly retorts simply because he was himself unmannerly.

"I beg your pardon," I said quickly. "I found the path by accident. The sun was shining and I liked the smell of the wind, and so I set out to find the sea."

Feeling that I was prating like a foolish maid, I stopped abruptly. How could I explain, and indeed why should I, the lure of the bright day and the sun-washed moors, the intoxication so close akin to madness which had brought me at last to the edge of the sea, and had then treated me to an ignominious drenching?

He did not speak for a moment. He stood looking down at me, a dark stranger with cold gray eyes and a hard mouth; and suddenly the wind struck sharply through my wet gown and I began to tremble.

"Come along," he said abruptly. "You're turning blue with cold."

He took my arm and marched me along the sand, and I soon saw how he had reached me so quickly after I fell. The precipice made a sudden turn to form a narrow cove edged with silver sand and bright saffron weed, and the cliff behind it levelled into a gentle slope which merged with the moorland above.

At the top of the rise I paused and waited for him to take his hand from my arm, but he seemed to have no such intention.

"Don't stop," he said, setting off across the moor and forcing me along at the same swift pace. "You've stood too long in those wet clothes."

"Your kindness is most gratifying," I said politely, "but Clennon House does not lie in this direction."

"I know quite well where Clennon House lies."

"Pray loose my arm," I persisted. "I've been away longer than I intended, and I must get back before they find I am gone and begin to search for me."

Too late I realized what I had told him. No one at Clennon House knew my whereabouts, not even the Highland Elizabeth; and if they discovered my absence it was unlikely that anyone would consider me fool enough to have ventured so far afield. And now I had blurted out my unenviable position to this somewhat sinister man who, from his demeanor, did not take kindly to lone women wandering the lonely moors.

But he seemed not to notice. Without a break in his stride he leaned down and took hold of my sodden skirts and threw them over my arm.

"You should wear a habit when you're on the moors," he said, "and heavy shoes. If you'd been sensibly dressed, you might have saved yourself a fall."

I looked down at my petticoats, torn and limply sodden, and at my wet slippers which threatened to fall apart at each step. The stony heath was leading me on to disaster; I might have been barefoot for all the protection or comfort afforded by the thin soles.

The prospect of the lengthy walk back to Clennon House was not a pleasant one, but I knew I must manage it even if forced to crawl the last mile. Wherever the man thought to take me, I was as resolved not to go with him.

"I should make you run," he said. "It would warm your blood and prevent a chill."

"You are forcing me, sir," I said, "against my will." When he did not answer, I added, to keep up my courage, "I dare swear I'd receive better treatment at your hands were I a horse, but I am not, and I'll thank you to unhand me."

"Aye, the best of treatment," he agreed, and for the first time I noticed that the angry contempt was gone from his voice. "I'd give you a good run to Torra, then a brisk rubdown and a pail of oats before I bedded you down in a warm stall. Would you prefer it?"

I did not turn, feeling my face burn at the unexpected turn of his humour; but I planted my feet and refused to take another step, and he was forced to a halt behind me.

His hand still grasped my arm as he turned me to face him.

"Mistress, your protests are growing wearisome."

In turning me toward him he brought me so close that I could discern the delicate weave in his shirt and see the steady rise and fall of the pulse in his brown throat. But when I raised my eyes I saw naught but the cold narrowed look of his eyes, like gray sea water beneath a wintry sky.

The day had grown, all at once, chill and threatening, and I began to tremble again. The shadows lay long beneath the trees and the sun was now pale and fitful, hidden now and again by the clouds which no longer raced with the wind but formed in melancholy slow-moving masses which seemed to roll in from the sea like a great herd of shaggy Highland cattle.

"I myself am growing weary," I said, taking a deep breath to quiet my shivering, "and my slippers have rubbed blisters. I should like very much to return to Clennon House."

One dark brow lifted, peaked like those I had once seen in an old painting of Lucifer after his fall from grace.

"You should have told me sooner," he said coolly, "instead of prattling away like a frightened virgin expecting to be ravished on the moment."

I wondered if he hoped to shock me into frightened compliance, for he must be well aware that I, who lived amongst sober and pious Covenanters, did not know how to cope with such indelicacy of speech. But I must confess that I was more wretched than shocked, and longed above all else to sink to the ground and rub my aching feet.

"I am not frightened," I said with what dignity I could summon, "nor do I expect to be ravished."

His mouth seemed less hard and austere, and for a moment I thought he might smile. "But I trust you are yet a virgin," he said, "if not an expectant one."

I said nothing, for there was nothing to say in the face of such impropriety. He took his hand from my arm and without his support I wavered, finally steadying myself with a great effort.

" 'Tis a good three miles to Clennon House," he said, "even through the glen, and the sun will soon be gone."

I think I had known for some moments past that I could not venture far without drying my clothes in some measure and attending to my ragged slippers; and the thought of the narrow glen in the dusk, its old lost path wandering beneath the dark trees and across the moorland where the lonely wind always cried and the rocks loomed like misshapen men, brought an added chill to my blood.

"It would seem to be a choice between two evils," he said, as if reading my thoughts, "and since you are in no condition to do so, I shall make the choice for you."

At that he moved, so swiftly that I had no time to guess his intentions, and swept me into his arms. I was too astonished to struggle, and indeed for the first few moments I was conscious of nothing but a vast relief that I was no longer forced to stand on my own two painful feet.

But fast upon the heels of relief came horror and disbelief. Surely, I thought incredulously, this could not be I, the sober Anne Lindsay, a respectable spinster of twenty-three respectable years who would never run away across the moors and fall into the sea, and allow a strange man of uncertain character to carry her off bodily as he might a disreputable tavern doxie.

But at that point my disbelief faltered, for I knew nothing of doxies and was beginning to think I knew less of Anne Lindsay. Sober and respectable I might be, but the unfamiliar sensation of being carried so closely, and with such ease, in a man's arms was oddly exhilarating, and I began to understand the alacrity with which some women became disreputable.

His long effortless stride was that of a man accustomed to the hills and rough moorlands, for despite the added burden of my weight he covered distance with a careless swiftness which gradually won my respect, unaccustomed as I was to such an unseemly mode of transportation.

Once I thought that I might pray for my safety. Had Margaret stood in my place, although an unlikely event, she would have retreated into the familiar comfort of her prayers and thus soothed her apprehensions in some measure.

But it occurred to me that if there were a god in that wilderness he would be an ancient pagan deity, one of those gods men worshipped in olden days with weird circles of stones and chants of exultation; and he would stride along the hilltops, his massive head and shaggy locks touching the sky, and toss aside great boulders as if they were pebbles, and call forth the furious gales sweeping in from the sea. His voice would thunder from the very heavens, and the sound of his laughter would echo wildly down the deep chasms and corries of the mountains.

And so I did not pray, fearing the consequences, but closed my eyes and tried not to think at all.

Thus we arrived at our destination almost before I realized it, and my first sight of Torra, that great mass of grim stone towering above the sea, consisted of no more than a brief glimpse of corbelled battlements etched high against the sky, and a round turret catching the sun in its embrasures while the sheer wall beneath lay in cold shadow.

Then I heard rough voices and the creak of portcullis, and like a mortified and woefully unnerved maid, I closed my eyes again and refused to face my fate.

This lamentable want of courage seemed to amuse my companion. He spoke to someone over my head, his cool voice warming slightly with laughter. "No, she is not yet dead. Evan, bring some wine."

We mounted some stairs and went on an interminable distance, and then he kicked a door open with his boot. Belatedly I opened my eyes and saw a high ceiling and carved panelled walls and the corner of an enormous tester bed. My fears, momentarily lulled by the amusement in his voice, sprang instantly to life again; but if he noticed that I stiffened in his arms, he ignored it as he walked across the room to deposit me in a tall chair by a fire which at once shared its warmth with an unsparing generosity.

He left me there and crossed the room to a heavy chest. I sat as if frozen, watching as he rummaged through the contents, keeping my eyes from the huge bed by a singular effort of will. Then he came toward me again, holding something of a deep crimson which he tossed across my lap, and went down on one knee before me. With a leisurely air of unconcern, he proceeded to remove my slippers.

Too stunned to move or protest, I stared while he replaced them with soft slippers fashioned of velvet. I could scarce credit my senses, seeing his dark head bent and his powerful hands deft on the laces of my slippers, this man of violence and angry humours betraying such a strange gentleness in his touch.

Standing again, my shabby slippers in hand, he drew a long bench before the fire. "Hang your clothes here," he said. "Then you may sit in comfort and sip wine while they dry."

I had not moved since he placed me on the chair, nor was I certain that I still possessed the wit to move at all. He must have noticed my quiescence at last, for he paused before me and remained standing there till I raised my eyes.

"Would you like me to do it for you? I've no objection, if you've none."

He made a slight motion with his hand, and for a desperate moment I thought I would cry. I did not know then his occasional way of seeming poised on the brink of violence, as if the power leashed within him was but loosely held in check, was but a deceptive guise to fool the unwary, or that he was at his most dangerous when he appeared to be lazily at ease, quite coolly dispassionate and unconcerned by the world about him.

But I did not cry, and my voice surprised me with its quiet composure.

"Mayhap I have earned your displeasure, but surely I've given you no cause for presumption."

He smiled at that, catching me unawares, and I wished childishly that he had done it sooner. His eyes were suddenly warm as gray smoke is warm, brought to life by the small flames flickering in their depths and the laughter touching his mouth.

"Aye, I've presumed too much," he said swiftly, "and teased you overlong. 'Tis a grievous habit of mine." His face became grave, but the warmth of the smile lingered. "You've nothing to fear from me, mistress, or any of my men. I cannot send you a maid, since there are no women at Torra, but once your clothes have dried I'll have one of my men ride with you to Clennon House." He added, as if I had protested aloud, "You'll find it no great distance by horse, and my man will see that you come to no harm."

Having thus disarmed me, he turned toward the door without heeding my murmured words of gratitude.

"You know my name," I said quickly. "Must I leave without learning yours?"

He paused on the threshold, his shoulders filling the doorway.

"Monleigh, mistress, at your service," he said, and bowed briefly. When he straightened the smile came back to his face. "The Clennons will doubtless tell you that a Covenanter brings out the worst in me. A fair accusation, and you may now reward their righteousness by describing your dire fate at my hands."

"I am not precisely a Covenanter, my lord," I said. Then I dared to retort, "I think you behave much like a small lad who cannot remember his manners."

"Aye, 'tis much like that," he agreed, unrepentant. "If you are not a presbyterian, you must be sorely tried by the company you keep. Did you never feel the urge to tweak their sanctimonious noses?"

Against every measure of my will, I laughed outright. "Now and again," I admitted.

"You almost laughed," he said, "when I stood glaring at you on the shore. At last I have proof that you know the way of it."

Then he was gone and the door closed firmly behind him; and I was alone with the enormous bed and the warm fire and a pool of crimson velvet spilling from my lap.

It was a dressing robe, I saw when I inspected it, but

such as I had never seen before, lined with satin and richly embroidered with intricate patterns of gold which formed a crest at one spot. He had said there were no women at Torra, and I wondered what woman had visited there and left behind so intimate and lovely a garment. Or may-hap, I thought, it was no unusual event for the master of Torra to bring a woman home in his arms, and doubtless he would find it politic to keep such necessities at hand.

I chided myself for entertaining such shameless specu-lation. Hastily shedding the wet cloak and gown, I hung them before the fire and donned the crimson robe. I also unloosed my coif and found it hopelessly rumpled and limp, and so I let my hair hang free and tried not to think of Margaret's reproach were she to see me thusly.

A tap on the door startled me; I drew the robe close about me and said, "Who's there?" in a voice which lacked any semblance of composure.

"I've wine for ye," a rough voice answered. "Mind ye open the door, else I'll drop it all. I've no' mastered the ways of a lackey."

He had not indeed, as I saw when I opened the door to a clansman bearing a silver tray, so gingerly that he seemed to fear it might shatter into pieces at his touch. I took the tray, which held a single wine glass and a delicate wine cruet of sparkling Venetian glass, and smiled at him for his kindness.

"I thank you," I said, "and regret you were forced into the role of lackey on my account."

He wore a saffron shirt and pleated kilt, and was short for a man so that we were almost of a height; and he was so dark-visaged that his black brows met in a scowling line across his face. He did not turn away after he relin-quished the tray, but stood and looked me over at his leisure.

"Simon must be daft," he said at last. "Still and all, I've never known him to be mistaken about a wench."

"Simon?" I repeated.

"Monleigh," the man said. "He's told me plainly ye were a pious presbyterian with a long face and a backbone stiffer than your stays." He looked from the crimson robe to my loosened hair, then sighed and shook his head. "The devil take me if I ever saw the likes of ye in kirk."

"The robe is not mine, nor am I accustomed to wearing any like it, at home or in kirk." Honesty, a trait I admired in others and determined to keep alive in myself, compelled me to add, "But even a long-faced spinster can appreciate beauty when she sees it. And when your master fished me from the sea, my backbone was no stiffer than jelly."

"The robe may not belong to ye," the man said, "but the face does, and 'tis not so long and pious a man would pass ye by in a crowd."

The conversation was ridiculous beyond belief, but I could recognize a plain compliment when I heard it. "Thank you," I said, and smiled again at his homely face. "Now I must ask you to tend the door for me. I am well used to playing the lackey, but I'd not risk breaking a valuable piece of Venetian glass."

He nodded and reached for the door, but said before he closed it, "Open it when ye think it time enough. My name is Evan Stewart and I'm to ride to Clennon House with ye. I'll be waiting."

If he was more plain-spoken than courtesy or propriety demanded, there was something about his ugly face and blunt speech that reassured me oddly; and I sat beside the fire and sipped my wine with a fine peace of mind. The fire was hot and my clothes dried rapidly—too rapidly, if the truth were known, for I was taking great pleasure, with a worldiness which would have displeased Margaret no less than would my uncoiffed hair, in feeling the luxury of velvet against my skin and watching the fire deepen the crimson until it was the colour of a black rose.

It was a brave hue, crimson. So rich, so proud and incautious that kings and rebels alike took it for their own— so passionate, so vibrantly alive that it bespoke another world infinitely distant from my own of worsted stockings and sober habits and frowning piety. I admired it and relished it and even stooped to covet it; but soon I was obliged to put aside the robe and don my spotted and soiled mulberry gown.

When I opened the door the man, Evan, came at once and handed me my slippers, neatly mended and dried, and so I replaced the bits of velvet with my own no-nonsense shabby slippers.

Then I was ready to leave, and it did not seem likely that my host intended to reappear. Evan led me down a long hall to a flight of steps which led to a courtyard below, and upon hearing a great deal of boisterous laughter and round masculine oaths, I looked neither right nor left but walked sedately beside Evan till he paused before two horses, one a docile-appearing mare with a high sidesaddle.

Evan put out his hands and boosted me into the saddle. But I sat upright and stiff, feeling as if I had suddenly been bewitched into madness.

"Do I hear a lute?" I asked amazedly.

I did not need his nod to confirm my guess. In a lull in the din of voices and laughter, the melody came clearly to my ears; it was a gay and lilting air which seemed as little at home in that rough masculine stronghold as did I.

"Aye, 'tis a lute," said Evan, "and from the sound of it he's well pleased with himself. I've no liking for the curst strings when he's angry at the world and all in it; he can bring the tears to my eyes, and me a man grown and past the age for greeting."

I did not ask who at Torra played a lute, gay or melancholy as the moods came upon him; even had Evan told me, I think I would scarce have given credence to his words.

"I must be on my way," I said firmly, putting the lute song out of my mind together with a wayward thought or two.

We moved our horses toward the massive gates and across a drawbridge which was deeply shadowed in the late dusk; but the thin thread of music followed me through the gates and would not be left behind. It haunted me long after the tall gray walls of Torra were hidden behind the hills; and only when Evan Stewart helped me dismount at the edge of the woods behind Clennon House did the gay lift of it fade away, as if it were obliged to cry quittance at the grim prospect of facing Margaret Clennon.

For Margaret was grim indeed, and the angry recriminations which met me at the door of her bedchamber were not so familiar that I did not shrink, as always, from the humiliation inflicted so ably by Margaret's malicious tongue.

But as I stood quietly under her reproaches, I realized that she was apparently finished with her illness; and I wondered what Walter had said or done to effect so rapid a recovery.

"Walter has left to see to important matters concerning the estate," Margaret said, "leaving only his secretary to protect me in this wild spot, and you spend your time wandering about the countryside as if you had no sense of duty or propriety." Her thin mouth tightened at the very thought of such ungrateful behaviour on my part. "It pains me sorely, Anne, that you should give so little in return for all that Walter and I have done for you."

"I am sorry, Margaret," I said. "I did not intend to go so far or stay so long."

Her eyes moved from my soiled gown to my loosened hair. "Have you enjoyed yourself? You look much like a kitchen maid whose conduct would shame her to speak of it."

"I am sorry," I repeated, for a defence was never possible before her accusations. She did not truly suspect me of anything improper, but it pleased her to make the implication.

"And well you might be," she said severely, "leaving me alone and ill in my bed." At this she recalled that during my absence she had miraculously been returned to better health and, as if I could not readily guess that Walter's absence made a show of ill health unnecessary, she added, "I am rid of my headache, but I feel quite weak from the harrowing pain of it. Small thanks to you if I had died in your absence, with no one to know or care."

"I would care," I said quietly. "I am glad your head no longer aches; it must be a grievous thing to suffer."

She turned abruptly and walked to the cushioned chair kept before the fire for her comfort. "Bring my potion, Anne," she said, her trenchant ill humour slightly mollified, "and a glass of sugared wine. Mind you pour it yourself; I suspect the cook waters the wine, the last you brought me was so sour and tasteless."

I looked at her rigid back as she settled into the chair, at the tight knot of hair and the scrawny neck only partially disguised by her high collar; and for a moment I remembered, with devastating clarity, how it felt to be carried in a man's arms and know the warmth that could spread from his smile to my blood.

And suddenly I knew why I had fled Clennon House that day. I no longer belonged to myself but lived at the bidding of those who would force me into a mould of their own fashioning; and the vision of Anne Lindsay a few years hence sat before me there in a chair by the fire, ordering sugared wine and potions that would never warm a barren soul or give life to blood already grown thin.

"Anne," said Margaret abruptly, "I trust you did not venture too far from Clennon House."

"Not so very far," I said wearily. "It has been a lovely day. I think the fresh air cleared my head."

It was the wrong thing to say. She frowned, her long nose crinkled with distaste. "I saw nothing lovely about it. But I cannot expect you to feel any sympathy for me. A healthy person cares nothing for those less fortunate." Then she added thoughtfully, "This west country is perilous for armed men. You should not walk out alone. Walter and I have both warned you against it. Strangers are not welcomed in the Highlands, you know."

"I'll be more careful in the future."

"Our nearest neighbours are Stewarts," Margaret said, looking over her shoulder at me. "They are scoundrels and ruffians, and I have warned the servants to admit no one by that name. You must also be on your guard. And their chief is a man to avoid at all costs."

I was well-versed in the art of appearing innocent. "I have never before heard of the man," I said, and comforted myself that it was only a very small lie.

"He calls himself Lord Monleigh." Then, with a bitter curl of her mouth, "The very name has come to be more hated and despised than that of Charles Stuart."

"Is he related to the royal Stuarts?"

"The King? We have no king in Scotland now, Anne." She shrugged, then pulled her collar about her neck as if the chill in her bones would never be warmed. "I think Monleigh claims some distant kinship; but no matter, it has gained him nothing to aspire to royal blood but an empty purse and an earldom of only a few years' standing."

"I will take care to avoid all Stewarts," I said easily. "They must be quite dangerous and desperate men."

She looked at me sharply. "Don't be insolent, Anne. The man is a rascal. I will not have you straggling over the moors with such a man in the vicinity. You must stay indoors henceforth."

"Yes, Margaret," I said gently. "I'll bring the wine. Now you'd best rest, else your head will ache again."

I went about my chores, sobered and thoughtful, but when I finally escaped to my chamber I found I had not, after all, lost all the carefree and impenitent joy I had known that afternoon. For there, waiting only for me to blow the candle, was the wanton lute melody which had followed me across the moors to Clennon House, and then, with a reckless impropriety, had come to keep me company in my prim and lonely bed.

⟡{ 3 }⟡

I slept dreamlessly that night, wearied as I was, and when I awoke in the dark hour before dawn I could not immediately force myself to rise.

Rolling over to burrow my head deeper in my bolster, I viewed with considerable reluctance the prospect of rising in my cold chamber, bathing in cold water, dressing with awkward fingers so that I might hurry down the stairs and take my place among the servants kneeling together for Margaret's morning prayers.

As I lay there, warm and drowsy in my bed, I could already feel the damp chill of stone which seeped through layers of rugs and skirts and petticoats; and so familiar was I with the pitiless way the hard floor rubbed sore spots that could not be assuaged by prayers that my knees soon began to ache from the mere thought of the discomfort ahead.

Then I suddenly sat upright, my eyes wide open.

A shot rang out, and then another, and a woman's shrill shriek came through my closed door with such undisguised fright and horror in it that my skin tingled unbearably with the sound. The scream came again and again, as if the woman had lost all control; and for a moment, alone there in the dark, I felt a terror so stark and elemental that I feared I might faint of it.

Then I heard shouts in the lower part of the house, and running feet, and a door somewhere slammed. In the stables just below my window, horses whinnied and stomped; and the air seemed alive with thunder as a great number of horses, or so I reckoned from the clatter, rode down upon Clennon House.

Now is the time to put my head under the bolster, I thought; but instead I lit my candle with unsteady hands

and climbed out of bed. The disturbance beneath my window was deafening, drowning out the hysterical screams
which had not diminished one jot but continued with unabated vigour; and so I pulled the curtains cautiously to
see what I might see.

Clennon House, built a scant twenty years before, did
not have a central courtyard, whereby the owner's possessions from his family to his cattle were protected by battlemented walls and turrets. It was a tall square building,
depending upon its high walls and narrow windows for
defence, and the outbuildings and stables were enclosed
by a stone wall which ran at right angles to the house
proper and formed a small courtyard beyond the postern
door of the kitchens.

This yard, eternally smelling of refuse and the stables,
lay directly below my window, and in the fitful light afforded by a pine flare held aloft by a horseman, I could
see the whole incredible scene quite plainly. Mounted
horsemen were everywhere, beyond the open gates, within
the courtyard, cantering around the house in a dark surging
line; and by the stable doors two men sat their horses calmly
as Walter's horses were herded past them.

I saw one horseman look up toward me and raise an
enormous pistol, and in the same instant I realized that
I must be clearly outlined against the candlelight behind
me. Sheer panic kept me motionless, as if my hands were
chained to the casement; I was about to be shot, murdered
in cold blood, and yet I could not move a muscle to save
myself.

But, small thanks to my witless curiosity, I was not
murdered. The man directed his shot into the air, and
others about him followed suit, making an intolerable din;
then the pine torch was suddenly extinguished and I could
see no more. There was a moment when only the sound
of horses could be heard, then the renewed uproar of wild
yells and boisterous shouting gradually lessened and grew
faint as the galloping horses surged away from Clennon
House into the darkness of the hills.

There was a long silence, broken by nothing more sinister than my own gasp as I let go the breath I had been
holding for such an interminable space of time. The
screaming, I realized, had abruptly ceased, and there were

no running feet or slamming doors; indeed, all was deathly quiet in Clennon House, and for a dreadful interval I was certain the entire household of people had been murdered below, leaving me the sole survivor of that awesome attack.

Forgetting my candle in my haste, I ran to the door and flung it open. I had no time for fear then, nor did I hesitate at the sight of the stairs, only faintly lit by the light from my door, descending into the black abyss below. I only knew that I must find Margaret and the man Robert who served as Walter's steward and secretary, and discover whatever dire fate had befallen them.

I stumbled twice on the dark stairs but caught my balance before I fell, and when I had safely put them behind me I moved less cautiously to the spot where I reckoned the door to the great hall should be. At last I found the huge handle, and I pushed open the door with a sense of mingled relief and apprehension.

But the hall was empty and silent. A single candle sputtered on the long table where we took our meals, but the chairs placed around it were empty. Beyond them the fireplace, holding only the cold ashes of last evening's fire, gaped an enormous black shadow toward me, and I ran past it without daring to look over my shoulder.

Just as I reached the door leading to the retiring hall, I heard a noise from beyond its stout oaken panels. A muffled sob, no more, but for the second time that dark morning my blood turned icy cold and the skin along the nape of my neck shivered as if a dank draught of wind had touched me.

Pausing with my hand outstretched, I listened intently, but the sound did not come again. My backbone was indeed made of no sterner stuff than jelly, I thought with shame; and so I gathered my resolve and what courage was left to me, and flung open the door, determined not to shrink before whatever faced me on the other side.

The bright glare from a dozen candles struck my eyes and I closed them involuntarily, but not before the scene had impressed itself quite clearly, even to the small detail of a drip on the end of Robert's long nose, upon my disbelieving mind.

Margaret stood before the fireplace, fully clothed, her

face rigid with disgust and repugnance as she looked at the woman sobbing quietly by the table. One of the maids brought from Edinburgh, I recognized at once, and no doubt it had been she whose earsplitting screams had first awakened me.

The servants were kneeling in a circle, as was customary, but few of them looked disposed to praying on the moment. Robert stood dressed and booted by the window, his pale face even paler, more pinched and wan than I had ever seen it.

"Anne," Margaret said harshly, and I opened my eyes.

The others must have been no less startled than I, for every eye in the room was fixed upon me with an incredulous surprise which matched my own.

"You are late for prayers," Margaret said coldly, "and you are improperly dressed."

I felt, for a desperate moment, as if I had gone daft. Then I remembered, too late, that I had somehow neglected to don my dressing robe in my haste, and now stood there before the assembled household in nothing more than a muslin night rail, with my hair still rumpled from sleep and loose about my shoulders in a most indecent manner.

"I thought you had all been murdered," I said faintly, hearing it in my ears as a woefully inadequate explanation.

Robert gave me an outraged stare and turned his back on my disgraceful attire. The servants, with the exception of the bold fellow who tended the stables, followed his lead and lowered their eyes. Then Elizabeth, that dour Highland woman, broke the strained silence by stepping forward to put her arms around the weeping maid from Edinburgh.

"Och, now," she said briskly, "stop greeting like a bairn. 'Tis over and done, and no harm's been done ye. Come away to the kitchen and we'll find ye a bit of something hot."

By taking the attention of the room to herself, Elizabeth gave me a chance to escape, and so I backed through the door and closed it without speaking again.

I stood quietly for a moment, somewhat dazed by the turn of events. The dawn had begun to thrust its pallid fingers through the windows, and in a few short minutes it would have scattered all but the most obstinate shadows; I could see almost the length of the stairs, and the high tapestries hanging above them.

There is something depressing and hostile about the onset of day, I think, before the splendour of sunrise appears to lift our spirits from the low ebb of that last hour preceding dawn. Or mayhap it is only the dissolution of night which saddens us, as any death, however impersonal, is likely to do, and we face the reality of hard truth without the veil of self-deception fostered by the night shadows. It is a dingy and lacklustre hour, when all the shortcomings of the world stand exposed to view: a carpet, rich and luxurious by candlelight, betrays its shabbiness and a greasy spot beside the table; a copper bowl of summer flowers becomes a bit of tarnished metal holding a dreary bunch of weeds; the warm fire, which danced and whispered the night away, is now but a handful of dirty ashes. All mystery, all dreams dissolve into the graceless evidence of stern reality, and we ourselves are suddenly weary and dishevelled and oddly sad, and older by another day.

It was thus on that morning, and even had I known what was yet to befall me on that strange day, it would not have cheered me as I went slowly up the stairs to my bedchamber and dressed as if it were like all other mornings and no wild horsemen had come in the dark to steal Walter's horses and frighten the maids witless.

When I descended the stairs again, less precipitously than before, I found the prayers finished and the servants dismissed about their morning chores. Margaret still stood by the fireplace, while Robert stared out the window as if he cared not a whit for the hot food Elizabeth had placed on the table.

It was exceedingly difficult to face Margaret's disapproving stare when I could smell the mouth-watering odour of roasted meat and hot bread, reminding me forcibly that I had not eaten since noon of the day before.

I spoke quickly, hoping to divert her attention before she rallied her forces to chastise me.

"I am happy to find you safe," I said. "Do you know why they came, and what mischief they did?"

"They emptied the stables, the ruffians, and attempted to molest the women in the kitchen," she said. "Robert managed to save that wretched little fool you heard screeching, else she would have lost both honour and life to the murdering knaves." She added, so outdone that her voice shook with unwonted emotion, "She deserved no better fate, the brazen wench. Slipping away to the stables in the night to see that vulgar stableboy with the dirty hands, and thinking to come straight from his bed to morning prayers!"

I thought of the lad with the bold eye and the quick smile, and remembered that the plump young maid from Edinburgh had a merry way about her when she was safely away from Margaret's stern frown. Small matter to her, I'd wager, if the lad had dirty hands and smelled of the stables; doubtless she was not the first lass to learn that a man's estate did not always determine his worth.

"So Robert is our hero," I said. "How did you save her, Robert, and how did you know her whereabouts?"

Robert's back stiffened. "She ran toward the kitchen door," he said. "I had only to pull her inside."

It would seem I had missed a bit of choice sport. The weary despair I had felt on the stairs in the cold light of dawn was immeasurably lessened by the vision of a pious Robert MacLeish saving a sinful maid from more dishonour.

" 'Tis fortunate you happened to be at the door," I said. "Were you of a mind to protect us, Robert? Margaret and I are indeed grateful to you. There were so many evil-looking men in the courtyard, I myself would never have dared to open the doors."

"That servant woman with the stone face opened the door," Robert said frigidly. If Elizabeth, just then entering the hall with another tray of food, heard his unkind remark, she gave no sign but continued around the table as if we were all invisible to her. "I was in the act of pushing the door closed when the woman reached it. Do you think me fool enough to challenge a wild mob of savage Highlanders?"

"I will hear no more of that shameless wench," said Margaret. "They must have known of Walter's absence.

I cannot believe they would have dared to attack Clennon House had not Walter left us alone here."

"We had Robert," I reminded her innocently, "and a good share of the men who rode as our escort from Edinburgh. Where were they during the fracas?"

"Abed," Margaret said flatly, apparently disturbed by her inability to command Walter's troop of men as easily as she did her servants. "Sleeping soundly in the guardroom, with their swords well out of reach."

"But how could anyone know of Walter's departure? He only left yesterday." I dared to add, my curiosity whetted by Robert's indignation, "Was anyone truly molested, or did the maid scream from nothing more dreadful than fear?"

If I had stood in her place, I thought, I rather imagine that I should have been far less frightened had a wild-eyed Highlander with rapacious and murderous intent been breathing hotly at my heels than at the dread prospect of having my misconduct found out by Margaret Clennon.

"I shudder to think," Margaret said, neatly ignoring my question, "what we might have suffered at the hands of that uncouth rabble had not Robert latched the doors against them in time. I warned Walter that we would not be safe here, I pleaded with him not to bring us from Edinburgh."

"But we are not harmed," I said quietly. "Perhaps they were bent on nothing more malicious than stealing the horses."

"Aye, 'tis sport with them," Robert said, his nose on the very edge of quivering. "They murder and plunder, and steal each other's horses and wives, and think it no more than a pleasant way to pass the time. May God wreak His vengeance on their wickedness!"

I noted another drip on the end of his nose, and tried not to stare as it stubbornly resisted the vehemence of his piety. Robert, of a sudden, seemed to bear a close resemblance to Margaret; as they stood there in the retiring hall, seething with outrage, their sensibilities affronted and illused, they were both so put out of countenance that their displeasure began to take on an identical bearing.

"Do they steal wives as well?" I asked incautiously. "Robert, you do mean to tell me that even an ignorant clansman would be daft enough to steal what he has in troublesome plenty at home. Surely you have it wrong; I wager they only trade their wives, and the sport lies in the uncertainty of it."

The two of them stared at me as if they had not heard aright.

"Doubtless they are properly punished for their wickedness," I added quickly, "when they learn they have only exchanged a lawful scold for an unlawful shrew."

I could not keep the sarcasm from my voice, try as I might. The erring maid would live to rue her transgression, I knew, for on Margaret's return to Edinburgh she would promptly report it to the Kirk; but it seemed unlikely that the raiding Highlanders stood in danger of Heavenly vengeance called down upon their heads by Robert's prudish indignation. Surely it would be more practical if he went to examine the extent of loss suffered in the foray, for the stables had held a large portion of Walter's most valuable horseflesh.

But my asperity, driven on by hunger, had carried me too far. Robert looked at me with disrelish and Margaret tightened her mouth and remembered my earlier disgrace.

"You were a laggard this morning, Anne," she said, "lying abed long past the hour for prayers. You know I care little for such indulgence." She looked at me closely. "Do you feel well?"

I felt quite well, except for the pangs of hunger and the odd sense of rebellion which accompanied them.

"I did not intend to be tardy. Our unexpected visitors delayed me somewhat."

"You are flushed," Margaret said slowly, "and your eyes are much too bright. I think you have taken a fever."

It did not seem wise to remind her that I had spent hours in the sun the afternoon before. "I think the excitement has affected me," I said.

"You aren't yourself this morning," she said, "and there is certainly a feverish look about you. The cook who died before we left Edinburgh looked much the same the day she took ill."

Robert took a hasty step backward before he thought, then turned his back as if I stood in deeper disgrace than before.

"I don't have the plague," I said. " 'Tis almost a month since we left, and I feel sure I'd have displayed some sign of it before now."

"You nursed the cook," Margaret accused. "If you are ill, Anne, I'll not soon forgive you. I advised you to stay away from the woman. There were servants enough to tend her, and your reason for being in my household is not to wait upon the servants, ill or not."

I knew the reason well enough. Margaret, the invalid, claimed the sole right to be ill in her household; and I was there to wait upon her wants and not to ape my betters by falling ill myself.

"I am not ill, Margaret," I said quietly. "Please don't fret yourself about it."

I wished that she would put aside her grievances with me and permit us all to fortify ourselves with breakfast; but the day had not, thus far, shown any signs of being a pleasant one, and I did not anticipate any good fortune from it.

"I think you had best retire to your room. It is quite selfish of you to come so near me when you are feverish and unwell."

Forgetting myself, I protested, "But I am not feverish, and I daresay my only malady at the moment is hunger."

"You are being obstinate," Margaret said coolly. "Go to your room, Anne. If you grow worse during the day, call one of the women from the kitchen. I cannot risk my health for the sake of yours."

Robert's sniff of disdain was clearly audible; and I was aware of Elizabeth still standing by the table, seeming not to listen but surely filled with scorn for anyone of so little consequence as I.

I did not trust myself to speak again. I turned and left them; and for the second time that day I climbed the stairs to my room and closed the door behind me, feeling the exasperated and bewildered anger of a·child who has been punished unfairly and without apparent cause.

Flinging myself across the bed, heedless of my fresh gown, I pillowed my head in my arms and wished I might vent my temper in throwing something against the wall, or cursing mightily at the top of my voice until my anger had exhausted itself. But I had few possessions I cared to

hurl at the wall, and the only objects within reach were
the pewter bowl and ewer on the table, unpolished for so
long that they were streaked with black much like the
leaden skies showing through the narrow window. Nor did
I know any curses vile enough to be shouted mightily, unless I employed the same invectives hurled from Mr.
Naseby's Edinburgh pulpit, which went under the guise of
God's direst wrath and so were doubtless not meant to be
borrowed at will by mere mortals.

To my annoyance, I felt hot tears beneath my closed
eyelids. I blinked them away with all the determination I
could muster, knowing too well that naught but disaster
lay in self-pity and remorse.

I thought of the small purse of coins locked in a leather
chest well hidden beneath my night clothes. The purse
was thin, for I had not been able to save much; Margaret
had always believed food and shelter to be payment
enough for my services, and while Walter kindly gave me
a monthly amount to cover my personal needs, it was
barely sufficient and did not often allow a margin for
saving.

It would be years before that handful of coins grew to
a size which might purchase my freedom, for there was
no place in the world for a gently born spinster with no
family, no accomplishments, no estate. I might serve as a
governess, or seek another position where I would fetch
and carry for a mistress doubtless as demanding as Margaret; but I would not have bettered myself and I would
be no nearer to freedom. My only hope, I had long ago
determined, lay in my fingers, for I was a fair seamstress,
and even the wives of sober Covenanters paid well to have
their gowns fashioned with care and skill. But a seamstress,
however genteel her name and breeding, must have a bit
of gold put aside, hoarded against illness and starvation
and want. I could not hope to survive without it, for I
would have no one in all the world, except myself, upon
whom I might depend.

And so I must bide my time, and face reality honestly
and without evasion, and never give way to anger, or
humiliation, or futile despair. And if I would keep what
self-respect was left me, I must not lie weeping in my bed
like a bairn for no more reason than Margaret's disagree-

able temper, and the loneliness in a gray dawn, and the foolish memory of a gay lute melody.

I fell asleep after a time, and did not wake until I felt a firm hand on my shoulder, shaking me back to consciousness.

It was Elizabeth, standing by my bed. "I'm sorry to wake ye," she said, "but I was sent to ask how ye feel."

I looked at my rumpled gown. "I feel quite undone," I said, "to have gone to bed without first removing my clothes. It will take me no less than an hour to freshen my gown, and I could easily have saved myself the trouble."

"The gown ye wore yesterday will take more than an hour to freshen. 'Tis spotted with sea water, and I doubt ye can do aught with it but tear it to rags for scrubbing."

I looked at her with a rueful chagrin, remembering too late that I had taken the mulberry gown to the kitchen to hide it from Margaret's sharp eye until I might examine it.

"A pity," I said lightly, as if the fate of a gown could not possibly concern me. "My slippers were also ruined, but I can think of no worthy use for them."

Elizabeth glanced briefly at the slippers on the floor by my bed where I had dropped them the night before.

"They were mended well," she said enigmatically. "I imagine ye might still find wear in them."

I dropped my eyes quickly. She was a Highland woman, one of several obtained to serve at Clennon House for the length of our stay, and she surely knew all about that stone fortress called Torra and its master with the cold eyes and hard mouth. I wondered if she had guessed at my misadventure and its surprising consequences, but decided she could not, without the gift of second sight, know all that had befallen me from no more evidence than a soiled gown and mended slippers.

"I feel very well," I said at last. "Who sent you to inquire?"

"The mistress and the gentleman are leaving," said Elizabeth, "and she fears for ye to undertake a journey with a fever coming on."

I stared at her. "Leaving?" I repeated inanely.

" 'Tis too dangerous to remain here without the master," she says, "since the knaves who came this dawn might come again to do more mischief. She thinks to ask the protection of a Cameron kinsman." The woman added impassively, "I know no more of her plans than that."

I remembered the kinsman, a Cameron related to Margaret and Walter through their mother, for we had stopped there the night before arriving at Clennon House.

"But she can't think to walk the distance," I said incredulously.

"There's no need for her to walk," Elizabeth said, shrugging. "Two horses were left in the stables."

"What of an escort? Surely she will not venture abroad with only Robert MacLeish to guard her!"

Again I saw a faint glimmer of a smile in her eyes, as I had seen it the afternoon before; but it disappeared, in the same way, before I was certain of its presence.

"She will take the master's men with her," she said, "and she thinks a long walk in the fresh air will do them no harm."

Standing up too quickly, I felt giddy-headed and weak from the emptiness of hunger. And mayhap something more, for I suddenly knew Margaret's intentions. I was not to go; she meant to leave me behind.

"How long have I slept?"

"Till almost midday." Then, "Do ye mean to go with them?"

"If I am as ill as Margaret would believe," I said, "she will order me back to bed. Do I appear feverish to you?"

"The pale look about ye is gone," she said only, "but the sun was bright yesterday when ye went out for a walk."

"Tell me," I said thoughtfully, "do you think Robert MacLeish would stay behind, so that I might ride the second horse, or else offer to walk with the other men?"

"Ye know the gentleman better than I. But I heard him say he intended to ride on to the English garrison. Mayhap he will seek their aid."

"A foolish errand," I said, "as well as a fruitless one. The English fear their own shadows once they leave the thick walls of their fortresses."

"Ye'd best make haste," the woman said, and turned toward the door. "They've been packed and ready to leave the better part of an hour."

"Were they waiting for me to awaken?" I asked with a faint stirring of hope.

"The mistress has had a bit of trouble persuading any of the maids to go along with her. 'Tis a long walk across the hills."

The hope died before it was scarce born. "She'll dismiss them all for such rank disobedience," I said, but did not quite achieve the lightness I had intended.

Elizabeth had reached the door before a peculiar thought struck me.

"Elizabeth," I said slowly, "why were two horses left behind? Were they too lame or sickly to deserve the notice of horse thieves?"

"They looked to be healthy enough," she said. "They might have been overlooked in the confusion. I believe they were found in the back stalls, well out of sight."

It was a reasonable explanation, and surely there was nothing in her words or voice to cause the queer chill which spread through my body until my very bones ached with it.

But as I followed her down the stairs, straightening my gown and hair as I went, I could not escape a persistent warning in my mind that something was awry in the scheme of things, something unnatural and strange I could not name but which teased my mind in much the same way the answer to a conundrum will hover on the edge of a memory and then dance away before one can grasp its meaning.

"Anne, you should not have left your bed. Didn't the woman give you my message?"

I paused there on the stairs, holding to the carved railing, and looked down at Margaret, bundled in her cloak until only her thin face showed beneath her coif and hood.

"Am I not to go?" I asked carefully.

She must have felt the weight of her conscience then, for her voice when she spoke again was less severe.

"I would not have you expose yourself to the weather, Anne. You might suffer a chill on the journey, and where would we find aid for you in such desolate country? I am only thinking of your welfare."

It was exceedingly plain that nothing I said or did would change her mind; I was to be left behind in an almost deserted Clennon House, alone except for a few sullen and taciturn Highland servants.

"How long will you stay?"

"Only until Walter returns," she said, looking at Robert. He came to her aid at once, raising his head to look down his long nose at me. It was an admirable feat, for my position above him on the stairs forced him to hold his head at a most uncomfortable angle.

"You will be quite safe here," he said coolly. "I daresay the villains will not molest you further, since there is nothing of importance left for them to steal."

It was but small consolation to me, who must remain there, that Robert deemed Clennon House stripped of importance once he and Margaret had departed; nor could I comfort myself with his reassurance that not even a murderous freebooter would attempt to molest me.

"I trust you will be as safe, Robert," I said, "behind the stout walls of the English fort."

He reddened. "Someone must report the malicious attack. I'm sure Walter would wish it."

"He would, indeed," Margaret said decisively. "The English are despicable swine and it pains me to call on them for any slightest aid. But they claim their garrisons are here to keep the peace, so I say, let them keep it. Come, Robert, we must be on our way. I've no desire to travel after nightfall." She did not look at me again, but spoke over her shoulder as she walked toward the doors. "I hope you will soon be fully recovered, Anne. Stay indoors and don't, I beg you, cause the servants extra work. They seem oddly disgruntled today, and I'd not be surprised to find the lot of them gone by the time I return."

"I find them an ignorant race on the whole, these Gaels," Robert said in answer to her callousness, "and lamentably indolent."

I could not have spoken had my life depended on it. Standing on the stairs as if carved there from cold marble, I looked down at Margaret's retreating back, still unbending and rigid, and at Robert's long face as he said with an odious nicety, "Remember your prayers, Anne, and I'm certain your afflictions will soon be eased."

The door closed sharply behind them, and the horses, with a cheerful jingling of harness and clatter of shod hoofs against the pebbled track, moved away from Clennon House. Then even that lively sound faded away, leaving only a vast and empty silence.

THROUGH the open door at the bottom of the stairs, I could see into the great hall. There was no fire in the grate, and the dank smell of a house too long closed against sunlight seemed to rise up the stairs toward me like a faint mist, enveloping me in a damp and fetid melancholy.

Of a sudden I was twelve again, standing in a cold library where no fire had been laid, waiting for a strange old lady to come and tell me that my mother had died, and that I was now alone in a world which had become as coldly empty as the deserted library.

Twenty-three years is not long enough, I thought; surely one must be vastly older and wiser to learn to accept with courage and indifference the knowledge that one is alone, and very lonely, and that the emptiness of the world is as true a reality as the emptiness of a house when all have departed it but a single one.

I turned to climb the stairs, with the cowardly hope that I might reach my chamber without encountering any of the servants. They would be more enigmatic and sullen than before, I suspected, and now contempt would flicker openly in their eyes. I had been left behind, not important enough to need Cameron protection nor yet a servant like themselves who might seek the comfort and warmth of their companionship. They had displayed little respect for Margaret beyond the mere obedience which she demanded, and now they were free of her thin mouth and endless orders, it would not surprise me to have little service, if any, and that rudely given.

But I could not hold them to blame for their dislike of us. Walter and his sister were Covenanters, and Walter had gained Clennon House and its properties through the forfeiture of some hapless Royalist. It was no secret that the Highlanders, many of whom had followed the Stuart fortunes to ruin and tragedy, still harboured as bitter a resentment against the Covenanters as against the English who had conquered both Royalists and Covenanters alike. Nor had they, like we Lowland Scots, been exposed to the amenities of the civilized world beyond Scotland's borders. In the wild fastnesses of their mountains they stood secure in their clan pride and self-respect, and were unaccustomed to being treated as lowly menials. And surely I should feel a sympathy for them, I who had also been forced by brutal necessity and hardship to strike my colours and abandon my pride, I who also harboured resentment and disliked to be ordered about.

Before I had reached the upper floor, the woman Elizabeth spoke to me from the bottom of the stairs.

"I'd like a word with ye, mistress."

"Yes?"

"A fire has been laid in the retiring hall," she said, and somehow there was less dourness in her voice than before. "If ye'd prefer to dine there, I'll bring the food on a tray."

I could not answer at once, fearing my voice might betray me. Until that moment I had refused to heed my hunger, thinking with dread of the dinner hour, of cold food consumed alone in the enormous hall while I faced the long oaken table and a host of empty chairs.

"I should like it very much," I said, and added quietly, "thank you."

"The two women from Edinburgh would speak with ye," Elizabeth said. "I told them to wait in the hall."

I descended the stairs. "Did neither of them go with Margaret?"

"They chose to stay here," the woman said dryly, "and now are ill with fear that their choice was no' the wise one."

They were indeed frightened, almost to the point of illness. Kitty, the plump little lass who had been chastised so severely for her sins, stood upright by the fire, her eyes bright with unshed tears and her mouth trembling beyond control. The other, a small thin woman of an indeterminate age who was called Elsie, was quite pale with dismay.

"Whatever are we to do, ma'am?" Kitty began at once.

"We'll all be murdered in our beds, and I've no wish to die!" The tears began to roll down her pink cheeks. "I should never have come, I should have stayed in Edinburgh!"

"Kitty, don't weep," I said. "We shan't be murdered, least of all in our beds."

Elsie clasped and unclasped her hands. "We've been listening to the others in the kitchen, and they've hinted of terrible things. I don't know what we're to do, indeed I don't."

"What terrible things? What have they been saying?"

"Those wild men who came this dawn," Kitty wailed, and I remembered with despair how she had screamed that morning.

"They've gone," I said hastily, "and I doubt they'll return. Please compose yourself, Kitty."

"They'll murder the mistress out in the hills," she went on, not heeding me, "and then they'll come back to murder us!"

" 'Tis no more than one can expect from Highlanders," Elsie said flatly, fear draining her voice of all expression. "Those in the kitchen will run away and leave us here alone, you'll see. We're the only three in this place from Edinburgh, and they've no liking for us."

"We've no men to protect us now," Kitty gulped, her sobs rapidly gaining in volume. "We'll be at the mercy of those dreadful Highlanders!"

"They've done nothing thus far but steal the stables clean," I said briskly, hoping I did not sound as much like Margaret as I suspected. "And did you never pause to consider, Kitty, that your friend the stableboy is a Highlander?"

She paused in her weeping, at any rate, to stare at me with round china-blue eyes.

"I don't expect to be murdered for no reason at all," I said firmly, "and you shouldn't allow the other servants to tease you so."

Kitty blinked her eyes at me. "Aren't you frightened at all?"

I disliked to lie to her, but it was my duty to appear unconcerned. "Of course I'm not frightened," I said, swallowing to ease the dry constriction in my throat. "The

mistress will not return for at least a week, and you'll
have few chores while she's gone. I'd advise you to enjoy yourselves, and not spend your holiday jumping at
shadows."

The reminder of so unexpected and pleasant a gift, an
entire week without Margaret, did much to restore their
courage.

"Would it be disgraceful," Kitty asked tentatively, "if
we sought out the friends we've made here?"

She was asking, I understood, if I would report her to
Margaret in the event she renewed her affair with the
handsome Highlander, and in all conscience I knew I
should not encourage her misconduct. But I also knew the
ways of loneliness, and how it went with a woman to have
naught for comfort in the long watches of the night but
slow tears and an empty heart.

"What you do is your own affair," I said, "not mine."
Then I smiled at her and added, "I like a man who smiles
often, Kitty, don't you?"

Elizabeth entered the room at that moment, a large tray
in hands, and the two maids curtsied toward me as if I
had been Margaret herself. Kitty looked mischievous and
murmured, "Thank you, ma'am," and Elsie, no longer
wringing her hands, said, "Since I'll have no other chores,
I'll be pleased to do your bidding during the mistress'
absence."

They left me feeling quite foolish and embarrassed, for
my composure was no more than a deceptive pose for
their benefit and I deserved no gratitude.

"I see ye smoothed their ruffled feathers," said Elizabeth.
"Addlebrained, they are, like all town women, and I'll be
thankful if ye'll keep them out from under my feet."

I was not deceived, for I remembered how she had comforted Kitty that morning.

"They're certain they'll be murdered in their beds," I
said. "D'you think it likely?"

"There's no way of telling."

"Does it happen often in the Highlands?"

"We're a ferocious lot, and that's a fact." She placed
the tray on a table by the fire. "Taste the food with care,"
she said, "else ye might find it too bitter for your liking.

If I were of a mind to be murdering today, I'd think poison much the easiest way to go about it."

I smiled, despite myself. "Aye, and it'd not spoil the bed linens."

But once Elizabeth had gone and I was alone again, the smile disappeared. A grim question had come unbidden to my mind, and I could not rid myself of it so easily as I had reassured the frightened maids.

Why were two horses left behind in the stables? Horse thieves, however inexpert at their trade, did not commonly overlook two valuable horses; nor did the men I had watched from my window, scoundrels who rode through the hills in the dark hours before dawn to fall upon their unsuspecting victims at will, appear so generously considerate they would provide means for those victims to later escape them.

Margaret had felt certain they knew of Walter's departure, and by the same token they might have known of Margaret's. Mayhap the kitchen gossip had truth in it, and the freebooters were even now preparing to fall upon Margaret as she rode through the hills.

But if such a miserable thing were true, why were two horses left behind, and only two, when there were three of us to ride away from Clennon House?

I shook my head at such morbid fancies. Margaret would arrive safely at her destination, Robert would reach the English fort, and I would spend an uneventful week alone; to imagine otherwise would surely invite more trouble to plague us.

And indeed I felt more cheerful after I had done away with an excellent meal of hot grouse and the better portion of a bottle of Walter's best wine; cheerful enough, in truth, to realize for the first time what Margaret's absence would mean to me. Before me stretched days of freedom, heavenly freedom such as I had not known since I first came to live with the Clennons three years past; and had the raiding Highlanders come to batter at the doors that very moment, I doubt it would have shaken my elation by one jot.

Forgetting my decorum completely, I propped my feet on the hearth fender and laughed, and hummed a snatch of song I had once heard. The exciting sense of being all

at once unshackled and set free proved vastly more intoxicating than Walter's wine, and so my memory of that
next hour is somewhat confused and hazy.

I have a notion that I opened the windows wide to let
in the clean wind, for thus I found them the next day;
and for a time I sat quietly by the fire, chin in hands and
feet tucked beneath me, to dream away the idle moments
in a childish fashion not allowed me for many years.

Then it was that my imprudent elation got the better
of me. I began to sing aloud, in that room where only
psalms and hymns were wont to be heard, and then began
to dance to the melody, closing my eyes and swaying back
and forth at the command of an invisible partner.

Dancing, a sin the Kirk considered grave enough to
warrant a stiff fine and a long day of misery in the stocks,
was not a familiar thing to me. But my conscience seemed
to have deserted me as I danced around the hall, whirling
and swaying, holding out my skirts on either side, feeling
so buoyant and disembodied that I might have been dancing to the thin piping of fairy music.

"A graceful performance," came a voice from behind
me, "but an intolerable situation. No man likes to see a
lass dancing alone."

I spun around to face the master of Torra, standing
scarcely more than a few feet from me.

"I heard you were ill," he said. "Have you recovered
so soon?"

Leaning insolently against the doorjamb, thumbs in the
wide leather belt at his waist, he regarded me with so
much amusement in the depths of his gray eyes that my
incredulous astonishment gave way to a swift embarrassment which set my cheeks aflame.

"Someday I shall teach you to dance the volta," he
said casually. "Would you like that?"

I wondered how long he had been watching me, and
how he came to be in Clennon House unannounced, but
I hesitated to ask. He seemed so much at his ease, I
thought indignantly, that it would doubtless appear a gross
discourtesy for me to question his behavior.

"Why are you here, m'lord?" I asked at last, and belatedly realized I was still holding out my skirts. I dropped

them and put my hands behind me, and retreated a step or two.

"I came to pay my respects. How do you like Clennon House without the Clennons?"

I stared at him. "How did you know the Clennons had gone?" Then, as another thought struck me, "Who told you I was ill?"

"Such news gets about," he said calmly. "It was also brought to my attention that Clennon House suffered an attack by a mob of ruffians this dawn. Since they've been terrorizing the countryside of late, I thought it only neighbourly to offer my assistance."

"We've no need of it, thank you kindly."

He lifted a dark brow. "Then my condolences," he said. "Did you fall ill from fright, or was it only a consequence of yesterday's misadventures?"

"I haven't been ill at all."

"Then why didn't you leave with Margaret Clennon?"

"I don't think it should concern you," I said, wondering how far his audacity would carry him.

"But it does," he said promptly. "The men who came this morning are dangerous reivers, and they've been known to do far more mischief than stealing a few horses. Has no one told you how they murder without conscience, and mistreat helpless women before they leave them for dead?"

"I don't believe it. They mistreated no one here today."

"They may come again. A lone woman is easy prey."

His dark face was quite grave, but some indefinable quality in his voice warned me that he was quizzing me.

"I shall be safe enough," I said. "Dire tales have a way of spreading faster than the plague. And some foolish women need only to have a man look at them and they scream they've been molested. Do you know for a certainty that such terrible things have happened?"

Laughter flickered in his eyes, and I knew I had been right to think him less than serious.

"I bow to your courage," he said. "Your tolerance also, a quality one seldom finds in a Covenanter." He took his hands from his belt and straightened up. "I take it Margaret Clennon agrees with you, else surely she would not have left you here alone."

My cheeks burned at the sarcasm in his voice; for a moment I felt a great irritation at his perception.

"The servants are still here," I said. "I'm not entirely alone." Still uncertain of his motives, I added, "I fail to understand your interest in my affairs."

"And I've no intention of enlightening you," he said. "Why is it that women must have everything explained to the smallest detail? Go and change clothes, Anne Lindsay. I've come to take you riding."

I could not have heard aright. "You jest, sir," I said, and retreated another step.

"Why should I be jesting? I can think of nothing in the idea to warrant amusement."

"Then you're daft," I said, "and I am not amused."

"Merely impolite," he said, unperturbed. "Has no one ever asked you out for a pleasant afternoon ride? You must learn the proper manner of accepting or refusing. 'Tis seldom politic to accuse a man of being daft when he requests the honour of your company."

I had never met any man so brazenly outspoken, but he had the truth of it.

"No," I said, ashamed of my discourtesy, "no one has ever asked me such a thing before."

"Did you think I had come to discuss the virtues of the Covenant with you, or mayhap say a prayer or two for your sins?" He stood there in the doorway, booted feet apart and hands on his hips, his eyes coolly distant and his dark face contemptuous. "God's love, you're not speaking to Robert MacLeish now."

"Do you know Robert?" I asked, amazed.

"Aye, I know him."

He did not sound as if he considered it in the least pleasurable to know Robert MacLeish, and for some unaccountable reason I warmed to him at once.

"His nose always drips," I said without thinking. Then I added hastily, "I should not be so unkind as to mention it."

"His nose is so long and thin from pushing it into other men's affairs," he said, "I'm surprised to learn it has the capacity to do aught but stand as a monument to his meddling."

"You are harsh. What has Robert done to earn your dislike?"

He shrugged. "I've no liking for fanatics of any breed." He seemed impatient of the subject. "Well, are you coming with me?"

Remembering his forceful manner of the day before, I was not at all convinced that a refusal would avail me.

"I have no horse," I said. "All but two were stolen, and those two left with Margaret and Robert."

"So that was the reason you stayed behind," he remarked impassively. "Why did no one send to Torra for the loan of a mount for you?"

"I imagine no one thought of it in all the confusion," I said carefully.

"Did you tell Margaret Clennon of your visit to Torra?"

I shook my head, but did not school my face quickly enough.

"But she must have warned you of the dangers of walking on the moors alone," he said, and once again I was put on my guard by his tone of voice. "Did she order you to have naught to do with the Stewarts of Torra?"

"She believes strangers are not welcome in the Highlands," I answered as tactfully as I could, "and I must be on my guard."

"To be more specific," he said, plainly amused, "you are to avoid the Earl of Monleigh as if he had the plague. You are not to speak to him should the occasion arise, or receive him at Clennon House. And under no circumstances are you to go riding on the moors with him."

I doubted if Margaret had even entertained such a fantastic notion as my riding on the moors with Monleigh or any man.

"I hope you aren't offended, m'lord," I said, for the small fear that he was making mock of me for his own purposes was enough reason to refuse him. "Mayhap she would feel differently were she to know you better."

"If you knew me better," he said, "you'd not expect me to be offended by Margaret Clennon. Never mind about a horse, I brought one for your use. Have you a proper habit for riding? The mare is docile enough, but she's not accustomed to skirts and petticoats. I've no wish to have her frightened."

He appeared as careless of Margaret's poor opinion of him as he did of my polite refusal to go with him.

When I did not move or speak, he said equably, "D'you want me to go down on one knee and plead with you?"

Since there was not the slightest possibility of this, I said nothing; I only wished that he would go away before I succumbed to my confusion and uncertainty and accepted his incredible invitation.

"I think you've forgotten how to think for yourself, Anne Lindsay."

With that he took one long stride forward and put his hands on my shoulders; he stood so close that, for one disturbing moment, I not only forgot how to think but also lost my ability to breathe properly.

There was no good or wise reason for a respectable spinster to feel such a tremulous excitement over the simple matter of an afternoon ride. I was behaving like an addle-pated maiden, all blushing and simpering at the very hint of masculine company; if I had never been faced with such a situation before, it was no excuse for my loss of dignity and composure.

So I stood quietly under his touch, knowing all the while that I should protest his habit of putting hand to me so carelessly and with such disregard for propriety, and repeated to myself with staunch resolve the many good and wise reasons why I should not go out on the moors with this stranger.

"The day made a poor showing at dawn," he said quietly, "but now the sun is bright and the wind is out of the west. Would you like to get away from Clennon House for a while and ride on the high moors above the sea? When one has so little time, it would seem unreasonable to squander it indoors."

I looked at him, at his dark face and hard mouth, his eyes cold as gray rain on a mountain tarn; and I felt the strength of his hands on my shoulders and remembered that first moment when I faced him on the shore and wondered at the nature of a man who betrayed such a ruthless violence in his face and bearing.

Now I might also wonder at his perception and understanding, qualities so alien to violence, and his odd kindness toward one who must matter less to him than the wind on the moors.

"I have the proper clothes," I said steadily, "and I'll not be long in changing."

He dropped his hands and I left him, but I was well aware that he followed me to the hall doorway and watched me climb the stairs.

He also watched me descend a few minutes later, clad in my sensible gray moreen habit, and I did not doubt he found my riding apparel as unappealing as my mulberry walking dress of the day before.

But he showed no indication that he cared what I wore, so long as it had no rustling petticoats to frighten his mare, nor did he appear to notice that I had exchanged my linen coif for a small cap I had once purchased in a reckless moment and never before found courage to wear.

"I told the woman in the kitchen you would be gone for the remainder of the day," he said, taking my arm. "She gave me a message for you."

The weight of my conscience was almost too great to bear with equanimity, so I said nothing.

"You are to beware of horse thieves and freebooters, and murderous Highlanders of any ilk or name."

I gave him a wary glance, wondering if the dour Elizabeth so disapproved of my riding out with the master of Torra that she had seen fit to warn me; but if such had been her intention, she must realize the futility of it as well as I.

Two horses awaited us beyond the door, and then I saw a third which carried my black-visaged friend, Evan Stewart.

"A good day to you," I said, oddly pleased to see him again.

"Aye, 'tis a good day," he said, "and looks to continue so. I think myself safe in wishing the same for ye."

Monleigh cupped his hands and boosted me into the high sidesaddle, and I noticed that the mare, a chestnut with two white forelegs, was not the same horse I had ridden home from Torra the evening before. I hoped she was as docile and well-mannered, however, for my seat was not so excellent that I cared to test it before such company.

We rode off down the track, the three of us abreast, and all at once I was fully aware of the bright sun and the wind and the lighthearted gulls above the loch. And my companions did not appear murderous in the slightest. Although I had noted the sheathed dirk at his waist, Monleigh did not wear a sword, and the brace of wicked pistols at his saddlebow kept strange company with a small and innocent-seeming lute which caught my eye at once and caused me an uncomfortable moment or two.

There it was, incontestable proof that the man who plucked the strings until strong men wept or laughed, and sober spinsters sighed, was none other than the imperturbable man riding so silently beside me. I had not forgotten my foolish whimsy about a certain tune played upon that selfsame lute; but since its owner, however much he knew of Clennon House, could not possibly guess at my innermost fancies, I accepted the lute with no great loss of composure.

Evan, the ugly fellow at my other side who looked so much a scoundrel, had not left off his sword, but his loud and tuneless whistle was hardly that of a man with villainy on his mind. Nor did his wide grin whenever he caught my eye seem any less kind than the one with which he had reassured me the evening before when he left me outside Clennon House.

"Ye look well enough to me," he said. "I didn't suspect ye were the sort of lass to suffer the vapours."

"Nor am I," I retorted, growing weary of the role of invalid.

"I was told in the kitchen ye had a raging fever and so could not travel."

So the kitchen help had been the source of their information. I felt ashamed of my earlier uneasiness.

"I had no fever, but must confess to a raging temper."

Evan shook his head decisively. "I'd not believe it. Ye haven't the heart for being ill-tempered."

Surprised, I said, "You are kind, but I imagine it's more a matter of not having the backbone for it."

I liked his great rolling laughter. "Aye, ye've jelly for a backbone," he said, "and no more courage than a mewling kitten. And if ye were the witless lass who screeched like a loon this dawn, ye deserve to be strung

from the nearest tree till the Devil himself comes to cut
ye down and show ye the way of true fright."

My throat was suddenly tight and dry, and I could
scarcely swallow; and I realized on the instant that we
were out of sight of Clennon House.

At my other side Monleigh broke his silence at last.
"Pay no attention to Evan's threats," he said. "He's in-
clined to bully, but he's not so fierce as he'd like to appear.
And the nearest tree of any size is a mile away."

I looked directly at Evan. "How did you know about
the woman who screamed?"

"I heard her with my own ears," he said cheerfully,
"and I don't mind telling ye the hairs stood straight up
on my neck. Did ye do the screaming, or were ye the
curious one who stood peering out the window in an old
woman's nightcap?"

"I don't wear a nightcap," I said indignantly. Then,
"What were you doing at Clennon House this dawn?"

The two men turned away from the track, seeming to
move their horses closer to me so that I must accompany
them whether or not I wished; and the barren hills, desolate and lonely, rose up about us on all sides.

"What did I at Clennon House? I stole Walter Clennon's best horseflesh, that's what I did, and if Simon had
not been so strong-minded about the matter I'd have
stolen me a pretty lass from Edinburgh town."

I stared straight ahead, trying desperately to hide my
dismay and consternation.

"You're forcing the pace, Evan," Monleigh said calmly.
"Would you have her ill with panic before we've more
than begun our ride?"

"She had to know sooner or later, and I'm a man who
likes to speak plainly."

"Aye," Monleigh said, as if the thought amused him,
"and you'll never win a pretty lass with it. Don't blame
my strong mind if women scream and flee at the sight of
you. Look at Mistress Lindsay; she's terrified after only
five minutes of your company."

"She's not screaming. I'm no' so ferocious as all that."

"Doubtless she lacks the spirit, you've bullied her so.
And in any event she knows no one will hear and hasten

to her rescue as Robbie MacLeish saved the poor lass from your clutches this dawn. Credit her with some wit."

"You might credit me with still being present," I said, nettled, "and refrain from discussing me as if I were deaf and dumb."

"She doesn't lack spirit," Evan said triumphantly. Then he scowled at Monleigh. "A jest is a jest, man, but ye well know I did naught but speak to that lass in the stables, and mannerly enough at that. She had no reason to throw her apron over her giddy head and run away screaming like a madwoman."

Monleigh's laughter echoed from the hillsides above us, taking me so by surprise that I clutched at the pommel of my saddle to keep my balance. In doing so I looked down at the mare, and of a sudden realized how many long hours I had spent looking at that same mane and dainty head.

"I rode this mare from Edinburgh," I said quietly. "Her name is Mally, and she has a mark on her right foreleg from a bad cut she suffered the last day of the journey."

"You'll find it nicely healed," Monleigh said. "Her nerves are still skitterish, but if you handle her mouth softly she'll not bolt with you."

His audacity left me with nothing to say; indeed, my wits were in such a state of confusion that had I an apron myself I would have been sorely tempted to throw it over my head and ignore the two of them until I came to terms with my predicament.

But I had no apron, and so I lifted my chin and said, "What do you want of me?"

"I thought we had settled that," Monleigh answered me. He drew rein beside me, reaching for the mare's bridle, and the three of us halted there in the sunlight. "D'you wish to turn back? You've only to say the word and Evan will escort you back to Clennon House."

He was not smiling, but neither were his eyes so distant as they were wont to be; he merely waited, face impassive, for my decision.

I had no reason to believe him sincere, but somehow I sensed that he did not intend to force me against my will. I had come to ride with him by my own choice; I could turn back if I so desired.

Looking at him thoughtfully, I remembered Margaret's scorn for his title. The Stuarts had repaid his services with an earldom only a few years past, yet his name stood in evil disrepute the breadth of Scotland. So Margaret had said, and I had been loath to believe her; but now I could scarcely ignore the evidence at hand. He was one of the ruffians who had stolen Walter's entire stable of horses, save two; and he had told me himself that the freebooters were dangerous men whose consciences balked at no crime however base and odious.

Yet I, a lone and unprotected woman, had met him by the sea, had been inside his fortress of Torra, had worn a crimson velvet robe and sipped wine in his bedchamber, had heard him play a lute with great charm, and had suffered no dire consequences. I was not such an innocent, of course, to believe that the latter was a convincing proof of character: a scoundrel may pat a child on the head before he robs the father, the most depraved fiend may hesitate to kick a dog, and a pair of brutal hands may strum a lute as readily as virtuous ones.

But he had also spoken to me of the sunlit day and the sweet wind blowing off the sea; and I had already made one difficult decision under that steady gaze. Who would know, after all, how I chose to spend my time, and in what company, and who would care or grieve but myself if ill fortune befell me?

"It would be very unwise," I said at last, "for me to ride with you."

"Very unwise," he agreed.

"I've no way of knowing your intentions."

"None whatsoever."

"You may be plotting more wickedness."

"We may, indeed."

"It is doubtless improper, as well as dangerous, for me to remain in such infamous company."

"Doubtless," he said gravely.

"On the other hand," I said, "my character is reasonably virtuous and untainted. I see no reason to fear it would be corrupted by your guilt."

I retrieved my bridle calmly, and beside me Evan Stewart gave a long sigh.

"Well now, I'll remove my wicked self and leave ye only

one of us to cope with. But ye'd best watch sharply, lass. Simon has a sly way about him, and I've known him to corrupt enough virtuous souls to fill a kirk house."

He grinned at me and raised his hand, and turned his horse to ride back toward the track.

The sun was hot on my head, and small insects droned in the heather. The chestnut mare moved impatiently, eager to be off, but Monleigh sat his horse without moving until the hills around us no longer gave back the clatter of Evan's horse.

Then he smiled at me, and I watched the tiny flames spring to instant life in his eyes.

"Come away, Anne Lindsay," he said. "We must see to our ride before the afternoon is done."

{ 5 }

THE sun was dropping below the hills when Elizabeth opened the doors of Clennon House to me.
Behind her the hall was in near darkness, but from the
rooms beyond the cheerful glow of candles made a brave
showing against the coming of night.

There was light enough to show her my disreputable
condition, however, and for a moment she stood and sur-
veyed me from head to toe. My habit, damp along the
hem and badly rumpled, was still open at the collar as I
had carelessly unbuttoned it in the warm sun, and my hair
was wind-blown into a hopeless tangle.

I put out a foot to show her my undamaged slippers.

"At least I saved my slippers this time," I said faintly,
in the face of her dour scrutiny, "and my habit is not
beyond redemption."

"Would ye say the same for your virtue?"

Her abruptness startled me, but I held my ground.

"My virtue is my own affair, Elizabeth, sullied or not."

"It would seem so," she said, "but I know those who
would disagree."

"You seem to know a great deal about many things," I
said slowly, remembering a question or two I had in mind.
"Did you admit Lord Monleigh to Clennon House today?"

"His lordship has made a bad name for himself," she
answered, "and all of us here have been ordered to refuse
him the door."

We looked at each other, and at last I was certain of
the smile on her face.

"I heard no one at the door," I said. "Did you?"

"I was in the kitchen, and the maids were in their
rooms." She added with a shrug, "I doubt he entered

through a window, but since no one saw or heard him, there's no way of telling."

"No way at all," I agreed. "He is a scoundrel and surely has many tricks at hand."

"When she returns, the mistress will not take kindly to the news of your outing. Have ye invented a proper excuse?"

"Will you tell her, Elizabeth?" I asked quietly.

"I've no liking for gossip, but I'd not speak for the two women from Edinburgh."

I had forgotten them, and the curiosity common to all such women.

"The one named Kitty is in disgrace enough," said Elizabeth, "and mayhap the scrawny one has a sin or two of her own to hide. But ye may have noticed that their tongues have a foolish way of wagging."

I smiled at her. "Thank you," I said, "I'll watch my own tongue when they're about."

She nodded her head and started away, a woman of few wasted words.

"I had a very pleasant afternoon," I said softly.

"Did ye now?"

"I believe the ride quite cured my fever."

"There's much to be said for the air on the moors. I've known it to cure worse maladies than a fever."

"D'you think I might do well to try the remedy again?"

"It looks to agree with ye," she said. "If it were myself, I'd prefer it to a draught of evil-tasting medicine." Over her shoulder she added, "I was told to expect ye when the sun went down, so there's hot food waiting in the hall. Make haste or it'll cool on the plate."

The unfamiliar sense of well-being, of having my wants attended before I was aware of them myself, was so pleasant that I scarcely felt my weariness. And when I went up to my bedchamber to find a brisk fire on the hearth, and silver warming pans beneath the sheets, and my night clothes laid out in great elegance despite their ridiculous muslin air of poverty, I was quite overwhelmed, and was fearful lest I waken and find I had been dreaming, after all, the whole day through.

I bathed my face, still flushed from the sun. Above my clothespress hung a mirror, small and irregular, and I paused before it, candle in hand, to stare at my wavering reflection.

"You are playing the fool," I whispered to the Anne Lindsay in the glass.

She stared back, saying nothing, her hair curling at her temples and burnished as copper in the meagre light, cheeks suspiciously pinker than they were wont to be.

"A giddy spinster," I accused, "throwing discretion to the winds because a man smiled at you."

There was no answer, but behind her dark lashes the reflected candlelight glowed like slanted fragments of jade.

"You have a great conceit," I said, "if you think he has any motive but kindness."

A small secret smile touched her mouth, as if my sarcasm had moved her not at all, and I was obliged to admit, with no little surprise, that she looked exceedingly young and fair and happy.

"You are shameless," I whispered again, my cheeks afire.

But it was difficult to cope with this new and heedless Anne Lindsay, whose dutiful mind was all at once at great odds with a mutinous heart.

Had it been very wrong and wicked of me to ride with him? Should I have turned back when he gave me the chance?

But then, I thought, I would not have discovered for myself what manner of man he was; I would never have known the stark beauty of the hills rising against a blue Scots sky, one behind the other as far as the eye could see, nor felt the spellbound delight of that moment when we topped a crest and I looked down on a small portion of Paradise tucked away in the hills above the sea.

He had halted his horse so that I might look my fill. There below us, in a hollow of the moor, a valley lay hidden from all but the blue sky and the hills circling it about. A stream, bordered by green bracken and clumps of whin, meandered its lazy course along the level ground and disappeared at the far end in a stand of slender trees, and beyond the trees the hills opened to a bright wedge of blue which was the sea.

We were still high in the uplands, surrounded by the gaunt hills with their wild moorland and rock-littered gorges, and yet below us the gentle valley led in a direct line, down through the green trees and hidden glens through which the stream must fall, to the western shore washed by the Atlantic.

"Any army of men could hide away here," I said, pleased beyond measure at the sight, "with sentries on the high ground to give warning, and a swift descent down to the sea in the event they must retreat."

"Thus far we've had no army faced with the dire necessity of hiding away here," he said, "but a goodly number of Stewarts have tried it over the years and found it convenient."

"I can't think why the Stewarts would find it necessary to hide from anyone."

"The reasons a man sometimes must absent himself from the world and its affairs are not for a woman to question," he said lightly. "Mayhap they stole too many sheep and the wrathful owner took it in mind to have his revenge. Or a battle went against them, as battles have a way of doing, and they deemed it wise to keep to themselves till they regained their pride." He added, with a faint smile, "Or it may have been the news that a pious Covenanting parson was come into the west to push his long nose into everyone's affairs. I've no doubt this valley has seen its share of miserable sinners hoping to escape the curiosity of the Kirk."

I bit my lip to keep from laughing. I should not, I told myself firmly, countenance his habit of ridiculing all things concerning the Kirk, for it came dangerously near to blasphemy; the folk I lived amongst were not wont to treat life in so careless and lighthearted a manner, for the reprisal of the Kirk was as certain as the wrath of its God.

He was doubtless a rogue and a blackguard, an adventurer who stood in great disrepute; but there was something about him that intrigued me in much the way a timorous coward is awed and amazed by the reckless courage of a more daring man.

" 'Tis a bonny spot," I said. "Are we far from Clennon House? Could I find it again, without your guidance?"

He moved his horse slowly down the slope, leading the way.

"We're only a few miles north of Clennon House," he

answered, "and no more than a good shout from Torra. But you're not to come here alone."

I was puzzled, for we had spent almost an hour in the hills. But in circling through the bens, avoiding the most hazardous slopes, we had apparently come no more than a few miles distance.

"Why not? If you showed me a more direct way, I'd not lose myself in the hills."

"There is no direct way, lass, unless you come from Torra."

"I think the Stewarts excessively selfish to keep such beauty to themselves."

"But there's the beauty of it," he said promptly. "Else it'd be overrun with Clennons and Camerons and Mac-Donalds, cluttering up the scenery and taking all the trout and making an unholy nuisance of themselves."

"And spying on Torra," I said, for now that we were almost on the level floor of the valley I could see, far below the trees and almost out of sight on its precipice of stone by the sea, a gray turret rising from the fortress of Torra.

"You've sharp eyes," Monleigh said, "and there's the truth of it. All Clennons have sharp eyes and a penchant for spying."

"I am not a Clennon," I said shortly.

"But you'll be so like them," he said, "after another year or two, that no one will be able to tell the difference." He turned in the saddle and gave me a slanted scrutiny. "You have the look of Margaret Clennon already," he said coolly. "Take a close look in your mirror one day, Anne Lindsay, and you'll see your fate there."

For a moment I could not speak. I had been too unwary, put off my guard by his pleasant manner and the glorious day; and so the pain he inflicted with such cruel and indifferent honesty cut even deeper because I had not expected it.

To my sorrow, I knew my fate without the need of mirrors, and if I had begun to look as barren and prudish as the company I kept at Clennon House, it only proved the more that I had no business riding on the moors alone with the black Earl of Monleigh, laughing at his blasphemous humour, enjoying myself enormously, pretending for a nonsensical moment that I could change into the younger and happier lass I might have been had life gone differently.

"Don't weep," said Monleigh. "Can't you face the truth without dissolving into tears? Women are damnably sensitive."

"I'm not weeping."

"I know," he said. "I only said it to rid you of that sulky frown."

"I'm neither sulking nor scowling," I said, at last brought to anger by his derision. "And you err in believing my feelings so delicate they would be crushed by any opinion you might have of me. 'Tis only that I'm unused to such bluntness of speech."

He saw through this subterfuge at once.

"It hasn't offended you before now," he remarked, unmoved. He had brought the horses to a halt, and now he rested his arm on his saddle pommel and gave me so speculative a look that my cheeks burned. "Don't wallow in self-pity. 'Tis poor consolation at best, and seldom a thing to restore one's pride."

The barb hit too close to the truth for comfort, and my anger abruptly turned inward toward myself.

We were both silent for a lengthy interval.

"Why don't you defend yourself?" he asked suddenly. "Have they left you no self-esteem? Ask me why the devil I brought you along if I've nothing to do but insult you. Give me a few sharp words for being so uncivil as to compare you to Margaret Clennon." He added casually, "You did better by yourself when I took you to Torra. Must I resort to violence before you'll stand up to me?"

My mind fastened on one sentence. "Why did you bring me?" I asked slowly.

"To see if I could make you angry, for one thing," he said. "I had begun to think you only partly alive."

We measured each other as fencers will, and as is ofttimes the case with those who resort to bared steel to settle their differences, one of us was wary and without confidence while the other masked his superiority with a lazy ease of manner which boded no good to his opponent. I was safe enough for the moment, being too unversed in the art of fencing to make the odds worth-while to him;

but I knew I must learn to look to myself if I would match wits with this man.

"You are an odious man," I said, "and insufferably rude as well. I can't imagine why I came, or why I don't turn back at once."

"Better, but not good enough. Try again."

"You are also ill-mannered, disobliging, and offensive." Aghast at my own ill manners, even in jest, I added, "M'lord."

" 'Tis high time you acknowledged my consequence," he said, "but it spoils the effect. You should fix me with a haughty stare, leaving no doubt of your loathing for me, and allow your nose to quiver daintily with fury. Have you never been in a hot rage, Anne Lindsay?"

"Frequently," I admitted, "but my nose does not quiver, rage or no."

"And you're incapable of a haughty stare. Did you know," he said carelessly, "that your eyes are green as emeralds?"

Caught unawares, I stared at him as if he had gone daft.

"No," he said thoughtfully, " 'tis more the colour of the sea, early on a summer morn, or mayhap a winter tarn when the snow is deep and the water is frozen quiet and green."

"Shall we ride on?" I said, retreating in panic from the incalculable power of mere words to stun one's emotions and then send them reeling.

He smiled at me, and because I could not help feeling very gay and heedless, I smiled back.

"Aye," he said, "you must see the hidden glen of the Stewarts and learn the way to escape a hotly pursuing enemy. 'Tis not beyond reason that you might one day have need of a similar trick."

So we rode down through the valley, closed about on three sides by the massive hills, those formidable guardians of the sunlit green meadows and sparkling stream and all the peaceful quietude of that tiny kingdom.

When we neared the trees I could hear a rush of water and see that the narrow end of the valley terminated in a rocky cliff. It would seem that we could go no further, for the stream disappeared in a tangle of fern and green

vines and the slim trees grew thickly along the edge of
the precipice and down its face, soon joining company
with the rough boulders to present an impenetrable barrier
across our path.

"We must leave the horses here," Monleigh said, "and
trust to our own feet the remainder of the way."

He dismounted and took his lute from the saddlebow,
slinging it over his shoulder, and then transferred one of
the pistols to his leather belt.

"That looks to be most uncomfortable," I said carefully.
"Must you take it with you?"

He looked up and smiled at me. "I doubt I'll have occasion to use it," he said easily, "but a man finds it difficult to break the habit of having a weapon close at hand."

"You have no sword," I said.

"A sop to your sensibilities," he said. "I had no wish to
frighten you when I appeared so suddenly in Clennon
House."

His hand moved to the sheathed dirk at his waist. "I
have a sword of sorts," he said, "a likely enough weapon
when handled properly. I've often thought a woman
should be taught to use a dirk; would you like a lesson?"

The dirk lay in his hand, glittering with a restless blue
flame in the sunlight, its carved handle and thin dangerous blade seeming even more deadly when held in a hand
of such obvious strength and capability.

"No," I said faintly, "I wouldn't care for a lesson. I
have a way of wounding myself when threading a needle.
It would be foolhardy indeed to trust me with anything
more lethal."

He replaced the dirk in its sheath with such dexterity
I could scarcely follow his hand. I would not choose, I
reflected, to be his enemy, facing that wicked point which
moved so swiftly and ruthlessly to his command that it
seemed to possess a life of its own.

Then he put his hands on my saddle, one on either
side of me, and I looked down into his tanned face and
clear gray eyes, narrowed now against the sun.

"You'd be of small use to a man," he said, laughter in
his voice. "So you see I can no longer rely on my dirk
alone. I must be prepared to protect and defend you
against all comers."

"Even here? On your own land, in sight of Torra?"

" 'Tis the Stewarts I must guard against," he said. "There's no' a man in the clan without an envious eye for a likely lass such as yourself."

Before I could object, he put his hands to my waist and lifted me easily from the saddle. For a brief instant he held me so, then my feet touched the ground and his hands fell away. A mannerly show of courtesy, giving me no cause for misgiving, and yet my breath caught suddenly and gave me a bad moment or two. Mayhap it was only a look in his eyes as they met mine, a momentary glitter that might have been no more than the sun's reflection; but all at once I felt uncertain and distrait, and was glad when he turned away to give a slap to the mare's flanks and send her toward the grass beside the stream.

He led the way beneath the trees and turned without hesitation to the rocky slope rising to the right of the gorge. There he held aside the underbrush and I saw that the way was clear, for the width of a foot or so, between the hill and the trees. The path led downward, twisting among the boulders, and I felt Monleigh's hand on my arm to steady me on the rough ground.

Then we reached the bottom of the incline and stood in a small glen, bounded by the steep hillsides and the green trees, carpeted with meadow grass and moss. It boasted a high waterfall, the sound of rushing water I had heard from above, and the boisterous stream surged whitely down the rock face and formed a small pool before dashing on through the glade to another cliff beyond.

" 'Tis a lovely spot," I said, delighted.

"And a safe one, which is ofttimes more important."

"One could lie hidden here forever, if he had food enough, and care not a whit for the rest of the world."

"Aye, I've known men who came here once and never wished to leave."

"The fairies," I said, pointing to a circle of scarlet toadstools. "The glen belongs to them, and they cast a spell over those who dare to enter here."

He smiled at my whimsy. "Then beware, Anne Lindsay, else you'll not return to Clennon House the same lass who left it."

That fact had been established some time since, but I did not say as much.

He dropped to the ground, slipping the lute from his shoulders, and stretched his long legs out before him.

"Take your ease, lass," he said with a grand sweep of his arm. "Consider my entire fortress at your disposal."

I strolled to the edge of the pool and sat on a flat stone. The water was clear, peat-brown in its depths and blue above with the mirrored sky, here and there flecked with white froth from the falling water. The sun had been hot in the valley above and on the bare slopes of the hills, and I removed my cap to feel the cool shade on my head. And because I had my back to Monleigh, I dared to open the high uncomfortable collar at my neck.

"A pity you can't enjoy the most pleasurable advantage of this spot," he said from behind me.

"And what is that?" I asked curiously.

"A cool swim in the pool."

Startled, I said, "Do you always swim here?"

"When I've no feminine companion," he said lazily. "Does it appeal to your tastes?"

"Perhaps, if I had no companion at all."

"Don't hesitate on my account. I'll not look."

I turned to see him put his hands behind his head and look up at the sky, and I remembered he had been in almost an identical pose the first time I laid eyes on him.

"You must know I could not," I said with an assumed dignity.

"Then take off your slippers and paddle. But first loop your skirt under your belt, else you'll have another ruined gown."

I had apparently become inured to his indelicate and outspoken ways, for with no more urging I caught up my skirt and tucked it under my belt, and carefully removed my slippers and worsted stockings.

" 'Tis unbelievably cold," I gasped as my foot touched the icy water.

"A Spartan diversion," he said, "walking in frigid mountain streams. It will undoubtedly strengthen your character."

"My character is quite strong enough," I retorted, but I put both feet in the water at once and bore the stinging shock bravely until the worst of it had passed.

It was a glorious pastime, paddling about in the clear rushing stream, my feet tingling cold and my head hot from the sun. I loved the feel of pebbles rubbed to satin smoothness by the eternal rush of water, and the velvet touch of moss, and once I laughed aloud with pure delight, like a child, when I spied the swift shadow of a trout in the deeper water behind a boulder.

"Are you happy with your lot?" Monleigh spoke quietly behind me. "Do you still regret being left behind?"

"You know I do not," I said as quietly. Then, because I could no longer avoid asking, "Why did you attack Clennon House and steal Walter's horses?"

" 'Tis an old sport in the Highlands, stealing horses."

"Why Walter's? Because he is a Covenanter?"

"A matter of revenge, you mean?" He had not taken his eyes from the sky. "No, lass, I've more to interest me than the dubious pleasure of needling a former enemy."

"Enemy? Then you must have been out with the first Charles when he rode against the Covenanters." I added, as if I did not know, "Have you always been a Royalist?"

"In a manner of speaking. When the choice is mine, I prefer to give my loyalty to the Stuarts."

"I should think the choice would always be your own."

"Once I was obliged to fight with a Covenanting army," he said, "and I had no choice in the matter. And the one time, I discovered, was more than enough to put any man's loyalty to the test."

"I remember," I said. "After Charles the Second signed the Covenant, and led General Leslie's army against Cromwell at Dunbar. Was it a terrible experience, fighting with the Covenanters instead of against them?"

"Very. We made strange bedfellows."

"You were fighting for the same king."

"On the contrary. The Royalists fought for the King, and the presbyterians fought for their Covenant."

"At least you faced a common enemy, the English."

"Well now, it took a canny man to tell friend from foe. The Scots clergymen quoted scriptures and the English puritans sang hymns, and we miserable sinners were caught between. God's love, it was enough to drive a man daft."

I smothered my laughter. "What did you do when the battle was lost to Cromwell?"

"Came back to Torra," he said shortly. "All the King's

men were mustered from the army by wrathful Covenanters who believed the sinners had lost their battle for
them."

"I've heard it said, even in Dundee, that generals who
must needs take orders from ministers find it difficult to
win battles. Not all the Covenanters blamed the Cavaliers."

He looked on the verge of laughing. "After that tactful
remark," he said, "it would doubtless be unkind of me
to point out that all Cavaliers, without exception, blamed
the Covenanters."

"Did you go south with Charles? To Worcester?"

"Aye," he said, "and was chased all the way back to
Scotland by Old Noll's Ironsides."

"It has been a difficult time for all Scots," I said, "living
under Cromwell's rule."

"Defeat is seldom easy."

"I imagine Charles Stuart finds it more galling than
most," I said. "Did you then go to France with him?"

"I did," he said, "and there learned to accept defeat
with better grace. A civilized country, France."

I did not think it politic to mention the ugly rumours
I had heard of Charles and his exiled court in France.
And if the truth were known, when I looked at the man
lying at his ease on the ground, hard-muscled and fit, it
was indeed hard to credit the tales of dissipation and wild
debauchery.

"If you had no motive of revenge," I said, "why did
you select Clennon House for your raid?" I resumed my
paddling, for the cold water seemed even colder when I
was not moving. "Or was it only one of many such
forays?"

"I've a stable full," he said, "but I'll have nothing but
the best horseflesh. It brings a better price."

"Do you sell them?" I asked incredulously. "Are you
so badly in need of gold that you must steal for it?"

"I always need gold," he said, unabashed, "and I've
many ways of finding it. But stealing horses is one of the
most diverting. As for my choice of Clennon House, you
were there. Can you think of a more reasonable motive?"

I looked up in time to see the grin touching his mouth.

"You are jesting, m'lord."

"When we come to know each other better," he said,

"perhaps you can persuade yourself to address me as Simon. Or in the Gaelic, Sim, which is even easier to say."

The grin widened as his eyes met mine, and not once did I remember that I was stockingless and barefoot, and that he had promised not to look.

"You left two horses in the stable on purpose," I said slowly. "You knew Margaret would leave me behind."

He shrugged. "Does it matter so much? I won a wager with Evan, Margaret Clennon has fled, and you are no longer chained to Clennon House. Only a few moments ago you seemed quite happy about it."

"I have a conscience," I said. "It is evident that you have misplaced your own."

"Fortunately for my peace of mind, I have never possessed one."

I turned my back on him and sat on the boulder beside the pool, holding out my feet to dry in the sun. The silence lengthened, and then I heard his fingers touch the lute strings, so softly that at first the sound was no louder than the song of a linnet off somewhere in the trees. Then a melody emerged, slow and sweet as the drowsy afternoon, and I sat in the sun and closed my eyes, and was filled with a fine content. He is a man of many moods and humours, I thought, with so contradictory a nature that there is surely no one in all the world who can flatly declare, "I know Monleigh well." And yet, when one is with him, it seems of no matter that one cannot read him as plainly as a simpler man; simplicity, when compared to Monleigh, becomes an exceedingly dull affair.

And if I am not careful, I admonished myself, I will find that he has put a spell on me by reason of that very charm he possesses in such great measure.

To bring my wayward thoughts back to a more decorous level, I deliberately shattered the mood of sun and lute and sweet enchantment.

"My father also rode with the Stuarts," I said. "He died at Marston Moor, fighting for the first Charles."

"Aye, I know."

I looked up quickly. "Did you know him, then?"

"No," he said gently, "I did not have the honour."

"Then," I faltered, disappointed, "how did you know he was a King's man?"

"Evan told me."

"And how did Evan know?"

"I never question Evan's methods of obtaining information."

"Did he . . . " I paused, afraid to hope again.

"No, lass, he did not."

"Was he at Marston Moor?"

Monleigh shook his head. "We Stewarts were in Scotland then, riding with Montrose."

"If Montrose had been with the King that day at Marston Moor, it might have gone differently."

"Perhaps," he said, "and perhaps not. It is easy to win battles with hindsight."

"I remember how frightened I was when Montrose stormed Dundee for the King. It was many years ago, and I was very small, but I shall never forget the red light burning in the sky after he set fire to the town, and the way the smoke crept into my chamber through the closed shutters."

"What were you doing in Dundee that April?" he asked lazily. "It was in '45, if I remember rightly, less than a year after the defeat at Marston Moor."

"My mother died that year," I said quietly, "and I had just arrived in Dundee to live with a distant kinsman and his wife."

"A Covenanter, no doubt."

"A minister of the Kirk," I said, "although he no longer preached. He was an old man," I added, "and his wife was not much younger."

"And how old were you?"

"Twelve, and three weeks over. My mother died on my birthday."

I had never told anyone before, and immediately wished I had not said as much to him; but he offered no conventional sympathy and did not appear to feel any great pity for me, as if he knew I could not bear it; and what would have seemed cold indifference to another was to me but a decisive proof of his instinctive understanding.

"Did the Anne Lindsay of twelve find it a dreary matter," he said, "acting nursemaid to two elderly kinspeople?"

"They were kind to me," I said, thinking back to those seven endless years in Dundee, "and there was no one else to tend their needs."

"And that is how you came to be a presbyterian."

I smiled. "My kinsman was too old to preach in the kirk, and so it fell to me to listen to his sermons. I used to sit for hours on a hard stool by his chair, fearing I'd fall asleep if I took a more comfortable seat."

"And if the congregation drowsed, I'll wager she had her pate rapped and was sent to bed without supper."

"Worse than that. He gave me another sermon, and then it was too late for either of us to eat."

I gave him a quick glance, wondering if he found great amusement in the picture of the young and dutiful lass who sat with a stiff spine for fear of nodding before the lengthy sermons were done, and who ofttimes went up to bed with the hunger of an empty stomach less painful than the hunger of a frightened and lonely heart.

But he did not look amused. "Were you there when Cromwell ordered General Monk to sack Dundee?"

I took a deep breath. "Yes," I said carefully, "I was in Dundee when the English came."

"Were they as bad as Montrose's Highlanders?"

"It seemed to me then," I said, "that Montrose and his men were as gentle as children compared to the English soldiery."

"I was with Montrose," he said, "and I assure you we were not gentle children. But you are right in one respect. We did not order our men to rape and plunder wantonly, or allow them to murder unarmed citizens, and the most ferocious Highlander would not be so depraved as to urge his sword to the kill to the tune of a pious hymn." He added, a grim chill in his voice, "Your Covenanters fight their wars in the same manner of the English puritans. Mayhap they deserved their fate."

I did not care to argue the point with him. "My two kinspeople were murdered when Monk took Dundee."

"How did you escape?"

"I was more fortunate than some."

Monleigh's eyes were narrowed and distant, almost as if he were not listening at all.

"Will you tell me about it?"

I hesitated, but there seemed no reason not to speak.

"They battered down the door to enter," I said, keeping the words steady by a rigid control. "All in the house were put to the sword, including a poor woman who had begged shelter for the sake of her bairn, born a month before."

"And you?"

"I held the bairn, hoping to save him, but the two English soldiers turned next to me. I think I had a desperate notion of reaching the door, but I doubt it would have availed me. They were lusting for blood, and had their swords still in hand."

"What saved you?"

"Someone called," I said. "Someone from the street below, perhaps an officer. They turned and ran down the stairs, and I was left alive."

Someone called. An odd and unimportant detail to so control a person's destiny. How strange that a rough voice, out of the brutal carnage of that dark night, should be the hand of Fate to stay my death by the sword; because a man shouted at a certain moment, I now sat in a small green glen and felt the sun on my face, and was very glad to be alive.

"What did you do when they had gone?"

"I'm not certain. I stood holding the babe, and listened to the sounds from the street." With my heart pounding against my ribs like an anvil, and the frightened babe, a warm bundle of life in that room of the dead, crying furiously in my arms. "Then I smelled smoke and realized they had fired the house. I threw my apron over the babe and somehow gained the door to the street, but a Redcoat caught sight of me and started toward me, shouting and brandishing his sword over his head."

My eyes happened to rest on Monleigh's face for a moment, and so I saw the muscle tighten along his cheekbone until the hard lines of his face seemed even harder, as if cut from granite and chiselled with an angry knife.

But his voice was even and cool, as always. "A miserable specimen of a man," he said, "like so many of the psalm-singing English. What happened then?"

"A soldier of the Dundee garrison lay dead across the steps," I said, low. "He had been run through from behind, and still held his pistol, primed and ready. I stooped and took it from his hand."

"Did you think to shoot yourself?" he asked quietly.

"At first. But there was the babe, you see."

"So you did not," he said. "You shot the soldier instead."

"Yes." I clasped my hands tightly together. "I don't believe I killed him, but I did not stop to see. I ran with the babe; then I hid in the cellarway of a burned house, still smouldering from fire, for three days and nights, feeding myself and the wee bairn on scraps I found in the gutters."

His dark face was expressionless. "Yet you have a spine of jelly," he said, "and cannot cope with anything more dangerous than a needle."

"The English killed eight hundred men of Dundee that night, and two hundred women and children. One does not need a mighty courage to fight for survival."

I felt weary and unsteady, but somehow greatly eased to have it spoken out after living with the burden inside me for so long.

"All life is a fight for survival," he said. Then, as if we had talked long enough of grim and painful matters, he smiled at me and said, "I was wrong, Anne Lindsay. At this moment you haven't the slightest resemblance to Margaret Clennon."

He had a way of catching me off guard. I sat there on the bank of the pool, bare feet tucked beneath my skirt and my collar carelessly unbuttoned, my face shiny and my hair untidy, and knew there was no retreat from his unswerving gaze and demoralizing smile.

"Don't look so startled," he said. "I'll not take advantage of your indiscretions."

"You have not yet told me," I said hastily, "how Evan learned of my father."

"I would not tell you," he said easily, "even if I knew."

"No one here but the Clennons knew my father was a Malignant."

"In my company, lass," he said, "you will henceforth refrain from calling a King's man a Malignant. 'Tis a discourtesy dreamed up by some long-faced wretch unable to curse properly, and we've no liking for the sound of it."

It was useless, I understood, to question him further about Evan. "Should I dub you a Cavalier then?" I asked. "I fear you're scarcely elegant enough for the title. You've no lovelock."

He grinned. "And no lace ruffles. Are you disappointed?"

"Vastly. I thought all Cavaliers went dressed like peacocks, adorned with velvets and lace and ribbons, and knew more of writing sonnets and combing their long curls than fighting wars."

His laughter startled the linnet in the trees behind him to instant flight.

" 'Tis only a rumour," he said. "The sort of tale they like to spread in towns like Dundee."

"Have you and Evan spent much time in Dundee?" I asked idly.

"Enough," he said, "to have developed a great dislike for it."

" 'Tis a long way from the west, and they care little for Royalists there. What do you do there?"

"You're a stubborn lass," he said. "Evan has been in Dundee more than once, and so have I, and doubtless it was there that he asked about your father. Any more questions?"

My cheeks burned. "I only wondered why you stay in the Highlands, when there is so little here to occupy your time."

"We retire to Torra to lick our wounds," he said lightly, "and spend our time scheming of ways to find more dragons to slay and more lovely maidens to rescue when we sally forth again."

"Then you are not always in residence here?"

"Only now and again."

"I had forgotten," I said. "There have been so many battles, and so much of war."

He stood up, moving with such careless grace that I was reminded of the lithe resilience of a cat. A very large and dangerous cat, I warned myself, perchance a tiger; and like the tiger, his charm was doubtless calculated to a fine degree, a cunning snare to dupe the unwary who did not perceive, until too late, the deadly menace of his true nature.

But I was not unwary, and surely was in no danger of being duped.

"We must go," he said, "if I would have you back at Clennon House before night."

"Yes, it is growing late."

I donned my hose and slippers, strangely reluctant to leave. The afternoon had gone too swiftly, and in a short time would be no more than a memory. But memories are not so perishable as actuality, and I knew I would not soon forget the hidden glen with its sun-dappled pool and scarlet toadstools, nor yet the man who had brought me there.

He gave me his hand and pulled me to my feet.

"Don't be sad, lass," he said. "There will be another time."

I shook my head.

"I shall come to fetch you tomorrow," he said, "and we'll go riding again."

"I think not," I said soberly. "My indiscretions have gone far enough."

He lifted a dark brow. "You have a weak conscience," he said, "if it will bear so little weight."

"It is not my conscience."

"What is it, then?"

His smile disappeared, as the sun had done, and his face seemed almost swarthy in the shadows of the trees.

I could not answer. We stood looking at each other, and suddenly the world seemed to recede like the slow wash of the outgoing tide, leaving behind a vast and breathless silence. The rushing sough of water faded away, there was no bird call, no faint rustle of wind in the trees; and I remembered the strange moment I first saw him on the moor above the sea, when I had known that same rapt silence and quietude.

Then he put out his hand and pushed back a wayward lock of hair on my forehead. I did not move, for all will to move had left me at his touch, and he held my chin and and lifted my face to his.

"Don't be frightened," he said quietly.

"If I am afraid," I answered, low, "I have reason enough."

"Are you sure?"

No, I was sure of nothing, except that for the space of a single afternoon I had been happier than I had ever been before.

"I'll meet you at midday in the hills behind Clennon House," he said, "and we'll have another look at the sea." His hand doubled into a fist and he pushed my chin gently with it. "I'll take care you don't fall into the water again."

"Why do you concern yourself with me?"

"That is a question no well-bred woman should ask a man," he said, "but since your curiosity is continually greater than your propriety, I'll be honest with you." He smiled, a white flash against his dark face. "I like the way you laugh, Anne Lindsay, and I've always been fond of green eyes. And if you're a good lass on the morrow, I may be persuaded to tell you more about your charms."

With that he took my arm and turned me firmly toward the path leading up to the moor, and in a few moments we were riding out of the valley.

His farewell at Clennon House was abrupt and laconic. "Say your prayers properly, lass," he said. "I'd like your conscience clear and unburdened when I see you again."

I stood and watched him ride away, sitting his saddle with the superb ease of a born horseman, and then sighed and went indoors to look into my mirror and tell myself firmly that it was the cheap and irregular glass which made my eyes appear so wide and brilliant, and set my mouth to trembling.

6

I awoke to the sound of wind, blowing in wild gusts against the narrow windows of my chamber; and the chill damp air on my face told me before I opened my eyes that the day was rainy and dark and drear.

"I've started ye a fire," Elizabeth said from the bedside, "and ye'd best make haste."

I opened my eyes wide.

"The master is below," she said calmly, "asking to see ye at once."

For a moment I was completely bewildered, so close was I still to the warm oblivion of sleep.

"Walter Clennon?" I said inanely. "Here?"

"He rode in a few moments past, and from the look of his horse he's had a long ride of it. I'd not keep him waiting if I were yourself."

All drowsy remainders of sleep left me on the instant, and I was coldly and wretchedly awake.

"No, I mustn't keep him waiting," I said, flinging back the covers. "Did he say why he returned so quickly? He was to be gone a week or more."

"No doubt he heard of the scandalous doings at Clennon House," she said, "and came hurrying back to learn the truth of the matter."

"Did you show him the empty stables?"

"Aye, I gave him all the bad news at one telling."

"Was he angry?"

"A bit ill-tempered and glum, as any man would be in the same circumstance."

I pulled my gown over my head. "I wonder how he learned of the raid," I said thoughtfully. "It was only yesterday at dawn, and no one but Margaret or Robert

MacLeish could have carried the news. Did he mention that he saw either of them?"

"He didn't say," Elizabeth said impassively, "but any news, good or bad, travels quickly enough in the Highlands."

"Do the gulls carry it? Or the wind?"

"No such thing," she said. "We've all the power of second sight and know what's to happen before it's begun."

I finished doing my hair and covered it with its linen coif. "But Walter Clennon is no Highlander, except by virtue of his Cameron kinsmen, and he surely possesses no second sight."

"Surely not," Elizabeth agreed, "else he'd not have left his fine horses behind to be stolen."

"Or indeed have come to Clennon House at all?"

She looked me in the eye. "I'd say he's been made welcome enough."

"Elizabeth," I said slowly, feeling a vague disquiet, "why do you dislike Walter Clennon?"

"I've no reason to like or dislike the master. He pays me well, and that's all I care about."

"He is a Covenanter," I said, "and some Highlanders seem to consider that a mark of blackest villainy."

"I care little how the man worships," she said. " 'Tis his affair, and none of mine."

I was no more able to fence with this dour Highland woman than with Monleigh. I walked to the door, but I bethought myself of another question and wondered what sort of answer she'd give me.

"Do you know," I said casually, "if the Stewarts hereabouts carry a grudge against the Clennons?"

"If they don't, they're not worthy of the name of Stewart."

Startled, I turned. "Why?"

"Did ye not know?" she said, not shifting her eyes from mine. "Clennon House has not always been called by that name. Once it was a stronghold of the Stewarts, owned by the chief of the clan."

"Monleigh?" I asked incredulously.

"I believe his lordship has always resided at Torra. 'Tis

said he gave this castle to his younger brother on the occasion of his marriage."

She deliberately turned her back on me and added a few faggots to the fire, but I waited stubbornly.

"I didn't know he had a brother, Elizabeth."

" 'Tis possible ye have a good deal to learn about the Stewarts," she said succinctly.

"Where is the brother, now that the Clennons own his fortress?"

"Why don't ye ask his lordship?"

With this short counterstroke, she effectively ended the the conversation. But I would not admit defeat.

"Elizabeth, are you a Stewart?"

She moved past me through the door. "My name is Elizabeth MacDonald," she said over her shoulder. "Ye must know the mistress would allow no Stewart within Clennon House.

I followed her slowly down the stairs, thinking of the proud Stewarts who had once walked the stairs and chambers of Clennon House and called it their own. Would they not hate the Clennons with a burning intensity, those arrogant Highlanders who must stand idly by while alien Lowlanders usurped their properties and purchased the castles they themselves had been forced to forfeit for lack of gold to pay the heavy fines levied on all Royalists? It would not be otherwise; and yet, the aftermath of war had ever meant ill fortune to one man and gain to another, and Monleigh had denied that revenge was his motive in raiding Clennon House.

But he had also given me a foolish reason, and I had foolishly believed him. I should have known that he did not steal the horses and frighten Margaret into leaving for no more purpose than his kindly desire to free me of her demands for a few days, and if I felt irrationally disappointed, it was no more than I deserved. Women, I reflected soberly, are absurd and simple-minded creatures who believe only what pleases them, evidence to the contrary, and then must needs suffer disillusionment and the humiliation of exchanging fatuous whimsy for stern truth.

On reaching the hall, I paused in the doorway. Walter stood by the fire, hands behind his back, absorbed in thought, and so I had a brief interval of grace before he became aware of me.

He had not had time to change his travelling clothes, yet he was as neatly groomed as if he had just stepped from his dressing room. His brown velvet doublet, impeccably tailored, was unwrinkled, his cropped and graying hair looked freshly brushed, his linen was as virgin white as when he first donned it. Only his high riding boots betrayed his unwonted haste by the streaked dust marring their perfect sheen.

But despite the rich velvet suit and his fastidious neatness, Walter suddenly appeared quite plain and colourless to me, his restraint no longer elegance but a rather pallid and unnecessary severity; and I understood, with a guilty twinge, that it was only because I had met, since last I saw Walter, a man with a dark vivid face and clear eyes and the look of a wild hawk about him, and so those men who were by nature less intensely and arrogantly alive must perforce suffer by comparison.

Walter turned as my skirts rustled slightly. "My dear Anne, come in," he said. "I am greatly relieved to see you. The servant woman tells me you have been ill."

I moved forward to meet him and he took my hands briefly.

"I trust you suffered no harm from the knaves who set upon Clennon House, else my conscience will plague me unmercifully. I should never have left you and Margaret here alone."

"I've suffered no harm," I said. "It was only a slight fever from a cold in the head."

"But surely you must still be weakened by it," he said mildly. "You've only just awakened, and it the Sabbath."

I sat in the chair beside the fire. I had indeed forgotten, when I had blown the candles and climbed into bed the night before, that the next day would bring the Sabbath. My last thought before sleeping, wearily and happy as I was, had been the knowledge that no one would call me during the night for a hot posset, or for a spoonful of medicine, and that I would not, when the gray dawn appeared, be aroused from my sleep for morning prayers and a hymn before breakfast.

"It seemed best to remain in bed till traces of illness had gone," I said, appalled that I must now add lying to my list of sins. "Margaret would not have me still afflicted when she returns."

He nodded as if he thought my decision a wise one. "I fear she will be quite undone when she arrives home, Anne. You must be patient with her."

The word "undone" vastly understated the case, I thought, but did not say as much.

"She thought me unfeeling to bring her here in the beginning," he went on, "and now it would appear she had the truth of it. I am told she sought the protection of John Cameron. Why did you not go with her, Anne?"

"I was too ill to travel," I said, and left it at that.

"She should not have gone without you," he said, frowning slightly. "If she felt obliged to leave, Robert could have remained."

"I believe Robert intended to ride on to the English garrison."

"I know." Walter sighed. "A good man, Robert, but ofttimes overzealous. I apologize for his lack of consideration."

"How did you know, Walter?" I asked, surprised.

"I met him on the way," he said quickly, "and gave him a round scolding for leaving you here."

So that was how he knew of the raid. It did not explain what business Walter had in the vicinity of the English fort, but that was none of my affair.

"'Tis of no matter," I said. "I've been quite safe."

He put his hands behind him and stood with his back to the fire. "I must ride to John Cameron's at once," he said. "Will you be satisfied to stay here another day alone, or would you prefer to come with me?"

"I have no horse," I reminded him, "and you will have no fresh one for the ride."

The corners of his mouth tightened and his face sobered, but he showed no other sign of indignation. I admired his control, and not for the first time; despite the press of business affairs and his sister's nagging, I had never seen Walter submit to the irascibility one would expect from a man so harassed. He frequently withdrew into absorbed thought rather than open a quarrel with Margaret, giving an impression of cold indifference which might well be only the consequence of careful and infinite patience; and now his forbearance of such long habit stood him in good stead.

"I'll have one of my men stay," he said only, "and you may use his mount."

I shook my head. "You are kind, but I must not run the risk of falling ill again." I added, knowing the value he placed on his stables, "I am sorry about the theft of your horses."

"An immeasurable loss," he said. "I had intended to keep my best mares here for breeding purposes. But now I shall be forced to start in from the beginning again."

"Perhaps you may yet recover them. Would you recognize any if you came upon them?"

"I would know any one of them, but I can scarcely approach a hotblooded Highlander and ask to examine his stable. He'd think it an accusation and an insult, and I'd be challenged on the moment."

I hoped that I looked more innocent than I felt. "Could you not demand restitution from his chief?"

Walter began to pace before the fire. "I would it were so simple. Even were I to find definite proof, I doubt I'd stand a chance of retrieving my mares." Four paces, turn, pace again and turn. "Unfortunately, such efforts have been fruitless before. No insolent Highland chief will admit that his men are thieves."

"Robert had in mind," I said, "that the English should make an investigation."

"Robert should have better sense," Walter said dryly. "The English can do nothing when their own fortresses are constantly challenged and they dare not leave the walls, even in regiment strength, for fear none will return alive."

"I cannot understand it. Are not the English the conquerors? How can they administer Cromwell's laws in the Highlands unless they prove their invincibility?"

"Invincibility, my dear Anne, is proved or disproved only at the point of a sword. And to their sorrow, the English have found more than their match in the west of Scotland. No Highlander lives who was not taught to fight before he could walk; I'll wager they cut their teeth on a scabbard and learn to handle the sword along with their porridge."

"But they have been defeated," I said. "Cromwell holds all Scotland, even the west."

"Defeat does not always mean conformity," Walter said,

and stopped pacing. He leaned against the lintel and stared into the flames. "They are all heedless rebels at heart, and have never known a restraining hand."

"Has not the Kirk restrained them?"

"It has tried, God knows, and will continue to try. But it is difficult to convert savages, the more so when ministers must go armed in fear of their lives." He shook his head slowly. "It galls me to take the side of the English, but in the case of recalcitrant Royalists, I find myself with no little sympathy for Cromwell's soldiers."

I had never known his tongue to be so loosened before. I would have suspected him of quenching his thirst after his long ride with an excessive amount of wine, but I well knew that Walter carried nothing to excess.

"Is it an organized resistance?" I asked curiously.

"They strike so swiftly, and at such widely separated points, that one would think it merely a matter of scattered forays. Not an unusual pastime, I am told, in the Highlands. But the damage has been so intensive, and the results so unsettling, that it would seem the work of a shrewd and cunning mind. As for myself, I believe one man is behind it all, and I warrant the English commanders have come to the same conclusion."

I looked up quickly. "Do they know the man?"

"They've offered a reward of ten thousand pounds Scots to anyone offering information as to his identity. They intend to hang him properly once he's caught."

"But it would seem a difficult thing to prove. How could they be certain?"

"I imagine they'll not be exceedingly demanding in the matter of proof," he said, "once they suspect a man. What does it matter to the English if they hang the wrong Highlander? One less troublesome Scot, more or less, and they may still justify their search for the real culprit."

"I cannot believe even Cromwell's men would be so craven."

He smiled slightly. "You must agree, Anne, that such a man who incites rebellion and leads a rabble of thieving and murderous Highlanders to wage their own small war against the English and Kirk alike, must accept the penalty for his misdeeds."

"The Kirk? How is the Kirk concerned?"

"I am a Covenanter," he said reasonably, "in good standing in the Kirk, and my domicile has been wantonly attacked and plundered. The ministers feel the one responsible for so much mischief to be possessed of a devil. I do not agree wholeheartedly, but I must admit him to be an uncommon rascal."

"D'you think," I began, choosing my words with great care, "that the raid on Clennon House was the work of this villain?"

"No one can say, least of all I."

"Would you see a man hung, Walter, for stealing horses?"

"I would not wish such a pitiless end for any man," he said quietly. "But if the rogue who snatched my horses from beneath my nose is the same who has been plaguing the English to distraction, he will hang sooner or later."

"The English must catch him first."

"Have you a secret sympathy for rebels, Anne?" he asked, smiling again. "But you are right. The English will do little chasing so long as they are the chased."

"I confess I feel a slight sympathy for anyone who defies the English," I said lightly, "but I regret the loss of your mares."

"The blame is mine, when all is said. If I had known the true state of affairs in the west, I would never have exposed Margaret and yourself to the dangers."

I could not resist adding, "Or the valuable mares?"

"Or the mares," he said, laughing; and it was the first time in three years I had known him to do so.

"Margaret will wish to return to Edinburgh at once."

"But I cannot attend her, and I dare not send her without my protection." He spoke of Margaret in an amiable, almost apologetic tone, as if we stood on a friendlier footing by virtue of our shared knowledge of his sister and her eccentricities. "I must finish my affairs here, and then we will all return to Edinburgh."

And henceforth Margaret will be very difficult to live with, I thought. Walter mistook my silence for disapproval.

"Was it so unpleasant an experience, Anne?" he asked. "You cannot know how deeply I regret that you and Margaret were obliged to suffer such distress."

"You've no need to feel concern for me," I said. "I've

lived through far more frightening events. You'd best see
to Margaret, Walter, and assure her you will take better
care of her in the future. Hers is a delicate nature, you
know."

"Yes," he said, "yes, I must be on my way."

I stood up, having reminded him of his responsibilities,
and felt a vast relief that all had gone so well.

Walter paused beside me, hands still behind him and
his head at an angle, so that he looked much like a serious
professor of a university.

"I must say, Anne, that you look extremely well. Not
every woman can look as fetching with a cold in the head."

He smiled at me quite kindly and walked to the door,
leaving me so astounded that it was a full minute before
I could compose my features and follow him.

His men appeared on the moment and he was once
again the preoccupied master of Clennon House, bidding
me an absent farewell, striding stiffly outside to his horse.

It was well, I thought with amazement, that Margaret
did not know how quickly Walter thawed when freed of
her icy domination, or how his stern resolve weakened
when she was not there to stiffen it. Fetching, indeed, even
with a cold in the head. A dubious compliment, mayhap;
but any compliment from Walter was surely to be wondered at.

I went back to the hall and the comfort of the fire, for
the rain and driving wind had made the day unseasonably
cold, and tried to overcome the sense of depression which
assailed me.

What did it matter, after all, if the day was wild and
I must stay indoors? Margaret would return on the morrow, and I must put aside all unseemly thoughts of a
hidden enchanted glen and long rides in the sunlight. Such
things belonged to yesterday and would not come again,
nor would I likely renew my acquaintance with the man
who shared them with me.

I looked out the window at the gray loch and the wind-
tortured trees, and sighed, and envied the gulls their delight in stormy weather as well as fair.

He would be waiting in the hills, for it was almost midday and he was not a man to give his word lightly. Would
it matter to him, sitting his horse there in the cold rain

when I did not come? Would he be disappointed, or angry, or relieved, or mayhap merely indifferent?

With all my heart I longed to go; and yet a small voice whispered that I must not, that I would regret each indiscretion, that one could not consort with evil without taking evil to one's self. I sighed again, confused and disturbed, and pondered the complexity of discerning right from wrong when it was so seldom a simple choice of black or white but took in the myriad shading of a rainbow.

Turning abruptly from the window, I went toward the fire. But my determination was sadly shaken when I thought of the long day ahead, with no book to read or chores to be done, and freedom resting on my shoulders like a heavy burden.

In the end, it was nothing more than a piece of needlework that decided me. A bit of tapestry, neatly folded with its skeins of sombre-hued wool on a taiffel table where Margaret had left it. I looked at it for a long moment, and then with no more ado went to change my clothes and fetch my cloak and tell Elizabeth that I had taken a sudden urge for fresh air.

Once outside, it was as if midsummer had departed in the night and autumn was upon the land. The birch trees shed their leaves wildly in the face of the wet wind, the hills loomed darkly against a sky which threatened like an ominous battle line of advancing gray banners, the air had a sharp bite to it.

I tied my hood securely beneath my chin and ran for the shelter of the woods, holding up my skirts to avoid the damp bracken. The burn was filled to its banks, a rushing spate of brown water, and I picked my way carefully from one large boulder to another and so to the safety of the opposite bank.

"Well done, lass. I see your sense of balance has improved."

I looked up to find him there before me, leaning his wide shoulders against a tree, his dark cloak blending so skilfully with the wet brown bark that I understood why I had not noticed him before.

"I was coming to fetch you," he said, not moving. "Knowing your cowardly habit of indecision, I had an idea you might not venture out on such a stormy day."

I caught a reasonably steady breath. "Had you come knocking at the door," I said, "Walter Clennon would have greeted you. He only just rode away."

"I seldom knock at doors," he said, "but I can see I would have met with ill fortune however I entered. Doubtless he would not have allowed you to come."

"No doubt at all," I agreed.

"So I have avoided disaster by a very thin margin," he said. "You will learn, however, that any margin at all will serve well enough for me."

He was teasing me, and I would never know how disappointed or indifferent he would have been had I not come.

"I prefer disaster at arm's length, not breathing down my neck."

"You have no sense of adventure, Anne Lindsay."

"But a fair sense of self-preservation."

"A dull affair," he said, "to preserve one's self to no avail. Are you afraid of the Clennons?"

The question was so unexpected that I had no ready answer. "No," I said at last, "I think not."

"Then why do you permit them to rule your life so completely?"

"I owe them my obedience," I said lamely.

"I suspect you owe them nothing," he said calmly. "A small amount of clear thinking would show it to be the other way around."

"I'm quite capable of thinking clearly," I said, finding it somewhat difficult to maintain any dignity with rain dripping from the end of my nose.

"But not of living your own life and making your own decisions."

"You've no right to be so scornful," I said. "We cannot all be lawless freebooters."

"Do I detect a note of envy?" he said, smiling faintly. "Never mind, lass, I shall soon teach you the way of it. Come along and I'll commence the first lesson."

"We cannot ride in the rain."

"On the contrary, I've spent more wet hours in the saddle than dry ones. But I've no intention of riding farther than the gates of Torra today."

My lips framed a refusal, but no words came. I only

looked at him, suddenly aware that the confusion and depression and guilty doubts had curiously departed now that I was with him.

"No protests?" he asked quietly.

"Protests are tiresome," I said. "I've done nothing else since I first saw you." I added honestly, "Margaret returns tomorrow. My holiday is almost at an end."

"Then you will agree that we must make the most of the time left to us."

"Which role do you play today?" I asked. "Gentleman or freebooter?"

He did not smile, but I was aware of his amusement.

"That is for you to discover."

"What shall we do at Torra?"

"I shall present you to my Stewarts, all of whom have betrayed a vast curiosity about you, and then I'll show you how they spend their time when they're not abroad stealing and murdering and molesting helpless women."

"And then?"

"You will see," he said. "If I tell you now, you'll have nothing to anticipate."

He put out his hand to take mine, and as his leather gauntlet closed around my fingers I remembered how the long dirk had looked in his lean hand, shimmering with a cold and dangerous blue light in the sun, and how it had come alive at his careless command.

We walked up the hill together, and he did not release me, and I knew that the time for turning back was past. I could no longer cavil or debate but must go wherever that strong hand led me; and whatever befell me, I must in all honesty admit that the choice had been a free one, of my own making.

So we came to the horses and mounted to ride across the moors and through the narrow glen with its weird stones leaning up against the thin rain, and came at length to the narrow track which ran above the sea and led to the gates of Torra.

Here Monleigh touched spur to his horse and set off at a gallop, and my skitterish mare followed suit, putting back her dainty ears as if to show me her disrelish for plodding tamely along to the rustle of petticoats. I grasped the pommel with both hands, not at all sure I would be able to halt the mare when we reached Torra, and entertained a vision of Anne Lindsay and her derisive mare pounding scorched leather across the moors until someone galloped after to stay the wild flight.

But the mare did not treat me so shamefully, after all. She shortened her stride and came to a trembling halt just as we reached a steep gorge which broke the ground before the gates of Torra.

I looked up and caught my breath, and thought that only a merciful Fate had prevented me from seeing this aspect of Torra on my previous visit. It sat on a rocky precipice above the sea, its massive bulk rising sheer from the edge of the crags, and the gorge below me circled the walls to join again with the sea and render the castle a battlemented island unto itself. The tide was high and the turbulent water surged and boiled through the jagged gorge, and above it Torra towered against the sky like a vast thundercloud, bleak and stark, its walls running black with rain and the arched gate scowling defiance at all before it, the sea and mountains and one awe-struck spinster.

I watched as the drawbridge creaked protestingly into place across the gorge. "It looks very like you," I said. "Did you design it yourself?"

He smiled. "The Stewart who built Torra has been dead two hundred years. He came home one dark night, so the story goes, and forgot to have the drawbridge lowered."

"Too much usquebaugh, I'll wager."

"Undoubtedly," he agreed, "and any man who cannot carry his whisky with a clear head deserves no better fate."

"There must have been a Stewart who threw his enemies over the battlements for the fish to devour," I said, "and perhaps one who jumped himself."

"And we have a ghost who walks through Torra on the stroke of midnight," he said gravely. "It was a matter of unrequited love, I believe."

"Nonsense," I said. "Not a Stewart, and not at Torra. Possibly an enemy took off his head with one cut of a claymore, and now his headless corpse wanders through Torra and reproaches all good Stewarts to take up the sword in revenge."

Monleigh threw back his dark head and laughed. "A

Stewart who allowed his head to be sheared off so easily would never dare to haunt Torra. He'd walk in terror of the living."

"Then I trust I will never be obliged to pass a night here," I retorted. "His ghost would surely seek me out, recognizing a kindred spirit."

The drawbridge still stretched before me, seeming no wider than a needle across the wicked gorge, and no amount of banter would circumvent the immediate necessity of crossing it.

"Well," I said, aware of his amused patience, "I am quite sober, having had no usquebaugh to addle my head."

So I put the mare to a walk, hearing her hoofs strike the planks with a hollow clatter, and kept my eyes on the heavy gates standing open before me. Then I had reached the safety of the dark passageway leading to the courtyard; I was once again in Torra, and could judge its reputation of vicious profligacy for myself.

7

THE mare halted just inside the courtyard, with a last sprightly dance to prove her mettle, and Monleigh dismounted beside me.

I looked about curiously, but there was nothing more to be seen than a large cobbled court, washed clean and empty by the rain, and the usual assortment of stables, kitchens, and various household buildings backed by the higher outer walls. It had the appearance of any other fortress inhabited only by man, no bleaker or more disreputable than a masculine world is wont to be with no feminine hand to soften the harsher edges.

While I stared impolitely about me, the rain became a hard downpour, as if the pointed turrets of the courtyard towers had caught and pierced the wet clouds.

Monleigh lifted me unceremoniously from my saddle. "The lads will be waiting," he said, taking my hands. "Are you drenched through? Come away, we'll make a run for it."

So we ran up the tall cut-stone steps hugging the keep, our faces running with rain and our laughter startling a reproachful gull from his perch atop the stable. Then the door opened before us and we stood in the crowded great hall of Torra.

Breathless and bedraggled I was, scarcely in fit condition to be appraised by a roomful of curious men, but strangely enough I was less unnerved by their scrutiny than I would have imagined.

Monleigh took my sodden cloak and stripped off his own, and a clansman appeared at his elbow on the moment to take them.

"My Stewarts," Monleigh said. "Lads, may I present Mistress Anne Lindsay of Clennon House and Edinburgh."

They bowed in unison, punctilious to a fault, and I put my hand on Monleigh's proffered arm and gave the entire room at large a deep curtsy, for all the world as if we were being formally presented at St James's and must accord one another the most exacting of courtesies.

Then, with more gallantry than I suspected one would find at St. James's with His Highness Oliver Cromwell in residence, they all returned to whatever activities had occupied them before our entrance, so that I was no longer the focus of all eyes. A dice game continued on the floor before the hearth, a dozen or so young men lounged around a long trestle table, and by the fireplace, a cavernous opening of stone which looked capable of holding a tree end to end, a stalwart lad turned his hand energetically to polishing a scabbard of chased silver.

I was vastly interested, never having guessed at the ways a troop of young men might spend their leisure time, but when I met my host's amused eye I imagined they were not wont to be so orderly in demeanor.

"Have you eaten, lass?"

"No," I said, remembering with surprise that I had not. "Where is Evan today?"

"Riding about the countryside," he said, "seeking out more information for me."

"I shouldn't think him very adept at such a delicate business."

"Don't be misled by his ugly face and blunt ways. He's the canniest man in all Scotland when it comes to guile and craft."

"Evan?" I said, disbelieving.

He laughed. "He has a dozen guises, lass, but I think he favours best the one he showed you. 'Tis odd how a man who lives by cunning prefers to act the slow-witted clod who possesses naught but good humour and a strong sword arm."

"Mayhap," I said tentatively, " 'tis more to his nature to be good-humoured."

"I've no doubt of it," he agreed promptly, "especially when he finds himself in your company. He's a man's man, is Evan, until a pretty lass appears on the scene."

"You're a craven friend," I said, "to so betray him when he isn't present to defend his character."

"Tell that to Evan and he'll love you for it."

The men had cleared the table by the time we reached it, and Monleigh pulled a chair forward and seated me with exaggerated ceremony.

"Display a huge appetite," he ordered, "else you'll lose face in this company."

So I was given the place of honour at the head of the long trestle table; and I dined on a fat roasted capon stuffed with mushrooms, and tiny green peas seasoned with sweet butter, and an unfamiliar drink of a deep tawny brown served to me in a tiny silver cup.

"Chocolate," Monleigh explained at my elbow. "Quite the rage in France. Do you like it?"

After the first bitter taste, I decided that I liked it very much, and so had a second cup sweetened with sugar.

"Do you always eat so fashionably?" I asked, no little amazed. "I thought men were satisfied with no more than a haunch of venison and a tankard of ale."

"I must confess," he said, "that we usually manage very well on meat and ale. But today we have a guest, and so felt the need to appear at our best."

He handed me a small golden pear, dripping with sweet juices, and I ate it with a fine carelessness for my face and hands.

"But where do you find such delicacies?" I asked when I had finished it to the last delectable bite. "Surely not in the west of Scotland."

He smiled and gave me another pear. "We smuggle them in, of course," he said, "along with velvets and damask and silver plate. And should the need arise, a cargo of guns and powder now and again."

I should have known better than to expect a serious answer from him. "Then perhaps one day I might persuade you to smuggle a bolt of crimson velvet for me. I've a great yearning for a crimson gown."

"An emerald green would become you better."

"But it would not satisfy my longing for a crimson one. And I should like a pair of Parisian slippers, if you please, fashioned of satin to match the gown."

"And a tiara of diamonds? You shall have them, Anne Lindsay. A Stewart could never deny a lass with a yearning heart."

"No," I said, "I don't care for diamonds. Pearls, I think, would be in better taste."

I laughed at him, and he leaned over to wipe my mouth with a linen square.

"You're smeared with pear juice," he said. "Next time I shall feed you strawberries. A crimson mouth will go quite well with a crimson gown."

Of a sudden I was very shy; and so I turned away from him and looked at the men below us at the table, all of them seeming quite pleased with themselves and the occasion.

"I told you once I would teach you the volta," Monleigh said. "Are you ready for the lesson?"

The pipes were skirling with abandon, and I could not escape the challenge in his eyes or the laughter in his voice.

"Yes," I said, "I am ready enough." And I thought to myself that it would be unreasonable to balk at one small additional sin when the list had already stretched to such lengths.

The men must have guessed at our intentions as soon as we left the table, for they cheered lustily and cleared the tables in a trice; and I was left facing an empty floor and an attentive audience of some size for my first lesson in the sinful art of dancing.

"Turn a pretty leg for the lass, Sim," a red-haired clansman shouted, and the entire company then proceeded to give freely of advice and derisive comment.

"Show her how it's done at Court, with the scented handkerchief to your nose."

"Aye, he can simper with the best of French fops. Watch closely, lads, and learn the trick in it."

"When ye tire of his great lumbering boots, lass, ye've only to call on me, who taught him all he knows of dancing."

"And that little enough, God help the poor lass."

Monleigh turned me to face him and laughed down at me as if he cared not a jot for the lack of respect accorded his consequence in his own stronghold.

"Pay them no heed," he said. "Ugly fellows, the lot of them, and so long without women that they've forgotten their manners."

Loud jeers and taunts greeted this insult, and a great deal of laughter, and the pipes took up the clamour and shrilled a lively air.

"We'll begin slowly," said Monleigh, "until you've caught the rhythm of it. 'Tis simple enough, requiring nothing more than energy and stamina."

It was a simple dance, in truth, and I faltered only once or twice before I saw how it was done. But it was also vastly exhilarating, for I was not accustomed to swinging back and forth in a wide circle, nor being lifted high in the air and twirled over a man's head, and so found myself growing quite giddy and lightheaded.

But the lesson was to be a thorough one, I saw, for soon the entire company joined us on the floor and each man took his turn as my partner; and while I was whirled from arm to arm, and lifted high by each new dancer who wished to prove his superiority before the others, I wondered if the general hilarity or my own exhaustion would prove my downfall.

Then it was Monleigh's turn again, and he held my arm firmly and brought me to a halt.

"No more, you greedy vultures," he said, and would not be dissuaded by the uproar of protests. "Would you send her back to Clennon House in a state of collapse?"

He led me to the door, and I smiled farewell at his Stewarts and wished I had the breath to thank them for treating me so kindly. We went through a long corridor and a small chamber boasting nothing but a table and candles, and so into a large room where a brisk fire burned on the hearth and tapestried hangings shut out the draughts.

The floor there was laid of a dark golden wood, a fashionable innovation I would not have thought to find in the Highlands, and the high-backed chairs by the fire had comfortable cushions of Flemish embroidery. It was a vastly cheerful chamber, with two windows facing the sea and two looking south, and I imagined that on fair days the warmth of the sun would be captured there from morning until night.

"My father valued his comfort secondly only to his King," Monleigh said. "He had a great distaste for stone dungeons."

He poured wine from a tall bottle and handed the glass to me. "You look as if you have need of it," he said, and pushed back a damp unruly curl which had fallen over my forehead. "You danced very well for a novice. Do you feel sinful beyond redemption?"

I sipped the cool wine gratefully. "Now that I have tried it for myself," I said, "I wonder why it is considered so wicked a thing. Surely one would have no energy left for sinning after a rousing dance or two."

"Sin often loses its terrors," he said, "when examined closely."

"I think the Kirk condemns anything which gives pleasure," I said thoughtfully. "Surely God cannot be so embittered and dour."

"And you are now doubly condemned, sweet Anne, for dancing on the Sabbath."

I almost choked on my wine. To break the Sabbath in any fashion was reprehensible enough, for presbyterians were forbidden to walk, or visit, or laugh, or pick their own gooseberries on the Lord's Day; to break it with dancing was a transgression so heinous as to be beyond belief.

"Don't look so horrified. We've no spies in Torra to report you to the Kirk."

"Do the English require you to pay a great deal to keep Torra?" I said, to change the subject.

"Aye, a fortune," he said, "and I must continue to dole it out each month."

"And the Kirk?"

"The Kirk," he said carelessly, "has no army mustered in the Highlands, and so I let them whistle for their gold."

I remembered that Walter had once said the Royalists were kept docile only by reason of their poverty, and the King himself wore a shabby doublet and cadged meals from his relatives on the Continent, and cursed the cunning of Cromwell's scheme to render the King's Scots harmless by taking their gold and their pride at one stroke.

"Will they take Torra," I asked, "if you once fail to pay?"

"I'll give them no such opportunity." He went to one of the tall windows and rested his hands on the casement. "Come here, lass."

I went to stand beside him and look down on the sea, an incredible distance below the window. The surf hammered at the crag of land and the wind came across miles of open sea to beat with furious ire against the thick walls, but Torra sat its island of stone and turned a face of cold scorn to sea and man alike.

"Look below you to the south," Monleigh said.

I saw nothing but wild headlands jutting into the sea, their black granite the only positive colour in a world of gray rain, gray water, gray tattered mists. A scene of lonely desolation, I thought, but somehow fascinating by virtue of that very stark and sombre beauty.

"Do you see the large flat boulder above the near cliff?"

"Yes, I see it."

"Beyond it is a narrow cove where the water is deep even at the ebb tide."

"It looks to be a dangerous spot."

"Quite deadly when one is unfamiliar with the coast hereabouts. But it provides an excellent harbour, protected by a chain of rocks and ledges across the entrance and furnishing draught enough for a barque-of-war."

"I should not care to navigate a ship through those ledges," I said, watching the foam tossed high in the air as the sea and land clashed together.

"Easy enough," he said, "with a skilled helmsman at the wheel and a leadsman lashed to the bowsprit."

"And a stout heart for each of them."

"If a ship were anchored there now, you could see only the topmost rigging from the ground. D'you see the advantage in it?"

"So Torra has a secret harbour," I said, delighted, "as well as a hidden glen in the hills." Then I added, "But I should think a ship there would be plainly visible to anyone looking down on Torra from the hills."

"I told you once that the Stewarts keep their hills and moors free of spying eyes," he said, "and you reproached me roundly for my selfishness."

I gave him a level stare. "Why does it matter? What would a man see if he spied on Torra from the hills?"

"A great deal he should not see," Monleigh said calmly. "Would you have me hanged for a smuggler?"

"I don't believe you."

"Does your disbelief spring from charity or hope?"

He was not jesting, after all. I had only to look at his dark face, to hear the chill suddenly returned to his voice, to know with certainty that he spoke the truth.

"The Earl of Monleigh," I said slowly, "a smuggler and a horse thief."

And yet I was not too amazed, for one was no worse than the other when all was said, and I had already known him for an unscrupulous rogue.

"If you think to shame me, you must do better than that."

"Is that how you keep Torra from the English?"

"A man must use his imagination," he said coolly, "when he is denied the right to his sword. I find it amusing to pay English taxes with English gold."

"The English are not amused," I answered, my eyes on the sea, "by the men who raid their garrisons and attack their patrols. 'Tis a graver offense than smuggling."

"War is a grave matter."

"The war is over. Cromwell rules Scotland."

"That is a matter of opinion," he said, and his voice was dangerously soft. "What do you know of such things as raids and attacks, Anne Lindsay?"

"Only what Walter Clennon told me today. A reward of ten thousand pounds has been posted for the man who has been plaguing the English."

"I am of two minds," he said lightly, "whether to consider myself insulted or flattered. What think you, lass?"

The cold wind off the sea penetrated the thin panes and sent a chill through my blood, and I felt an astonishing urge to weep.

"They mean to hang you," I said, low.

"Would you rejoice," he asked lightly, "to see this villain receive his just reward?"

I met his eyes at last. "There is naught in hanging to jest about. Why do you tell me these things? I have only to repeat them to the Clennons to bring the English down about your ears."

"And receive ten thousand clinking pieces of gold for your pains. Does the thought appeal to you?"

"Perhaps," I said.

He smiled. "But you will not repeat anything to the Clennons," he said quietly.

"You have no reason to trust me."

"Reason enough," he said. "You will see."

I left him and walked across the room to the fire, at such a loss for words that I needed to widen the distance between us before I could compose myself.

I bethought myself of the gibbets I had seen at the Mercat Cross in Edinburgh, tall and thin against the sky, their pitiful burdens swaying uneasily in the wind. Tattered rags, a distorted bundle of terrifying inertness which once was a man, and all the crooked houses staring down at the market place, at the mute warning to the living that here was one beyond all pride or arrogance, beyond even the last painful humiliation, one whose miserable flesh must remain to bear the shame his spirit had left behind.

I turned to look at his dark head and powerful shoulders outlined against the window, and wondered if it would be blasphemous to pray that I would never live to be told that this man, as alive and proud and arrogant as no man I had ever known, had come to death at the end of a hangman's rope beneath the Mercat Cross.

"You've changed a great deal since I first saw you," he said. "All of two days ago, was it not?" He walked to the table and poured a glass of wine. "You are not so easily shocked now, and you've lost that tiny frown between your eyes. And now and again you have the look of a lass who would like to toss discretion to the wind and cry good riddance after it."

"I think you deal in witchcraft," I said. "I only change when I am with you."

"A sorcerer? Perhaps so, but I did not cast the first spell." He smiled at me. "I remember thinking, when I met you on the shore, that I would like to be the one to bring you back to life."

"Is that why you came to Clennon House?" I asked unevenly, moving so that one of the tall chairs was between us. "Did you think to entertain yourself by showing the respectable spinster the error of her ways?"

"Do you really wish to know why I first sought you out?"

I said, with great care, "No woman likes to play the fool."

Arms resting on the carved back of the chair, he regarded me with his eyes narrowed and dark, hooded against the firelight and my own searching gaze.

"Pity came first," he said, "and then contempt."

"Pity?" I whispered, and my cheeks flamed.

"Pity for you, and contempt for Walter and Margaret Clennon. Does that answer your question?"

I put my hands behind me and clasped them tightly together. "Yes," I said.

"You wished to know why I first sought you out."

"And you have told me. I am grateful for your honesty."

"Are you? Will you be honest with me in return?"

"Honesty," I said quietly, "must sometimes be taken in small measure, like a bitter medicine."

"But the bitter taste seldom lasts beyond the moment, and then one begins to feel immeasurably better."

"I am quite aware that honesty is an admirable virtue."

"Yet you shrink from it, just as a child will shape his mouth into a button and refuse to take his medicine."

"You, of course, would know nothing of such cowardice."

"I have a vague recollection of it," he said, "but I was very young at the time. Now that I am older I know the folly of turning my face from the truth."

I was obliged to protest this injustice. "I have no quarrel with the truth."

"Then you must finish what you begin. Have you mislaid your curiosity?"

I wished, somewhat desperately, that he would move or look away from me, but he did neither.

"Now that I am older by a moment or so," I said, "I know the folly of it."

"And you should also know the folly of taking your medicine by sips. It only prolongs the agony."

"All this talk of medicine. My mouth is turning inside out."

The firelight glinted in his eyes, still narrowed, still inscrutable. "You asked only one question, and that one of small importance. Don't you care for my answers?"

"No," I said, "I do not."

"Do you really believe," he said inexorably, "that you are here today because I feel so great a pity for you?"

"You said it yourself," I said, at last stung to anger. "Have you changed your mind? Pray don't compromise your honesty on my account, m'lord. I assure you my feelings are not so sensitive."

"The devil take your feelings. Stop hedging, lass."

"I don't want your pity. Keep it for yourself, I've no need of it."

"You no longer have it," he said, no whit perturbed. "We are speaking, I believe, of my original motives for seeking your company."

I stared at him. "Have you others?"

At once I regretted my heedless question. I should never have asked it, I should turn away from his dark face, and the quiet implacable voice, and the truth I had known all along to be hidden behind those narrowed eyes.

"You are a woman," he said. "You should understand such matters without having to be told."

I unclasped my hands, feeling a cramp in each separate finger.

"But you are an innocent, sweet Anne, lacking the most rudimentary knowledge of feminine wiles, and so I shall explain it very carefully to you. I want no misunderstanding between us."

He placed his wine glass on the table and moved around the chair, and because there was no retreat unless I stepped backward into the fire, I was obliged to hold my ground.

"You are still afraid of me," he said coolly. "Or is it, perhaps, only a fear that you stand too near the fire and might burn yourself?"

I found that I could not be less than honest with him, after all, by pretending that I did indeed misunderstand him.

"A little of both," I said faintly.

"Whatever happens," he said, his voice gone low and hard, "it will be less painful than you imagine."

"It is foolhardy to seek pain."

"No pain is unbearable," he said, "except that of regret."

Putting his hand under my chin, he lifted my face as he had done once before, in the quiet glen in the hills, and I knew the same breathless sense of being alone with him in a world where nothing had substance or reality but his touch and the sound of his voice.

"I admit you stand in dangerous company," he said, unsmiling, "and will likely come to grief before you've done with the Stewarts. No one can promise happiness to another, however much he may wish it, and no man can measure the torment he may cause a woman." His hand held me motionless there before him, but I had no will to move. "But I shall take care that you'll never live to know regret on my account."

I might know nothing of feminine wiles, but some inner instinct told me that such matters were not usually decided between a man and woman in so blunt and deliberate a fashion.

"You cannot expect me to make a decision here and now," I said, shaken.

"The decision was made some time past," he said. "It has been out of your hands since the moment you left Clennon House that first day to walk on the moors."

If I searched my heart, I was obliged to admit that he spoke the truth. Why else had I gone riding with him, and run to meet him in the rain, and come to Torra in so brazen and unseemly a manner? He had given me every opportunity to turn away from him, to refuse his company, yet from the beginning I had heeded nothing but the inexplicable fascination which drew me to him.

"You are daft," I whispered. "If I have no choice in the matter, what are you asking of me?"

"I want you to trust me," he said. "It will make it easier for you."

It did not occur to me to remind him that he was not a man the world would consider it wise to trust without reservation, for at that moment the world's opinion of him mattered not a jot to me. I knew only that he had spoken to me with explicit honesty, and so had put me to shame.

"If I am too hesitant," I said, "it is only because I am cowardly and shrink from the burden of responsibility. You are too honest with me, you see, and henceforth I can blame no one but myself if I suffer from my misdeeds."

"You have forgotten," he said, "that I promised there would be no regrets."

"And no self-reproach?"

"Only if you dissemble," he said calmly, "and are untrue to yourself."

"You give no quarter, m'lord."

"Neither do I ask it."

"But you have no need of it," I said childishly.

"Would you grow old, Anne Lindsay," he said softly, "without once daring to taste life for yourself?"

For an instant I thought that he intended to kiss me, and I drew a deep breath and tried to make my mouth less tremulous than it felt. But I could not breathe properly, and my trembling would not be stayed; and I suddenly understood all he had tried to tell me, all I had denied in mistrust and apprehension.

"No," he said, and smiled. "I'll not force the pace."

He dropped his hand and the tiny flames in his eyes flickered with laughter. The moment was gone, and my first intoxicating taste of life was, to my way of thinking, far too brief and fleeting.

"Then we are agreed," he said, "that you will no longer cavil and protest. We will think on ways for you to escape Margaret Clennon's eagle eye, and you will come to Torra whenever you can." As if this was not incredible enough, he added, "And we will take our pleasure as we find it, with no terrible guilt on our consciences for our sins."

He held out his hand, and without ado I took it. And so the outrageous bargain was sealed with no more than the simple masculine gesture; and if I immediately began to entertain certain private doubts of my sanity, he allowed me no time to vacillate.

Taking his pear-shaped lute from the table and propping one booted foot on the hearth fender, he said without looking around, "Sit down, lass."

I sat, feeling a sudden need for it.

"What shall I play for you?"

"Something gay, if you please," I said. "Do you also sing?"

"If you were anyone but yourself," he said, "and we had not bargained to be honest with one another, I might say that I sing infrequently, and only when I've an appreciative audience. But the truth of the matter is that I think myself to have an excellent voice and sing on the slightest pretext, until my Stewarts hate the sight of me and threaten to stuff their ears unless I desist."

"Such honesty," I said. "You set a poor example for me to follow."

His fingers touched the lute strings with a careless skill, making it difficult for me to remember that they were equally skilled at handling a sword hilt or a carved dirk, or mayhap at closing in violent anger about a man's neck.

But I would not allow myself to be disturbed. We had made a pact between us, however foolish, and I was content to watch his hands on the lute and his face absorbed and relaxed over it, and listen to his deep clear baritone as he sang a ballad or two for my amusement.

"If you had no title or estate," I said idly when he paused, "you might earn your bread and keep by singing in the streets. Or going from castle to castle, like the old bards, entertaining the nobility."

"I'll remember that," he said gravely. "It may be I'll need to earn my bread and keep honestly one day."

"Doubtless you'd prefer the dishonest life of a smuggler."

"Surely," he said mildly. "But it has its disadvantages. Hard work to break a man's back, miserable rations, long hours at the watch, foul weather more often than fair, and the chance always at hand of meeting an English man-of-war."

"A singer of ballads, on the other hand, has nothing more strenuous to do than to strum his foolish lute."

"And nothing more dangerous than rhyming a pretty verse for a pretty lass."

"It would become you famously," I said, laughing at the thought.

"Perhaps," he said, "when I am old and gray, and can no longer cope with the ache in my bones."

He struck up a rollicking air I had never heard. "A sailor's chantey," he explained, and laughed down at me. "Unfortunately, we smugglers can seldom sing to our work aboard ship. We're too eager to escape notice, and must preserve a great silence at all times."

He sang the coarse and lusty verses with a fine disregard for my sensibilities, but the deep lilting accent he assumed, as if he were one of his own Highland sailors, was so cheerfully infectious that I soon joined in the chorus, admitting my sensibilities to be blunted beyond recognition.

I slipped to the floor before the hearth, and found the rug and the warmth of the fire vastly more comfortable than the stiff, intricately carved chair.

"You've a fair voice," Monleigh commented, "but a woeful habit of slipping off key."

"And you have a great conceit," I retorted.

"Never mind, lass. Sing loudly enough and it'll never be noticed."

We sang again, and exchanged an insult or two, and I discovered, with no great surprise, that I was very happy.

"The lute was not designed for such vigorous treatment," he said. "One day I must play the pipes for you."

"And wear a kilted plaid? Your Stewarts often wear skirts, I've noticed, and I'd hoped you would don one for my benefit."

" 'Tis no' to be ridiculed," he said, grinning. "We take a great pride in the wearing of it."

"Like children dressing in women's clothes, or barbarians who know no better."

"We ha' a purpose," he said firmly. " 'Tis a coat of arms, the tartan, worn proudly for all men to see and take warning. And the plaid is an admirable piece of invention, serving as a suit of clothes or a blanket for sleeping or a braw protection against the wildest storm. Try that with a pair of Lowland breeks and see for yourself what will happen."

"I've no intention of trying it, either in breeks or plaid."

"You stand in ignorance of such matters," he said, "and have no right to be insulting."

"If you think so highly of the belted plaid, why aren't you wearing one?"

His grin returned. "There are times," he said, "when I've no wish to wear my name emblazoned in scarlet and green on my back. It would make it too simple for some dolt of an Englishman to collect ten thousand pounds of bounty."

We fell silent then. The fire mulled quietly and the wind battered with an angry futility at the windows; and the lute was only a slow sweet thread of melody, as if his mind was intent on other matters and so his fingers were obliged to draw from some lost and forgotten corner of memory. And I realized that the music of his lute served more purpose than I had imagined, that he used it as another man will absently drink wine and then toy with his glass until it be filled again for him, yet never taste the wine or see the glass before him on the table. It was a matter of concentration, of keeping his hands and the outward portion of his mind occupied with ordinary affairs, thus leaving a quiet and secret part of himself free to think clearly and unencumbered.

After a long while I said, "You said there must be no misunderstandings between us."

He said nothing, waiting.

"But you have not yet told me what the Earl of Monleigh sees in the spinster, Anne Lindsay."

"When you call yourself a spinster," he said lazily, "I presume you refer to the fact that you are still unwed. I see no tragedy in that, since you are scarcely in your twenties, nor do I discern the attraction in being wed to some pimply-faced lad before one is well out of the cradle."

"It is the accustomed thing, being wed when young."

"The accustomed thing is not always to be admired or desired," he said, "and you are still exceedingly young. As for myself, I find it most convenient that you have no husband glowering in the background. It would make matters slightly more difficult for me."

My eyes widened. "Would you have done the same had I a husband?"

He put his lute aside. "Aye," he said quietly, "I would have brought you to Torra and danced the volta with you and watched you laugh. And I would have told you that you are absurdly lovely, especially when you sit cross-legged on the floor before the fire and sing an unseemly sailor's air with me."

"You will turn my head, m'lord," I said unsteadily. "I am unused to such flattery."

" 'Tis past time your head was turned a trifle," he said. "A fair lass deserves no less. And my name is Simon. Try it once, if only to taste the sound of it."

Forced to the issue, I did so, and we both laughed at my awkwardness. Then he took my hands, pulling me to my feet, and told me it was time to see me home to Clennon House; and that is all that happened, no more or less, the day I went to Torra and spent a long rainy afternoon consorting with evil.

{ 8 }

WE sat in the small hall, Margaret and Walter and Robert MacLeish and I, and the endless day dragged out its endless hours and minutes.

Margaret plied her needle with great industry, having already examined my own embroidery work and found it gratifyingly inferior to her own. "What did you do with yourself, other than lying abed, while I was gone?" she asked, sighing at my indolence, and I did not remind her that she had ordered me to remain in bed till I had recovered from the illness she had fashioned for me.

I was kept busy enough the first day she arrived back at Clennon House. The entire house must be aired, the linens cleaned and counted, the supplies in the pantries checked and rechecked for fear the thieving Highland servants had made away with a boll of meal or a pinch of salt, Margaret's riding clothes freshened and cleaned of dirty Highland mud, and Margaret herself cozened and placated to restore her good humour after two days of Cameron hospitality which did not include an Anne Lindsay for her comfort but only an ignorant woman of the clan who sniffed down her nose at Margaret's demands and spoke only Gaelic.

Now that she had been enthroned in Clennon House again for the best part of twenty-four hours, Margaret had exhausted her immediate list of chores for me. I was called to the hall to keep her company, and to be close at hand should she need a shawl for her shoulders or another skein of thread for her needlework; and since no woman might sit in Margaret's presence with idle hands, I kept my head lowered above my imperfect needlework and welcomed the opportunity to sit quietly for a fleeting moment.

Robert had been holding forth for some time on the

subject of morning prayers, and the lamentable habit of
the Highland servants to avoid such Christian practices
whenever possible.

Then he cleared his throat and began to swing one leg,
a nervous affectation as much a part of him as his long
nose.

"I heard something of your neighbour," he said, "while
I was away."

Walter turned from the window, and Margaret raised
her eyes to fix Robert with a cold stare.

"Neighbor?" she repeated.

"Lord Monleigh," said Robert, looking at his restless
foot.

After an astonished silence, Margaret said firmly, "We
do not discuss the man in this household."

"I should think not," Robert said. "The name itself is
a vile abomination, and the man who bears it a spawn of
the Devil. The Kirk is aroused to his infamy; I met a
minister on the track to the English garrison."

"Is he coming in this direction?" Margaret asked. "Can
we look forward to a visit from him?"

"No doubt. Indeed, it was the mention of that very
thing which led us to a discussion of the Earl." He added
casually, "I would imagine the Kirk sent the minister to
these parts for no other reason."

He had Margaret's full attention now; her pale eyes
gleamed with the opaque glitter of sun on a pane of glass.

"For what reason, Robert?"

"To see what can be done about Monleigh, of course.
The man blackens the very name of Scotland."

"It would be blackened beyond repair were every
scoundrel's sins to show there. They have only to arrest
him, you know."

"I fear it is not so simple as that."

"Indeed?" Margaret said thinly. "And why not? I see
no good reason why he has gone free till now."

Walter spoke from the window. "He resides in an impregnable fortress, sister, and the Kirk has no army to
storm it."

Margaret's needle flashed in and out with a restrained
fury. "The English have soldiers. They use their army to
take whom they please, and why not Monleigh?"

"Those they take," said Robert, "are then tried in English courts with English judges. Do you dream a nonbeliever, a Dissenter, would convict a man for being untrue to the Kirk of Christ? On the contrary, Margaret, I fear they would condone his heresy, being no more than heretics themselves."

"Have they no score against him? Did he not fight for the King with Montrose's Irish rabble? They have only to seize his estates, force him to forfeit his title. It has been done to Royalists far less despicable than Monleigh."

"He pays his fines to the last groat," said Walter. "They've nothing to hold against him thus far."

The last two words echoed in my mind, then clung there like a limpet and would not be dislodged.

"What does the minister think to do?" asked Margaret. "They should have sent an elder, someone with proper authority to chastise the man."

"He will watch," said Robert, "and see what can be done. He is one of the ministers who travel through the Highlands, and he has been in the west before. There will be less suspicion aroused by his questions."

I smoothed the round of tapestry on my lap. A bird, two figures dressed in clothes fashioned of bright thread, a colourful scene which brought Margaret's disapproval whenever she caught sight of it; and yet the bird would never sing, never know a single golden note, and the man and woman standing there were but woven puppets possessing no life, or breath, or any passion.

"His name is Peter Finlay," Robert went on. "I believe that he once stood for the Kirk in a parish in Angus. He is not precisely the man I would have chosen for the task of ferreting out Monleigh, but doubtless he is well qualified as a minister."

"I quite shudder," I said, with an unwonted audacity in my heart, "to think that I stayed here alone for two days and nights and never suspected such a monster existed close by."

Margaret said, "I warned you of him."

"But you only warned me," I said, "and did not go into detail. Are his crimes so terrible that I would know him at first sight for the villain he is? I trust he hasn't the lo of an ordinary man, else I might not be able to escape him in time."

"You run no risk of seeing him," Margaret said. "He'll not come to Clennon House."

"Unfortunately," Robert said, with a look down his long nose at me, "there have been women enough who did not see him for the villain he is, and they did not escape him."

There was a long silence. I looked up from my tapestry, suddenly aware of a strange undercurrent of emotion in the room which had not been there before.

"You frighten me, Robert," I said quietly.

"No need for that," Walter said. He gave me a kindly glance. "I'm certain Robert had no such intention. Monleigh is a heretic and a renegade, but no inhuman monster. You and Margaret stand in no danger from him, else I'd not have ventured to bring you to Clennon House."

Margaret was quite angry; I knew it from the set of her face and the chill in her voice. "I'll tell you his crimes, and you may judge for yourself if he's human."

"Margaret," Walter said mildly, "I think it unnecessary to dwell on the subject."

She ignored him, as was her wont. "He murdered and plundered the length of Scotland under the false Montrose. He still dares to profess loyalty to the King, that loathsome son of Belial. He flouts his heresy before the world, making his castle a vile place of adultery and carousing, and the tales of the orgies held secretly in the dark of night at Torra would turn your blood cold in your veins. 'Tis said he deals in witchcraft, and I've no doubt of it. Those who have come to a violent death at his hands would seem to bear witness to evil given him by the Devil's hand. He forces himself on helpless women for the sole purpose of defiling them, and seduces them from all virtue and reason, and has scattered a brood of unnatural children to perpetuate his shame."

It seemed that she would never pause for breath, that she needed none but spoke on one long wave of resentment; but Walter came across the room to stand with his hand on her shoulder and the spate of words ceased for a single moment.

"You have said enough," Walter said. "It will only upset you."

"I have not finished," she said flatly. "His hands are stained with blood. He took a wife, a pure and innocent lass no more than a child, and when he tired of her he had her foully murdered."

Walter frowned. "Margaret, we know all these things. Pray don't make yourself ill by thinking of them. It will serve no good purpose."

"Anne does not know them. No monster, you would have her believe, but I say it will only serve evil if we allow delicacy to hide the truth from her."

I stared at my lap, at the scrap of tapestry with its stiff lifeless figures and silent bird, and struggled desperately to keep my balance in a room which swirled and danced giddily before my eyes.

"Yes, it is always well to know the truth," I said, hearing my voice as from a great distance.

"Anne, you look quite pale and faint," Robert said unsympathetically from the midst of the fog. "Have you still signs of a fever? I should think you would keep yourself away from others until you are quite well."

Then Margaret's cold voice, "Anne has not been well for several days. She has been of no use to me whatever, and it would seem she has no thought for anyone but herself."

I stood up and said, "By your leave," and walked to the door, feeling my head grow clearer with each step I took away from them.

Behind me Walter said in a low voice, "She has been suffering from a bitter cold, sister. Don't be too hard on her."

I closed the door on Robert's snort of exasperation, and thought on Walter's reckless impulse to defend me. I knew of no reason for his sudden kindly attention toward me, but doubtless Margaret would soon put him to rights and he would return to that air of preoccupation which normally set him apart from the world. And I could not blame him; he was a temperate man, with a strong aversion to strife. It was not irresolution, I imagined, so much as compliance, not evasion so much as an ability to adjust to the winds of chance. In the heat of battle, Walter would be the first to seek a truce and offer a compromise; and who was to say that such reasonable prudence was not to be admired?

I did not go to my bedchamber, but went down the long corridors to the kitchen. There I found Elizabeth, as I had anticipated, alone in the vast room designed to accommodate the horde of cooks, stewards, spit boys, maids, and serving men who crowded it at mealtime. She was busily scrubbing an enormous table which had long since been scrubbed to a furry white cleanliness, and she was humming a song as she worked.

"Have you no leisure, Elizabeth?" I asked. "Do you always labour so diligently?"

The humming ceased. "I've naught to do with leisure but sit and twiddle my fingers."

"Margaret will wish to take you back to Edinburgh with her. The kitchen has never been so tidy before."

"Wishing is one thing," she said, "and doing, another."

"What did you," I asked idly, "before you came to Clennon House?"

"I cooked and kept a tidy kitchen."

"A large kitchen, such as this?"

"My peat fire would fit snugly into the corner of yon hearth."

"But you are accustomed to feeding great numbers," I said. "Did you learn that over your peat fire?"

"I've had a brood of bairns most of my lifetime," she said, "and a man to feed."

"And who feeds them now, while you cook for the Clennons?"

She scrubbed energetically at some invisible spot. "They ha' their great stomachs filled, never fear."

If I had a secret of life or death, I thought, I would surely entrust it to Elizabeth and be assured it'd be kept safe.

"A man was just here asking for ye," she said, "but I told him ye were too busy to bother with the likes o' him."

"How very wise of you," I murmured. "Did he leave a message?"

"Aye. 'Tis a fair day, he said, and mayhap a walk in the sun would be of some benefit to ye."

"What sort of man was he?"

"No' the sort I'd care to go walking with."

"An ugly fellow, with a broken nose?"

"And a nasty brace of pistols," she replied. "It were a

pity ye ha' no more handsome gentleman than he to come wooing ye."

"A pity," I agreed. I rubbed my fingers along the satin surface of the table. "Elizabeth, why did you not tell me of Lord Monleigh's wife?"

After a pause she said, "Ye know it now. Who was I to tell ye?"

"Will you tell me how she died?"

"She died," Elizabeth said flatly, "and that's all I know."

"I've been told . . ." I stopped and swallowed, and took another breath. "They say she was murdered."

"Ye can hear anything," she said impassively, "if ye lend your ears to gossip long enough."

I raised my head and found her eyes on my face, and so we stared at each other for a lengthy moment.

"And if you were inclined to gossip," I asked slowly, "what would you say?"

"I'd say a woman deserves what she gets, and that not often enough."

My heart beat painfully in my throat. "Then you believe he did indeed murder her."

"I said nothing of the sort."

"Do you know him well?"

"He's lord of all the land hereabouts," she said briefly. "I've lived here the best part of my life, would ye expect him to be a stranger to me?"

"Then you knew his wife as well."

She looked me straight in the eye. "Aye, I knew her."

"How did she die, Elizabeth?"

"Why don't you ask his lordship?"

"You always return to that. 'Tis not an easy question to ask a man."

And yet, I thought, he gave me his pledge to be honest with me, and he had asked me in return to trust him.

"If it were easy, ye'd know without having to ask."

"Do you think him a man to murder?" I persisted, and the word seemed unreal and without meaning when spoken aloud.

Elizabeth gave me one last stare and went back to her scrubbing.

"No one knows a man like the woman who shares his bed," she said. "If ye fear to ask him, why not ask her?"

"But she's dead," I said with tolerable patience.

"Then mayhap ye've no business asking questions in the first place."

I might as well be seeking information from an oyster, I thought with exasperation. But she had the truth of it.

"I am sorry," I said. "I've no right to pry."

"Ye've no apology to make to me."

"The apology is due Lord Monleigh," I said, "but I can scarcely apologize to him without giving reason, and that would be a second discourtesy."

"Then I'll take it," she said, "and hope ye'll learn better manners."

I knew I had redeemed myself in her eyes, and was not at all surprised by the smile in her eyes. Then she turned her back on me and went to work scrubbing a black pot.

"If you happen to see the fellow with the pistols again," I said, "wouldst tell him a walk is impossible today?"

"Like enough," she said, "ye're shivering at the thought of being murdered on such a fair day. That's the way of things, and small blame to ye."

"I'm not shivering."

"Ye might consider that he's not known ye long enough yet, and would scarcely do away with ye before he's had his bit of entertainment."

"I cannot get away. You know Margaret would not allow it."

"Ye've only to ask," she said, "and no harm done."

"Then I will ask, and prove I am not so craven as you'd have me."

She said nothing more, and so I turned and went back to the door of the hall. I did not hesitate, fearing I'd lose my nerve, but opened the door and stood facing the three of them with no more than a very small and treacherous tremor.

"What is it now?" Margaret said impatiently.

I decided on the moment that to ask permission would be to invite refusal. "I think I shall take a walk," I said. "Mayhap the fresh air will clear my head."

Margaret stared at me. "I begin to suspect, Anne, that you need more than fresh air to clear your head. You'll exhaust yourself, and then I'll be obliged to nurse you. Have you no consideration?"

"I'll not go far."

Walter hesitated, then said firmly, "It will do you no harm to get out in the sun. But I might suggest that you take a horse, Anne. It will not tire you so much."

And that has done it, I thought hopelessly. Margaret's sharp scrutiny went to Walter and back to me and settled on her needlework. She said nothing, but her silence was enough to daunt the boldest heart.

"I prefer to walk, Walter," I said, "but I thank you for your kind offer."

"Nonsense. Take one of the horses. They were not ridden hard on our return from John Cameron's, and you'll not exceed an amble. But don't go beyond sight of Clennon House."

Astounded, I left them before disaster fell on Walter's head and mine alike. We would both suffer for such effrontery, but I would have another afternoon of freedom first.

When I went through the kitchen again, I smiled at Elizabeth. "You had the truth of it," I said. "I had only to ask, and no harm done. When I return I shall doubtless be confined to my chamber, and fed on bread and water, and I'll languish away till I'm pale and wan. But no great harm done."

"None at all. I've heard it said a delicate lass catches a man's eye quicker than a robust one. Get ye gone, now. Even an ugly fellow will wait only so long for a lass."

It was as simple as that. The stableboy saddled a horse, giving me a bold look obviously tinged with remembrance of the morning I had appeared at prayers in my night rail, and I rode off through the woods and up the hill to the moors beyond.

Evan Stewart, leading the mare Mally, waited for me there.

"What kept ye so long?" he said with a wide grin. "I'd begun to think ye wouldn't come without Simon to persuade ye."

He turned the horses without waiting for an answer and started off at a fine clip across the moors.

"No laggards today," he called over his shoulder. "Any man dragging his stirrups will be left behind."

With this cryptic remark he turned his attention to the way ahead, leaving me to follow as best I could.

Crossing the drawbridge at Torra was easier the second

time, with the tide at low ebb and the sea an innocent
blue, and I entered the courtyard with a comfortable sense
of familiarity. It was no longer empty and quiet, however;
a troop of horses milled restlessly before the stables, paw-
ing the cobbles and the air, and the Stewarts tending them
had no leisure to turn their attention to me.

Evan led me to the chamber, with its sunny windows
and golden floors, where Monleigh and I had spent the
greater part of that rainy afternoon; he did not announce
me, but opened the door, motioned me inside, and strode
away about his business.

I stood there for a moment, undecided, but Monleigh
did not look up. He was absorbed in a large piece of
parchment unrolled on the table before him; one outstretched hand held the curling corner of the paper, the
other moved across it in a slow arc.

Looking at his dark head bent in deep concentration
and the ruffled shirt opened carelessly almost to his waist,
making his skin appear very tanned against the white
linen, I forgot that I had not spoken or given any indication of my presence. I simply stood quietly and looked my
fill, and felt my heartbeat quicken beneath my rigid stays.

"So you managed to escape the Clennons," he said
without raising his head. "Did you have any difficulty with
it?"

"No," I said faintly, "no difficulty at all."

"So? I cannot believe the Clennons have had a change
of heart."

"You know them better than that."

"Aye," he said, moving his finger across the paper
again. "I know them far too well to expect any such
miracle. Did you slip away while they looked in another
direction?"

"I am riding in the sun to benefit my delicate nature,"
I said, "and I'm to stay within sight of Clennon House."

"You're a clever lass. How did you contrive it?"

"I must give Walter the credit. He kindly insisted that
I take one of the horses."

"That sounds little like Walter Clennon."

"He has been behaving strangely," I admitted. "Almost
human, now that I think of it. I can't imagine what has
happened to change him so."

"Can't you?" He looked up, surprising me with a cool appraising stare. "I could tell you if you'd like. 'Tis plain enough to any man with half an eye in his head."

"If it's so plain," I said, "I will learn the reason myself sooner or later."

He went back to the parchment. "I imagine you will," he said briefly.

After a moment I ventured, "What are you doing?"

"Looking at one of Evan's maps. Would you like to see it?"

I went to stand beside him at the table. At first glance the map was only a muddle of finely detailed lines drawn in delicate blue ink on the parchment, but gradually I saw the outlines of a loch, and an irregular, greatly indented line which must represent the coast. The Atlantic, to the west of the land, was identified by a sea serpent humping his back and rolling a gleeful eye toward a galley which hastily plied its way toward the edge of the map and the unknown beyond.

"Did Evan do this?" I asked.

"We work together," he said, "since we've both a liking for the task. Evan scouts the land and I draw the maps according to his findings, then we change about."

"Where is Torra?"

"Here," he said, putting his finger on a tiny crooked line which bore no resemblance to the rough crags and cliffs of Torra.

"It brings one down to size," I commented wryly. "Torra is only a small dot beside a calm blue pond, and you and I might not exist at all. Even the hills resemble nothing so much as ant heaps."

His brown finger moved across the map. "And here is another dot, the English fortress to the east."

I laughed. "I once saw the head of a pin engraved with an entire psalm. 'Tis probable, if you look closely, you'd find an entire regiment of soldiers swarming under that certain dot."

"Most probable," he said, "and we have a slight score to settle with that certain regiment."

I looked at the tiny circle, at the conical squiggle of ink behind it which was one of the highest mountains in all Scotland, and I remembered the restless horses and men below in the courtyard.

"Do you intend to settle it soon?"

"Tonight," he said. The map rolled up with a loud crackle. "D'you think we will have moonlight?"

"There is a price on your head. Is it wise to storm an English garrison?"

"You have illusions of grandeur, lass. I'd not attempt to storm any garrison without reason and means to retain it once I won it." He tied the map with a leather thong. "A man must recognize his limitations."

I could not prevent a smile. "I was not aware," I said, "that you consider yourself bound by any limitations, even Monk's army."

"I may be a rascal, Anne Lindsay," he said easily, "but I am no' a fool."

"Granted," I said. "Tell me how you think to settle your score with the English."

"Simple enough. They are busily engaged today at cutting trees. A pleasant occupation, you'll agree, for a fair summer's day."

"Cutting trees?" I echoed. "Whatever for?"

" 'Tis an English pastime more popular than dice. Clear Scotland of its trees, they imagine, and the miserable Scots will have no cover to hide them."

"You cannot be serious."

"I assure you the English are quite serious. They've cut down the best forests in Scotland and used the wood to reinforce their fortresses. And we base Scots must now cower in the open with no' a single tree to hide our shame."

"Doubtless," I said, "they have ventured beyond their stout fortress today."

He smiled at me unexpectedly, and I drew a deep breath.

"Aye, and they have," he said, "and the Stewarts must give them a proper welcome."

He sat on the edge of the table and idly swung a booted foot. The silence lengthened; and I thought of the men and horses waiting in the courtyard below and wished, with a strange and unbidden yearning, that I were a lad and could go riding out of Torra with the Stewarts to give the hated English soldiers a proper Scots welcome.

"It will be fine sport," I said wistfully.

"Aye," he said again, "the finest."

The yearning became a sharp envy, tinged with disappointment as intense and illogical as a child's.

"Women must always stay behind," I said, "and drink of life as though it were naught but watered wine."

Monleigh said nothing, but his eyes did not leave mine.

" 'Tis grossly unfair. We are not the frail and craven weaklings you would have us."

"Only a stupid man," said Monleigh, "would make so grave an error of judgment."

"Then why is it," I asked, "that all men, stupid or wise, must needs wrap their women in layers of dullness, like silken cocoons, and deny them the barest glance of the world beyond?"

"Do they, indeed?" he said lazily. "I fear I've had little time of late to examine the habits of other men."

I remembered, for a fleeting moment, that I spoke to Monleigh, and that he bore little resemblance to other men.

"But you must agree that we are miserably cheated," I went on. "We are allowed only the tasteless dregs, after you have done with the finest essence of the wine."

I walked to the window and put my chin in my hands, propping my elbows on the casement. Below the castle walls the blue water reflected the serene blue of the sky, and a white bird wheeled indolently in the same gentle wind which touched my face with the warm salt scent of the sea.

"Perhaps our Highland women are of a different breed," Monleigh said. "They ride off to war with their men, on occasion, and I've a kinswoman who thinks nothing of leading the boldest of her clansmen on a fast cattle raid now and again."

I caught the amused lift of his voice and realized full well that he was teasing me. But the unfamiliar sense of rebellion still surged inside me; and an incredible notion came suddenly to mind and grew, in the space of that instant, from the tiniest of impulses to an urgent inexplicable determination.

I turned swiftly. Facing him, and his dark sardonic face and knowing eyes, I almost lost my courage. But once intoxicated, whether by wine or an impulsive wish, one finds it exceedingly difficult, if not impossible, to return to sober reason immediately.

"M'lord," I began tentatively.

His voice, oddly gentle, cut across mine. "No, lass."

Startled, I said, "But—"

"No," he said, firmly.

"Your kinswoman," I pointed out. "You said—"

His slow grin set my face to burning. "My kinswoman is approaching threescore years. On the death of her husband, some twenty odd years past, she was forced by harsh necessity to defend her life and lands against all comers. She lifts a claymore with ease, and she boasts a moustache on her upper lip and a wart on the end of her nose. I admit," he added gravely, "that I'd prefer her to a regiment of soldiers were I caught shorthanded in a fight. But I refuse, Anne Lindsay, to compare the two of you as women."

"Please," I said breathlessly, "please be serious."

"I might ask the same of you."

"I have never been more serious."

"Or more ridiculous and foolhardy."

"Is it so very dangerous, then?"

He shrugged. "A certain risk is always involved."

"No more for me," I persisted, "than for you and your men."

"There is a slight difference."

"Yes," I said bitterly, "I am a woman."

"Then we are agreed on one thing," he said, his grin deepening, reaching his eyes. "However, you have overlooked a point or two of importance. You are not merely a woman; you are Anne Lindsay. Secondly, I have not yet taught you the way of being a proper freebooter."

I sighed, recognizing defeat. "I see what you mean," I said sadly. "I would only be a nuisance."

"Surely," he agreed. "I'd be obliged to leave one of my men to see that you were kept safely away from the scene of action, and I'll wager he'd think you a terrible nuisance."

"And I haven't the character to be a reiver. I'd be

frightened, doubtless, and weep to be back in my bed-chamber at Clennon House."

"You'd also tire, and begin to nag and scold. We ride hard and eat lightly when we've a night's work ahead."

I turned back to the window, not wanting him to see the sudden tears which threatened my poise. Surely, and surely again. He had the right of it, I was playing the fool. He had bewitched me, mayhap, or else I had been possessed by a devilish imp; no respectable woman would dream, even in her most secret fancies, of asking such an incredible thing.

But I could feel the staid womanly chains of convention and propriety closing about me again, binding me fast, and knew, with a miserable certainty, that I would not likely be permitted another glimpse, however brief, of that glorious tantalizing freedom which lay just beyond my prison; and so the tears would not be stayed.

Then his voice, cool and quiet, came from just behind me. His hands touched my shoulders, then fell away to my wrists.

"Why is it so important to you?"

For a moment I could not answer. How did one say it, how did one find the proper words to describe the hope-less, maddening, stifling dullness of being Anne Lindsay?

"I thought it would be a fine reckless way to spend an evening," I said at last.

He ignored my flippancy and went straight to the hard core of the matter, as was his wont.

"I think you've the heart of a rebel," he said, "and the misfortune of living in a world that despises all rebels and outlaws."

"Only now and again," I said honestly, "and even so, 'tis more envy than rebellion. I may rail at my lot, you un-derstand, and pity myself greatly, but I haven't the cour-age to do aught but submit meekly."

He was silent for a long while. His hands still held my wrists, and the warmth tingled through my blood and re-minded me, once again, that I was the most foolish and ridiculous of women.

"You are always right," I said, "and righteousness is a tiresome virtue. But I am obliged to agree that a raid is no place for a woman."

Unexpectedly he said, "Nor is Torra. If you think to be a proper lady you'd best go back to your needlework and the Clennons."

I gave a reluctant thought to my needlework, with its two silent figures listening through eternity to a bird that could never sing, and to the Clennons who doubtless still sat in the hall I had quitted and lamented the evil abroad in the land.

"I see I must teach you," he said, the amusement returned to his low voice, "that there is a vast difference between being right and righteous."

He turned me to face him, and his dark lashes hooded his eyes as he looked down at me.

"I have many faults," he said, very quietly, "and the worst might well be my refusal to put aside a riddle before I know the answer. Quite often I find the answer not to my liking, and not nearly so entrancing as the riddle. But I must have at the truth, however unpleasant, and the devil take those who would turn their backs on it."

"I am no riddle," I protested.

"We are all strangers to ourselves at one time or another."

"And you needn't accuse me of turning my back on the truth. I thought we had settled that matter fairly the last time I saw you."

"So we did, and now the time has come to test our theories." He dropped his hands, stepped back, smiled at me strangely. "Perhaps I shall change my mind, after all. Give me two promises, Anne Lindsay, and you shall have your small rebellion."

I stared at him, a wild flare of hope neatly routing all my hard-gained reason. "What are they?" I asked heedlessly.

"You will tell me truthfully, when it is finished, how well it suits you to be a rebel for a brief night."

"And the other?"

"You will follow my orders precisely, else you will endanger my men as well as yourself."

"I promise," I said, elated beyond measure. "I promise to be truthful and obedient, if only for a single night." I looked down at my habit. "I fear I cannot ride far like this."

"Would you like to be a lad for the ride, dressed in breeks and shirt?"

"I should like that very much."

" 'Tis as good as done."

He put his map under his arm and took my hand, and led me down the long corridor to another room. It was the chamber where I had dried my clothes the first day I came to Torra; and I bethought myself that the large chest there must hold a magic genie who presented a change of apparel for every occasion.

He searched until he found a pair of leather breeks and a white shirt, and two small leather boots. These he tossed across the counterpane of the bed, and followed them with a plumed hat.

"Hurry with it," he said. "You'll receive ten lashes for each minute you're tardy."

"You frighten me," I said, and held the shirt against me for size. " 'Tis a proper fit, however did you guess?"

"I've come to know you fairly well," he said, and grinned.

Then he was gone and the door slammed behind him, and I went about the task of sloughing my respectable identity as one Anne Lindsay for that of a Stewart free-booter. A scrawny one, in truth, whose trousers must perforce be gathered by a belt to prevent them from falling about his knees and whose white shirt bulged muscles in all the wrong places—an unnatural and ill-begotten lad who would never pass muster if an enemy looked too closely.

Evan Stewart, however, did not appear to think too poorly of the lad when he met him in the corridor outside the door.

"God's wound, ye're a likely sight." He whistled appreciatively. "The men will pay little heed to the business at hand this night."

Behind him, his master laughed. "This comely lad rides with me," he said. "Find your own company, Evan."

We walked down the corridor together, and I set my plumed hat at a rakish angle, and felt vastly free and unencumbered in my breeks and supple leather boots. I did not precisely swagger, I trust, but I rather imagine I

walked a bit straighter and took a longer stride for not
being hampered with stays and skirts.

"If ye remember," Evan remarked, "I told ye Simon had
a way of leading the virtuous astray. Too bad there's no
parson handy to pray over your downfall."

"The time for prayers," said Monleigh, "would seem to
be past." He looked down at me and smiled. "I begin to
understand why the Devil keeps such a tight hold on some
men. There is something far more intriguing about a fallen
angel than a virtuous one."

"I have not fallen," I said with dignity, "nor been led
astray."

"Surely not," Monleigh said promptly. "It is only a very
small sin, after all, a mere nodding acquaintance with
evil."

They looked at me in the foolish breeks and laughed
immoderately, and so my dignity went for naught. We had
come to the steps, and so descended to the courtyard
where the men waited beside their horses. There was some
amusement among them at my appearance, but it was
good-natured and did not embarrass me; they appeared
neither boisterous nor grim this afternoon, merely alert
and on their mark for the task ahead.

Monleigh gave me a hand to my horse. Mally was
spared the ignominy of the high sidesaddle; on this ride,
I saw, I was to be treated like the men, and I soon found
that it was not uncomfortable, or unduly mortifying, to sit
astride with the freedom allowed me in my breeks.

We clattered across the drawbridge, fifty strong or more,
and the late afternoon sun gleamed quietly on the horses'
flanks, on a silver scabbard and the chased metal of pistols
and long wicked spurs, and dyed to a deep crimson, like
the colour of blood, the scarlet lining of Monleigh's dark
cloak.

I was somewhat surprised that we took to the track, and
it soon became apparent that our way would lead us to
the lochhead and directly past Clennon House unless
Monleigh turned away into the hills within a few minutes.
But he showed no such intention, nor did he appear in the
least apprehensive that curious eyes might see the Stewarts
riding in such force and wonder at the reason.

Such boldness was not one of my dominant traits, how-

ever, and I could not resist the temptation to pull my
plumed hat lower over my face and shrink down a bit, as
if by doing so I might be less conspicuous.

Monleigh, with his uncanny way of seeing all within his
ken, laughed by my side.

"You cannot disappear by cowering in your saddle," he
said. "That alone will give you away. All Stewarts are excellent horsemen, you will note, and ride with as proud a
swagger as they walk. Straighten your shoulders, lass, and
look as if you've no fear of anything on earth."

"I'd still look like nothing so much as Anne Lindsay," I
retorted, "masquerading as a lad."

"And catching a whiff of a most unpleasant odour. Be
easy on't, I'll not let them find you out."

I had not been aware that my features were tensed into
an unseemly grimace, and so I laughed and lifted my chin,
and immediately caught sight of a group of advancing
riders.

"Then you'd best put your sorcerer's art to good use,"
I said, "and conjure me out of sight on the moment."

He was not one jot perturbed, and I suspected he had
known of their approach long before I spoke.

"You're only to fall back," he said easily, "and take
cover. Go slowly with it, and use Mally's mouth gently.
You'd not wish her to bolt and attract undue attention to
yourself."

I did as he bid me, tightening the reins with great care,
and Evan moved forward to take my place. The ranks of
mounted Stewarts opened around me and then closed
again, and in a matter of seconds I was screened on either
side, as well as before and after, by men whose most
precious virtue suddenly appeared to me to be their ability
to tower in their saddles like heroes of Homeric proportions.

The pace slowed perceptibly, and from beneath the
wide brim of my hat I saw Monleigh's raised hand which
signalled us to halt. Then I could hear nothing but the
sound of the approaching horses and the slow sough of
the sea somewhere to the west; and on either side of me
the men threw back their cloaks to show their swords
sheathed and no weapons in hand.

But we did not go in peace, I reflected, despite the gal-

lant gesture; it was a deceptive, if honourable, truce. The
hoofbeats came to a stand and the silence stretched interminably; I dared not move my head to look around the
man directly before me, and so could only surmise that all
concerned were taking one another's measure with great
wariness while the flimsy truce held, and in all probability
none would be loath to end the amenities on the first
provocation.

But the swords remained sheathed. Monleigh's curt
voice came back to me with startling clarity.

"What business have you on Stewart land, Walter Clennon? Can I be of any assistance to you?"

"Perhaps you can, m'lord. I am searching for a woman
who has apparently gone too far from Clennon House and
become lost. Have you seen anyone riding hereabouts alone
and unattended?"

"We've only just come from Torra," said Monleigh,
"and met no one on the track. Has she been long missing?"

"Only an hour or so." Walter's voice was more abrupt
than usual. "But I fear for her life were she to remain in
the hills after nightfall. She is delicate by nature and would
be unable to protect herself."

"Come, Walter, we've no wild animals in our hills. I
warrant you'll find her none the worse for wear, if frightened a bit by the dark."

"I was not speaking," Walter said, "of wild animals who
walk the night on four legs."

There was a silence. It did not seem possible that Walter, that mild and tactful man, would knowingly insult a
troop of hot-tempered Highlanders to their faces; and I
held my breath for Monleigh's reply and hoped he would
not take it for a deliberate affront.

"I am well acquainted with the beasts who prowl my
land," Monleigh said carelessly, "human or otherwise. I'd
advise you to take care."

"I intend to do so."

I fought the urge to push back my hat so that I could
see better; it was much the same suicidal impulse that
grips men's souls when they stand on the edge of a cliff
and hear a treacherous inner voice urging them to take
another step.

"Then I wish you good fortune in your search," Monleigh said, and in my mind's eye I saw his face, lean and sardonic, looking at Walter with that arrogant inscrutability he affected so well. "I regret I cannot offer more aid, but I am riding south in some haste and cannot be delayed."

Walter was not yet finished. "You are reckless, sir, in these days of English laws and penalties. I'd say you had no less than twoscore armed men behind you."

The English might forbid men to ride abroad in armed troops, I thought with amusement, but how else did one go about fighting battles with English soldiers?

"I go to visit the English tax collector," Monleigh replied briefly, "and he'll not quibble that I wish to protect his gold." Then, as if he tired of both Walter and the conversation, he raised his hand in its leather gauntlet, and said, "Your servant, sir," and so took his leave of both.

Walter and the men with him sat their horses without moving as we rode past. My heart pounded until I was certain it would betray me, and my mouth was so constricted I could not swallow past the great lump in my throat. I controlled my bearing and my hands by only the most rigid effort, longing to pull down my hat, to avert my face, to turn and flee so that I might avoid passing in review before Walter Clennon for him to ferret me out in my sins.

But although I did not once make the fatal mistake of glancing in his direction, I somehow realized that Walter was not scrutinizing the troop of Stewarts with any great care. He would not, in his wildest imaginings, suspect to find me among them; and had I spoken out to him, he would doubtless mistrust his senses.

But not until the men from Clennon House were left far behind, and Evan fell back to give me room to ride beside Monleigh, did I breathe with any degree of ease.

"Well done," Monleigh said gravely. "I'd have been hard pressed for an explanation had Walter caught a glimpse of my newest apprentice."

"Apprentice in what?"

"In the art of deluding and confounding one's enemies," he said, "or if you would have it another way, learning how to be sly without taking on the look of a fox."

"Now that I think of it," I said innocently, "your ears are oddly pointed."

"An unlikely apprentice on all counts," he said sternly. "You are delicate in nature and cannot protect yourself, and you have no respect for your master."

"I've too many masters and cannot respect them all at one and the same time. You see how it has turned me into a lying jade."

"I see only a handsome lad in a plumed hat, who will shortly begin to complain that the journey is too lengthy and he has discovered a sore spot or two from riding astride."

He had the truth of it, but I would not confess to being such a weakling. I rode past a silent Clennon House with my head and shoulders as proudly straight as any Stewart's, and hoped that Robert MacLeish was not casting a curious eye from the high windows.

We rode through the burnished glow of sunset and the cool northern gloaming which followed, past clumps of stunted fir and fragile green birch, past the barren hills turning an unearthly shade of intense blue as they came between us and the setting sun; and in all that quiet world of hill and sky and moor there was no sound but the wind and the clattering hoofs, and the creak and jangle of leather and bit. We went riding on, each one occupied with his own thoughts, silent and bemused as if we were pounding unchecked to an inevitable destiny none might change or care to circumvent.

Just as the sun dropped behind the hills a dozen men left the troop to turn their horses south, and I knew they went to lay Monleigh's gold before the English exciseman, thereby proving the tale he had given Walter. He did not trust to chance, that much was plain, and I began to understand better why the English had not yet managed to outwit him.

Before the twilight shaded into the pale night, we paused to rest and eat. We had long since left the track and taken to the hills, and the secluded moor where we dismounted was hidden from all but the wide view stretching before it in unbroken miles of wilderness.

Evan, closest to me when we halted, gave me a steadying hand as I slipped to the ground; and indeed, I had need of some such support. I managed to stagger to a boulder and ease myself down, however, without making a sorry spectacle of myself.

After he had spoken in a low voice to the men, Monleigh came to sit beside me and share a meagre meal of cheese, bread, and long cool draughts of wine from a slender silver flask.

"We'll have better to offer you later," he said. " 'Tis never wise to eat too heartily before a raid, nor could we light a fire without risking detection."

"Are we so near the English?"

"Not so near that you must whisper," he said, amused. "How do you feel?"

I took a bite of cheese, and looked before me at the mountains lifting one behind the other, the awesome peaks shading into violet against the blue twilight sky. A new star hung above a gorge, like a lanthorn lighting the dark fastness lying so quietly below, and to the east the pale moon cast a tentative light before it to test its welcome.

"I am very well, thank you," I said contentedly. "What do you intend to do with me now that the witching hour approaches?"

"I'll leave one of the men with you, and you must be prepared to ride on an instant's notice should something go amiss." He stood up and stretched, and pulled me up beside him. "Stay where I leave you, lass, no matter what happens. We may return in some haste, and I'd like to retrieve you without the delay of a search."

I did not realize that Evan had been gone until that moment, when he came up behind us so silently that I did not hear him at all until he spoke.

"All goes well," he said.

Monleigh nodded, but did not speak; and all about me the Stewarts swung into their saddles as if they had just arisen from a night's rest, no whit weary or reluctant. The true purpose of the ride lay just ahead, and they were more than eager.

I myself found it exceedingly painful to mount the mare again so soon, but I tightened my belt and lifted my chin, and so avoided any sigh or groan to give me away.

We waited there in the growing darkness, it seemed to me, for an interminable length of time. Monleigh sat his horse with an almost indolent ease, one arm carelessly across the pommel, and I could not take my eyes from this new and different aspect of the man. His face was impassive and self-contained, a familiar expression to me, and yet there was no hint of the latent violence one ordinarily sensed about him. It had been subtly replaced with an icy restraint that was frightening to contemplate, so ruthless and implacable that mercy was surely an unknown value to him.

This, then, is when he is most deadly, I bethought myself, for he controls his strength, as a fighter will, and fashions it into a weapon which is ever at his command. No violent, hot-headed rage is his, after all, that would render his judgment foolhardy and rash, but rather a cold and dangerous force tempered as finely as the edge of his sword.

I think I did not know him at all in that moment. The man who smiled with so devastating a warmth and teased me into laughter was only an unreal figment of my imagination, and this stranger of the cruel quiet face and hooded eyes was the true Monleigh, the black earl who held so much of Scotland in dread fear of him.

We began to move, slowly and with great care, and neither Evan nor Monleigh appeared to give me a second thought. But when we had reached a narrow ravine, thick with birch and ash which straggled over a rise ahead, a Stewart reached out for my bridle and pulled Mally to a halt, and Monleigh turned to me.

"Keep a good heart, lass," he said quietly; and, incredibly, I saw the white flash of his smile. "We'll be with you shortly."

They were gone, a silent line of men and horses disappearing among the trees, filtering through the night so quietly that the men might have been spectres and the horses merely ghostly shadows of no substance, no shod hoofs to ring against stone, no harnesses to jingle on the night air. There was no sound at all, and I was left alone with an equally silent clansman whose only claim to reality lay in the almost tangible reproach he directed at me for having kept him behind.

[9]

WE waited, he and I, there in the dark glen where nothing stirred but the sighing wind; waited for a sign or sound, a cry, the clash of steel; and so caught was I in the spell of the whole astounding affair that I was not at all terrified when that sign came suddenly out of the night.

The cry came first, a shrill warning from a surprised English throat, and it seemed no further away than just over the rise before me. Then a great shouting arose, and the reverberating echoes of gunshot as many pistols were fired at once. The metallic clatter of swords was carried on the night air so clearly that my nerves grated with the harsh sound; and Mally, completely unnerved by the unexpected uproar, reared her forelegs to the sky and came near to unseating me.

"Hold her in tightly," the clansman shouted, deeming the time for silence had passed. "Don't give her a chance to fall on ye."

I held as tightly as I could without bruising Mally's mouth, but it did not calm her. She gave a frantic snort, dropped her forelegs only to dance sideways and toss her mane restlessly; then, as another round of shot rang in her ears, she threw all training and good sense to the winds and leaped forward.

I might have jumped clear, that first moment, if I had kept my head; but I was too startled to do more than try to retain my balance on the distrait plunging mare. A birch limb caught at my hat, then slapped my face with a stinging blow; I heard the clansman shout another warning behind me, but before I could consider my unenviable position, Mally had topped the rise and galloped straight into the wild scene of confusion before her frightened eyes, in much the same manner a night moth will be mesmerized by sudden light and so fly blindly to its destruction.

I saw few details of that violent scene of battle. In a later and safer moment, I remembered the glitter of swords in the dim moonlight and a great deal of noise and a surging shapeless mass of men and horses. But Mally, finding a strange wall of noisome humanity barring her flight, stopped dead; and before I had more than a glimpse of my unsavoury surroundings, I flew over the mare's head to land on the ground with a resounding thud which shook my senses as well as my unfortunate head.

What does one do when precipitated so unexpectedly into the midst of a bloody fray? Alas, I followed my instincts as blindly as the foolish mare, and stood up unsteadily to ascertain if all my bones were still knit together. And I heard a Stewart shout boisterously to the grim tune of his sword; I became aware of the tide of battle surging around me; and I was suddenly caught up in the intoxicating spirit of the fight.

But I have no sword, I thought angrily as I looked down at my empty hands; I have no sword to protect myself, and no horse to lead to the charge. Niggardly men, those Stewarts, I cannot fight the English with my bare hands.

Then, standing alone and furious in the midst of the strife, I saw the man lunge forward, coming toward me with a fierce yell swelling in his throat, an Englishman with a bared sword in hand and a look of stark hatred on his face.

He means to run me through, I thought clearly, he fully intends to kill me.

I do not yet know what sustained me in that awful moment. All anger, all fear left me; there was only the crystal-clear certainty that I faced a sudden death with no hope of escape. I stared at the wicked point of the sword and could not move, and waited for the end.

Of course, it was all a bit of nonsense. I was not truly there, in a small clearing under the moon, dressed as a lad, staring at a man who meant to kill me before another moment passed. I would awake in a trice and find myself in my staid bed at Clennon House; I would laugh, shame-faced, and blame the cheese I ate at the evening meal for the nightmarish turn of my dreams.

But the clammy coldness gripping me spoke ill of prayers offered too late to be of service; and I had only to look at the advancing soldier to know that I was not dreaming.

Since I must confess what it was like, I must say in all honesty that my last thought was not of the Clennons' horror to learn my fate, nor was it a terrible disbelief that I would soon know how it was to lose one's life in battle. I merely wanted to weep, with a frantic disappointment, because I would also lose something I had never had, that taste of life Simon Stewart had so carelessly promised me.

But I did not die. I instinctively took a backward step, and the malevolent sword point came after me and stung me lightly on the arm. He will follow through now, I told myself coldly as I waited for the feel of a blade in my heart; but suddenly there was no time for him to finish the chore.

A long sword materialized out of thin air to strike so telling a blow that the English weapon turned a complete circle in the air before clattering to the ground. Then, before my incredulous eyes, the attacking sword, its supple blade seeming to move of its own accord with no hand or heart to guide it, pierced the soldier's side just below his shoulder, and he fell with his face stiffened into eternal lines of surprise and anger.

Then I saw the gauntlet, dark like the shadows, holding the sword, and I realized why it had hitherto been invisible; a horse loomed above me and turned so abruptly that the warm nostrils brushed across my face, and I was swept up to the saddle in an arm which encircled me like a band of steel.

Stricken with relief and remorse in equal measure, I did not move but kept my face hidden against his leather jack. I heard him shout and felt his horse break forward into a hard gallop, and the thunder of horses behind us shook the earth and made me quite giddy-headed.

After a time my arm began to throb. I became conscious of a sticky wetness in the palm of my hand, and was obliged to accept the astonishing fact that the English sword had done more damage than a stinging scratch. I was wounded, God ha' mercy, and were it not so precisely what I deserved for making such an appalling fool of myself, I'd have considered the situation very droll indeed.

Monleigh, I'd warrant, was not amused. I'd spoiled his plans and forced him to draw back; and I'd caused him to kill a man in cold blood. At that point I closed my mind to all that had happened; it was not a thing to bear with pride, and I was suddenly too weary to weep.

When we had ridden for what seemed like endless miles, Monleigh reined his horse and I lifted my head at last to face his wrath. But he paid me no slightest attention.

The men were close behind us and Evan was at our side.

"How did we fare?" Monleigh asked briefly.

"We're all of a piece," said Evan. "But we lost the mare. She was no' to be found, and I was loath to linger behind to search for her."

"It can't be helped," Monleigh said. Then, "The men will remain here. I doubt if we've been followed, but they'd best keep their ears open. You come ahead and join us; I may have need of your aid."

We went over a hill and rode down into a glen, wooded along the banks of a stream. The moonlight touched the trees and water with gilded silver, and the shadows were velvet soft and black. There was no wind there, only the quiet night and the sweet fragrance of bell heather still warm from the sun.

He dismounted without a word and lifted me from the saddle. Feeling giddier than ever, I was grateful for the strong support of his hand, but I would have gladly exchanged it for some small indication that he did not consider me quite the odious and bungling fool I felt.

Evan followed us, his horse making no sound on the thick grass.

"Sit down, Anne," Monleigh said finally.

I sat on the grass, obeying him on the moment, and the heavy dew was cool and wet beneath my hands.

Monleigh knelt on one leg, Evan close beside him, and the two of them examined my arm in the moonlight.

"Thank God," Evan said bluntly, " 'tis a clean cut."

"Not much more than a deep scratch. She caught only the point as he lunged past her."

Monleigh began to work my shirt away from the cut, and I could not stifle a gasp as the skin tightened and pulled.

"We'll need to bind it," he said, "till it can be properly dressed. Have you any clean linen, Evan?"

Evan went to his saddlebag and Monleigh waited beside me.

"I'm sorry to be such a nuisance," I began hesitantly.

He might not have heard me at all for the attention he paid my apology.

"Bring me your flask," he ordered Evan. Then he turned back to me and, before I had any notion of his intention, began to unbutton my shirt.

I stared at him, too startled to protest, and his eyes were black and shadowed as they met mine.

"I cannot dress the wound," he said quietly, "unless you remove your shirt."

It was Evan, in the end, who shattered the spell of horrified dismay which held me motionless.

"Don't be squeamish, lass," he said. "Ye're among friends."

He grinned at me, and I came to my senses and unbuttoned my shirt with as casual an air as I could affect on the moment. But I did not look again at Monleigh, nor could I meet his eyes when he slipped the shirt from my shoulders and left me exposed to the chilly night in no more than my thin chemise.

He took the clean linen from Evan and wet some of it in the cold burn water, and went about the business of cleaning my arm. I did not flinch again; I sat and watched his brown hands on the white skin of my arm, and thought him as impersonal as if he had been treating his horse.

"Give me the flask," he said to Evan, and his left hand closed over mine in a hard numbing grip. "This will hurt," he said. "Close your eyes and take a deep breath."

Aye, it hurt like the very devil, and I bit my underlip until I was certain the blood would begin to drip from it. The whisky ran cold on my skin and burned inside the long cut like a liquid fire; and I tried to catch my breath only to find that I could not breathe at all. Only Monleigh's hand kept me upright, the firm grip holding me steady, bracing me against the fierce burning pain.

Then the pain slowly diminished and I opened my eyes to find the world settled again on an even keel. The black trees were still edged with silver, the horses loomed against the sky, and Monleigh, his dark face outlined into high chiselled planes, was deftly wrapping my arm with linen strips.

Then he was done and there was no time for embarrassment. He held my shirt for me and buttoned it to my neck with an unhurried skill, and his eyes flickered over me for no more than a brief instant before he lifted me to the saddle and swung up behind me.

We were off again, with the Stewarts clattering behind us, and I was vastly more comfortable than before. When he considered we had put a safe distance between us and the English, Monleigh called a final halt on the high moors; here, I gathered, we would spend the remainder of the night.

I sat quietly on a large plaid spread on the ground for my comfort and watched as the men built campfires, widely separated, and prepared food for themselves. Evan cooked over a fire directly at my feet, his concentrated skill not a whit perturbed by my close scrutiny; but when he had finished with it, Monleigh was across the moor with his men, and I saw that I was to sup with only Evan for company.

So I sat with my back to a boulder, across the fire from Evan, and dined on juicy browned plovers washed down with a strong red wine, and thought myself tolerably at peace with the world. The harsh lines of moor and gaunt rock around me were softened by the moonlight, and the air was as clean and cold as the hill burn we had paused beside earlier.

But a curlew cried suddenly, a plaintive sound; and the wind, never absent from the hilltops but sighing eternally as from the beginning of time, touched my face with a cold hand. I shivered, feeling all at once as lost and lonely as the curlew crying in the night, knowing a desperate hunger for something I could not name, but which tore me with a need and a longing so painful it brought me close to tears.

Then Monleigh came and knelt beside me. "How is the arm?"

"Not so painful now. I wager I'll recover in good order."

"When one of my men disobeys orders," he said, "he goes back to Torra in disgrace. A captain cannot allow mutiny in the ranks."

"I did not intend to be disobedient," I said. "The mare bolted." After a moment I added, "I'm sorry the mare was lost. Did I spoil everything for you?"

"Our purpose was accomplished," he answered, "and that is all that matters. So Mally wanted a taste of battle. Do you think she found it to her liking?"

"I'll not speak for Mally," I said, "but as for myself, I found it an amazing revelation of character."

He sat beside me, leaning his weight on one arm while the other rested casually across his knee. "What did you learn about your character in the press of battle, lass? Were you very frightened?"

"I was furious because no one had thought to give me a sword."

"And what would you have done with it?"

"Held it above my head, doubtless, and charged into the fray shouting 'Set on them, lads!' at the top of my voice."

The laughter finally escaped; he threw back his head and gave himself up to it, and Evan looked across the fire and grinned as if he would like to share the jest.

"But I fear I'd not make a good soldier," I went on. "The intoxication did not last very long."

"So you froze, and found you could not move a muscle."

"A terrifying experience," I admitted, "to face the point of a sword and realize the man behind it means to kill with it."

"What were you thinking, Anne," he said quietly, "in that last moment before he lunged at you?"

"I prayed it was a nightmare, and I'd soon awake to find myself safe in my bed at Clennon House."

"Was that all?"

I did not look at him. "I don't remember," I said untruthfully.

He said nothing. He did not tell me that I lied, or that I was guilty of evasion, or that such dishonesty was only a furtive and awkward form of self-defense. But his silence spoke for itself, and I suspected that he knew quite well what I had been thinking in that last moment.

"A raid is no place for a woman," I said. "You see how much trouble I have caused you."

"Don't brood over it. You'll not come again."

"I would I had never come at all."

"Your conscience is clear. You may have wished for a sword, but you carried none."

"I saw you run the man through," I said carefully. "It would not have happened except for me. You were very angry that I had forced you to it."

The curlew sounded closer, almost above me, and the uneasy cry hung on the wind and wept over the rocks and moorland.

"Look at me, Anne."

I turned to meet his steady gaze, his impassive face.

"More than one Englishman died tonight. The fortunes of war, no more or less, and you waste your sympathy. Were it the other way around, they would have spared no one."

"But only one died because of me," I said miserably.

"Does it matter so much why he died? I have killed many men, and doubtless will kill many more before one returns the favour."

I winced at his callousness. "Then why were you so angry?" I whispered. "Why did you say I would not come again?"

I knew, somehow, what his next words would be.

"He might have killed you," he said.

A moment passed, and then another. Shaken, I wondered if all my heart was writ upon my face for him to see, and knew from the narrow look of his eyes, the smile touching his hard mouth, that this was so.

"If the English find you out," I said hastily, "it will be another crime on your head."

He shrugged. "They can only hang me once."

"Once," I said, "is more than enough."

"These are bitter times," he said, "and all men must die sooner or later."

I shivered again, but not from the night air.

"Did you know that the Kirk is sending a minister to spy on you?"

"I've been expecting it. We've not had a curious parson in these parts of late. Do you know his name?"

"Peter Finlay," I said.

"A good man," Monleigh said. "I'll be pleased to see him."

I stared at him, amazed. "He is a minister, a Covenanter."

"I am not so narrow," he said, with a cynical smile, "that I cannot recognize a man's worth, whatever his sympathies. A good many of my friends may be counted as presbyterians."

There was no understanding him. "Then you do not despise the Kirk?"

"I despise intolerance," he said, "wherever it appears."

"Do you know Peter Finlay well?"

"He has been in the west before," he said, "and I've met him once or twice. He is a devout minister, and lives his creed. I can find no fault with that." He added, "He has a great love of men, sinners and virtuous alike. It has given him a bad name in the Kirk, and so they send him among the savages as a penalty for his compassion."

"Are you not afraid he will pry too closely?"

He laughed softly. "No, lass, I am not afraid. Are you?"

I sighed. "Aye, to my sorrow."

"You are a sweet wench, and I thank you for your concern."

"You would be more wary," I said, "had you listened to the Clennons and Robert MacLeish today."

"But I am always wary," he said coolly, "and keep my wits about me in better fashion than you seem to believe. What have the Clennons said to upset you now?"

Now is the time to ask him, I thought clearly, for he will surely give me an honest answer. Whatever I have wished to know, he has told me the truth; and if the truth does not always please, it is myself I must blame.

But I could not find the words to ask him. "They said you were one of Montrose's murdering army."

"You know that already."

"You are a heretic," I went on bravely, "and care not if the whole world knows it."

"I care most of all that you should know," he said, "that I have never believed in tyranny or cant."

"Is that why they brand you with heresy?"

"Their Solemn League and Covenant was designed to protect the liberty of men's consciences," he said, "but it has come to mean only the liberty to bind men to their own convictions. And they scream like wrathful vultures because I'll not permit my conscience or my mind to be bound by other men, as mortal as myself, who have taken the word of God to themselves and think to make all others worship as they see fit."

"You are past praying for, m'lord."

"So will you be," he said, "if I have my way."

"They also say that Torra is a vile place of adultery and carousing and wild orgies held in the dark of night."

"You have caroused there yourself, but not yet in the dark of night. D'you feel yourself slighted?"

"And you deal in witchcraft."

"A sorcerer of no mean cunning," he said calmly. "Look at yourself, Anne Lindsay, and admit you've changed since you came to the west of Scotland."

I hesitated, remembering what Margaret had next said.

He was plainly amused. "Out with it."

"You force yourself on women," I said faintly, "and seduce them from all virtue and reason."

I had kept my eyes resolutely on the fire, but when he did not answer at once, I turned to look at him. I had not expected shame or remorse, knowing that such emotions would sit uneasily on his wide arrogant shoulders and proud head, but neither was I prepared for his smile, flashing swiftly across his brown face.

"You have more trust in me than you profess," he said, "if you would come to Torra after hearing such gossip."

"Is it only gossip?"

"I think you must decide that for yourself."

"Well now," I said, "I have surely been seduced from all reason, if not virtue."

"Given time," he said gravely, "I might yet manage to uphold my reputation."

My cheeks aflame, I murmured, "Your conceit is equalled only by your indelicacy."

"Tell me, lass," he said lazily, "d'you think I'd be obliged to force myself on any woman?"

He sat there beside me with his lithe and careless grace, the firelight glittering in his dark eyes and throwing into bold relief the high cheekbones and the line of his chin, the laughter curving his hard mouth, the powerful thighs and shoulders; and I knew with an unequivocal clarity that no place on earth which had known his presence would remain unchanged with his passing, nor any woman such as myself, no matter the desperation with which I might fight against it.

"I suspect," I said, "if the truth were known, it might well be the other way around."

"Aye," he said, laughter warming his voice, "I've fought them off from John O' Groat's to Edinburgh. 'Tis a wearisome affair."

"I imagine you also find it wearisome," I said, "to be reminded of the bairns you've left behind."

Because my eyes were on him at that moment, I saw the almost imperceptible change in his face, the brief narrowing of his eyes.

"Not so wearisome," he said, "as revealing. Did Margaret Clennon give you an exact accounting of them?"

I wished miserably that I had left well enough alone. "I believe," I said hesitantly, "she used the word 'brood.'"

"God's love, she has a high opinion of my virility."

I gave him a slanting glance. "'Tis not so farfetched a notion."

"You flatter me, lass," he said amused again. "Not that I can swear innocence on all counts. I'll wager most men have fathered a bastard or two without knowing it, but that's the way of things. 'Tis a hard world for a woman."

"And a harder one for the wee bairns."

"I think you've a heart like warm butter," he said. Then he added quietly, "Are you sure you want the truth? We made a bargain to be honest with each other, but I'm not yet convinced that you know the way to deal with it."

"I've no wish to pry into your affairs."

"'Tis no secret," he said, shrugging, "except, God willing, to the Kirk. I've a small lass in Dundee, standing no

higher than her mother's hand, and at last counting I've
only the one to my credit."

"A lass?" I said softly, forgetting to be shocked.

"Aye, with blue eyes and a mop of black curls. I would
I had her safe at Torra, but doubtless she's happier with
her lot as it stands. She has a father now, on the face of
things, a braw lad who cares for her as he would his own,
and I'd not ask her mother to part with her."

I stared at him incredulously. "Did he wed her, knowing the babe was not his own?"

"Not all men are warped by intolerance," he said easily.
"He loved her, and she returned it. He considers himself
fortunate to have gained a daughter in the bargain."

"Do you know him?" I asked, still thinking him daft.

"He was one of my troopers when we rode with
Montrose, and we value our friendship as highly as we do
the wee lass."

"And the mother?"

He smiled. "Are you truly so innocent of life, sweet
Anne? She was a bonny wench, and a clean one, and we
spent a happy hour or so together long ago. But she's
happily wed now, and I'll wager she considers she has the
best man of us."

Mayhap I knew nothing of life, but I would have
wagered him all I owned that he was wrong. No woman
who had known him, and borne him a bairn, would ever
be fully satisfied with less; I was a woman myself, however innocent, and I felt a great pity for a certain bonny
wench of Dundee.

"You amaze me," he said. "I thought to scandalize you
with my sins and be treated to a stern sermon in return.
Have you forgotten the proprieties?"

I smiled. "I should like to meet your small daughter."

"I promise you shall, one day. You would get on
famously together."

"Do you play your lute for her?"

"She'll have naught to do with me otherwise. I taught
her to dance a reel before she was scarce walking, and
now she begs for a tune at the very sight of me."

It made a strange picture, the tiny gay lass who loved
to dance to a lute song and this man of such infamous
character, and behind them the dreary backdrop of that

dour Covenanting stronghold of Dundee. Strange and incredible, aye, and one to warm the heart.

"Have you finished?" he asked suddenly. "What is the next crime on the list?"

Ask him, a small voice prompted inside me, ask him about the other bonny wench, the one who wed him and died within the year. Ask him how she died, and why, and watch his face carefully as he answers.

" 'Tis past time I remembered my manners," I said, and looked at the dying embers of the fire.

I was not aware that he had moved until his hands closed on my shoulders, forcing me to face him.

"We've no use for manners," he said curtly, "you and I. Are you afraid to speak?"

Afraid? Perhaps. And yet his hands, so brutally strong, so accustomed to violence, were oddly gentle on me; and I was unnerved from no more than the nearness of him, the hard mouth so close to mine, the aching hunger in my blood.

"I'm not afraid," I said truthfully.

He waited, his eyes searching my face, but I was determined to say nothing more. It no longer mattered that he understood me far too well, or that his perception was such that the words I left unsaid were as clear to him as those spoken between us. Let him see the questions in my mind, the struggle between heart and icy logic, the cowardly evasion; let him see and do what he would. I was wearied to death of questions and strife; he had asked me to trust him, and it would be a heavenly comfort to shift the burden to his wide capable shoulders.

"Aye," he said, low, "I think you've done with fear."

He smiled then, and I saw the tiny flames come alive in his eyes, warming me as no fire had ever done. It was for me alone, that smile, for I suspected that few were privileged to see it; and it left me shaken and entranced, unprepared for the feel of his mouth on mine, the kiss I had shamelessly wanted for such an endless length of days and hours.

It was a long while after, when he had left off kissing me and my eyes were still closed against the devastating effects, that he said against my face, "Have you never kissed before, lass?"

"You must know I've not," I whispered.

"I know you're far too expert at it to be a novice," he said lazily. "Have you been practising with Robbie Mac-Leish?"

I opened my eyes wide, and met his teasing grin, and was obliged to laugh. I did not realize until some time later how adroitly he handled that dangerous moment, returning my poise to me intact when he had only just finished shattering it to a perilous degree.

"You must sleep before the dawn comes," he said, and shook the plaid free of my shoulders to wrap it around me. "D'you think you might be weary enough to overlook the absence of a feather mattress between your bones and the hard ground?"

"Here?" I said uncertainly, for surely he did not mean that I should sleep beside him there.

"Here," he said decisively. "I warrant I'll make a fair pillow. I've had no complaints thus far."

Wordlessly I watched as he rolled a plaid into a bundle to put beneath his head and took his cloak from the boulder behind us. Across the fire Evan was apparently asleep, wrapped like a mummy in his plaid; and I could see the scattered shadows on the moor which were the other men, silent and prone under the moon.

Then Monleigh took my hand and gently pulled me down beside him, spreading his cloak over the both of us, and slipped one arm beneath me to hold me close against him. My head rested on his leather jack, so that my cheek felt the steady beat of his heart, and the warmth of his body communicated itself to mine and enveloped me in a serenity so rapt and tranquil that I would have been asleep on the moment had it not been for the thunderous misbehavior of my own unsteady heartbeats.

"The stars are close tonight," he said quietly.

"Close enough to pluck down," I said, "if one wished for a star to wear as a bauble."

"And do you, lass?"

"At this moment, I've no wish for anything more," I said drowsily, and then regretted I had no wit to think before I spoke.

But he only said, "I'm reasonably content myself, having only one small quarrel with the world."

"And what is that?"

"If I told you, sweet Anne, you'd take fright like a startled fawn. It can wait. I said I'd not force the pace."

It was a long while before I trusted my voice again.

"Are you dreaming," I asked, "when you lie so quietly and gaze at the sky?"

"All men dream, else life would ofttimes be unendurable."

"What sort of dreams are yours?"

"Not uncommon ones. I think on what life has been, and what it will be, and what it might have been had I been a different man than I am."

"Do you never wish that you could change what has been, so that what is to come will be more to your liking?"

"I've no time to waste on foolish regrets."

"All dreams are foolish."

"No," he said, "only the dreamers." He did not move or tighten his arm, but I felt its presence there against me like a caress, holding me safe and protected from the night beyond. "Tell me," he said softly, "what Anne Lindsay of the green eyes and sweet mouth dreams for her future."

"Something of my own," I said, "my very own. A home, children, happiness. And peace, above all else."

"Peace does not always bring happiness."

"It keeps one safe. Safe from want, from fear and loneliness. If I were forced to a choice, I'd prefer it to happiness." I laughed a little. "When I was younger I fashioned a very pleasant dream for myself, complete with a knight in shining armour who came to wed me and carry me away from Dundee. I knew the castle he built for me down to the last larder and dairy room, the last scrap of linen in the pantry. I even planned the number of jam jars I'd preserve each year. Our children were all fair and dimpled, and were never naughty, and each day was like a small perfect pebble dropped into a placid pool. Oh, it was a fine foolish dream, and it kept me sane for years on end."

After a brief silence he said, "When did you first begin to think it foolish?"

"When I discovered there were no shining knights for such as I, and no perfect placid days to be found in all the world."

"Nothing is so bitter as disillusionment," he said. "You must find another dream to take its place."

"I am older now, and wiser. I've no use for second-best dreams, slightly tarnished at the edges."

"I've heard it said that the moon casts a spell on any lass who sleeps in its light. Go to sleep, sweet Anne, and mayhap you'll dream a new dream for yourself."

We were quiet then, and I heard the curlew cry once again from the heather. But the sound was no longer desolate and lonely; and I felt very warm and drowsy and beguiled and oddly amused.

No one would believe such a fantastic tale. They would call me liar, brand me with a scarlet letter of sin, think me a wretched fool caught in the spell of his evil witchcraft. No woman, they would cry in horror, could spend a dark night on the moors in a man's arms, and that man the black Earl of Monleigh, and come to no harm or suffer any loss of virtue.

And yet that is precisely what happened, and if no one called me liar it was for the very good reason that I never breathed the tale to a single soul.

❧{10}❧

FAILING, for once in her life, to find adequate words
to express the depth of her wrath, Margaret took to her
bed. And since I was the cause of her relapse into illness,
she studiously ignored me and chose one of the Edinburgh
maids to scatter the herbs upon her bedchamber floor and
sit beside the curtained bed.

It had been a difficult scene. Margaret's anger I had
faced before, and so I found it no more humiliating than
I had expected; nor did I feel crushed by Robert's scornful exasperation, for if he had behaved differently I would
have immediately suspected his motives. It was Walter's
reaction that pricked my guilty conscience and set me to
stumbling over my words. Walter, who had patiently and
tirelessly searched for me, who had worried for my safety
after nightfall, who listened to my tale of woe with no
reproach, only an air of weary relief that I had come to
no harm.

If Walter believed me, I had no reason to think that
Robert or Margaret would distrust my explanation. I had
been carefully coached by Monleigh before he set me
down within a mile of Clennon House to make my way
home on foot; but my sense of guilt, added to the discom-
fiture I felt when obliged to tell my story before three
pairs of amazed eyes, did more to give a proper impression than the glib words I had prepared. I faltered more
than once, and could not prevent a sigh, and was no doubt
the very picture of a frightened and shaken miscreant.

I had ridden further than I intended, I told them, and
did not realize I might lose myself in the hills. When my
horse stumbled in a hole, throwing me to the ground, I
had slashed my arm open on a sharp boulder, and so
could not run down the horse. And since Monleigh had

taken care to have the horse I rode to Torra released on the moors behind Clennon House, that part of my tale had stood without question. I learned later from Elizabeth that it had been the stableboy who first brought word that a riderless horse had returned to the stables, and he had also gone out in the night to search for me.

When I told them I had come to a rude hut as I tried to find my way home, and that the woman there dressed my arm and fed me and gave me a bed for the night, promising to direct me to Clennon House on the coming of dawn, only Robert showed any untoward emotion.

"A dirty hovel, I'll wager," he said, staring down his nose and seeming poised to step away from me should I show any sign of contamination. "You should not have allowed her to touch your arm, Anne. I fear it will be rather the worse for the treatment. I've seen men whose wounded limbs withered and died from being touched with such filth."

"It was an exceedingly clean bothy," I said, "and the woman there was as clean as I."

We had stopped there in the crimson dawn while Monleigh spoke to the woman in Gaelic, and as she smiled and nodded her head at his words, I noted a plain cairngorm brooch at the neck of her saffron dress. It was a crude trinket, but somehow I sensed that she must treasure it greatly; and I was taken aback when she insisted that I accept it as a gift.

"Simon," I said, "I cannot take it."

But he said quietly, "You cannot refuse it without doing her a grave discourtesy."

So I took it gracefully and asked him to thank her. I think she gave it to me because I rode with her lord and chief, for I saw her eyes rest on him with a fond affection; and when we took our leave of her, she rested her hand on his boot for a brief moment, and looked quite proudly pleased when he smiled down at her.

When I left Torra again, dressed in my habit which Evan had carefully ripped and soiled, I put the brooch in my pocket; and the entire time I faced the Clennons and Robert I kept my hand in the pocket, my fingers closed around the brooch as if the mere touch would somehow work as a charm to ward off disaster.

Mayhap it was of some aid to me. Margaret, quite beside herself and no whit sympathetic, had left me to my own devices; and after several days of idleness, of being ignored by all but a kindly Walter, I was obliged to admit that the punishment could have been far worse.

But I was wary, and somewhat disconcerted. Margaret was too shrewd, I knew, to think that a mere show of displeasure would be chastisement enough for my misbehavior, nor did she imagine that I would feel any dismay at being freed from my chores. For reasons of her own, which I did not understand and therefore mistrusted, she had chosen a temporary course of leniency; and I was not misled into believing the delay would lessen her wrath when the stick fell upon my head at last.

I sat in the small hall one afternoon, absently plying my needle, and wondered what the Stewarts might be doing at Torra on such a fair day. Evan had come for me once since the night of the raid on the English, but I had instructed Elizabeth to tell him I could not risk leaving Clennon House again so soon; if he had come again, she had said nothing to me about it.

"What are you thinking, Anne," Walter said from the doorway. "I've never known you to sigh so deeply."

I looked up, startled to be caught at my daydreaming.

"I need a skein of red thread to complete my embroidery," I said, "but I can think of no place to purchase one this side of Edinburgh."

He came to the fire and held out his hands. "Could you not use another colour? I've never cared for red; 'tis too blatant for my tastes."

"Perhaps I shall use black instead. Margaret would be better pleased."

"You must not judge her too harshly, Anne."

"She has every right to be angry with me," I said quietly. "It was very remiss of me to cause so much unnecessary worry."

"A regrettable incident," he said, "but one that is over and done with now. It is only that Margaret cannot endure such anxiety and excitement." He crossed his legs, his eyes on the buckles of his shoes, and added, "She was quite grieved, you know, to think that you might have suffered some dire misfortune."

I looked up, surprised that he should think me so gullible, I who knew his sister as well as he.

"How is your arm?" he asked, changing the subject abruptly. "I trust it is almost recovered. Has it caused you much pain?"

"It has healed nicely, thank you."

The conversation appeared to have dwindled into oblivion at that, for Walter kept his eyes on his buckles and said nothing more for a lengthy time. Then, as I despaired of finding anything to say myself, he raised his head and smiled at me.

"I am completely at a loss," he said, "to know how to converse with you, Anne. You have changed since we came to Clennon House."

I did not think it the apt moment to remind him that he had never before conversed with me, other than the day he had come to Clennon House to find his stables raided. A greeting, a good night, a polite exchange while dining—I could count on the fingers of one hand the times his preoccupied attention had settled fleetingly on me.

"It is the mountain air," I said lightly. "It can be very exhilarating to one who has always lived in towns."

"Do you like it here?"

"It can be a fearsome place," I said, "this western portion of Scotland. But I have found it pleasant enough."

"I had hoped your distressing experiences would not turn you against it. I expect to spend a good deal of time here in the future."

I could not resist a single pointed remark. "Surely it could not matter," I said softly, "whether I like it or not."

"It matters to me," he said. "I would not have you unhappy."

Struck silent with astonishment, I struggled to keep my mouth from hanging agape.

"Margaret and I have grown very fond of you," he went on. "We would not care to have you leave us now that we have come to consider you as a sister."

That was more than enough. I looked up, my eyes wide, to find his kindly gaze even more disconcerting.

"I don't need to tell you, Walter," I said, "that I have no choice in the matter. You know very well that I have no intention of leaving your household until I am asked to do so."

My bluntness did not seem to offend him. "I cannot blame you for being bitter," he said. "It cannot be an easy life for anyone with pride or spirit. I fear we have taken advantage of your good nature, Anne, but we will try to mend our ways. Perhaps we can persuade you that we are not by nature selfish and unkind."

"Indeed, you are most kind," I murmured, incapable of saying more.

"I must ask a more personal forgiveness, however. I am well aware that Margaret is inclined to be upset by mere trifles, and it is you who must bear the brunt of her displeasure. I am often able to calm her, but now I can see I have been too lax in my efforts." He put his thin fingers together to study the large ruby on his forefinger. "I think you will find her more amiable in the future."

The black wool did not become the embroidered woman in my tapestry; she appeared even more dismal and lifeless in the sombre gown, as if the sun had gone behind a cloud and cast long shadows across the bird, the man watching her, the very shape and colour of her being.

But I worked busily with my needle, my mind just as busy with this puzzling mystery of Walter's unwonted behaviour. And yet, as I sorted snips and bits of thought as I sorted the skeins of wool in my lap, I saw the truth of his words. Margaret was never so rigid in her ways when her brother, the only person she held in any affection, was at home; it was only when his brief visits came to an end that she resorted to the petty and arbitrary persecutions which made life so unpleasant for all who came near her, as if she must in some way, however disagreeable, unload the irritations and burdens of her empty life upon someone else.

It was not beyond belief that Walter was, after all, the master of his household; I had thought him ruled by Margaret's demanding invalidism, but it might well be that he was no less canny than his sister. If she gained her way through stubborn determination, it might be that Walter held out with equal determination until her way suited him as well; and while he seemed to surrender grudgingly, he always managed by such a stratagem to placate her demands for another interval of peace.

He stood up, held his hands to the fire again, and came to my chair to put a hand on my shoulder.

"Beyond my anxiety," he said, "which was considerable, I was greatly hurt that you found it necessary to run away from Clennon House. It gave me pause to wonder how we had failed you."

"I was not running away," I began quickly, then knew I could not finish so obvious a lie, even to Walter.

"Give me time, Anne," he went on as if I had not spoken, "and I will try to make life more cheerful for you. I owe that much to you, if only for the service you do me in staying by Margaret's side. It is good for her, you know, to have the companionship of one so young and pretty and pure in heart."

I was too astonished to feel any pricking of conscience at his words; I answered his smile and bent my head again immediately, and listened to his footsteps as he walked slowly across the room.

Young, pretty, pure in heart. I stared at the black-gowned tapestry lady and wished, for a foolish moment, that my life was as simple and uncomplicated as hers, as barren of feeling and emotion and bewilderment.

To quiet my turmoil in some way, I went to the kitchen to find Elizabeth. She was not alone; Kitty, the maid with a fancy for the stableboy, was assisting in the chore of cutting dried fruits for a pudding, and she smiled at me with a merry tilt to her mouth, no doubt having learned in the way of all servants that I was in as much disgrace as she, and gave me a handful of dried plums to chew.

"Run along wi' ye," said Elizabeth, "else we'll have no pudding for supper. I'll put Mistress Lindsay to work at the cutting."

Kitty dimpled and said, "Will you need me for a short while?"

Elizabeth snorted indelicately. "Ye're small use to any-one. I'll not see the day I'd need a town woman in my kitchen, dirtying it with her slovenly ways." Then she added, "Ye'll find him in the stable, but I'll put my own hand to your backside if ye keep him from his chores."

Kitty laughed and danced through the open door, and I could not but admire her lighthearted disregard of the fate hanging over her head at the hands of Margaret Clennon and the stern parson of a certain Edinburgh kirk.

"Would you give aid and comfort to such a brazen sinner?" I asked innocently. "I thought Margaret gave you orders to keep Kitty away from the stables."

Elizabeth shrugged. "She gave me other orders this morning," she said, "concerning another sinner."

"What sort of orders?"

"I'm to see that ye don't leave the house. And should ye slip away before I can warn her, I'm to send one of the others to follow and spy on ye."

I chewed a dried plum and pondered this latest development. "Did she appear very suspicious of me?"

"I'd say, offhand, that she is beginning to lack the entertainment of having ye neatly under the ball of her thumb. Ye're a disobedient lass, she led me to understand, and stand in insolence of your elders."

"Then perhaps it is as well that I've foregone the pleasure of my walks," I said quietly. "It will do me no harm to stay indoors for a few days."

"Roll up your sleeve," said Elizabeth, "and I'll take another look at that arm. Is it beginning to itch?"

"Long since," I said. " 'Tis enough to drive one senseless."

"Ye were senseless enough," Elizabeth said, "to cut it open on a rock."

I rolled my sleeve above my elbow and said nothing. Elizabeth examined it with no expression on her face, in much the same manner she had dressed it the morning I stumbled into the kitchen and repeated the tale I had told the Clennons and Robert MacLeish.

She removed the thin bandage and put it aside. "I think we'd best leave off the bandage. 'Tis well enough to do without a dressing."

"I must say," Robert MacLeish said from the doorway, "it looks to be a nasty wound. I'm surprised it has healed so quickly."

I did not jump at the unexpected sound of his voice, nor did Elizabeth, although her mouth tightened as she raised her head.

"It is unseemly of you, Robert," I said easily, "to walk into a room without announcing yourself." I rolled down my sleeve, hoping that I showed no haste except that of modesty. "No gentleman would confront a lady when she is unprepared and in a state of disarray."

Robert flushed. "Then must you disrobe in the kitchen?"

"Elizabeth was merely looking at my injury," I said mildly. "Aren't you pleased that it has healed with no unpleasant complications?"

"It would have been no more than you deserved," he said loftily, "if you had lost the use of your arm altogether."

"Mayhap," I said, "but I do not think I deserve to hear a sermon from you, Robert."

"You have felt the sword of a wrathful God," he said. "A sharp boulder, you say. I say it was an instrument of Divine justice, and before you scoff you might do well, Anne Lindsay, to look at the scar you bear upon your arm. The wound of a sword, a mighty and avengeful sword, and it is there to remind you that our Lord God will not permit the wicked to go unchastened."

I bit my tongue to keep from betraying myself with the laughter strangling in my throat. Robert turned on his heel and stalked from the kitchen; and I put both hands over my mouth and looked at Elizabeth.

"Don't laugh," she said soberly, "he's no' a man to ridicule."

"I'm not laughing at Robert," I said, and wished I might share the jest with Elizabeth. The margin between laughter and anxiety was a thin one; but if Robert had come dangerously close to the truth with his pious declaration of an avenging sword, it was yet amusing enough to lighten my heart.

"What have ye done," asked Elizabeth, "that appears so wicked to him?"

"I have been disobedient," I said, "and wilful, and have caused a disturbance far beyond that due my meagre consequence in the world. And he has caught me, twice over, nodding at morning prayers."

But Robert did not begin to suspect the worst of it, I reflected; doubtless he would consider me quite beyond redemption were he to know the truth.

"He is a curious man, that one. I hear he has been riding the moors of late, asking many questions."

And my laughter was stilled on the moment, and I was obliged to forego my certainty that Robert did not suspect.

"Questions?" I repeated slowly. "What is he curious about, Elizabeth?"

"He has been searching for lonely sheilings, and a woman who acts the Good Samaritan and offers her roof to those who stray from home."

After a moment I said, "Did he find the bothy he sought?"

"Aye, and the woman also."

"Did she answer his questions?"

"I've no way of knowing," said Elizabeth, with the inevitable shrug, "but few folk hereabouts speak aught but Gaelic."

"Thank you," I said thoughtfully. "I can see I must be on guard against Robert's sly ways."

She gave me a brief glance. "He's not the only man with sly ways and curious questions in the back o' his mind."

"But it was you," I pointed out, "who called me a coward when I hesitated to go riding with Lord Monleigh that day. You can see what your interference did for me. I think you might have warned me then."

She put her hands on her hips, and I saw a flare of exasperation in her eyes.

"I was not referring to him," she said. "He's sly, on occasion, and the good Lord knows he has a plaguing habit of posing questions without end, but it's no secret to any that knows him. He'll not trick ye, never fear of that."

I stared at her. "Surely you cannot be speaking of the master, Elizabeth."

Elizabeth said, "The world is full of pitfalls for the unwary," and went back to her pudding.

I was very subdued for the remainder of the day. It surprised me somewhat that Elizabeth did not trust Walter any more than she trusted Robert MacLeish; but it was little wonder that Walter's aloof and impersonal manner had not endeared him to the Highland servants. I did not give it a great deal of thought, however, for it was Robert who worried me, and I knew I must take seriously the threat of his curious suspicions.

The evening meal was a quiet one, for Margaret was still abed and neither Walter nor Robert seemed inclined to conversation. I bid them good night immediately the meal was finished, and went up the stairs to my bedchamber.

Bemused and abstracted, I closed the door behind me and lit my candle. I stood by the press for a moment, staring at my reflection in the wavering glass, seeing Robert's thin pale face instead of my own.

"You are far too lovely to frown at your mirror so bitterly."

I whirled around, stunned, to see Monleigh stretched across my bed, so insolently at his ease that one might have thought he belonged there.

"You are daft," I whispered; then, "What are you doing in my bed?"

"I'm not daft," he replied lazily, "and I find your bed far more comfortable than that hard chair by the fire. Waiting for a lass is a dull affair at best, and I thought it only fair to take my ease as I found it."

"You are daft," I repeated inanely. "What if someone finds you here?"

"You've been disgraced long since," he said. "I'll wager no one would be too surprised to find you entertaining a man in your bedchamber." He swung his boots to the floor. "Don't look so anxious. I'll not be discovered unless one of the Clennons walks in unannounced, and surely you don't allow such unseemly licence."

"That door leads to Margaret's apartment," I said, "and she walks where she pleases in Clennon House."

"Not in the next few minutes," he said calmly, "else she is more expert than I think at faking a sound sleep."

"She is not necessarily asleep. She spends hours in her bed when she has no intention of sleeping."

"All alone?" Monleigh said. "What the devil does she do?"

I ignored his grin. "She thinks," I said.

"I give you my word she is fast asleep at this moment," he said. "I took a close look."

"What of the maid who sits with her?"

"She must have slipped away for her supper. God's foot, that room has an unpleasant smell. What does Margaret think to cure with that stinking incense?"

" 'Tis nothing but dried herbs," I said, and came near to laughing aloud at the vision of a startled Margaret opening her eyes to find the Earl of Monleigh looking through her bed curtains. "If you're not daft, you're a reckless fool."

"Aye," he said, not at all insulted, "that may well be. How is your arm, lass?"

"Almost healed. Elizabeth removed the bandage today."

"I had thought it might be causing you unwonted pain," he said casually. "You've avoided Evan so cleverly that he's been obliged to return to Torra without you on three occasions." He went to the window, gave a cursory glance at the stables below, then turned to face me, leaning indolently against the casement. "The Stewarts have been most apprehensive. They hold me to blame, you see, for your unfortunate mishap."

I had no ready answer, and so I said, "Please lower your voice. Margaret or the maid will certainly hear you."

"I doubt it. Are you able to hear Margaret without standing your door ajar?"

Considering it, I said, "How did you know I could not?"

"I am well acquainted with this room," he said easily, "having romped with two loud and unruly nephews here long past their bedtime, without being found out by either stern parent. I assure you the walls are thick enough for safety."

I remembered all at once what Elizabeth had told me. "Did your brother reside here?"

"Aye, at one time."

I understood then that he knew the corridors and apartments of the house so well it was small wonder he could move about without detection.

"Where is he now, and the two unruly nephews?"

I wished, a moment later, that I had retained my curiosity. His expression did not change; only his voice became low and hard, with a faint chill in it that warned me I had probed a touchy portion of his past which might better have been left alone.

"He is dead," he said, "as well as his two sons."

"I am sorry," I said quietly. "I had no right to ask such a question."

"You had every right. Would you like to know how they died?"

"Not if it pains you to tell me."

"The time for pain has passed," he said, "nor did it ever serve any good purpose. I learned at an early age that weeping over the dead is as futile as wishing them alive again."

I did not wince at the bitterness in his voice; somehow I understood that it had taken him a good many years to speak on the matter with anything approaching an impersonal moderation.

"They died at Philiphaugh," he said. "John was killed in battle, as honourable an end as a man could hope for, but the two lads were shot down later in the courtyard of a Covenanting fortress, alongside the other prisoners taken after the battle."

"Shot after they had been taken prisoner?" I said, disbelieving.

He shrugged. "Not an unusual practice. The Covenanting army found it easier to do away with Montrose's rabble than to feed and convert them."

"You speak from prejudice," I said. "I cannot believe such a terrible thing actually happened."

"John's wife, Ellen, also died on the battlefield," he went on relentlessly, as if I had not spoken. "All the women who followed Montrose's army, caring for the baggage and cooking for their men, were slaughtered after the defeat. Ellen was but three months before being confined for the birth of her third child."

Horrified, I exclaimed, "But she should not have been with an army at such a time."

His eyes flickered over me with something akin to scorn. "A Highland woman can be of great solace to her man during a campaign," he said. "In Ellen's case, however, she had come to bring food and clothes badly needed by her sons, and was to have returned to Torra as soon as John or I found an opportunity to escort her in some degree of safety. Neither of us foresaw she would be driven to the river with the other women, and there cut open by a sword and held under the water to drown."

I gasped and put my hands over my face. Surely he lied, surely not even a wrathful Covenanting soldiery would commit such inhuman atrocities.

"Their battle slogan was 'Jesus and no quarter,'" Monleigh said, as if he were explaining to a child and must therefore simplify his words for a childish mind. "The clergy preached on the text, 'They shall fall by the sword; their infants shall be dashed to pieces, and their women with child shall be ripped up.' Did you never hear such pious sermons, Anne Lindsay?"

"Aye," I whispered, stunned, "many times. But I did not dream they meant it so literally."

"They walked in blood to their anklebones," he said, "and then rubbed their hands gleefully and demanded more blood. The ministers looked about them at the slaughter and sent word that 'the Lord's work goes bonnily on.'"

I could not explain or justify; there was nothing to say, nothing in all the world. But I tried to find a reason, if only for my own peace of mind.

"I've heard many tales of the terrible deeds done by the wild Irish and Highland men of Montrose's army," I said. "Mayhap it was a matter of revenge."

"We killed many men in fair battle," he said flatly, "and that's the way of all wars. But in all the lists of the dead, you'll not find the name of a single woman or child. Nor the names of unarmed citizens, and men taken prisoner and then murdered in black hatred. We had no inclination to do the Devil's work in the name of the Lord."

"Please," I said, feeling very ill, "please don't."

"Have you heard enough of the truth for one time? Let it go, 'tis over and done with. You asked about my brother, and I've told you."

"You must go," I said, forcing my mind back to the present and its equally sickening dangers. "I'm not certain they believed my tale about the night I spent on the moors."

He raised his dark brows. "Are you so poor a liar?"

"Robert found the bothy where I claimed to spend the night," I said. "Elizabeth told me he asked the woman there a suspicious lot of questions."

"But she told him nothing he had not heard from you," Monleigh said calmly.

"But don't you see, he is not content that I told the truth. He will be watching me now, and mayhap Walter will do the same. Robert must surely have discussed it with him."

But even as I spoke I remembered how Walter had talked to me in the hall that afternoon, how kindly he had smiled. If he had discussed me with Robert, he had certainly shown no sign of suspicion or mistrust.

"But you have an idea Walter is no' so skeptical as Robbie MacLeish," Monleigh said softly, as if my face were so transparent he could see into my mind merely by glancing at me.

"He has been very kind," I said only.

"I will mark him down as a man of great kindness and amiability," he said. "Benign, charitable, and filled with a Christian love toward all men. Have I overlooked anything?"

I looked at him closely, but his eyes met mine with an amused blandness, and I could detect no sarcasm beyond that small hint of it in his voice.

"I think you are quite as intolerant as Elizabeth," I said, "on the subject of Walter Clennon."

"Intolerant? I think not," he said idly. "Only cautious."

"There is no need for caution where Walter is concerned," I said. " 'Tis Robbie MacLeish who would catch me out in my sins."

"On second thought," Monleigh went on, "perhaps I would be wise to leave the list open to suggestion. Walter is a man of many moods and manners, and when you have come to know him better you may discover another quality or two worthy to note."

"I believe I know him well enough," I said. "I've lived beneath his roof for three years; it should be long enough for me to take his measure."

"It should be," he said, "but you are much too innocent to judge people at their true worth. And you've a soft heart which accepts the most flagrant lie for the truth until it's been proved othehwise. You're gullible, lass, and I stand here as incontestable proof of your failings."

"And how else would you have me? Women were not born to live by the cold logic of the mind."

"I'd not have you any other way," he said, and smiled at me. "So there have been too many curious questions asked, and you have lost your nerve."

"Margaret has forbidden me to go outside the door, and the servants are instructed to spy on me from morn till night. She would know the instant I left Clennon House."

"Then you think Margaret suspects also?"

"She has ever suspected me of indolence and shiftlessness," I said. "It angers her that I should have the leisure to go chasing about the moors when I should be tending her needs."

"Have you retired for the night?" he asked abruptly.

I found that amusing. "Such was my intention when I came to my room."

"When do the others customarily retire?"

"They were considering the matter when I left them."

"Then I'll take my leave," Monleigh said. "I've no wish to meet them outside your door." He stood erect, but there was no air of haste about him. "I'll give you an hour, lass. By then Robbie and Walter should have donned their nightshirts and said their prayers, and all will be quiet in Clennon House."

"An hour?" I repeated inanely.

"Would you prefer to come with me now?"

"Come with you, m'lord?"

He was tolerably patient. "Must you repeat everything I say?"

"When you speak in riddles," I said uneasily.

"I think you understand me well enough."

He would not allow me even a modest evasion. "You must know I cannot leave Clennon House tonight," I said. "I'd not dare."

"If you are clever with it," he said coolly, "no one will see you leave or return."

"I am not at all clever, and it is much too dangerous."

"There is no' a pillory in the west," he said, "if that is what unnerves you. The Clennons would be obliged to take you a good many miles, and the Stewarts would have ample opportunity to snatch you from their clutches."

"Don't tease," I said. "I'm not so craven that I fear only for myself."

"Then for me?" he said, smiling faintly. "Tell me, lass, what punishment you think the Clennons might contrive for me."

"You know as well as I the crimes they've marked against your name."

"Aye," he said, "but I fail to see any crime in meeting a lass in the moonlight. Mayhap the Kirk considers it an unnatural sin, but the Kirk does not rule supreme in the Highlands."

"If there were no other considerations," I said, "I must remember that a lady does not run across the moors in the dark of night to meet a gentleman."

"But I am not a gentleman," he said, amused, "I admit to the other, against my will, but grant me the hope that I may one day persuade you that you are less a lady than a woman."

"I've often heard it said," I remarked, "that a lass who is too forward only succeeds in lowering her worth in a man's eyes."

"You've heard a damnable lot of witless things in your lifetime," he said. "Don't be a fool. We both find pleasure in your coming, and that is all that matters." Then he smiled at me and added, "When you have wearied of being with evil freebooters, you will refuse to come. Until then, we must remember our pledge to be honest with each other. Would you have me call upon you in the proper manner, and converse with you under Margaret's sharp eye, and kiss your hand circumspectly when I take my leave?"

"You know I would not," I said quietly.

"Then you will remind yourself, now and again, that you also promised not to cavil and protest. Don't plague yourself with so many worries, Anne Lindsay. I'm quite capable of taking care of you."

But he would not be the one to listen to Margaret's recriminations, I thought soberly, nor would he likely understand why I should care a whit if I were to be banished from the Clennon household. He could not know as I did, with the dreadful knowledge of experience, what it meant to be lonely and friendless and without means in a world which gave solace to none but the strong and bold who most readily found solace for themselves. And because he lived by strength and incautious boldness, he could not share my anxious fear that someday, in a stealthy way unbeknownst to me, I might be the cause of his downfall at the hands of his enemies.

He took a single long stride which brought him close beside me.

"I once told you," he said softly, "that I might bring you to grief. But I spoke only of the torment of soul and heart; I did not mean that you would suffer for my sins, or that I'd stand idly by and see you hurt by anyone, least of all the Clennons."

He was saying, I understood at last, that I was no longer alone or friendless, that I no longer need fear the world beyond Clennon House or the equally cruel world inside it. It was surely a pleasant solace; and yet, I bethought myself, how long would it last?

"Solace for only a brief moment," I said, "can be worse than none at all. It leaves one strangely vulnerable and defenceless."

He did not ask me what I meant; he seemed to know quite well without asking.

"Solace cannot be measured in terms of time," he said. Then curtly, "I'll meet you beyond the trees in an hour. Give me your promise."

"D'you think you need it?"

His brown hand lifted my chin. "Do I, Anne Lindsay?"

I sighed. "Aye, you'd best have it. I promise."

He paused at the door to listen, then gave me no more than a casual wave of his hand before quitting my bedchamber.

I sat on the edge of my bed, trying to think with some reason and logic now that his disturbing presence was no longer there to befuddle my mind. But I had spoken the truth; a woman was not born to reasonable logic. I had only to look at my rumpled feather bolster to recall how his dark head had looked resting there; I sat in a silent room and still heard his voice, bringing so urgent and passionate a breath of life to my maidenly chamber that the very essence of it remained, even after his departure, and insolently drove from my mind all thoughts of logic.

When I deemed I had allowed enough time for a necessary margin of error, I fastened my cloak with uncertain fingers and blew my candle. My courage almost failed me, even then, when I opened the door in the darkness and faced the black night engulfing corridor and stairs. But Walter and Robert would be well in their beds, and so I went on with my heart thudding in my ears, and my hands, as they felt the way along the wall, were so unsteady I was suddenly more taken with shame than apprehension.

Down the corridor and gallery I crept, down the stairs and through the myriad doors to the silent kitchen, past the great hearth with its flickering peat fire, to the postern door opening to the courtyard. The chain and bolt almost proved my undoing, being heavy enough to protect the house against marauders of any ilk, but I struggled manfully, determined not to fail so ignominiously at the kitchen door.

Then I was out in the cool night, and my feet flew over the courtyard as if Margaret herself had been at my heels. It was not until I reached the gate that I realized I was still within the confines of Clennon House and would likely remain there; for the gate was tall and heavy, and latched with a stout plank across it which creaked and groaned when lifted as if the entire foundation of Clennon House were being pushed out of place. Ordinarily, when the yard was crowded during the day, the gate stood open; but I stood no chance of opening it myself in the dead of night without risking detection.

Feeling an almost unbearable disappointment, I leaned my head against the gate and wondered cynically if Monleigh had expected me to scale the wall as he himself had doubtless done on his departure. It would not be too difficult, in truth, were I a long-legged Stewart with the litheness of a cat and the nerve of the Devil; but I had no intention of trying it merely to dangle there helplessly till Robert came to haul me down on the morrow.

Then, with an amusingly apt timing, the gate moved slightly under the pressure of my unhappy face, and I realized that it had not been latched after all. It stood ajar, and by pushing it a foot or so, I managed to slip through. I did not pause to wonder at Monleigh's ingenuity in contriving it, even as I remembered that the gate had also been left open the night the stables were raided. He must certainly have an accomplice within the house, but it was no affair to puzzle over when the dark woods loomed just ahead and beyond them stretched the moors, sweet and wild beneath the night skies.

I ran through the woods and across the whispering burn, and Monleigh waited just beyond the woods. He put his hands to my waist without a word and lifted me to the saddle. Then he sprang up behind me and touched spurs to his horse; and we were away, riding like the wind across the hills, while the stars rode their white stallions in furious pursuit across the wide arc of the sky.

❧ 11 ❧

MONLEIGH took my cloak from my shoulders, and I walked to one of the windows to look out across the sea. Behind me a fire burned on the hearth, but the windows were opened to the cool wind. The room was washed clean of stale air and the dankness constantly fostered in stone walls eight feet thick; it seemed filled with the sweetness of the night, with the clean salt air brought by the wind over countless leagues of sea water.

"'Tis a lovely night," I said softly. "Isn't it a pity that we must needs lock ourselves in stone dungeons to sleep the night away, when beyond the walls such loveliness exists, free for even the most wretched of men?"

"We shall go out again presently. Would you like that?"

"Very much. I cannot remember a time when I might walk abroad after dark without fear. It was forbidden in Dundee, and Edinburgh is so unspeakably evil the streets are unsafe even by daylight."

"You'll be safe enough on Stewart land. We discourage visitors with evil minds and habits." Then he laughed and said, "Come here, lass. I've something to show you, as a reward for not breaking your promise."

I turned to see him undoing the heavy leather straps encircling a sea chest which sat against the wall across the room.

"What is it?" I asked with a surge of feminine curiosity, and went to stand beside him.

"Treasures from far Cathay," he said, teasing me by taking his time with the straps. "Fabulous gems from the Orient, gold doubloons from a ship of the Spanish Main, and a few ancient hasty puddings stolen from under the nose of His Highness the Lord Protector of London town."

"Ill-got plunder," I said. "I'll have none of it."

But then he threw back the carved lid, and I drew a long unsteady breath. The firelight caressed the rich velvets, the glowing satins, the gay profusion of colour in embroidery and damask and brocade; crimson there was, and tawny gold, green with the deep fire of an emerald, palest blue and rose and yellow, and in all that giddy whirl of colour not a single thread of sombre gray or black.

"May I look at them?" I murmured politely, but did not wait for his answer.

I sank to my knees and began to pull out the gowns one by one. Here was one of gold cloth, with enormously puffed sleeves and lace ruffles; here a delicate blue satin encrusted with pearl and boasting several petticoats of Flemish lace; here a dainty white cambric sprinkled with tiny roses much like a spring garden after rain; here a crimson velvet, elegant and luxurious, glowing with exquisite colour.

This last I held to my cheek in wordless longing, quite forgetting that I was not alone. One thinks of softness in many terms—the cheek of a wee bairn or the nape of his moist little neck, the downy underside of a goose, the feel of a snowflake against one's face, the first stirring of a summer breeze, the pale-green tree moss in the northern woods. But none of these, I'll warrant, could compare with the wondrous feel of velvet held in hands long accustomed to worsted and muslin.

"The choice is yours," said Monleigh. "You must decide which pleases you the most."

I looked up at him, leaning there against the wall with his eyes steady on my face, and my sudden shame at displaying such a covetous greed faded away on the moment. He understood, that much I knew from the compassion in his face; and by his perception, untinged with pity, he once again gave me the courage to be myself, free of restraint or self-reproach.

"You are kind," I said, "but I could not. The joy is not in possessing. Whatever would I do with a crimson velvet gown in Clennon House?"

"I would I had a portrait of you," he said levelly, "just as you are at this moment."

I laughed up at him, the crimson gown still in my hands

and the others strewn about me like fallen petals of some exotic flower, and felt very wantonly happy.

"And what would be its title? 'Downfall of a Lady,' mayhap, or 'Seduction of the Innocent'?"

"It would be more apt," he said, "to call it 'Portrait of a Sweet Wench.' " He reached for my hand and pulled me up. "If you can't take it home, you can at least wear it while you're at Torra. I regret I haven't the Parisian slippers to match."

I smiled to think he had remembered that foolish bit of banter. "Go away, then," I said, "and I shall exchange my dull gray plumage for that of a very bright peacock."

So I took off my sober spinster's gown and coif, and donned the velvet gown; and not once did it occur to me that I was making a dangerous and imprudent mistake. I forgot the remarkable events which had followed the occasion of my changing into a freebooter's breeks and boots and plumed hat; I forgot that one tends to discard old habits of mind, old notions of behavior, once the staid boredom of the familiar has been traded for the exciting novelty of the unknown.

I was much too enchanted with the gown to be bothered with such trifles. The bodice was cut rather low for respectability and the extravagant width of the skirts gave me pause to shake my head at such a waste of expensive material; but it was a near perfect fit, and I felt vastly elegant and fashionable.

In a pleasant rustle of stiff lace petticoats I went to the door and opened it, but Monleigh was not in sight. Evan Stewart, however, a dark bottle of wine in each hand, was making his way toward the boisterous gathering in the great hall.

At the sight of me he halted abruptly. "God's foot, ye're enough to take a man's breath away."

I whirled before him. "Do you like it, Evan?"

"It becomes ye famously. I'm drunk at the sight of ye."

"If you're drunk, you've had too much wine," I said, "and if you're not careful with your flattery, I shall grow exceedingly vain."

"How else does a man speak to a pretty lass," he said, "if not with cajolery?"

"Does cajolery serve you well?"

He grinned. "I'll admit there's a trick to it I've not yet learned. Simon, the black dog, has only to turn his mind to an insult and a nasty leer, and he wins all."

I laughed. "Don't despair, Evan. Somewhere there must be a lass who'll succumb to your charms."

"To my sorrow, one has already done so."

"Are you married, Evan?" I asked, surprised.

"Aye, but ye needn't spread the word around." Then, changing the subject abruptly, he said, "How did ye come to be wearing a red dress?"

" 'Tis my favourite colour. D'you approve of my taste?"

"I once knew another lass who had a liking for red," he said slowly, "and I've noticed it has a strange way of showing a woman's true nature." He regarded me for a moment. "She was a fair enough wench, but now I see she was no lovelier than ye."

Thoughtfully, I asked, "Did she have a crimson velvet gown like this one?"

"She may have had. I've not much of an eye for gowns and such."

I looked down at the wide skirts, a cold despair creeping over me. The sea chest, the fabulous gowns, even the one I wore, had likely belonged to that other lass, who had also had a wanton liking for crimson red. I would not have thought Monleigh to be so tactless.

"If ye're thinking ye might not be the first to wear it," said Evan, "I'll tell ye how that gown happened to be in Torra. It came by mistake, with a dozen others, when we should ha' got a long box of muskets, and not till this minute do I understand why Simon was so pleased. When he likes he can curse the stupidity of men with as fine a rage as I've ever known."

I felt a vast relief; and yet I could not but wonder why Evan had mentioned the woman at all. He was, Monleigh had told me, a man of great cunning and craft, a man of many guises, who did naught without a purpose.

"The other lass you spoke of," I said slowly, "was she as happy at Torra as I have been?"

"I doubt she was ever happy," he said, "whether at Torra or elsewhere. A dozen scarlet gowns would no' have satisfied her." Looking at me blackly, he added, "Women are a foolish lot."

Foolish I might be, but I was not stupid.

"Then you think I, too, am a fool," I said quietly, "to talk of happiness as if it were so readily obtained as a pretty gown."

"From what I've seen of ye," he said, "I'd say it takes very little to make ye happy. But I'll tell ye this, Anne Lindsay, because I've grown quite fond of ye. All women are fools who think to barter their charms to their own purpose."

"It cannot be fondness," I said, oddly hurt, "to think so ill of me."

"I'm not accusing ye. But think on't."

Surely, I thought miserably, he did not believe I would attempt to bargain with Monleigh. I was not so great a fool as that, nor did I have such confidence in my paltry share of charm.

"You have misjudged me, Evan," I said.

"And ye have misunderstood me. I'll put it to ye this way. I've seen many a comely wench think to chain him to the hearth, but not a single one had the wit to see how she had failed." He looked at me with that inexplicable air of kindness so much at odds with his ugly face. "A man may look on a lass and think himself well quit of the world for a night. But if she has naught but a fair body to offer, and the instinct to use it as a whore will, for her own gain, she'll not hold him past the dawn."

I should have been horrified at his unseemly choice of words, but I was not. He was giving me a warning I would do well to heed, and he was telling me something I would hear from no one else.

"What should she have done," I asked, feeling my way cautiously, "to hold him?"

He shrugged. "No man is held against his will."

"He would not have wed her," I said slowly, "if he had no wish to be held."

"So she believed," Evan said flatly. "She thought she possessed the whole of him, body and soul. But she overlooked one small important trifle. Having no heart of her own, she gave no consideration to his."

"You are harsh with her memory."

"I've a word of advice for ye, and all women who learn of men from other women. When beauty fails, ye'll need more of a trick than turning into a nagging scold, or weeping, or hating blindly."

"We are only friends, Monleigh and I. I've no need of tricks."

He looked me up and down. "Well now," he said, "is that the way of it?"

My cheeks aflame, I said, "I'd not lie to you."

"Only in innocence," he said, "and I think ye're far too innocent a lass for Simon's sinful ways."

"Did she have a child?" I asked suddenly.

Our eyes were at a level, and Evan's black brows drew together in a scowl. "No, she had none."

"Perhaps a bairn would have tied him to her."

"D'you believe that?"

"No," I said faintly, "I do not believe it."

No, he would not be tied to any woman, I reflected, no matter how beloved, and the bairns she bore him would make little difference. He would cherish the woman, mayhap, and adore the bairns; but when all was said and the love-making done and the bairns all tucked away in their trundle beds, he would be off again, and to hold him back would be much like catching the hill winds in a bag or halting the sea waves with a scrap of silk. Only the woman would feel the chains, tying her securely to the hearth and the bairns that cried in the night and the empty pillow beside her on the bed.

"But he was kind to her," said Evan. "Even to the end, and it was more than she deserved."

Kind? Surely no man, not even Monleigh, could be kind to a woman and then turn so violently against her that he would have her murdered. Surely the gossip lied, it could not be true that she died by his hand.

There was something mocking in the set of Evan's mouth. "Are you surprised?" he asked. "Did you think otherwise?"

After a long while I said, "I have heard many tales."

"You should not listen so indiscriminately," Monleigh said from behind me.

I turned hastily, and my skirts rustled against his boots. How long he had stood there, and how much of the conversation he had heard, I did not know; his face was closed and guarded, giving nothing away, and his dark eyes

scanned me carelessly as if his thoughts were only of me
and the way I looked to him at that moment.

"Get you gone, Evan," he said, not taking his eyes from
me. "Each time I leave my lass unattended I return to
find you skulking about in the shadows."

Evan grinned, his geniality restored on the moment. "I've
no choice," he said, "when ye hide her away as if ye fear
to lose her should she see any man but Monleigh."

He walked unsteadily down the corridor, but I well
knew he was neither unsteady nor drunk. But I could not
puzzle over it, nor think on his strange warning, when
Monleigh stood beside me, looking down at me like a
father whose child has exceeded his fondest expectations.

"I did not imagine," he said, "that a gown could make
such a difference. I'm overwhelmed."

"Was I so terrible before?" I asked, suddenly shy.

"A shabby way of begging a compliment. But if you'll
be better satisfied, I'll admit that you could wear sacking
and still be lovely." Before my head could be turned by
such a pretty speech, he added, "Only to a discerning eye
such as mine, however. You must remember that I am
acquainted with the beauty of your soul."

"As I know the iniquity of yours," I retorted, put at my
ease again.

"Such ill-bred manners. If I didn't know you so well I'd
suspect you of being a presbyterian." He took my hand.
"Come away, we must have our walk in the moonlight."

It was a glorious night, pleasantly warm without a hint
of the treacherous rain and cold winds that sometimes
plague the west coast even in high summer, and the crushed
heather, wet with dew, beneath our feet scented the air
about us with a haunting sweetness.

Monleigh's hand was under my arm, steadying me on
the uneven heath, and so he kept me from stumbling that
moment when I first heard the thin enchanting thread of
sound coming unexpectedly out of the night.

It seemed so close to me, almost under my feet, that I
halted abruptly and looked around me for the musician
who strummed his lute so lazily in the moonlight; but
standing on the high moor with a clear view in all directions, I could see no man or lute in sight. It was an eerie
feeling and an eerie melody, and I wondered if I should
distrust my senses.

"Fairy music," I said. "D'you hear it?"

"I hear it," said Monleigh, "but I must warn you that the one who plays that particular lute is a rough fellow with horny fingers and a broken nose who bears not the smallest resemblance to a fairy."

Bewildered, I said, "But where is he?"

Monleigh led me toward the sea, on my right hand, and for a moment I thought he intended to walk me straight over the precipice. But at one and the same instant I perceived the slender masts etched against the sky, only the topmost portion visible as if they sprang from the very ground at my feet. Then I saw the narrow path winding among the boulders to drop steeply out of sight, meeting the sea somewhere below.

"Your ship is returned," I whispered, delighted.

"Two nights ago," he said, "and your stubbornness almost lost you the chance to see her. She'll weigh anchor again in a day or so."

"So soon? You give the crew little time for pleasure."

"They'd deem it small pleasure to be hauled to Edinburgh in chains," he said briefly, "and that is what happens to unwary smugglers who linger overlong in port."

He began to descend the path, no more than a narrow foothold clinging to the side of the cliff, and his strong hand pulled me along behind him and gave me no time for apprehension.

On the tiny beach below, a shingled half-moon of sand and pebbles scarce ten feet wide, a longboat was pulled up beyond the high-water mark. A man in canvas breeks and a dark woolen jerkin uncoiled himself from the shadow of the gunwale and stood up, awaiting our approach.

"We'll go aboard," Monleigh said quietly to him, and when the sailor moved toward the boat he added, "No, lad, I'll handle the oars myself."

The man nodded and shoved the boat into the water, holding it steady while Monleigh lifted me across the intervening space and deposited me firmly on the stern thwart. I watched him bend his back to the oars with an easy regularity of pace that rippled the muscles in his shoulders and brought us to the anchored ship in short minutes. He shipped his oars in her shadow, and I looked up entranced at the graceful flare of her sheer, and the

tall, tall reach of the masts toward the sky. It had the bold
reckless lines of a pirate ship, a privateer, and I thought
it a suitable ship indeed for Stewart smugglers.

"What is her name?" I asked softly.

"The *Marie*."

"Why?" I asked. "Why not a Scots name?"

" 'Tis only the French version of Mary, and a most tactful name for a ship that spends a good part of her time
stealing in and out of French harbours. Even the English
can understand it, despite its foreign flavour, so you can
see it serves us well."

"And what do your Stewarts think of it?"

"We have our own Marie to remember," he said lightly.
"A queen named Mary Stuart, who held the name in such
affection she kept four Maries with her until she died."

"Is your ship named for Mary Stuart?"

"Aye, but I trust we'll have better fortune with it than
she."

Remembering how the lovely and hapless Mary Stuart
had come to ruin at the hands of Scots and English alike,
I said, "Then take care you don't make the same mistakes."

"I shall, lass," he said, and reached for the rope ladder
lowered over the side. "Can you manage those skirts?"

"I should have worn the breeks again. They'd be better
suited for climbing about a ship."

"But not nearly so enticing," he said, and without ceremony sent me on my way up the ladder before I could
dwell on the immodest view I would present to him standing below.

A lanthorn was held over the side to furnish more light
for us, and a pair of jersey-clad arms lifted me clear of
the last few rungs of rope and set me gently on the deck.
Then Monleigh's dark head and white shirt appeared and
he jumped down beside me.

"Secure the longboat, Ian," he said, and when the fellow
had left us he took my arm and led me across the deck.
"You'll meet Ian later," he said. "He's my mate, and captain when I'm ashore tending to other matters."

"Do you sail the *Marie* yourself?" I had not thought of
him as also a seafaring man; there was no end to his accomplishments, and I wondered when he had found time

between battles and wars to live so varied and endlessly fascinating a life.

"I prefer it to anything else," he said quietly.

He said no more, but led me up narrow steps to another deck. "The quarter-deck," I said, proud of myself for knowing, and he smiled down at me. "Have you never been aboard a ship before?"

I shook my head, too excited to speak. The ship was clean and sweet-smelling, but I could not identify the enticing scents beyond that of wood and hemp and planks scrubbed diligently with holystone and stout muscles.

I went to the great wheel and put both my hands on the spokes, rubbed to the feel of satin by countless rough hands; and I allowed myself a brief moment of pretence. The *Marie* was no longer in a snug harbour but lifted her sails before a fair wind somewhere out in the wide reaches of the sea; and Monleigh and I stood together on the slanting deck and set our course by the stars, sailing free of all the dangerous cares of the dark land behind us, alone with the lovely ship and sweet wind and far horizons.

"Stand by to come about, sir," Monleigh said against my ear. "Starboard the helm when I give the command."

He put his hands over mine, facing me across the wheel, and smiled at me in the moonlight.

"Never mind," he said, "perhaps one day you'll sail my ship."

"Perhaps," I said quietly.

"Would you like to see the captain's cabin?"

I took his hand and we moved across the deck. The lanthorn had been extinguished and the shadows were long and dark, and the lute somewhere beyond us on the deck was muted and quiet. We went through a swinging door and down a companionway, and then the darkness ended in another door which Monleigh opened.

The cabin was neat and clean, from the polished table and chairs to the brass fittings on the lockers, and I had not expected it to be so like a room in a land-bound home. The lockers beneath the ports were cushioned, furnishing narrow beds which looked amazingly comfortable; and a leather lanthorn hung above the table and cast a warm light over the smooth golden planking, the charts on the wall, the pewter tankards and trenchers held in place in the open cupboard by a raised wooden edge. Opposite the door the wall was broken by windows stretching across the stern of the ship, and the moonlight reflecting on the water below threw rippling patterns against the panelled walls.

"When you are aboard the *Marie*," I said, "is this your cabin?"

Monleigh went to the cupboard and took a wine bottle and two wineglasses from it. "Aye," he said, "I eat and sleep here, and study my charts like any wise captain. Do you like it?"

I walked to the window and leaned out, watching the gentle surge of waves and the intricate designs of moonlight etched on the dark water.

"I envy you," I said. "Why do you linger on shore when you have this waiting for you?"

"A man cannot always live as he pleases."

There was nothing to say to that, for I understood too well. But I had not thought him to be bound by anything but his own desires and ambitions.

"But why must you stay in Scotland?"

"I am bewitched," he said lightly, "by a lass with green eyes and a crimson gown."

He handed me a wineglass and sat on the edge of the table.

"But now that you have been here," he said, "I'll have no escape left me. You will possess this cabin, as you have come to possess Torra, and I'll never be rid of you."

If his voice teased me, his eyes did not; and I wished I could look away but did not dare.

"Will you think of me, then, when you sail away from Scotland at last?"

"I expect you will always haunt me, Anne Lindsay. But the hours are ofttimes long and lonely on a ship, and you will be good company."

Would he remember me in the crimson gown, I wondered, sipping wine in his uncluttered masculine cabin; or would the fleeting reminder be of a spinster disguised as a slender Stewart lad, a silly wanton woman who had longed for a single taste of life before settling down to the dreary business of growing old? Would he laugh and shrug pityingly at the memory, would he never know any regret that things had not gone differently for us?

"I will haunt you for as long as it takes to fetch another port," I said, "and another lass."

"You can be quite absurd," he said evenly, "when you choose to be."

We looked at each other, and the world grew still and hushed, faded away into oblivion beyond us. I smiled, inexplicably happy, and felt the smile grow tremulous and unsure; and the breathless moment seemed to last forever, as if all existence and all life had ceased to be for that one span of time belonging to us alone.

It was he who broke the spell at last.

"Do you find it such a diverting game," he said quietly, "to toy with disaster?"

I could not pretend to misunderstand him. "I very much fear that I do," I said, drawing an unsteady breath. "I don't know what possesses me. I've never thought of myself as one who flirts with danger."

"When one walks along the edge of a precipice," he said, "there is often a great temptation to see how close one may venture to the brink without falling."

"Perhaps I have learned that you will pull me back to safety before I have taken a fatal step."

His face was unsmiling, and I remembered how he had looked to me the moment before he led his Stewarts against the English troopers.

"I had a purpose," he said, "but it was no' so gallant as you imagine."

"You wanted me to trust you," I said softly. "I have done so for some time past."

He put his wineglass on the table behind him, moving with easy deliberation, and came toward me.

"Trusting me," he said, "is far more dangerous than walking the edge of a cliff."

"I know, but you once said it would make matters easier for me."

"So it has," he said coolly, "until now."

He was so close that his wide shoulders shut out the rest of the cabin; I could see the small steady pulse in his brown throat, and so I fastened my eyes on it and would not raise them to be further disconcerted by his unswerving gaze, his mouth, the heavy fringe of black lashes shadowing his eyes.

"But this time I'll not pull you back to safety," he said, "and you will know the meaning of disaster after all. It will not be easy for you, and nothing will make it so."

He took the wineglass from my unresisting fingers and placed it beside his on the table.

"Is it so surely a disaster?"

"Speaking from conceit and pride," he said, "I would not deem it so."

"Then why should I?"

"You are a woman," he said, "and a chaste one at that."

"If it is so wretched a thing for me," I said, choosing my words with care, "how can you find any pleasure in it?"

"Unfortunately for you, my dear Anne, that is the nature of a cruel world."

I was uncertain and shaken, the more so because I could not understand why he thought it necessary to be so ruthless.

"I should not have come," I said at last. "Will you take me back to Clennon House?"

But I knew before he spoke that such a craven retreat was impossible. I had long since lost any chance to turn back; I had known, as had he, that sooner or later I must face this moment and make the best of it. If I yearned desperately to avoid it, to delay the inevitable, it was only a final cowardice, one last instinctive defence urged on by panic. I was not ready, I thought desperately, it had come too soon.

"No," he said.

"I was right," I said. "You give no quarter."

"Did you expect it?"

"I don't know," I said, trying to regain some semblance of poise. "I don't know what I expected."

His hand held my chin firmly, lifting my face to his.

"You will soon find out," he said, his voice dangerously soft. "I am done with patience, lass."

"No," I whispered.

"No," he said, mimicking me. "No, kind sir, you must unhand me. You have mistaken me, I am not that sort of a lass. I am a lady, surely you will not force me against my will."

Beyond the mocking implacable voice I could hear the sea murmuring against the hull below the windows, and on the deck above my head the unseen sailor played his plaintive lute.

I will not plead with him, I thought clearly, I will not shame myself.

"You seem quite familiar," I said, "with the protests of unwilling ladies."

But it was a flimsy courage at best, and my voice betrayed me with its slight tremor.

"I thought we were agreed," he said carelessly, "that I had no need to force myself on any woman."

His hands, strong and ungentle, moved from my face to my shoulders; and wherever they touched me a flame streaked along my nerves. They paused at the velvet neckline of the crimson gown, slipping it slowly from my shoulders, and the tiny rustle was incredibly loud in the silence. The soft breeze from the sea was cool against my bare skin, but where his hands held me the warmth spread to my blood with a fierce unbearable intensity.

His mouth came down on mine and his hands bruised my shoulders, and the flame within me began to burn with a slow sweet languor, consuming in its blaze all protests, all fear, all will to live apart from his mouth and hands and the urgent demand of his powerful body against mine.

It would not save me from condemnation, nor restore me to grace, to say that he took me against my will, at his own pleasure, and spent the violence of his passion with a careless disregard for my innocence, my painful chastity, my frightened tears, seeking only his selfish satisfaction at the expense of my helplessness.

For it would not be the whole truth. He took me, aye, and against my will; and I cannot deny I was frightened at first, and struggled against hot tears. I was also helpless before his violence and the strength of his hands, as all women must be in that last moment when passion, unleashed and savage, sways thinly balanced on the crest of a towering wave, when naught in the wide world could prevent the inevitable triumphant crash upon the shore.

But when it was finished and his dark head rested

against my breast, and I lay watching the shimmer of
water ripples on the polished wood above me, I remembered something Elizabeth had said to me. "No one knows
a man like the woman who shares his bed," she had said
in her dour way; and I who had shared Monleigh's by
force and cruel mockery, had come to know that he was
neither cruel nor mocking, nor merciless, nor selfishly in-
considerate.

At last he lifted his head, and for a long moment we
looked at each other without speaking.

"Do you understand now?" he asked quietly.

"Yes," I said, "you know me very well."

I was grateful that he had not insulted my intelligence
by offering an explanation. He had routed my conscience
in the only way possible, knowing that my fears could
only lead me to endless evasion, and my irrational and
trembling happiness was proof enough that he had made
no error in judgment.

"I know you better now," he said with a lazy smile.
"We have wasted a good deal of valuable time, Anne
Lindsay."

"I am not to blame," I said. "I am the shy one, and you
the man who has only to smile at a maiden to have her
swoon in your arms. Why did you wait so long to practice
your skill on me?"

"Have you been so eager, lass?"

I looked at his dark face, no longer wary and closed
against me, at the warm laughter in his gray eyes; and the
unfamiliar look of tenderness about him, existing for me
and because of me, was enough to take my breath away.
After this moment, I thought with a dazed enchantment,
I could die and be well quit of the world.

"Well," I said, "you took long enough about it."

"I've not begun yet," he said, laughing down at me.
"Shall I show you the way of it?"

"I should think," I said, "that you had already proved
your point."

"Any lass can be taken by force," he said. " 'Tis no test
of a man's skill."

We smiled at each other; and the look in his eyes, steady
on mine, set my pulses to leaping again, and my smile
faded away into that rapt moment of silence I had come

to know so well whenever we looked at each other and felt the aching fire spring to life between us.

And so he set out, deliberately and with consummate skill, to show me what he meant. He succeeded very well, being a man to whom the art of persuasion came so easily that he might in truth have been born to the secrets of witchcraft and sorcery. But he must have discerned, almost at once, that he needed no further art to spellbind me than to put his mouth on mine, and speak certain quiet words against my throat, and let me know again how strangely gentle his hard hands could be.

The lute played on and on, dreaming the night away, and the sea still murmured faintly below the ports; and the smugglers' ship, the fair *Marie,* rode quietly to her anchors in the hidden cove.

{ 12 }

MONLEIGH refused to leave me outside the gates of Clennon House but escorted me to the postern door of the kitchen, pointing out that a man could do no less when he brought a lass home in the middle of the night.

"Even a smuggler and a freebooter," he said gravely, "has some idea of the proper amenities. We are no' barbarians, Anne Lindsay."

"You may not be barbarians," I said, "but you are all scoundrels. And if you're not careful, you'll be attempting to explain the difference to Walter Clennon."

"I'd not waste my time," he said. " 'Tis an unwise scoundrel who would plead innocence to one who knows nothing of guilt."

I sighed at the cynical note in his voice. "You dislike Walter because he is unlike you," I said, "and yet I should think that very dissimilarity would be proof of his good character."

"A good proof of character, in any case."

He had twisted my words only slightly, yet the meaning at once took on a vastly different shade of meaning.

"I would like to believe you jealous of my high opinion of him," I said lightly, "but I know you too well to feel in the least flattered."

He laughed softly. "No, lass, I must disappoint you. I'd have a small opinion of myself had I naught to arouse my jealousy but poor Walter Clennon."

"Then it is only an arrogant superiority," I said, "and it will blacken Walter's character less than your own."

He laughed again, dismissing the matter, and put his finger on a truant curl which had escaped my coif.

"Do you know why I've grown so fond of you, lass?

You're a changeling, and give a man no time to tire of you."

"It would scarcely do," I said, feeling a faint regret for the lovely gown I had left behind at Torra, "for me to go to bed with a worsted gown on the chair and awake to find it changed into crimson velvet. I'd be accused of witchcraft."

"You'll be accused of far worse if you don't get yourself to bed. Good night, lass. Sleep well."

He lifted my face and smiled at me, and gave me a fleeting kiss which was little more than a caress; and stood on the stone steps, hands on his hips, until I had opened the door and slipped within.

I stood there for a moment in the darkness, leaning against the stout panels of the door. Then I sighed, and slipped off my slippers, and started the lengthy journey through the corridors to the stairs. The peat fire, carefully banked for the night, still afforded a faint light until I had left the kitchen; but then I was forced to find my way by memory and the diligent use of my hands along the walls.

I reached the stairs with no mishap, and felt for the balustrade. Then, with no warning, a great flood of light caught me and held me motionless there, my hand still outstretched, my bare foot on the first step.

I was too shocked and astounded to feel any sudden fear; I merely stood as the light had found me, realizing without conscious thought that it came from the great hall behind me and meant the door had been opened by someone, and thought that a butterfly must experience the same bewildered disbelief when captured and pinned ruthlessly to a board.

At last I turned, slowly and dreamily, and faced Walter Clennon. He stood with the light behind him, and so seemed taller than before, and because his face was in darkness I might have been confronted by a towering shadow which repeated itself across the floor in a mis-shapen, grossly exaggerated figure of darkness.

"Come in, Anne," he said. "I think we must talk before you go up to bed."

It was truly Walter, then, and not a grotesque figment of my imagination. He stood aside so that I might enter

the hall before him, and as he moved I caught the dull
flash of the blood-red ruby on his forefinger.

"Sit down," he said in the same passive tone of voice,
his poise unperturbed, his composure no more or less
ruffled than it was wont to be.

I paused by a chair to slip my feet into my shoes, and
went to sit by the fire. I was silent, for there was obviously nothing I might say with impunity, and so oddly
subdued that I could not feel my heart beat at all; but
now that the worst had actually happened I was not so
much fearful as relieved that there could be no worse
disaster than this. I had been caught, found out in my
sins, and no further misfortune could befall me.

Walter did not sit down, but rested one arm on the
lintel of the fireplace, the other behind him, and stared
into the fire.

The long trestle table, with its heavily carved legs which
formed the massive paw and claws of a lioness, held several branched candelabras of silver; and the brilliant light
shone across the table, the squat chairs with their high
cushioned backs, the arras hanging on the walls, then
finally disappeared in the shadows lurking in the tall
corners of the room.

"Where have you been?" Walter asked mildly.

I had sufficient time to prepare the first answer.

"Walking on the moors. 'Tis a lovely night."

"Were you not afraid to go out alone so late in the
evening?"

"I did not go far," I said, and wondered why the lie
did not stick in my throat. I had travelled, in a few short
hours, a world away from Clennon House, a lifetime, a
brief eternity.

"I am loath to read you a sermon, Anne, and especially
so at this late hour. But you must know I cannot countenance such misbehavior."

"I am truly sorry," I said. Another craven lie; I would
soon be quite proficient at it.

Walter turned slightly, so that he might better observe
me. "Have we been so harsh with you that you must slip
away in the dead of night? Did you fear, perhaps, that I
might refuse to allow you the innocent pleasure of a
walk?"

I shook my head wordlessly for want of a better answer.

"You look different," he went on, in the same idle tone of voice, "most unlike yourself. Surely the moonlight did not put that becoming flush in your cheeks."

The flush became a hot flame, despite all I could do; but I resisted the impulse to put up my hands to hide my telltale face.

"An assignation, Anne?" he asked softly.

I could not allow him to guess until he hit at the whole truth; I could not sit like a clod of mud and say nothing to throw him off the scent. But there was so little to say. My only defence was to stand firmly by the lie, for it could never be proved as a lie except by Monleigh or myself.

"You flatter me, Walter," I said, proud of my steady voice.

"It is not my flattery," he said, "that has given you that look of beauty."

I was oddly breathless, as if I had run the last mile to Clennon House. "The air here on the coast is the most invigorating I have ever known," I said quickly. "I think it has greatly improved my state of health."

"I am pleased to hear it," he said, still temperate. "For a time I feared you would be as distressed as Margaret over the wretched condition of affairs here." He looked at the fire again, but somehow I felt no relief from the tension rising in my throat like a great lump. "That harrowing night when the stables were raided, the irksome weather, your frightening experience of being lost on the moors, the proximity of a rather odious neighbour—I had thought it enough to make your visit here quite intolerable for you. But I am beginning to understand that you are an independent person, more than capable of finding solace for yourself."

There was no reproach in his voice, only a curious blank politeness. But in that moment, I think, I was certain that it was no longer a matter of suspicion. He knew the truth. Some instinctive sense of caution warned me that he knew, and I had best beware.

"I have always enjoyed a walk," I said, "even in Edinburgh."

"Perhaps one day you will allow me to join you. I, too, have a fondness for simple pleasures."

Uneasily I wondered when he would show his anger, accuse me, remind me of the certain punishment meted out for such heedless misconduct.

But he turned from the fire and fixed me with his mild blue eyes and said only, "I have almost completed my business in the west. We shall return to Edinburgh shortly."

"Margaret will be pleased."

"And you, Anne?"

I managed a creditable shrug. "My life is much the same," I said, "wherever I might be."

In a moment he said, "How long have you been with us?"

"Three years, Walter." Now it will come, I thought, he will tell me that they no longer have need of my services.

"You must have come to know us very well in that length of time."

"I think I understand Margaret better than when I first came," I said uncertainly.

"She is an unhappy woman, Anne, and has known little pleasure in her lifetime."

He did not need to defend his sister to me. "Yes," I said, "I know."

"You have helped to share her burdens, and I am deeply grateful. It cannot have been easy for you to retain your good humour."

"It was my duty," I said. I disliked the word, but it was one that Margaret had not allowed me to forget.

"Have you also come to a better understanding of me?"

Still unsure of his purpose, I said, "I have seen very little of you, Walter. You are seldom at home."

His voice had regret in it. " 'Tis the price a man must pay when he can trust no one to handle his affairs properly but himself." He hesitated, then said, "I feel that I know you very well, Anne, despite my meagre time spent at home."

The warning clamoured in my mind again; the tension inside me stretched dangerously close to the breaking point.

"I am well aware that the moment is scarcely auspicious

for such a question," he went on, "but I can wait no longer."

I clasped my hands tightly together and tried to breathe normally.

"Will you do me the great honour, Anne, of becoming my wife?"

For a moment, too stunned to school my face, I could only stare at him.

Then, quietly, he said, "I realize it must be somewhat of a shock to you, but I pray I have not distressed you."

I could not speak; I could only attempt, as best I might, to hide my incredulous surprise.

He went on speaking in that calm reasonable voice, as if he would give me time to recover my poise. "It is not only Margaret," he said, "who needs a companion. I have been very lonely, Anne."

"I am overcome," I said, low, "by your kindness."

"Kindness does not enter into it. I admit to my selfishness in asking you, but I have hopes that we might both find much to offer each other."

I looked at him, at the thin pale face and well-groomed hair, at the questioning blue eyes, at the spotless linen at his chin. "You cannot imagine that you love me," I said hesitantly.

"Love is an illusive quality," he said. "There are other things of greater importance to people such as we. I have been alone, more or less, for many years, and I am growing no younger. I would like someone to share my life, sons to bear my name. Is that so foolish a wish, Anne?"

"No," I said quietly. "It is only that I never suspected you to need anything, or anyone. You have always seemed sufficient unto yourself."

"No man can be that," he said, "and still be human."

But I had never thought of him as a man with ordinary desires and unspoken yearnings; he had always been Margaret's indulgent brother, harassed, preoccupied, intent upon the pursuit of wealth and valuable horseflesh, a mild and tolerant figurehead who paid the household bills and submitted to Margaret's demands, then absently went his way again, a man shrewd in the ways of business but sadly ignorant of the business of living.

"I would not ask the impossible of you, Anne. Perhaps you might come to care for me, but I would ask nothing of you but your companionship, your graciousness as a wife and hostess. I have observed you well these past years, and my decision is not a hasty one. Any man would consider himself fortunate to be wed to you."

He came closer, he stood almost above me. "I don't know," I said desperately. "I had no idea, I did not dream of such a thing."

"You would be the mistress of my household, of course, and would not be expected to tend Margaret's needs. I feel certain we could find a suitable woman to take your place."

He was daft, he had gone mad. Usurp Margaret's role as mistress, sit in her chair at table, rule the household in her stead, while she graciously stepped aside for one who had been no more to her than her servant and maid in waiting? It would never be, I thought numbly, he could not be serious in his proposal.

"In the future," he said, "I intend to spend a part of each year at Clennon House, and I think Margaret might be happier to remain in Edinburgh. But perhaps it would not be too difficult for you to enjoy Margaret's companionship for only a few months of the year."

I understood his meaning; politely phrased, it was yet plain enough. I would be mistress of Clennon House, while Margaret would still be free to rule her Edinburgh household as she had always done. Walter was a canny man, and an understanding one; but he was right, it would not be too unpleasant to live under her stringent domination for only a part of the year.

"Is there a chance, Anne, that I might persuade you?"

He meant it, he was deadly serious. He wanted me to be his wife—I, Anne Lindsay, the spinster with no estate, no dowry, no future except the drab certainty of being lonely myself.

Then I thought of Monleigh, and the world steadied around me.

"I cannot give you an answer on the moment," I said at last.

"Of course not. I did not expect it."

There was a perceptible note of relief in his voice, and

I wondered if the past few minutes had been as much of a strain for him as they had been for me.

"By the way," he said, "I have a piece of good news for you. I recovered one of the stolen horses. The mare named Mally, if you remember her."

I did not gasp, but I felt the blood drain from my face; and I was very glad that he had his back turned to me.

"Yes," I said, "the horse I rode from Edinburgh."

"I thought you had favoured her, and so I was doubly pleased to have her returned to me."

"Where did you find her?"

"I visited the English garrison this past week," he said, "and learned that they had recently suffered a foul attack by raiding Highlanders. Later the mare was found wandering loose on the moors. I asked to have a look at her and immediately recognized her as one of the horses stolen from Clennon House."

"Do you think the same men who raided your stables," I asked casually, "also were insolent enough to attack the English?"

"There would seem to be little doubt of it." He gave me a slight unexpected smile. "They shall soon catch the culprits, and mayhap I'll be fortunate enough to recover a good share of my horses. Then you may have your choice, either the mare or another, and I shall consider it my first gift to you. When we return to Edinburgh, I'll purchase a saddle made to your order."

"You said the English will soon catch the thieves," I said. "Have they identified them, then?"

"I was not given that information," he replied, the smile lingering on his face as if he were most pleased with his thoughts. "But I was favourably impressed with the intelligence of the commanding officer, and he led me to believe they would soon close the net."

The fire was stifling me, the candles burning my eyes with their unwavering brilliance. I was utterly confused, I could not think clearly; I only knew I must retreat to the blessed privacy of my bedchamber and find some measure of quiet in which to calm my shaken nerves.

"Perhaps you will allow me to exercise the mare," I said. "We were great friends, and I have missed her."

"You might come to harm," Walter said. "I'll not soon

forget the anxiety of that night when you did not return
from your ride."

"But I had disobeyed you," I said, marvelling at my
courage, "and deserved no better. I'll only follow the
track a short way, and see if the Highlanders treated Mally
with consideration. She has a sensitive mouth, you know,
and must be ridden with a gentle hand."

The smile was more ingratiating than I had intended;
Walter returned it, and his eyes lingered oddly on my
face. "Then you have my permission," he said. He added,
"Perhaps it will help you to come to a decision. It is hard
to think when one is surrounded by other people."

"Thank you, Walter," I said, and stood up.

"Good night, Anne," he said. Then, as if it were an
afterthought, "Will you do me a favour in return?"

I could not hesitate. "Certainly."

"Will you take no more unnecessary risks? You have
my future in your hands, you know, and I would be
desolate if you came to any misfortune."

It was easier than I had expected. "I'll take no risks,"
I said quietly. "I am sorry if I have caused you any
anxiety."

He stood by the chair, watching as I took a candle to
light my way to bed. I said, "Good night," and smiled
uncertainly at him; the distance to the door stretched
interminably before me, but I walked it under his benevolent gaze and closed the door gently behind me. Then
I drew a deep breath and ran up the stairs, holding one
hand before the flickering flame, and so reached the
safety of my bedchamber.

I threw off my clothes and put out the candle, not
daring to glance at my mirror. The lass who would stare
back at me, with flushed cheeks and slanting green eyes,
was long since a stranger to me. She it was who had
gone aboard a smuggler's ship and lain there in a man's
arms, and then come home with her mouth still soft and
warm from his kisses to face another man's honourable
proposal of marriage. And she it was who would lie
awake, eyes wide and entranced in the darkness, thinking
not of Walter's kind courtesy at all, who would finally
sleep only to dream of a dark face and ungentle hands
and a smile that began a slow sweet flame burning inside
her.

But when I awoke in the dawn, a sobered Anne Lindsay once more controlled my mind and heart. I felt a vague apprehension, the more frightening and malicious because I could not immediately put my finger on the cause; and I put my hands behind my head and stared at the velvet hangings of my bed, and tried to think clearly.

I put aside the plain fact, however astounding, that Walter had asked me to marry him; it was vastly more important to reason why he had asked. I had been so certain, for a single brief moment, that he knew about my meetings with Monleigh; but if that were true, did he intend to ignore it, pretend that it made no difference to him? Indeed, he had never displayed a hatred comparable to Margaret's, he had even been mildly tolerant. But no man lived who was tolerant enough to ask a woman to marry him after learning that she had wantonly kept company with a man of Monleigh's reputed character, and certainly not Walter Clennon.

He did not know, then; there was no other conclusion to draw. It was not improbable, however, that he suspected Monleigh to be the villain who had so plagued the English, and doubtless the shrewd English held a suspicion or two of their own. Monleigh was well known in the west, he was hated and feared by countless enemies; the most innocent and naïve of men had only to look at him to know that here was one who submitted meekly to no one, who stood in the humbled company of the defeated and yet walked with a high arrogance and pride, who held his personal rights on the point of his sword and dared any man to trample them.

His would be the most likely name to head the list of suspects; and now that Walter had established a connection, however tenuous, between the raid on the English and the raid on Clennon House, it would not be long before some canny mind turned an inquiring look toward the Stewarts of Torra.

The sun was shining in a pale curve from the window to my bed, but the day seemed all at once to be cold and dreary and infinitely melancholy. I forgot Walter completely; I only knew that I must warn Monleigh. I must ride to Torra again, before a troop of English took it in mind to ride hence, and tell him that I had brought him ill fortune he had not reckoned for.

After breakfast I found time to speak to Elizabeth in the kitchen.

"I am riding this morning," I said idly. "Did you know the mare Mally had been found? Walter Clennon has said I might ride down the track a short way. 'Tis a lovely morning, don't you think, to be out?"

"Aye, and that it is," she replied. "Take care ye don't take another spill."

"I shall be most cautious." I added, "Lonely, too, unless I find some sociable gentleman to keep me company."

"I shouldn't think ye'd have lacked for company all this while ye've been gadding about the moors."

"I spent last evening in very pleasant company," I said, "and doubtless am expected to lie late abed today. You must agree I cannot have an assignation without sending word ahead."

"I reckoned some wicked spirit had been prowling in the night," Elizabeth said dryly, "when I found the door unlatched this dawn."

"Do you think," I asked slowly, "that the word might go before me? Perhaps I have only to begin my ride and hope that another hearty soul will also be riding out to enjoy the sunny day."

She raised her head and gave me a brief glance. "I've told ye before," she said sensibly, "that news always travels in a hurry in the Highlands."

She turned her back on me deliberately and went about the chore of scrubbing; and so I left her and went back to my chamber, and waited impatiently until the sun had climbed in the sky and no longer struck my window, but slanted with a hard glance across the shingled roof of the stables below.

When I slipped from my room and descended the stairs, I was vastly relieved to encounter neither Robert nor Walter. They were, from the snatches of conversation I heard as I passed the partly opened door of the great hall, discussing a great lot of boring details concerning high finance and the precarious state of monetary values in a land smothered beneath Cromwell's iron fist; and I hoped that Walter would not think again of my plans for the day.

The stableboy with the dark bold eyes was unaccount-

ably absent, so that one of Walter's men was obliged to
saddle the mare for me; and I was slightly amused that
I had not given Kitty's friend a closer consideration
before. I also better understood why the pretty maid from
Edinburgh had so fallen under his spell; Kitty and I were
much alike, it would seem, and had come into the company of a reckless breed of men who had taught the both
of us that it was more fitting to commit one's sins in the
grand manner, disdaining any miserable and furtive
pettiness.

I rode slowly along the lochside, allowing the mare to
nibble daintily at her pleasure by the track, and forced
myself to betray no air of haste or stealth. Therefore it
was some time before I was in the beech woods border-
ing the loch, out of sight of Clennon House, and could
put my slender whip to the mare. After a mile or so,
before the track turned to wind over the moors, I halted
Mally and sat quietly for long minutes; but there was no
sound of a following horse.

The way did not seem long after that, so engrossed was
I in my thoughts. I would see him soon, I would once
again attempt to reckon his mood by the look of his
tanned face, the warmth or coolness of his smile, the
shape of his words, his gray eyes; and as before, when I
sought to understand the contradictions of his nature, I
would have a singular lack of success.

But what did it matter, after all, if I could not place
him in a neat drawer in my mind, comfortably labelled
and filed away, his moods and humours, his ambitions,
his dreams, his passions all noted and tallied with the
smug assurance bred by familiarity? It was a lamentable
feminine trait, the desire to know a person wholly and
without reservation, as if the knowledge might serve as a
safe guidepost to avoid the pitfalls of the future.

No, it did not matter. What mattered was the unruly
delight inside me whenever I thought of him—the hidden
exultance, the reckless urge to laugh aloud whenever I
heard his name; that strange rapt moment of peace, of
utter surrender, that engulfed me now and again when I
looked at him and felt my world complete, come clock-
wise to a full circle.

He had enthralled me, bewitched and enraptured me;
and I knew I played a dangerous and deadly game by so
giving myself into his keeping. He was no god, in truth,
or even godly. He was only a man, a mere mortal, who
went in leather breeks and a dark cloak lined with scarlet,
wearing a long sword at his side and a wicked blue dirk in
his belt—who felt anger, boredom, indifference, who loved
and hated as other men; who stood taller than most and
held his dark head with a greater pride. He could die
in a moment's time, like other mortals, could be reduced
to a common dust, could learn at last that courage and
a quick wit and a skilled sword arm could not save him
from an entire world leagued against him, the narrow,
fanatical, hostile world he regarded with such a careless
insolence. He could go down to defeat, languish in a
squalid prison, hang at the end of a rope; and I would be
left bereft and lost and tormented.

And yet, I reflected as I rode the mare Mally along
the track above the sea, it was difficult to face the dangers
honestly. I was under his spell, as I had come to be under
the spell of this west coast of Scotland. And his was the
nature of a Highlander, after all, a man forever fighting
for the possession of himself. There was a dark heritage
in his blood, that same heritage of violence and disquiet
which had seethed through Highland history since the
beginning of time; and I would imagine that this unrest,
this dark vein of passion, must be guarded with a constant
vigilance lest it stealthily conquer a man's soul and
abandon him to the darkness.

There was no portion of land in the world with so
contradictory a nature as the Highlands. Now it was a
land of sunlit moors stained red with heather, knowing
only the peace of the quiet sky and the heart-shaking
beauty of the blue hills; now it was a harsh and awesome
place where silent mists obscured the peaks and a bitter
relentless rain came down from bitter skies, where an
angry sea washed against the shore, and sullen clouds
reflected in sullen gray lochs.

Scotland in the sun and Scotland in the rain—it was as
true a description of Simon Stewart as anyone might give.

I saw him then, riding his big gelding down from Torra
to meet me; and the plaid over his shoulder was of a

tartan that blazed red in the sun and dazzled my eyes, blinding me for a moment.

Putting my whip lightly to the mare, I rode toward him with an impatient eagerness that must have been communicated to the mare, for she lifted her head and skimmed down the track like a bird in flight.

He reined his horse, waiting for me, but I had forgotten that the giddy mare, once begun, disliked to be stayed from her headlong pace; and so we went pounding on along the track and I prepared to give Monleigh a rueful greeting as I galloped past. But he sat his horse in the center of the track, poised and ready, and as the mare swerved, he reached for me with a deft sense of timing.

I was lifted from my saddle, I was in his arms; and our laughter followed the mare and disconcerted her so greatly, after having just lost her rider in such a precipitous manner, that she faltered and slowed to a halt, looking back at us with a ridiculous expression of bewilderment.

"An old Highland trick," Monleigh said in my ear, "and a fine reckless way to grab a wench from under the nose of an eagle-eyed father."

"Reckless, to be sure," I retorted. "And what would have become of me had you missed?"

"I never miss, lass," he said, and smiled down at me.

He is pleased, I thought with a vast relief, he is very glad that I came. "I can't imagine how your Stewarts bear with so great a conceit," I said. "Have they never tried to take you down to size?"

"Well now, they've tried a time or two," he said, "and ha' a few broken heads to show for their pains."

He shifted me adroitly in his arms, so that I sat on the saddle before him, and turned his horse. His white shirt, opened carelessly at the neck, smelled clean and fresh so close to my face; I noted the single initial on the collar and wondered, with a childish envy, who sewed his elegant shirts and then washed them with such loving and painstaking care. They were hung to dry in the sun, I knew from the faint scent still clinging to them, and blown by the sea wind and the hill wind, then folded into snowy white piles; and when he donned one, he took it intimately to himself as he did everything he touched. If I

could tell little of his character from his face, his linen
shirt told me a great deal about his scrupulous cleanliness, his innate sense of quiet good taste, his disregard
of pretension. And that was a great deal, when I considered it, to know about a man.

"You are very sober," he said, "for such a braw morning. Didn't you sleep well?" Before I could answer his eyes
fell on the mare, close ahead of us. He lifted one dark
brow. "I see we have Mally with us again."

I had not thought to tell him so soon, to spoil the fine
morning before it was well begun.

"She appears to have suffered less from her bout with
the English than her mistress," he said. Then he looked
down at me and smiled again. "How did the foolish little
baggage come to be at Clennon House again?"

I hesitated, and with his unerring perception he noted
it at once.

"Never mind. I've no great desire to hear about Mally's
misadventures. You had a strenuous night, lass; do you
feel strong enough for a walk in the hills?"

My cheeks burned. "Aye," I said faintly.

He laughed at me and spurred his horse to a gallop,
Mally following close behind, and I watched the tall
turrets of Torra go by above my head. When we had
gone a short distance beyond the castle, Monleigh paused
to put me gently to the ground, then dismounted himself
and slung his lute over his shoulder.

"'Tis a hard climb," he said. "I'll wager a pound
Scots you'll be lagging behind before we've reached the
top."

I looked at the rippling stream, hurrying down the last
slope of rocky hillside to the sea below, and then with
my eyes followed its course upward through the barren
hills. Somewhere above, hidden by the gaunt granite
heights, was a small glen where this selfsame stream
foamed over a precipice and formed a cool amber pool,
where the sun dappled the grass and a linnet sang, and
one could look down on the sea like a deity from his
heaven.

"I haven't a pound," I said, "Scots or otherwise. But
you'll not find me a laggard."

We set off up the glen, lifting into the heart of the

hills. The sun was warm on our heads, and the silence, the solitude of all such lonely places, stirred in my blood and filled me with a fine happiness. A cock grouse crowed once, and above the hills, rising against the sky on both sides, an eagle drifted with the wind and cast a moving shadow across our path. But it was not a threatening omen; it was only an arrogant bird wheeling silently in a silent blue sky, and Monleigh walked beside me and held my hand.

Soon we came to the trees, alder and birch hugging the damp earth at the edge of the stream; and the climb began in earnest, twisting higher and higher, following no visible path, leading through scattered boulders, and finally ending at the bottom of a fall of water much like the one in the small glade.

We crossed the stream by way of several flat stones, wet despite the sun, and I almost lost my footing. But Monleigh's hands were firm, as was his balance, and he lifted me clear of the water and held me against him for a long moment.

"I was wise not to take your wager," I said, shaken. "You know all the tricks to weaken a maiden's resolve."

I had long since removed my coif and tucked it in my belt, and he rumpled my hair with his brown hand and laughed down at me, and let me go again.

"I'm a gentleman at heart," he said. "I'll give you a hand the rest of the way."

He set me before him, giving me a stout push from behind whenever I paused, and we made the last steep ascent in high good humour.

Then we were in the green glen again, where the trees clustered thickly by the water; and I collapsed on the grass and tried to catch my breath, and was thankful I had not been pursued up that steep glen by a troop of vicious enemies.

Monleigh dropped beside me, putting his lute to one side, and lay back with his hands behind his head. I wondered if it was a habit he had acquired as a small boy, spending long lazy hours in that quiet place, alone with his dreams and the patch of blue sky overhead; for surely he had found meagre time to spend there once he came to a man's estate.

He turned suddenly, resting his dark head on one elbow, and the movement brought him so near to me that I had the chore of catching my breath to do all over again.

"What are you thinking, Anne Lindsay?"

"That I am exceedingly happy."

"It takes very little to make you happy."

"So Evan told me, just last evening."

"He also told you that you were too innocent for my sinful ways."

It was difficult to meet his scrutiny, knowing that he had in truth overheard that strange conversation; but I saw no mockery, no amusement in his gray eyes, only a quiet tenderness that I had not expected from him and so found doubly unnerving.

"Oddly enough," I said, "I don't feel in the least sinful when I'm with you." I added candidly, "Nor very innocent, if the truth were known."

He threw back his head and laughed. "Didn't you learn in kirk," he said, "that the Devil makes wickedness attractive for the sole purpose of corrupting the virtuous?" His face was suddenly very young, the hard lines less embittered; he put out his hand and touched mine, and smiled at me. "Don't worry with it, lass. If you know your Scriptures, you'll remember that one repentant sinner causes more rejoicing in Heaven than a regiment of virtuous parsons."

"You've twisted the phrasing a bit," I said, "and any parson could tell you that even the Devil can quote Scriptures to his purpose."

" 'Tis near enough," he said, "and I've as much right to misquote as a parson."

"But I've nothing to repent," I said softly.

He still held my hand; he pulled me down beside him and put one arm across me, his face so close that I could see the tiny image of my face reflected in the black pupils of his eyes.

"And before God," he said, low, "you never will."

The laughter was stilled in his face, but not the tenderness. He put his mouth on mine, and when he raised his head at last, we looked at each other for a long silent moment. But the face of love is an awesome and heart-shaking thing to look upon, and I closed my eyes against the wonder of it.

At this moment, I thought exultantly, he is mine; he has forgotten to be wary, his defenses are down. This is the man he might have been were there no wars, no bitter aftermath, no reason to kill and hate and fight constantly against overwhelming odds—a man with warm gray eyes and a mouth of exceeding sweetness, more inclined to laughter than violence, a man whose great strength has as its balance wheel an abiding and compassionate gentleness. This is Monleigh the lover, unguarded and vulnerable; and I have only to ask and he will speak the truth, I have only to wish and he will give me all of that portion of the world which he possesses.

But not for all the world and its kingdoms would I have been so underhanded as to take advantage of that brief interval of time. I had enough to compensate for a lifetime of want, and mayhap a similar dreary future; it was all I needed or desired merely to know that I had been the one to please him, I had brought the warmth to his eyes and the tenderness to his smile. And to my eternal credit, it was not until much later that I remembered Evan's warning and finally understood what he had meant when he spoke to me of that dangerous moment when a woman first realizes the hold she has on a man's heart and passions and must withstand the temptation to use it to her own gain.

Afterward I lay in the grass, my head pillowed in my arms, while he lazily played his lute for me.

"What are you playing?" I murmured, and raised my head.

"An old ballad," he said, "written many years ago by an unhappy king of Scotland."

"How does it go?"

In a low careless voice he sang the words for me; and the sun was suddenly less bright, and all the brave happiness was gone from the afternoon, and I remembered why I had come to Torra and the things I must say to him.

> An' we'll gang no more a-rovin',
> A-roving in the night,
> An' we'll gang no more a-rovin',
> Let the moon shine e'er so bright.

I sat up and brushed away the bits of grass and twigs clinging to my rumpled gown.

" 'Tis a sad ballad. Why was he so unhappy with his lot?"

"He wanted to be free to live as he pleased."

"Don't all kings do as they please?"

"They've less chance of it than ordinary men, what with their kingdoms and ministers and sacred traditions."

"And I, who am quite ordinary, have my Margarets and Walters and my weary conscience."

His brown fingers moved over the lute strings, making them weep for all unhappy souls, kings and commoners alike, and I was not so far from weeping myself.

"Tell me about it, lass," he said quietly.

So I knew I could no longer ignore it. "The English recovered Mally," I said. "While Walter was away this past week he stopped at the English fort and heard of the attack. Then he asked to see the mare and recognized her as one of his missing horses."

"I know all about Mally," he said.

So the stableboy had told him or mayhap Elizabeth. He had known all that went on in Clennon House since we first arrived; I should have reckoned that he would not be remiss in hearing of the mare's return.

"They suspect you," I said. "I'm certain of it."

"Aye, the trail is growing warm. Before long I'll have them breathing down my neck."

"I must bear the blame," I said miserably, "if you come to any misfortune. I should never have ridden with you that night."

He smiled. "Don't flatter yourself. D'you think it is so easy to bring me to ruin? Fortune is a fickle jade, lass, and the man a fool who would trust her with his fate."

"Can't you sail to France with the *Marie*?"

The smile deepened, was very amused. "They've not caught me yet. It will take more than a suspicious Englishman to trace Walter Clennon's mare to my gates."

"But Walter seems to think they have more damning evidence than the horse," I said, my anxious fear for him outweighing my prudence. "He is quite pleased with the progress of events. I swear you are in great danger."

He shrugged, his fingers still engrossed with the plain-

tive ballad of an old forgotten and unhappy king; and I
realized the futility of asking this man to run away from
any danger.

"Was that all you wanted to tell me?"

I clasped my hands together. "No," I said, low, "there
is something more."

He waited patiently for me to continue, his eyes almost
closed; and I looked at the black lashes against his brown
face, the dark curve of his brows, and longed to trace
them with my finger.

"Walter was waiting," I said steadily, "when I returned
to Clennon House last evening."

He was silent for a moment, then he put his lute aside
and leaned back on his elbow.

"That must have been a shock for you."

"I was terrified," I said. "He opened the hall door and
there I stood, slippers in hand, preparing to creep up the
stairs."

"Like an erring chambermaid. Did he beat you?"

"He was most kind."

"You've told me before," he said coolly, "of Walter's
great charity and kindness. Must I hear it again?"

He had changed, in the space of a moment or two. The
unguarded happiness was gone from his face; his eyes
were once more inscrutable and narrowed, his smile
slightly twisted as if he enjoyed a secret and cynical
amusement at my expense.

"We are leaving for Edinburgh shortly."

"Indeed," he said softly. Then, "Did he guess that you
have been coming to Torra?"

"I was sure of it at first," I said. "But he said nothing,
he gave me no reason to think that he knew."

"What reason, then, did he give for his decision to drag
you off to Edinburgh so precipitously?"

"He has done with his affairs in the west," I said only.

"I doubt that," Monleigh said carelessly. His eyes were
steady on me, missing nothing, seeing all. "You've not
finished," he said. "What else?"

I took a deep breath and stared at my hands, seeing the
knuckles taut and white.

"He has asked me to marry him."

He was silent for so long that I lifted my head again;

meeting his eyes, so coldly distant and sardonic, took all the courage I could summon, and I knew with a very small and bitter triumph that my words had touched him at last, but whether in anger or contempt I could not say.

"And what was your answer to Walter's honourable proposal?"

"I had no answer."

"What would you have said a month ago?"

"He would not have asked me a month ago," I said, "and in any case, I have never considered such a thing before."

"Aye," he said slowly, "you have changed. Not even Walter Clennon could fail to notice it."

I said nothing. If I had changed, Monleigh was responsible for it; knowing him, having met him, I would never be the same again.

"You are a fortunate lass," he said easily.

A sick uneasiness gripped me. "Am I?"

"You'll no longer be obliged to suffer Margaret's abuse, or run her errands, or act the drudge at her command. You'll be the mistress of Clennon House, Anne Lindsay. D'you know what that means?"

For a moment I could not control my voice at all. Then I managed, "Yes, I know," and the hot tears were so close behind my eyes that I feared lest he see and be further amused. Tears would not avail me, Evan had said, nor acting the scold, nor yet hating blindly.

"Walter is a wealthy man, and you'll have your own purse filled with clinking gold pieces. There's your security for you, lass, the safety you've been seeking. Life can be unco' pleasant when one has an ample supply of gold to smooth the way."

It was incredible that he could speak to me in such a manner. Only a short while before I had been in his arms; we had been very happy, we had belonged to each other. But then, I told myself dismally, he is Monleigh, the man of the contradictory nature I will never come to understand.

I put my arms around my knees and rested my cheek against them. "It could not be so pleasant as life aboard the *Marie*," I said daringly.

"Surely not," he agreed. "Do you covet my ship, lass?"

I sighed. "I would gladly exchange places with the least of your Stewart sailors."

"'Tis a good life, sailing the seas with a fast ship beneath one and fair skies above."

"Tranquil days, one after another," I said, bemused.

"Like perfect pebbles dropped in a placid pool."

At once I caught that indefinable quality in his voice which always warned me; and I remembered quite well when I had spoken those selfsame words to him.

"Why are you laughing at me?"

"Because you are so fond of turning your face from the truth when it does not please you. There are more stormy days than fair, as you well know, and there is little security or safety aboard a smuggler's ship."

"Must it be a smuggler's ship?" I whispered.

"I don't need to be reminded," he said, "that you seek a knight in shining armour."

He stood up with a single lithe movement and leaned against the tree behind him, thumbs in his wide leather belt. I could not turn away, nor hide from his cool voice that slashed so mercilessly at my dreams and exposed them for the foolish fancies they were.

"The *Marie* is not a castle," he said, "with pantries of linen and jam jars for you to count, and there is no place aboard her for a brood of bairns, well-mannered or otherwise." He added, his voice gone curt and hard, "And you have forgotten, it would seem, that my armour is slightly tarnished from hard usage."

"That was only a childish dream," I said, "and I have done with it long since."

"Have you, Anne?"

I was no longer sure of anything. Except this—there would be no tranquility, no peace, no security aboard a ship that ran dark-hulled before the wind in the dark of night, that carried illegal cargo below her hatches and a hunted captain on the quarter-deck; nothing to possess, nothing of my own to hold tightly against the fear of want or privation or unhappiness; no single charm to ward off that dread moment when the wind might change, the skies grow stormy, when the hostile faces that waited on the unknown shore, behind the cannon on an English ship, in every strange harbour, might finally destroy all that I held dear and leave me once again with empty hands and an empty heart.

"And yet," I said, "if you asked me, I could not refuse."

"But, my sweet Anne, I have no intention of asking you."

The sun was too hot, almost stifling me; and the rocky walls of the glen threatened to close in about me, a stone prison from which there was never any escape.

"I did not tell you about Walter," I said, almost inaudibly, "for the purpose of bargaining with you."

Some of the chill left his voice. "I know you did not."

I felt his strong hands on my shoulders, lifting me to my feet, and he spoke against my hair.

"Will you still be honest with me?"

I nodded, undone by the touch of his hands. He stood behind me, holding me against the length of him, and I could not see his face.

"Do you love me?"

It was too late to lie to him, even had I any such wish. He knew very well that I loved him, and how desperately much.

"Yes, I love you."

"And you thought I would carry you away," he said softly, "and refuse to allow you to marry Walter Clennon?"

"No," I said slowly, for if the truth were painful it must still be faced and dealt with. "I somehow knew you would not. But you cannot blame me for hoping foolishly that you cared enough to do so."

"I care a great deal," he said. "Too damnably much."

My heart sang, and an unbidden happiness burned sweet and fierce inside me. But it was only a fleeting happiness, after all.

"I've other affairs to tend, of vast importance to myself and my King, and I cannot risk being diverted from them."

"Am I so great a distraction? I admit I am a coward, but mayhap I could learn to be an adventuress."

"You would soon tire of the role and wish yourself back in your safe bedchamber at Clennon House, free of men with ungentle ways and a price on their heads."

"I have already proved you right, have I not," I said,

defeated completely, thinking of that moment when I faced an Englishman's sword and immediately lost all love of adventure and excitement.

"You've not changed so much as you'd like to believe," he went on relentlessly. "You are lovelier than before, in God's truth, and there is a look of radiance about you that comes to a woman when she's been loved by a man who's not too clumsy at it. But you've still a conscience to cope with, lass, and it'd give neither of us enough peace to count as happiness."

"But you have none," I said, reduced to a childish petulance.

"I have a sharp nose for survival, without which I'd have lost my head long since."

So that was it, I thought miserably. "You are wise to distrust me. I have brought you enough ill fortune."

"If I distrust you, lass, it is for none of the foolish reasons you've concocted for yourself."

Stung by the amused patience in his voice, I said, "You must forgive me for being so muddleheaded."

"Never mind," he said. "I did not expect you to understand. One day, perhaps, you'll discover for yourself how simple it is."

I bit my lip and so kept the tears in check, but the tight lump in my throat gave my voice a rough husky tremor which could not be disguised.

"Simple enough for you," I said. "I envy you vastly."

"You are a woman. It holds its disadvantages."

"One of which," I said unevenly, "I have only just begun to understand."

"I would I could make it easier for you."

"You told me at the beginning it would not be easy." I tried not to tremble while he still held me. "Since you are a man, with a man's advantage in such matters, will you tell me how one goes about forgetting?"

His hands turned me gently, then tightened on my shoulders. I stood facing him, memorizing every line of his face, his tall powerful body, the arrogant lift of his head.

"You will never forget," he said quietly, "but it will be less of a torment with the passing of time."

"Then you think I should wed Walter Clennon," I said,

already feeling the stunned anguish like a sickness inside me, "as if I had never met you, never come to love you at all?"

"The choice is yours," he said. "He has a great deal to offer you. You deserve to live your own life, to take whatever happiness you may find in it." His hands fell away, and I was lost and forlorn without them. "I've no right to hold you from it."

It was a bleak, cheerless, painful thing he asked of me. But his world was harsh and accepted no compromise, no weakness, no halfhearted indecision. He knew that I loved him, despite all the hostile world and its gossip, he had said that he cared for me; and yet when the *Marie* sailed away from Scotland he would be alone aboard her, and I would be left to marry Walter Clennon or not, as I chose. He did not, I suspected, want me to marry Walter, but he intended to do nothing to prevent it. He would offer no alternative, no escape. The price of a lass came too dear to him.

And yet I was still bewildered. The cold wintry gray of his eyes betrayed him, for I had come to know how much of bitterness and anger and savage violence lay hidden behind that implacable mask.

I would try once again. "No right?" I whispered. "Who has more right than you?"

"I do not possess you," he said briefly, "as a man possesses cattle, or a ship, or slaves to do his bidding."

That was all, then; there was nothing left to say. He did not, I realized numbly, mean to touch me again; but even as I longed quite desperately for one last kiss, I knew as well as he that it would be past enduring.

"I must go," I said at last.

"Aye," he said, his eyes never moving from my face. Then, "When do you leave for Edinburgh?"

"Within the week, I imagine."

We might have been strangers, remote, impersonal, courteous to a fault. He leaned down to pick up his lute, and I turned toward the steep descent which followed the course of the reckless stream, wondering what he would do were I to behave with the same abandon as that mountain burn.

If I were to throw myself on his chest and cling passionately to him, and weep profusely, would he feel the least compassion for me? Would he dry my tears and try to comfort me, would he listen to my pleas, would he say again that he cared a damnable lot for me, even above his King and his own important affairs?

Such fancies, such wishful thinking, such feminine nonsense. I bethought myself of the other lass who wept and whined, who clutched at him with nagging reproach, who finally fought his indifference with a fierce hatred, and who came in the end to a lonely and unmourned grave. He was kind to her, Evan had said, even when she did not deserve it; but I knew in my heart that such kindness would only be a final and unbearable torture.

We came at last to the horses, dragging their reins on the moor, and Monleigh held his hands for me to mount.

He was right, of course, always right. It was best to end a thing abruptly and decisively, leaving no entangling strings, no unfinished scraps of mood or conversation to later haunt the memory and bring unnecessary pain. But I looked down at him with a rebellious disbelief; it could not be good-bye, it could not be finished so abruptly. Surely he would not let me go back to Clennon House with no more than this brief unsatisfactory farewell.

But he was still imperturbable, still merciless.

"Take care, Anne Lindsay," he said quietly, and stepped back.

I looked down at him. "Why?" I asked. "Why must it end like this?"

"I promised you once," he said, "that you would never know regret on my account."

My laugh was ragged. "Regret? You know nothing of such things. I shall live with regret the rest of my life."

His voice cut levelly across mine. "Be honest with yourself," he said, "and one day you will understand."

I looked at him one last time, and turned my horse and rode off down the track, and struggled against the urgent impulse to look back yet another time.

Now, I thought wearily, I may weep at last. But the tears did not come, they were frozen and stilled as if I would never weep again; and so I rode back to Clennon House with my eyes burning wide and dry, and my heart a cold leaden weight within me.

{ 13 }

DURING the next few days I came to know my bedchamber well indeed.

I knew how many narrow panels were required to cover
each wall, how many strips of tapestry had formed the
faded arras opposite my bed, how many steps from wall
to window and back again. I knew by rote how the sun
crept across the threadbare carpet, when it reached the
bed hangings, the bolster, my face; I knew how the rain
trickled down the windowpanes and blurred the tiny gray
patch of sky, how the wind whispered or roared against
the outside walls; and like the princess in the nursery tale
who could detect a tiny pea beneath her feather mattresses,
I knew each lump in my bolster and each wrinkle in the
bedclothes so by heart that I could have drawn a map to
locate them one by one.

But while I tossed and turned, and lay awake in the
long watches of the night, and awoke each dawn, heavy-
headed and dishevelled, to face another endless day of
soul-searching, I came to no decisions, no conclusions.

I was always one to turn my face from the truth when
it did not please me, Monleigh had said; and because the
truth was so squalid, so tedious, so intolerably final, I
could not bring myself to face it with any degree of composure. I argued with it, I schemed to circumvent it, I
devised a dozen different ways to prove it false; only to
admit in the end, with a weary loathing for my lack of
pride and resolution, that only shame lay in further evasion.

I had been under a spell for countless days, wandering
in an enchanted land where the cruel exigencies of life
could not enter in to plague me; but the play had ended,
the audience had departed, the stage was empty and de-

serted. The glorious world of make-believe had ceased to be; it was but an illusion, a mummery, a shadowy farce without substance. I was the patron who, begging the price of admission, crept into the playhouse and shared, for a brief enraptured hour, the high passion breathed into life by that exalted company who lived on the lighted stage—and who perforce went out again, bemused and saddened, into the muddy streets, returned abruptly to a world where a husband or wife shrieked abuse, and supper was meagre and cold, and the bed linens were soiled and alive with vermin, where there was no nobility or passion but only the petty sordid actualities of living.

I was the disappointed child who must finally learn that benevolent fairy godmothers do not exist, the stricken woman whose lovers discard her for a younger, lovelier mistress, the bewildered king who is beheaded to the jeers and taunts of those he thought to be his beloved subjects. I was Anne Lindsay, a sober spinster who had known a giddy moment, been foolishly indiscreet, and who must now mend her conscience with a reluctant needle.

He had never said he loved me, after all. He cared, in truth, I had pleased him for a fleeting hour or so. But I was not so important as bonny Charlie across the water, or his dangerous game of annoying the English, or his renegade ship. He had not pretended otherwise, from the beginning; it was I who dreamed, who fashioned pretty notions from a word, a kiss, a slanted look. I should have been forewarned; whatever misery and torment raged in my heart, I should have anticipated it from the first moment I met him by the sea.

Oh, there was no denying it. I might be foolish, but I was no fool. I had known, I had been forewarned; but I had a lamentable habit of indecision, I hid my face from the truth. And now I could no longer hide from Walter, as I had done for the past few days; I must give him an answer without delay, he deserved no less.

But still I vacillated, and went to my small leather chest and sat on the floor in the sun to trickle the coins through my fingers, making grand plans and concocting great schemes. And then I counted them once again, the pitiful hoard of gold standing between me and a dreary

future, and was obliged to weep a few tears for the ill-
fated schemes and plans.

But I think, even now, that I would not have decided
as I did if Margaret had not angered me so that certain
afternoon.

I do not blame her, nor can I excuse my stupidity by
saying that I was very weary and unhappy and wrung
empty of emotion. I did a terrible thing, I was terribly
wrong. I know it now, and if I would be honest, I knew
it then. But admitting one's guilt does not absolve it; it
merely serves to blunt the bitter edges of despair, and
makes it possible to live with one's mistakes in the dark
hours of the night.

It was the Sabbath, and under Robert's guidance we had
prayers at dawn and prayers at noon and, I did not doubt,
would have them again at sunset.

Soon after noon Margaret, in her usual unfathomable
manner, rose from her bed as abruptly as she had taken
to it and pronounced herself greatly improved. Walter
had gone to her chamber earlier and talked with her there
for a lengthy time; but I could not be sure that he had
confided to her that he had asked me to wed him.

I did not expect her to call me; she had ignored me
since the morning I stumbled into Clennon House with my
tale of a night spent on the moors, and the two maids
from Edinburgh had been kept running up and down the
stairs at an exhaustive pace.

But Kitty came to tell me, with a rueful smile, that I
was wanted in Margaret's bedchamber; and so I put on a
clean kerchief and coif, and stifled my sighs, and went
to do her bidding.

She sat before her mirror, her thin hair straggling over
her shoulders, her arms modestly hidden in a muslin robe.

"Come and brush my hair, Anne," she said, her voice
petulant with irritation. "My head is quite sore from
Elsie's clumsy hands. I cannot endure her any longer."

Elsie, flushed and sullen, stood to one side, and I took
the brush from her hands. Kitty, busily brushing lint from
a dark russet gown, did not look up.

I brushed as gently as I could, forcing my hands to the
task, restraining my instinctive withdrawal at the touch of
her hair, not entirely clean after her long stay abed. I

thought of the robe she wore, fully as ancient and worn as my own, and wondered why Margaret cared so little for Walter's wealth. It was well within her means to wear velvet or brocade, or if she had a taste for muslin, to keep her wardrobe fresh and dainty with newly sewn material. But she clung to the symbols of poverty as a parson will his steepled hat and shabby black suit of clothes, as if such austere self-denial were virtuous in itself and so bespoke the virtue of her soul.

"Pin it as you always do," she said. "No, not like that. Have you six fingers to a hand? Can I find no one to dress my hair properly?" She pulled the hair tightly away from her face, holding it taut until I had secured the pins. "You are all clumsy dolts. I might better have done it myself, weak as I am."

There was to be no sermon, then, merely the petty grievances that would stretch from dawn till dusk, driving one near to madness like the small but persistent torture of a midge.

"Fetch my slippers, Anne," she ordered, and when I had done so, "There is a spot near the heel. Do you expect me to wear soiled slippers?"

So I removed it as best I could, and was sent to the kitchen to fetch a damp cloth to freshen the slippers where I had soiled them with my hands in working at the spot. Then Margaret remembered that she needed a clean kerchief, and I made another journey down the stairs to the kitchen. But the kerchief was not ironed to her satisfaction; I must search through her chest for another, and was obliged to remove everything before I found the pile of kerchiefs at the very bottom. But the kerchief from the chest was too yellowed, after all, and so she donned the one I had brought from the kitchen.

I adjusted it about the neck of her gown, and tied her coif while she watched with critical eyes in the mirror.

"Now I would like my tapestry," she said. "I've not felt well enough to bother with it of late, Anne, so you will doubtless find it in the hall where I had it last." She added, with an exasperated flick of her hands at the coif to better adjust it, "It has been almost a fortnight since I was taken ill. What have you been doing all this while? Lazing abed, or gossiping with the servants?"

I was thinking, with some ill humour, of the needless trips up and down the stairs; it was a moment before I caught the subtle undertone of hostility in her words, masked so well by her normal caustic manner that neither Kitty nor Elsie seemed aware of the sudden attack.

Her pale eyes met mine in the mirror. There was a quality of blankness about them, as if the glass had drained them of all betraying emotion before giving back her reflection.

"I have kept myself occupied," I said quietly, "one way or another."

Her smile was not a pleasant thing to see. "Yes, I think you have been very industrious. I underestimated your ability to accomplish so much in so little time."

So Walter had told her. Somehow I felt only a great relief. She knew; let her do her worst.

"I've not accomplished much," I said, deliberately misreading her insinuation. "A bit of needlework, some mending."

"You think not? What an ungrateful girl you are." She pushed a slender mirror, one of her most valuable possessions, into my hands. "Hold it there; no, higher." She examined the back of her coif with sharp eyes. "Don't move it. How can I see when your hand shakes so nervously? You will never make a well-trained ladies' maid, I warn you. When you leave my service, I'll be hard pressed to write a suitable recommendation for you."

I was too startled to think of a rejoinder. I stared at her complacent reflection in the large mirror and wondered if she truly thought she might defeat Walter's purposes so easily.

"Give it me," she said, and turned with a captious abruptness to take the mirror.

My hand had been too lax upon the handle; when she turned, brushing against my arm; the delicate mirror slipped from my hand and fell to the floor, and for a lengthy moment there was no sound in the room but the tinkle of broken glass.

Margaret said, "You clumsy fool," beneath her breath and stood up in the same instant. Then her hand moved, as swiftly as the pronged tongue of a coiled snake, and slapped my face with such force that the pain brought quick tears to my eyes.

No one moved. Kitty and Elsie stood frozen in the positions they had held when the mirror splintered against the floor: Elsie, her mouth sliding agape, and Kitty, in the act of smoothing the counterpane, still bent over the bed, her eyes going slowly from Margaret to the dull red imprint staining my face.

I myself stood very still. If Margaret Clennon were a man, I thought clearly, and I the same, I'd have my sword in hand this moment. I returned her stare, feeling her hatred like a tangible thing between us, as I had felt the flat of her hand against my face. But I was not intimidated. I was angry myself, and close to hatred.

I gave her one last look, then turned and walked to the door, letting my silence, my scornful deliberation speak for itself. Not bothering to close the door, I went to the stairs and down them with the dreamy detachment of a sleepwalker.

I did not think, I did not reason, I was neither hesitant nor reluctant. But in the back of my mind, I remember, were many disconnected images, vivid and unforgettable, finally merging into a shifting kaleidoscope which moulded my decision, stiffened my resolve, and directed my feet unerringly toward the great hall door.

A bit of this, a bit of that. A certain Sabbath when the cold damp of the kirk penetrated my clothes to the very marrow of my bones, mocking the thin protection of my shabby gloves, so yellowed with age and frequent mending that the newest split was a tragedy to bring tears; a memory of the Clennon House in Edinburgh on a dark winter's day, tall and bleak, its chimney pots shadowed by the Castle, and my small room beneath the eaves as cold and dismal as the streets without; the unmoved finality on Monleigh's tanned face when he said, "But I have no intention of asking you"; an hour or two of a lonely dawn not long past, when I wept scalding tears, and beat my pillow, and shamefully wished myself dead. A smattering of seemingly unimportant details, such as the ragged hem of my old mulberry gown, the black thread fashioning the tapestry lady in my needlework, the pitiful scrawniness of Margaret's neck, the kindliness in Walter's voice when he told me I looked quite fetching even with a cold in the head.

I reached the hall door and flung it wide open, and came face to face with Robert MacLeish, on the point of opening it from the opposite side. Looking at him from my remote height of calm, I succeeded in routing him without a word; he lifted his pointed nose, flared his nostrils, and stormed by me as if my appearance were a deliberate and personal affront to his dignity.

Then I saw Walter standing by the fire, and realized they had been quarrelling. His face was sober, marked with more than a trace of anger; but whatever the argument, it was clear that a dour and furious Robert was not the victor. Everyone was distrait and upset, I thought with a flash of amusement; we all had our problems, may God have mercy on the lot of us, and doubtless the staid constraint of Clennon House was considerably jolted by such an excess of turbulent emotion.

"Walter," I began, and paused just inside the threshold, "have you a moment to spare?"

He came forward, a slight smile warming the gravity of his face. "I shall always have time for you, Anne."

"You are kind."

"I've not seen much of you these past few days," said Walter. He took one of my hands. "May I dare hope," he said, "that you have come to give me my answer?"

Aye, that had been my purpose; but now that I was with him I was suddenly wordless, so wrapped in that vague detachment that I did not know how to go about telling him.

"Well, Anne?" he prompted me.

In a cool clear voice I said only, "Yes."

"My dear," he said. Then, "I shall try to make you happy."

He went on saying the usual things, I imagine, that such men have always said to the women who have consented to wed with them—the proper words and phrases, eager without exceeding the bounds of courtesy, triumphant but not blatantly so, sheering delicately from any undertone of intimacy for fear it might still be deemed offensive.

But dear God, I whispered silently, don't let him ask me to seal the bargain with a kiss. Not now, not yet. The detached calm had disappeared as it had come, with no warning or reason; I could breathe again, I felt the draught from the door behind me, I knew a slow tightening of pain in my heart.

"I have a pleasant surprise for you," Walter said finally. "Do you remember the minister that Robert spoke of not so long ago. He will reach Clennon House soon. We have no reason to wait until our return to Edinburgh, Anne, if you would prefer to be wed here."

I swallowed, but it did not ease the constriction in my throat.

"Such haste might appear unseemly to him."

"I will talk to him," Walter said. "He is a man, and human. Surely he will understand that we do not wish to wait longer."

"And Margaret?"

"I will tell her," he said kindly. "You need have no anxiety on that score. You will forgive her, I hope, if she has displayed signs of possessiveness; it is only the affection of a sister for an older brother. But she will come to accept the idea with a good deal of happiness, I assure you."

I was not assured, but it was no longer my problem. Walter must shoulder the responsibility; now it would be he who must bear with her petty tyrannies.

"Can you be ready in so short a time?" he asked, and his smile was that of a man amused by feminine foibles and yet willing to grant even the most trivial. "I imagine all women like to be given a lengthy time to prepare for a wedding, and I'd not care to deprive you of that pleasure."

At that moment I felt a deep and sincere affection for him, for his consideration and thoughtfulness.

"With Margaret's help," I said quietly, the smell of burning bridges thick in my nostrils, "I would need only a very little time."

"Then I will speak to her at once."

"You are very kind, Walter," I said haltingly, and knew it would be more fitting that I display some other emotion instead of constantly referring to his kindness. But I could not play the hypocrite; he had said nothing of love, he had promised he would not ask that of me.

"I have only begun," he said, "to try to atone for the unhappiness you have known." He went to the table, coming back to me with a small leather purse. He put it in my unresisting hands and closed my fingers about it. "I want you to have this, for your own, to spend as you wish. You must not feel that you were obliged to marry without a farthing to your name."

My cheeks burned hotly; my fingers burned at the feel of the heavy coins within the purse.

"I cannot take your gold," I whispered.

"Consider it a partial payment for your services during the past few years," he said matter-of-factly. "To my eternal shame, I have been much too miserly with it. You have worked unsparingly, and have given freely of yourself. I can do no less in return if I would live with my conscience."

But it would not be so easy for me to salve my own conscience, I thought miserably; not everyone could purchase atonement with a few gold coins.

"I will go up and speak to Margaret," he said again, and we turned and went up the stairs together, Walter's hand firm under my arm.

His smile was a trifle absent when he left me at my door; doubtless he was turning over in his mind the various words he might employ to stay Margaret's wrath. But I felt only a slight curiosity; whatever he said to Margaret, and she to him, I wanted no part of it. I had served notice, I was done with craven acquiescence; I would never again tremble before Margaret's arbitrary demands.

But I walked across my chamber and leaned my arms on the casement, and looked at the barren hills hiding the wild moors and glens beyond, and knew that I must come to stern terms with myself.

Monleigh was beyond my reach, I must live my life without him, I must plan ahead and be done with memories. Marriage with Walter would be a good thing. I would be able to lose myself forever in respectability, I would never again be lonely or hungry or frightened of the years ahead. What did it matter if I disliked the pale lashes framing his pale eyes, or the thin narrow shape of his hands? I trusted his kindness, his tolerance; I had noted that he sometimes moved restlessly during morning prayers, he frequently smiled.

And if my heavy conscience whispered that I came to

him less than a bride, I might remind myself that he was a lonely man, he longed for a companion, he had given me a careful scrutiny and deemed me the proper one to bear his name. A marriage of love was the exception, not the rule; and mayhap it was the more stable and comfortable for not being rent and torn by violent passion. We would not reach the heights, Walter and I, but it was not beyond possibility that we might find tranquility in the placid meadows below.

Oh, I argued and quarrelled with myself, and was vastly proud of my fine logic, and embroidered an endless number of platitudes with the thread of wisdom and lofty convictions.

But I was not deceived. I did not convince myself at all. My face, looking out on the mountain walls of my prison, may have been calm and serene; but my heart twisted with pain, and cried slow tears that welled from deep inside me, and gave me no peace.

And so the fortnight that followed is as foggy and unclear in my mind as the mists that crept down from the upland corries to veil the hills. It may well be that my mind, being less addicted to logic and reason than most, thinks itself well rid of that hapless interval of time and will not relinquish those of its locked memories which might bring a renewal of pain. Or perhaps my long-suffering heart is the culprit; no stranger to pain, it has ever chosen to forget the most intolerable of wounds. Just so did my injured arm heal, the pain almost forgotten, with only a faint line of skin, tougher than before, remaining as proof of the event.

I remember that Margaret came to my room shortly after Walter had spoken to her. Her face was as bleak as before, her eyes as chilly, and the stiff constraint of her words yielded not a jot to such a wretched being as I. But the fierce hatred had been driven underground by Walter's authority, subdued for the moment by strict necessity; and as she put a bolt of white satin across my bed and told me shortly that Kitty might be spared to help me sew a wedding gown, I understood quite well that it was but a temporary truce. I had presumed too much, I had dared to steal her brother from her; and she would never allow me to go unscathed.

I also remember the day, heavy with rain, when Peter Finlay, the minister, arrived at Clennon House. I could not forget the look of his strong young body in its black garb, his fair hair and quiet face, the compassion in his deep-set eyes.

In the privacy of the small hall, he asked me, "Are you certain that you do the right thing?" And because he had seen beneath my calm to the turmoil and hurt, I smiled and answered, "No one is certain of anything in life," and thought that I liked him very much.

He asked me an endless number of questions, softly spoken and never overly personal; and I tried to save myself by holding him to ridicule, telling myself that here was the prying and long-nosed parson Monleigh had told me would come into the west to convert the savages. But Monleigh had spoken of Peter Finlay as a man he liked, a man who had a great love of all men be they sinners or saints; and I longed to tell him all my sins and all my sorrows, and ask him to pray for me now and then.

But I did not, and at length he only sighed and said, "If you have made your decision, I will see to the marriage."

Elizabeth had nothing to do with me during all that time. I went in search of her once, when the world seemed too much for me, only to be told by her that she had more to do with her time than to spend it foolishly gossiping over affairs that did not concern her. She did not approve of my decision any more than did the wise Peter Finlay; but what odds, I did not approve myself.

Kitty, however, spent many long hours in my chamber, sewing a fine seam and chattering like a magpie.

"You're the fortunate one," she would sigh, "to be marrying the master, and he the fine gentleman with so heavy a purse." Then she would fall silent, doubtless remembering that I was of genteel birth myself and no servant marrying beyond her estate in life; but her merry tongue and teasing eye would not be prim for long. "Has he been in love with you all this while, and you never breathed a hint of it? Mercy on us, the mistress must have been vastly surprised to hear the news."

"I imagine so," I said only.

"Well now, it'll be easier on you once you're a Clennon yourself. She'll find another poor lass to do her bidding, and likely you'll have a maid of your own."

" 'Tis likely," I agreed. Then, because I liked Kitty and had not forgotten that Margaret would hand her to the Kirk once we returned to Edinburgh, I said, "What of yourself, Kitty? If you were my maid, Walter might persuade Margaret to be more lenient with you."

Her pause was a brief one. "Oh, you're very kind and I thank you, but I doubt it would help matters."

I stared at her, suspicion become certainty. "Are you not returning to Edinburgh with us, Kitty?" I asked slowly. "Have you other plans?"

Her eyes became quite grave and candid. "Aye," she said, "I've other plans."

If I hated her a bit in that moment, it did not last.

"You'll not betray me, I hope," she said.

Her needle was poised over the wedding gown; and I stared at it, and wanted to weep, and felt oddly stricken. She would go with her stableboy, he with the bold black eyes and knowing grin; and she would be very gay and happy and heedless of all she had put behind her.

"You know I would not," I said quietly. "You are very brave and wise, and I envy you exceedingly."

We looked at each other, and I saw that she had known all along. Her lighthearted gaiety had been but a kindly gesture to help ease the burden of one who had not been so fortunate as she, after all.

"Is there no other way? Can you not change your mind, even now?"

"It would serve no purpose," I said wearily.

"God be with you, then," said Kitty, and bent to her sewing.

"We must not speak of it again."

She nodded, and so we spoke of other matters as we put the final stitches to my gown.

I heard no word from Torra, nor did I expect any. He must know of my decision, since he knew all that went on at Clennon House; but he had also made a decision, that afternoon in the glen, and so he put me from his mind and led his Stewarts on another raid against the English, and when I heard of it I had no guilty conscience and could not smile secretly because I had been one of those gay raiders myself.

The die had been cast, the guests had been invited, the gown was finished and hung between muslin sheets, the final preparations were made. Even Robert treated me with a bare civility, as if his disapproval was too futile to be wasted on me, and I suspected that Walter had contrived to keep us apart those last few days so that I would not, in my tense and irritable state of nerves, be tempted to speak my mind plainly each time Robert looked down his long white nose at me.

The day before the wedding came, and at last I faced the inevitable truth that no shining knight would come down to carry me away, nor a dark one in tarnished armour. We would stand together on the morrow, Walter and I, facing the grave face of Peter Finlay, the minister; and we would be made man and wife, we would say the final vows to cleave us together for the remainder of our lives.

It would be over. I would be wed to Walter. But at that point my mind, unused to so much cold and bitter truth, shied away and dishonourably closed away all further thoughts, and so I was able to greet the wedding guests with some small measure of frozen poise.

There were to be no festivities, for marriage was a sacred and solemn occasion in the eyes of the Kirk, and no papish rite to be celebrated with riotous high spirits. Margaret had invited her Cameron kinsmen to Clennon House; but if they, being Highlanders and so less stringent in their observance of presbyterian ways, deplored the severity of my wedding preparations, they kept their complaints to themselves.

On that night, the eve of my wedding day, we gathered in the great hall for a restrained toast or two, and I stood by the fireplace with my hand on Walter's arm and tried to appear unconcerned by the curious stares turned in our direction. I looked sufficiently pale and chaste, as any nervous bride might appear; and if they went their ways sympathizing with Walter for marrying a woman of no charm, no beauty, no winning graces, it was no more than I deserved for my inability to speak or smile that entire endless evening.

Even Walter noticed it. "You look quite pale," he said in my ear. "Would you like another glass of wine?"

"Thank you," I said, feeling quite ill, "but I think not. It is only my head, it aches abominably."

"You are tired, my dear. But take heart; it is almost time for you to retire."

He showed only patience for my vapours and ineptitude as a hostess. But for all his consideration, he could not delay that moment on the morrow when we must walk down the long stairs to the chapel and a waiting Peter Finlay; he could not know that my heart ceased to beat whenever I thought of it.

Then, as if in answer to my cowardly hope for some deliverance, however brief and futile, Margaret's carefully planned day went astonishingly awry.

A servant stood in the door, and in one of those lulls in the conversation, his voice seemed unnecessarily loud and discomfited.

"The Earl of Monleigh."

Before the words were well out of his mouth, the un-invited guest stood in the doorway.

Had I not been jolted into a state of shock myself, I would have been vastly amused. There was not a sound; the horrified silence seemed to stretch to the very rafters. To a man, the company stared incredulously at the man standing in the door, their mouths stupidly agape and their eyes bulging like so many bewildered woodchucks; one startled Cameron even choked on his wine and looked too frightened to cough.

Beside me Walter stiffened and drew a sharp breath, but my eyes were on Monleigh, advancing across the room toward me.

He would have dominated the room even without the dramatic surprise of his entrance. All other men were sud-denly absurdly vulgar, bedizened in extravagant colours, or else they appeared quite dowdy, shabby to a fault. Even Walter, with his costly brown velvet wedding suit, grew unfashionably staid on the moment, his quiet ele-gance reduced to utter dullness.

Monleigh wore a black velvet suit, its stark severity only emphasized by the wide falling collar of white lace and the embroidered sword baldric slung over his shoulder and

fastened on his hip. His short cloak, swinging carelessly
from his wide shoulders, was also black, as were his boots
and gauntlets; but as I had expected, the cloak was lined
with scarlet, an insolent swaggering blaze of colour which
caught the eye whenever he moved and made mock of all
things dull and cautious.

I have never seen him like this, I thought fleetingly: the
courtier, the fashionable cousin to a king, the Cavalier
with his plumed hat and disdainful smile, the proud peer
of the realm whose arrogance cared not a whit for a
Commonwealth which acknowledged neither rank nor
realm, the black earl of the west Highlands, the chief of
his clan and master of his fate.

But it was only a role he assumed, a game played for
his own cynical amusement. The man, Monleigh, looked
out from the disguise of elegance and hauteur, gazed im-
placably from the dark hooded eyes at the guests gathered
in the great hall of Clennon House; and the women there
flushed and could not turn away, and the men were
strangely pale and silent.

Then there was no time for thought. He was only a few
feet from me; his unswerving eyes scanned me with an
aloof courtesy, went through me as if I did not exist, and
he presented himself to Walter with a brief bow which was
a subtle masterpiece of amused contempt.

"Don't halt the festivities on my account, Walter," he
said blandly. "Have I blundered into a state affair?"

After a moment's hesitation, Walter said, "Tomorrow
is my wedding day, m'lord."

"My felicitations. Is this the fortunate bride?"

"Lord Monleigh, Mistress Anne Lindsay."

The triumph in Walter's words, saved from blatancy
only by virtue of his lowered voice, puzzled me; but I
had no time to think on it. Monleigh bowed before me;
his dark head was close enough for me to touch, had I
succumbed to that bit of insanity, and the exaggerated
sweep of his plumed hat reminded me of a certain day
when I, too, had been a Stewart with a rakish hat and a
reckless nerve.

Shaken, I watched as he straightened. "Your servant,
mistress," he said with no slightest hint of recognition in
his voice.

I had not been aware of Evan behind him. But now
Monleigh stood aside, presenting Evan with a brief, "My
kinsman, Evan Stewart," and I suffered another shock to
see that ugly fellow dressed in velvet and lace. His bow
was perfunctory, little more than a curt motion of his
head.

Walter's voice was stiff, but his poise was fully recovered.

"You will wish to pay your respects to Margaret," he
said to Monleigh.

"By all means."

"She did not expect to see you here today."

"Surely Margaret knows me better than that."

"However," Walter said, "not even the unexpected will
avail you now, m'lord."

"That remains to be seen." Monleigh spoke softly, but
the smile touching his hard mouth did not reach his eyes.
"Overconfidence, Walter, is a dangerous weakness in a
man."

"I think you know more of that than I."

"Perhaps," Monleigh replied calmly, "but I can recall
a time or two when it served you ill."

"The past is done with," said Walter, "and I'll seek no
quarrel with you on the eve of my wedding."

His voice was quite cold, unlike his usual mild tolerance, and I remembered the day he and Monleigh had
met on the track to Torra. They had sparred in much the
same manner then, with the same undertone of malice in
their voices.

"Be at ease, Walter," Monleigh said, and laughed. "I
came with my sword sheathed."

The laugh only served to irritate Walter the more; I
stole a quick glance at him and saw his lips tighten, as
Margaret's were wont to do when she felt a terrible fury.

I looked at them standing there together and was astonished at my lack of perception all this while. Monleigh,
at least, had been plainspoken in his dislike of Walter;
and I well knew that Walter, for all the tolerance he displayed, cared little for the man Monleigh was reputed to
be. But now I could clearly understand that it was more
than a mere antipathy between them. They were desperate
enemies, they faced each other with a hatred of such long

standing that it had burned down to a harsh and grinding antagonism. It had little, if anything, to do with me; it must have begun long before I met Monleigh, before I came to live with the Clennons. I had not recognized it before, and now I found it vastly bewildering and painful to contemplate.

"Where is Margaret?" Monleigh asked, as if he could think of no one person he had rather pay his respects to, and when Walter said, "If you will pardon us, Anne," I received only a flickering glance from Monleigh and a murmured, "By your leave."

He left me and sauntered across the hall beside Walter, and I stood alone by the fireplace with Evan Stewart.

"Why did you do it, lass?"

I was obliged to look at him, at the contempt in his face which he made no attempt to hide. Nor would I, I thought, try to hide anything from this black-browed Stewart who had once been my friend.

"I was tired," I said. "I no longer cared about anything."

"You cared enough for the bribes he offered."

The truth was ofttimes a cruel and hurting thing. But what did it matter, all life was cruel and endlessly plaguing.

"Yes, I took his bribes," I said, "and a purseful of gold as well."

"You are a coward, after all. I would not have thought it of you."

He might have struck me, so stinging was the scorn in his voice; and I noticed that he was angry enough to drop the thick burr he usually affected, so that his English was as clear and concise as Monleigh's.

"On the contrary," I said, "we were once agreed that I had a spine of jelly."

He was in no mood for banter. "That afternoon in the glen. Did you refuse him then?"

"I did not," I said steadily. "He refused me, quite plainly."

He stared at me. "You lie," he said.

My hands were clammy and wet. "Ask him," I said stubbornly, "if you don't believe me."

I saw the slow dawning of a puzzled belief in his eyes,

and so felt obliged to pity him. The shrewd and cunning
Evan had been outwitted at last, as had a foolish and ad-
dleheaded spinster.

"I thought you were the one to tame him," he said
slowly, "you with your green eyes, and sweet ways, and
your way of laughing."

"And I think he is not a man to be tamed by any lass."

"There's no such man living," said Evan. "What did you
do to change his mind about you?"

"I took your warning to heart," I replied, "and did not
cry, nor scold, nor become a nagging shrew. But you can
see that it did not avail me." Then, "Neither of us knew
him as well as we thought," I said carefully, "and perhaps
I did not know myself. I will be happy now; find it in your
heart to be glad for me, Evan."

"You lie, Anne," he said again, but now he was not
referring to anything we had said of Monleigh, and we
were both aware that I was lying.

Then I remembered a persistent question that had long
been in my mind. "Once you told me you were wed," I
said. "Will you tell me her name?"

He shrugged. "'Tis of no matter. You know her well."

I nodded. "I am almost as fond of Elizabeth," I said,
"as I am of you."

"Then you'll miss her cooking and her dour face," he
said. "I've been without both for too long."

I could not have expected anything else, and yet my
heart sank and I gave a weary sigh. "Will she be leaving
Clennon House?"

"Aye, on this very night."

"I had hoped," I said sadly, "to keep her with me. She
has a way of making life more bearable." I smiled faintly,
unable to ignore the unbidden comparison that came to
my mind. "Maybe Monleigh sees the same virtue in you."

"You'll have to bear your life alone from now on," said
Evan bluntly. "'Tis of your own choosing, I'd think you
would be pleased with it."

"Yes, one would think so," I said dully.

"You'd not listen to anyone, not you. Stubborn and
headstrong as all the other foolish women in the world."

"I know the Stewarts have no love for Walter," I protested, "but that does not make him a villain. He will be

kind to me, Evan, and I stand in great need of a small portion of kindness."

"That's not all you'll get from the man," said Evan, "and I'll warrant there'll be precious little of that, when all's done."

A faint chill went through my blood, and I struggled against the involuntary urge to shiver, as though I stood in a cold draught. But I deemed it no more than a reaction from the miserable weariness which had begun, it seemed, to settle in my very bones.

"We sail for France on the morrow."

I stared at him, my heart beating against my ribs. My wedding day, I thought miserably, he is leaving Scotland on my wedding day.

"Then he has come to know," I said at last, "that he stands in great danger."

Evan looked his scorn for me. "He leaves by order of the King," he said. "What's danger to Simon that he should run from it?"

What was it, indeed, I asked myself, but an added fillip to give spice to the already turbulent and headlong pace of his life? Mayhap he had looked on me in much the same manner; now he could make boast that he had entertained himself by seducing a sober presbyterian spinster, he had once dallied with Walter Clennon's wife and found her so lamentably wanting that he had carelessly refused her.

But the thought was unworthy of him. It was born of misery and despair and cold panic, and it died of quick shame that I could so malign him in my mind when my whole heart knew the lie in it.

"When did the orders come," I asked, "and why?"

"With the *Marie*. I'll not tell you why; 'tis none of your affair."

"Then he must have known all this time," I said slowly. He had known he must leave, he knew it the night he took me aboard the *Marie*, the afternoon we climbed to the glen in the hills.

"Aye, he knew."

"Why did he linger, Evan? He could have been safe in France by now."

"You know as well as I why he stayed," Evan said

flatly. "But I'll be pleased to see him on his way. Charles has plans for him that don't include swinging at the end of a gibbet."

I could not resist a smile. "He would laugh if he could hear us, clucking over his safety like two mother hens."

"He doesn't know the meaning of the word. He's lived in peril from his cradle, and likely he always will."

"You are small comfort, Evan."

"Keep your fears for yourself, you have need for them. Simon wants no prayers said over him."

"But I shall say them," I said quietly, "for the rest of my life."

"I'd wish you good fortune, Anne Lindsay," he said, "but I doubt you'll find it with Walter Clennon."

"Do you think I'd have found it with the Stewarts?"

He looked at me closely and shrugged, and said flatly, "Well now, you can say good riddance to the Stewarts, and think of us now and again if you've the courage."

"I'll think of you sailing away on the morrow," I said with care, "and wish that I were with you."

He seemed to recall what I had said to him earlier, and the lines of his face softened somewhat.

"God be wi' ye, lass," he said gently, lapsing once again into the warm burr of the Highlands. "I'd have wished a happier fate for ye, but it can't be helped now. We're none of us without a devil riding our backs."

I watched him stride across the floor to the door, never faltering in his pace as the guests fell back in unison to let him pass.

"I fear Evan will never forgive you for deserting the colours so cravenly," a low voice murmured in my ear. "His opinion of women has never been exceedingly high, you understand, and now he appears to be permanently embittered."

I drew a long unsteady breath and turned to face Monleigh. "I did not desert," I said, "and now Evan knows it."

A dark brow lifted. "Then we have sadly misjudged you. Did you tell poor Evan that you have decided not to become the mistress of Clennon House after all?"

"No," I said shortly, wishing he had never come, wishing he would leave me alone, in peace, to do the thing that had to be done.

"No? Then perhaps Evan is justified in his bitterness."

"Have you come to taunt me?" I asked quietly. "I would not have thought it of you."

"I have come to say farewell," he said promptly. "Not a lingering one, however, under the circumstances. You must forgive me if I seem to put less than my whole heart and soul in the gesture." Then, with a small cynical smile, "I would not care to blacken your reputation in the eyes of this noble company."

I stood quietly, my head high and my cheeks, which burned as if I had come too close to a hot fire, doubtless stained a betraying and brilliant red, and with one breath I damned him silently and with the next prayed desperately for him; and all the curious gaping wedding guests left off their chattering and stared openly, wondering what words had passed between us, waiting to see what might happen next.

Then, incredibly, he offered his arm for my hand. When I hesitated, knowing it was dangerously daft to risk touching him, he said easily, "Come along, Mistress Lindsay, we shall promenade the hall." In a low amused voice intended for my ears alone, he added, "Walter Clennon is bearing down on us with a nasty gleam in his eye. Quite remiss of him, indeed, when I've only just begun to pay my respects to his lovely bride."

I walked slowly beside him, clutching at the last thin shreds of my poise; and all the while my hand clung to his arm and felt the hard flesh beneath the velvet, and my heart clamoured in my throat like the staccato thunder of a drum roll.

"I trust," said the Earl of Monleigh, "that you have completed your preparations for the wedding."

I smiled stiffly at a glaring Lady Cameron; my escort bowed politely.

"Have you counted the household linen and the number of jam jars in the larder? I'd not imagine that you would overlook so important a detail, or neglect to attach the proper consequence to such valuables."

John Cameron stood directly in our path, his long thin face even longer with its scowling anger, his neatly clipped beard seeming to quiver with outrage.

"Your servant, sir," said Monleigh, deftly leading me

around John Cameron and a bunched knot of silent Cameron womenfolk as well. "And doubtless you have checked the contents of the pantries," he went on smoothly, "and the upstairs wardrobes. Only a slovenly mistress would neglect to make a thorough inventory before accepting a new position as housekeeper and chatelaine."

Another perfunctory bow, an elegant leg for a red-tartaned Campbell chief.

"And the children. How many was it to be? One for every day in the week, surely, and twins on the Sabbath. On the other hand, there are those who might object to such strenuous activity on the Lord's Day. Perhaps you should schedule the twins for a Saturday morning."

"You are talking nonsense, m'lord," I said at last, between a brief nod and a brief smile for two guests who had imbibed too freely of Walter's wine and bowed so deeply as we passed that I feared for their balance.

"I think not," he said carelessly. Then, as if I had not spoken, "You could name them for the days of the week, of course, but that might lead to some difficulty in the event more than one arrived on the same day. Fair and dimpled, I think you described them once; I pray you will take the necessary precautions to prevent an ugly black-haired goblin from snarling your well-laid plans."

"Fair and dimpled," I said coolly, trying desperately to hate him and succeeding not at all, "and well-mannered as well. You should not forget that most desirable of virtues."

"Is it a virtue to be well-mannered, Mistress Lindsay?"

"I am convinced it would be both foolish and futile," I said, "to attempt to explain anything so foreign to your nature."

"And I refuse to believe it possible for you to be either foolish or futile," he said blandly, his eyes on Walter Clennon standing in our path only a few feet distant. "I must commend Walter for choosing such a lovely and virtuous bride. And well-mannered, for a certainty."

Walter's face was carefully blank, devoid of any tinge of anger or antagonism.

"Anne," he said, his eyes on Monleigh, "I think it time for you to retire. You would not wish to suffer from an aching head on the morrow."

Monleigh immediately assumed an expression of courteous concern. He shook a delicate lace handkerchief from
his velvet sleeve, but to my vast relief he merely held it in
one indolent hand, carelessly and yet quite properly elegant, so that all eyes in the room seemed to fasten on that
single square of exquisite linen.

"Indeed not," he said. "I would offer my sympathies,
Mistress Lindsay, were I not certain that all your afflictions will depart in the happiness of your wedding day."

"You are kind," I said faintly. "I warrant I shall recover."

"Do you care for lute music? I am told it soothes one's
pains quite as well as a draught of medicine. Perhaps," he
said to a stone-faced Walter, "you might engage a musician to lull Mistress Lindsay to sleep despite her aching
head."

"But I do not care for lutes," I said, "nor yet for players
of lutes."

Monleigh shrugged. "No accounting for tastes," he said,
his gray eyes so close to laughter that I felt an uncon-
trollable urge to turn away before I succumbed to a certain
wild laughter myself. "I rather fancy the instrument, as a
matter of fact. A man of my clan plays a bit, now and
again, and deems himself well-versed in the art."

"I should think," I said, not to be outdone, "that men
who waste their time and abilities strumming lutes must
be exceedingly vain and light-minded creatures."

"No doubt of it," he agreed gravely. "This fellow is an
undoubted rogue and blackguard, light-fingered as well as
light-minded."

Against every measure of my will, I repeated, "Light-
fingered?"

"On the lute strings, of course," said Monleigh, "and on
any valuable possession left lying about by a careless
owner. He would steal me blind, were I not on my guard
against his villainy, but I have long since discovered that
his eye gleams brighter for a pretty lass than a heavy
purse. Convenient, you'll agree, since we have no lassies,
pretty or no', at Torra."

"A villain, indeed," I murmured, feeling Walter's hand
close warningly on my arm. "You would be wise, m'lord, to
keep him well in hand before he meets disaster."

"At whose hands?" he asked lightly. "You must mean my own, since I alone am his master. And who knows, perhaps the knave finds it a diverting game to court disaster. A young Stewart lad of my acquaintance has developed a theory about such matters; he once met disaster at his master's hands and found it somewhat less than terrifying, and now no amount of logic can persuade him that all masters are not so lenient, nor all forms of disaster so unexpectedly pleasant."

"You speak in riddles, m'lord," Walter interrupted, his voice as curiously blank of expression as his face. "A good night to you, Anne. My lord Monleigh will understand if you take your leave of him now."

I dared not linger. Curtsying briefly, I held out my hand and waited for Monleigh's large one to close over it.

"I doubt your young Stewart lad is so innocent and foolish as you would have me believe," I said, proud of my steady voice, "nor his master so kind. These are bitter times, and we all learn to face the hard truth sooner or later."

"Aye, bitter times," he said, "and bitter truth." His mouth brushed my hand; and the small smile burned against my skin. "Your servant, ma'am."

"Good night, Walter," I said, and left them both without a backward glance.

Lady Cameron moved forward to stand in my way and I was perforce obliged to speak to her.

"The Devil himself," she hissed, not so quietly as she imagined, "would be more welcome in Clennon House than that man. What did he say to you? Why did Walter not order him away at once?"

I do not know what I said to her. My mind was too benumbed, too stunned with misery and shock to pay more than a cursory attention to her gabbling. Why had he come, why did he persist in turning the wretched point of the knife in my back? What did he think to accomplish with his cynical smile, his teasing double-edged remarks, his reckless baiting of Walter's long-suffering forbearance? No, he was neither kind nor gentle, this Monleigh; and the man who had given such tender understanding to a young Stewart lad belonged to another hour, another world, another universe.

I turned to leave Lady Cameron and saw him across the room, almost at the door, talking to the minister, Peter Finlay. He was leaving, sailing for France on the morrow, and I would never see or speak to him again. And what was there left to say, we had finished with words that afternoon in the quiet glen with the sun hot on our faces and the smell of heather drugging our senses. He was leaving, and I would be left alone—only not quite alone, because the morrow brought my wedding day and a new husband to dry my tears and ease my afflictions with happiness.

My mouth was hot and dry, as if I had been suffering a fever, and I found it suddenly difficult to swallow. I felt sick but could not swallow to ease the nausea; and in another moment the tears burning behind my eyelids would stream unchecked down my face. I could see their stares, hear their amusement, only faintly veiled with sympathy, as they patted cool water on my face and loosened my stays. "It is the usual thing for a bride," they would tell me, and behind my back, "Poor Walter, she is quite undone by her good fortune, do you think he will be able to cope with her vapours?"

Lady Cameron, still close by me, looked at me strangely, and I saw Margaret begin to push through the crowd to reach my side. She might hate and despise me, I thought, but she would not allow me to embarrass Walter before the guests she had invited to Clennon House.

But he was not leaving yet. He turned before he reached the door and spoke again to the minister; he laughed, and the sound of his laughter, brief though it was, cut through the voices and the clink of Venetian goblets, and touched my nerves like a flicker of fire.

Then, without warning, he turned toward me. His eyes met mine for a moment; and in the space of that instant the world faded away, there was no one in the great hall but Monleigh and I. He might have been close enough to touch me, so surely did I feel the renewed courage and strength, the reassurance that swept through me in that moment when he looked at me and I knew that he was not scornful, nor cynically amused, nor filled with a bitter contempt.

As I straightened my shoulders and felt the nausea disappear, leaving my pulses calm and normal once again, I heard the sharp report of a gun somewhere outside Clennon House, and then a high-pitched yell followed immediately by a great clamour of horses.

The crowded hall was deathly silent, held in an immobile grip of shock and disbelief. The same thing had happened before, when Monleigh appeared in the doorway; but now the return of reason came more swiftly on the heels of consternation. In the next breath, all was confusion; the men ran for the doors at the same moment, struggling to free their swords from the clutter of lace and velvet dress scabbards, and the women reacted simultaneously to raise their voices in a single shrill wave of terror.

I did not move, nor take my eyes from his. The room swirled and flowed about me, eddying like a swollen river in spate; a woman grasped my arm with frightened hands and was then borne away by someone even more frightened; a voice, perhaps Margaret's, called my name sharply. But I paid no attention to any of it.

I looked at him, and he smiled at me; and I knew whose Highland men had come down from the hills to raid Clennon House on the eve of my wedding day.

⟨14⟩

I stood in the door of Walter's chamber and laughed till
my eyes were wet. Whatever the consequences, I
could no more have prevented the laughter than I could
command my heart to cease beating; all the tension and
strain of the past days dissolved in a trice, and I was left
weak and shaken with unseemly mirth.

Walter had sent me abovestairs to wait for him; and
having been met with a shower of feathers as I climbed
the stairs, I rather suspected the mischief done by the
Stewarts. But I was unprepared for the ridiculous sight
that greeted my eyes when I stepped inside Walter's door.

Feathers festooned the bed hangings and carpet, clustered in drifts before the fireplace, clung thickly to the
tapestry on the walls, and danced lazily through the air
until the room resembled nothing so much as a mountain
glen in the midst of a winter blizzard.

"Do you find it so amusing?" Walter spoke from behind me.

I turned to find him standing in the doorway, Margaret
and Robert close behind him. Two feathers had caught on
the top of Robert's head, giving him much the look of a
scrawny bird furious to be seen at his moulting. I bit my
tongue, and composed my face, and prayed that my voice
would not break with laughter.

" 'Tis an amusing sight, don't you think, after the first
shock has worn off." I looked about me, and the faint
movement of my skirts stirred a small whirlwind of
feathers to eddy about my feet. "You see?" I began again,
but my voice failed me.

"I regret that I haven't your sense of humour," Walter
said. "Perhaps you will explain the jest to us."

His face was more drawn and pale than I had ever seen

it. The three of them advanced into the room, and for an eerie moment it seemed that Walter was one with Margaret and Robert, he was part of an army of the godly come to chastise me for my wickedness in daring to laugh at the odious work of the Devil.

Then the moment was gone, and I blamed my imagination for it. Walter was angry, of course; but he would surely never turn his hatred of Monleigh toward me.

Robert was also angry; the white lines about his nose made it even more similar to the sharp beak of a bird.

"Where shall we sleep," he asked, "and what of the guests?"

"On the floor," Margaret said tautly. "We've blankets and quilts enough, and I daresay there's no Cameron here who is so accustomed to feather mattresses that he can't abide the floor for a single night."

Walter walked to the fireplace. He scuffed at the deep pile of feathers with his boot, but they flew into the air only to drift downward again and cover the shining leather toe of his boot. He clenched his hands as if he felt maddened by frustration, then consciously loosened them and rested one hand against the lintel.

"Then see to it, Margaret," he said crisply. "You, Robert, may wait in the hall below until I have further orders for you."

He was master of Clennon House, and his voice implied that he expected them to obey his commands as instantly as if they had been among his old regiment of dragoons. It was yet a new Walter, one I had not previously encountered; and so I could not but be amused at Robert's alacrity in leaving the room.

But a feather blew against his nose and he sneezed mightily, and the feathers at his feet immediately swirled up into his face. I kept a stoic face through sheer determination, and wondered if he had ever surrendered to an unholy but satisfactory urge to curse. But he disappeared with his head high and his spine unbending, and I reckoned that temptation was too slight a matter for his notice.

Margaret, unaccustomed to orders other than her own, was not so prompt. She hesitated just inside the door and looked back at Walter.

"Are you certain you'll not need me?"

"I can manage without your help, sister," Walter said. "Pray look to your guests."

So she left us, closing the door behind her, and Walter and I were left alone. It was a moment I had dreaded and avoided for several days, but I realized, with a vast gratitude to Monleigh, that the soul-cleansing laughter had done away with my aching head and frightened uncertainties alike.

"There are a few matters we must put straight between us," Walter said.

Unsure of his meaning and so not daring to commit myself, I said nothing.

"Was it by your invitation that Lord Monleigh came to Clennon House this evening?"

I stood very still, my hands clasped before me. "That is a strange question to ask me, Walter."

"Not so very strange. Did you expect him?"

"No," I said truthfully, and my mind worked at a frantic pace to ascertain his purpose. "Nor did I expect the horde of ruffians that descended upon us. Was anything stolen? Did they do any damage beyond the—" I hesitated, then forced myself to finish smoothly—"beyond the beds?"

"A large amount of gold was taken from this room," he said, "as well as important papers. The gold I can spare, but the papers are of great value to me and cannot be replaced."

"I am very sorry that it happened," I said, seeking a tone of gentle regret. His calm words were only faintly tinged with anger; but his unwonted emotion was betrayed in the tight lines of his face. What sort of papers were stolen, I wondered uneasily, and why should their theft so upset the even-tempered, long-suffering Walter Clennon?

"Are you sorry?" he asked unemphatically. Then, "I must confess to a certain admiration for his cleverness. I did not expect him so soon, nor did I imagine that he would brazenly announce himself."

My mouth was parched. "Why did you expect him at all?"

"You needn't pretend such an unbecoming stupidity, Anne. No one with more than a passing acquaintance with his lordship would be foolish enough to think he would fail to make an appearance here before the wedding. Surely you know him better than that."

I was not defeated. "I don't know him at all, and I had no reason to think he would come here."

"Come, Anne," Walter said with a weary sigh, "lies will serve no purpose. Have I been mistaken in you? Are you more a fool than I believed?"

I fought for time, even as I knew that delay would not save me.

"Perhaps you will explain," I said evenly. "I am quite confused by your riddles."

He smiled with a certain amount of kindliness, as though he could not rid himself of the habit.

"Gladly," he said. "The trap was baited and set, but unfortunately Robert and I overlooked a fundamental rule of nature. Animals are ofttimes craftier than the men who seek to trap them; I would imagine it to be an acute sense of danger which all wild creatures must possess if they are to survive." He shrugged before adding, "But in the last stand, no animal is more cunning than his pursuer. I shall have him yet."

A cold draught touched my spine; but the windows and doors were tightly shut, no air moved in the room, the white feathers did not stir.

"What has he done to you?" I asked slowly. "Why do you hate him so?"

"Hate? 'Tis a mild word to describe my feeling for Simon Stewart." He moved his hand briefly. "Sit down."

I went to the chair directly before him and sat down, too dazed to resent his peremptory tone of voice.

"You knew, of course, that he was once married?"

I nodded warily, my eyes on his face. "Margaret told me."

"Her name was Lucy Gordon. She was my betrothed; we had planned to wed in the autumn. But I made the fatal mistake of presenting her to Monleigh that summer."

So many things became clear in that moment. "In Edinburgh?"

"We encountered him on the street. It was a Sabbath, just after kirk."

I could not resist murmuring, "Monleigh, in kirk?"

He gave me a cold glance. "He was merely passing by, I believe."

"And she fell in love with him," I said softly.

"I prefer to call it seduction." His face had subtly changed, become a remote mask of fastidious disdain. "A deliberate and ruthless seduction of an innocent girl."

I thought I understood his hatred. "Did you love her very much?"

I did not, after all; he gave me a pitying look, his voice was laced with scorn. "Quite the little romantic, aren't you? I cared nothing for the girl, once Monleigh had despoiled her. But I have been obliged to live with humiliation for an intolerable number of years."

This could not be the Walter I knew. He was still restrained and withdrawn, his face looked at me with the same expression I had so frequently deemed kindly and tolerant, his voice had not yet been raised in anger. But I sensed somehow that there was no kindness in him now, no tolerance, no amiable compliance; these qualities had disappeared as if they had never been, replaced by a grim unfamiliar vindictiveness. And I found it even more repellent for being hidden behind a pleasant façade, secreted in the torturous depths of his mind to await, with devious stealth, the proper moment to strike.

It was incredible that it should be so, that a person could live beside another, break bread with him, sleep under the same roof for years, know so well how he behaved in anger or boredom or indifference, recognize each individual trait of dress and habit, each like and dislike, and yet never suspect that behind the familiar face might exist such an intensity of hate and twisted wrath.

After a pause, Walter continued, "I owe him a long score, and I'll see it settled before I die."

"Because of Lucy?"

"That, surely, among other things. Do you blame me? He took her from me, with no regard for my feelings; then when he had tired of her, he murdered her by some foul means. It seldom pleases a man to have his possessions treated with such disrespect."

I remembered the day he had returned to Clennon House to find his stables raided and his best horseflesh stolen; he had displayed only a certain glum chagrin, and

I had admired his self-control. But doubtless a consuming
fury had raged beneath the deceptive mask of his composure; for he was apparently a man to whom the humiliation of being outwitted came as a more galling affront than
the actual loss of his possessions, whether horses or
women.

"And do you also consider me a possession?" I asked
quietly.

His eyes moved over me. "A bit tarnished and ill-used,"
he said calmly, "but mine nonetheless."

My cheeks did not burn; I felt instead a vast and ener-
vating sadness. A small voice repeated inside me, over
and over, a few words I had once heard: *I do not possess
you, as a man possesses cattle . . . you have a right to your
own life, to take whatever happiness you may find in it.*
But that was in another life, another world. I was to wed
Walter, I must bear his name and share his bed; and in
some manner I could not immediately foresee, it must be
endured.

"I am amazed," I said slowly, "that you would consider
me worthy of your name."

"You are worthy enough," he said, "in the eyes of the
world. And I have better means than most men to insure
your good behavior henceforth."

I understood. Whatever I had done, he did not intend
to discard me; by the same token, it was not the fact that
Monleigh had, in Walter's eyes, despoiled Lucy Gordon,
but the humiliation that the whole world knew of it.

"You need have no fear," I said dully. "I will be a dutiful wife."

"I am sure of it."

I could not fail to understand him; and yet for a moment disbelief struggled with astonishment inside me.
Whatever he knew or suspected, it was a potent and dangerous weapon he held over my head; and I would be
playing the fool to think he would not stoop to use it at
will.

But I was not so beaten I could not fight back.

"It would seem that you would hesitate to risk the same
humiliation a second time."

"The humiliation will not be mine, dear Anne, but yours
and Monleigh's. I would stand to gain a great deal of

prestige in the eyes of the Kirk were I to denounce the guilty sins of my own wife. And I might add, since you are doubtless interested, that a large share of my wealth depends upon my excellent position in the Kirk. I will not allow it to be jeopardized."

"But surely the exposure of my sins would only reflect upon yourself."

"In the opinion of the Kirk, a man can demonstrate his piety in no better way than to exorcise the evil in his own home. And I have many friends of no little influence in the church; your punishment, whatever it might be, would be known only to myself and a few others."

"And so the world would still consider me worthy of your name," I said slowly.

"I place a high value on the opinion of the world."

"Did you receive Clennon House," I asked, "in payment for the black mark Luck Gordon made against your name?"

His eyes were chilled almost white. "A partial payment," he said, "for the crime Simon Stewart committed against me."

"A partial payment?"

He smiled slightly. "One day I will have Torra also."

Despite my horror, the disbelief was slow in fading; old habits of thought, opinions of long standing, are doubly hard to discard.

"You would use me," I asked, "to further your schemes against Monleigh?"

"You are too harsh, Anne. I admit I thought I might make some use of you to trap him, but he was too clever for me this time. However, I will have Torra without your help. The Kirk has no use for renegade Royalists."

I began to see how Walter had managed to acquire so many valuable estates. The spoils of war went to the victor, and before Cromwell invaded Scotland with his English army, the victor had been a triumphant and avengeful clergy. And the armies of the clergy had been filled with the eager grasping ones, those who cozened the influential members of the Kirk with a great pretence of piety and devoutness, who professed a virtuous humility to match the expediency of the moment, who used their assumed godliness with the shrewdness of horse traders. I had never before questioned Walter's fortune; in my innocence, I had deemed it a just reward for his diligence and perseverance. But if he were truly diligent, I had learned in the past few minutes that he was not in the least godly or pious; and I thought of the leather purse he had given me, and knew that the gold coins therein were more sullied and illegal than the smuggler's gold in Monleigh's purse.

"But why do you hesitate to give me to the Kirk? Think of your reward were you to announce the latest injury he has done you."

"I have told you," he said, "that I shall gain Torra without exchanging a wife for it. And you must agree that Margaret and I can make good use of your services under the circumstances."

So Margaret, too, would have her revenge; she would go on having it for the rest of her life and mine.

"I would prefer the punishment of the Kirk."

"I've no doubt of it. But we shall get on famously together, Anne, never fear."

"How can you think to marry me," I asked, stunned beyond emotion, "when you think so ill of me?"

"I admit to being intrigued by that streak of wantonness in your nature," he said. "It galls me that Monleigh was the first to notice it, but I shall benefit from his perception." He looked carefully at his nails, toyed with the ruby ring on his forefinger. "The irony of Fate can be most amusing. Perhaps I'd not have been so hasty in bringing you to bed had I not foreseen the opportunity to repay a favour. It is Monleigh who must writhe this time."

With his words, the oppressive guilt weighing my conscience fell away. He was the evil one, the unscrupulous sinner; he was the one who cheated, who hid his duplicity behind a mask of false virtue, who openly condemned wickedness and secretly practiced it. Scotland hated and feared Monleigh, branded him evil, preached against his heresy; and yet the Walter Clennons went unscathed, waxed wealthy and influential, were praised for their piety, and all the while indulged their depravity behind closed chamber doors.

I closed my eyes, and said a small prayer, and saved my sanity by fashioning a picture for myself of the *Marie*, her clean deck aslant and her white sails taut with a fair wind, her rakish hull showing eager heels to the sombre land at its back, sailing away from Scotland in the bright morning sun.

We were not such sinners, after all, I thought clearly; I could have taken his hand and walked the world over, holding my head proudly, and I would have known no shame or dishonour.

"Perhaps you should know," I said at last, "that you will have taken nothing from Monleigh."

My words gave him pause; then he said, "I fail to understand you."

"He refused me," I said. "He would not have me. Indeed, he advised me to take advantage of your proposal of marriage."

"You lie," Walter said. "Unless," he added softly, "I have been mistaken, and he has never cared for you at all."

"That," I said, "can only be answered by Monleigh."

"No odds," Walter said. "You know little of men. It will gall him enough that I have prevented him from taking his pleasure of you."

The words were horribly obscene to me, and I took courage from some unexpected source of strength.

"Does it gall you so little, Walter, that you would wed one of his castoff women? He had finished with me, you understand, discarded me at his own will; he was entirely unmoved by the prospect of my marrying you."

And if that were a small lie, I thought, the situation surely warranted it. I saw Walter's composure crack slightly; he frowned, looked at me sharply from narrowed eyes.

"He hadn't enough time," he said, almost in a whisper. "I didn't allow him enough time to win you. Not even Monleigh could manage to lie with a woman in so short a time."

"You know little of women," I said.

He took a long stride and stood over me; his hand closed on my shoulder with a rough, deliberately hurting grip.

"Tell me," he said coldly, "has he ever possessed you? Tell me the truth, else I will kill you here and now."

"He will always possess me," I said quietly, and knew

that it was so. He had let me go free, for reasons of his own, and in doing so had bound me to him for the rest of my life. What did it matter that I did not understand, that my heart was sickened that he would hand me over to a man such as Walter Clennon, then sail away without a backward look? None of it mattered, when all was said; it was not his fault that I had come to belong to him, body and spirit.

Walter did not speak for endless minutes. But his hand did not loosen its brutal grip; and his heavy breathing above my head was somehow monstrous, belonging to a stranger I did not understand and so could not cope with.

"I shall kill him for this," he said. "But I'll not make it so easy for you." His voice sounded as though he were smiling, and I was glad that I could not see it. "On the morrow we will be wed lawfully, in the eyes of the world and the Kirk, and since you have been cast aside by such a man as Monleigh, it will scarcely behoove you to be shamed by whatever use I make of you now."

He let me go, but did not move away. His brown velvet suit was still unrumpled, still neatly groomed.

"Leave it be, Walter," I said quietly. "I have no intention of wedding you now." The very words seemed to lift an intolerable burden from my shoulders, so simple and true were they, so blindingly clear that I felt bathed in clean hot sunlight. "Whatever my future holds, I am still capable of choosing it for myself."

He laughed. "You have no choice in the matter."

"You cannot force me into marriage."

"You think not? Consider the consequences of your misbehavior, and you will come to see the folly of defying me."

The consequences? A tortured interval of punishment inflicted by less kindly members of the Kirk than Finlay, a long year or so of shame and degradation, a slow starvation in some filthy almshouse—these were the inevitable consequences of sinful misbehavior such as mine. And yet, I thought, I would gladly suffer it to free myself of another single moment of Walter Clennon.

"No," I said, "it will not be folly at all."

"You are a fool," he said calmly, "if you dream Monleigh will come to your aid. You are in Clennon House, beyond his reach, and I shall be prepared for him henceforth." Then, more thoughtfully, "Now that I think on't, the idea has a certain merit. The man has no conscience, but he would scarcely wish ill fortune to befall one of his former wenches."

"You cannot threaten me," I said, weary to the point of illness, "for we both know that it would serve you to no good purpose to kill me. And he will not attempt to come to my aid, he cares nothing for me."

The lie was an empty one, for I well knew that Monleigh and his kinsman, Evan Stewart, would not hesitate were they to hear of misfortune befalling any poor lass within Clennon House.

"In any event," I added, "he is leaving Scotland tomorrow. You may conquer an empty Torra, but never its master."

"Tomorrow?" he said quickly. "By ship, mayhap?"

Too late, I realized what I had told him. But it could not matter; Walter and all his Cameron kinsmen could not hold back the *Maria*.

But Walter went to the door and flung it open, and shouted for Robert MacLeish. The feathers whirled and eddied, like clouds of white dust about his feet; and I stood up, watching him numbly, despising myself for a stupid loose-tongued fool.

Robert came to the door at once. He did not look beyond Walter, nor show any indication that he was aware of my presence.

"Saddle a horse, Robert," Walter ordered. "Ride to the English fort and inform the commander there that our quarry thinks to slip from the net. He sails tomorrow."

"Sails?" Robert repeated.

Impatiently Walter said, "You heard me. If we're quick enough we'll have his ship. 'Tis all the evidence the English have needed."

Robert did not deserve Walter's impatience; if he was overly curious, he was not dull-witted. He understood the prize in the offing if he but reached the garrison in time, and his long nose fairly quivered with anticipation.

"I'll leave at once," he said eagerly.

His eyes rested on me for a brief moment, and I was amazed at the expression in them. An honourable man,

Robert, who could be triumphant and still feel a twinge of sympathy for his defeated enemy.

And despite my dislike of him, I felt a certain faint affection for him, for his unyielding integrity, his strict conscience. I might disagree with him, disdain him, deem him a narrow and bigoted fanatic; but it was a vast relief to know that his face reflected his soul precisely. He would never dissemble, feign a piety he did not feel, turn before my eyes into a mocking and deceitful stranger. One always knew where one stood with Robert MacLeish.

Then he was gone, with a nod to Walter. I could not cry out to Robert, ask him to stay, to delay his ride for another few minutes. He would be unconcerned by my fate; even had he stood beside me for the past hour and watched Walter's artful mask crumble with the force of his rage, Robert would doubtless tell me that I deserved no less for my sins.

And mayhap it was so. But I lifted my head as Walter closed the door and latched it, and prayed desperately for courage to face him without flinching.

"I am quite capable," I said, "of announcing to the world that I belong to Simon Stewart and no one else."

"Capable now," he said, "but who can predict how you will feel on the morrow?"

I said nothing; I had used my last weapon, and it had not availed me.

"When I spoke of ill fortune," Walter said softly, "I was not speaking of death."

And even so, I watched him advancing toward me and refused to surrender to the urge to close my eyes against his glittering pale eyes and scornful mouth.

I am reluctant to think, even now, about the long hours of that night. But what happened between Walter Clennon and me is not to be spoken of in the clear clean light of day; it belongs to the dark cankered hours of the night, to the strange nightmares one finds on the edge of sleep, to the hard past I would forget.

For a time afterward, I deemed it a scourge, a devil riding my back, a pitiless hair shirt to rub forever against my complaining flesh, a cruel penance for my sins. But only for a short time. He was only a man, when all was said, with a tortured mind and an unhappy soul that would give him no peace until he died. My mind was elsewhere, as well as my heart, and so was Walter Clennon's; and he must have realized that the game was too tame for him, that he could not have his revenge upon a woman who had closed her whole being away from him and refused to be concerned or frightened by a thin scrawny man who wore a long nightshirt and knew less of that sort of evil sin than he might have imagined.

I lay beside him and watched him sleep, fitfully and with dreams which must have been vastly unpleasant to so disturb his slumbers; and my tears and my heavy heart were not for the man there, or for the night I had just spent, or for the dreary prospect of the years ahead. They were familiar tears, born of a sense of utter loneliness, and by their very familiarity seemed in some measure to comfort and console me.

When I awoke in the pale dawn, immediately aware of the hard floor beneath the single quilt I had slept on, I ached in every painful joint, and the air was chill and damp, and a feather lay against my cheek. I cannot look at a white feather to this day without a feeling of depression, but that morning I was too wretched to care, too disconsolate to weep again.

A soft voice pressed insistently against my lethargy, my closed eyes. "Anne, please wake," the voice whispered in my ear. " 'Tis only I, Kitty."

My eyes opened wide. In that first moment, although my whole being shrunk from the unexpected candlelight, I knew that Walter was not in the room. Kitty stood over me, half crouched, wrapped snugly in a dark cloak; and the candle in her hand betrayed every pitying line of her face, the depth of compassion in her unwontedly grave eyes.

"What are you doing here?" I whispered in like fashion, as if Walter might suddenly appear behind her in the room were I to raise my voice.

"I'm leaving now," she said softly. "Our horses are waiting in the wood. But I had to see you again."

"That is very kind of you, Kitty," I said, and could have wept for her to find me in such a condition.

"No," she said swiftly, "you don't understand. The master is gone; I thought you should know."

"Gone?" I could not think, my mind was too befuddled and hazy.

"He rode away an hour past. Lachlan saddled his horse."

I sat up and pushed my tousled hair from my face. So Lachlan was the name of that stableboy with the reckless look in his eyes and the gay smile.

"In which direction, Kitty?"

"East. He almost caught me in the stables, but I hid myself in time. He seemed to feel a feverish haste, and Lachlan at last decided I must come and tell you."

I stood up, frankly grateful for her supporting hand. "And where do you and Lachlan ride?" I asked her. "Will you go past Torra?"

"No, we ride north to Lachlan's home." With no hesitation, she added, "If you wish to send a message, we will go to Torra for you."

It was a temptation, but I could not ask such a sacrifice of them. Walter had gone to meet the English soldiers, I was certain, and it would never do for Kitty and her Lachlan to be lingering in the vicinity. She had already taken a great risk for me, for she stood to lose her freedom before it was won should Margaret discover her.

"I will go," I said firmly, and suddenly I wanted nothing in the world so much as a cool cleansing ride in the dawn. I would think no further than that; Monleigh must be warned, and I must be the one to warn him.

Kitty helped me dress, then placed a cloak about my shoulders. Together we stole down the stairs in the pallid light while Clennon House slept about us, and took pains to keep our feet silent and stealthy so that no Cameron, disgruntled from a night on hard floors, might hear and challenge us.

But not all Clennon House slept. In the kitchen, standing by the postern door, was the minister, Peter Finlay; and I sighed a sigh of complete defeat, and considered that God had answered my prayers in a most unkind fashion.

Then he stunned me by saying quietly, "Do not linger, Anne. You have very little time."

I stared at him in the meagre light. "Do you know where I go?"

"I talked with Robert MacLeish before he left last evening. I delayed him as long as possible, but I fear he will bring the English soldiers within an hour or so. You must hasten."

"But you are a minister of the Kirk," I whispered. "You have no reason to help him."

"I am a man of God," he said softly, "and that is reason enough to save any man from hanging." He put out his hand and touched my head, and it was a blessing I had not reckoned for. "Simon Stewart is my friend," he said, "and he is not so ungodly that I could turn my back on him in his time of need."

"I think you would not turn your back on any man," I said, close to tears, "whatever his sins."

"I could do no less than He," said Peter Finlay, "if I would show men the meaning of His word."

The white bands of his calling, the dark suit of clothes, ceased to have meaning for me; I saw only his compassion, his tenderness, his humble and devout goodness that would go with me the rest of my life and warm my heart.

"My prayers go with you," he said, and stood aside; and Kitty and I ran across the courtyard and slipped through the gates, and there in the dark shadows of the wood Lachlan waited with three of Walter's horses.

He lifted me to the saddle without a word, and I whispered, "Godspeed," to the two of them.

"God speed yourself," said Lachlan. "There's no time to spare. Are you certain you'd not like me to go in your stead?"

I shook my head, and bid them farewell with a smile and a lifted hand, and spurred my horse across the burn and up the hill.

My head was clear, my hands steady on the reins, and I was not afraid. Whatever happened, it could be no worse than I had already known. And it was good to be riding across the moors again, smelling the wet heather and peat, feeling the clean wind against my face.

Riding, riding past the mute incurious faces of the tall rocks, past the clumps of trees and all the high barren hills. Riding through the last narrow defile leading to the moor and the track below, then pausing briefly to stare down the track and know a great relief that no horses were in sight. Galloping across the track and the moor to the woods beyond, thinking that the *Marie* would be closer than Torra and some Stewart there would carry my warning in time.

But I had not reached the woods when I heard the horse behind me, the clatter of its hoofs muffled by the thick wet grass but carried plainly to me on the still morning air; and the merciless thudding suddenly assumed monstrous proportions, as if all the hounds of Hell were pounding after me across the empty moors.

I dared not look behind me, and yet I knew I must. I hit desperately at the mare's flanks with my whip, feeling her lunge forward with nervous resentment; then I turned my head and saw the rider emerge from the glen behind me, following me so closely that he must have been only a short distance behind me for some time.

It was Walter. I did not need to see his white face, or to recognize his billowing brown cloak; I had only to see the manner in which he was driving his horse to the limit of endurance, with such a grim and ruthless set to his shoulders and hands that I imagined his large spurs must be bloodied with his determination to overtake me.

I could not take Mally through the woods at such a breakneck pace; by the same token, neither could Walter keep his horse once he reached the underbrush beneath the trees. So I reined in the mare abruptly and slipped from the saddle, and held my skirts high so that I might better run like the wind. Faster than the wind, it must be, else he would surely catch me; and my desperation put wings to my feet and propelled me over the rough ground with no regard for the branches that slapped me in the face, the damp boggy spots that clutched at my slippers, the sharp fingers of the young alders that tried insidiously to entrap me. I was almost at the strip of moor between the wood and the sea; I could hear Walter behind me, but with a last spurt of tremendous effort I could make it, could get close enough to the cove where the *Marie* lay hidden and shout a warning.

There was the stretch of rock-strewn moor where I had first seen Monleigh, lying with his hands behind his head; there, in another moment, were the distant turrets of Torra etched against the dawn-streaked sky; there, just beyond a sloping ridge of heather, were the rugged boulders that belied the existence of a tranquil cove below.

I could not lag, so close to victory; I could not collapse, or surrender to the burning torture of my lungs. I
must not think of Walter, so close on my heels that his
rasping breathing sounded quite loudly in my ears.

I gained the top of the ridge, but I went no further.
Walter's heavy hand closed on my cloak, almost ripping it
from my back; I was thrown off balance, and his hands
caught at me again, scrabbled at me with an animal's wild
ferocity. I had not made it; he had caught me, after all.

He flung me around, and for the rest of my life I shall
not be able to forget the look in his eyes, the shape of his
face, the feel of his hands. He had lost all control, after
so many years of rigid discipline; he was no longer human,
no longer recognizable as Walter Clennon. He was a beast
of prey, his hands were long claws reaching for my throat,
he intended to kill me.

I think I screamed, but I am not certain of it. I tried it,
surely, and in my terror I heard no sound issuing from my
throat. Then there was no chance to try again; I felt his
hands close about my neck, tighten there until I could no
longer breathe but knew only the great choking pain of
death staring me in the face.

I had given up in that last moment, had admitted defeat.
And it is somehow good to know that I did not flinch in
the final accounting, or close my eyes and turn my face
away. Perhaps it is only that the fearful anticipation of
death is far greater than the actuality; when it is come
upon us, and naught can be done to prevent it, we get to
know a calm and stoical desire to leave life with the same
innate courage with which we enter it.

But I did not die. Someone came between us, flinging
Walter away from me with such force that I went reeling
backward, coming up against a hard arm which immediately went around me to steady my balance.

Monleigh stood there, sword in hand, facing Walter
Clennon in my stead; and it was Evan who steadied me
and held me upright. I had no strength left to wonder
how they came to be there. I only knew that they had
come, they had appeared out of thin air to snatch me
back from a certain and terrible death.

For a moment no one moved or spoke. The sea murmured and a breeze stirred in the treetops, and I caught
my breath on a long sobbing sigh.

Monleigh was bareheaded; he wore a white shirt and a scarlet plaid belted into a kilt, and the fiery sky behind him took up the colours and repeated them in a thunderous blaze all across the wide arc of the heavens. He towered over Walter; there was such strength and power gathered up in him that I did not wonder that Walter still crouched, immobile and bemused, on the uneven ground where Monleigh had thrown him in that first moment.

Then the spell was abruptly broken. Walter straightened to his full height, reached for his sword. There was no expression on his face, only a blank icy fury that he had been interrupted. He did not speak, nor show any recognition of Monleigh; but all four of us standing there knew that his sword was poised for the kill, that there would be only one survivor of the battle to be joined between the two men who had waited so long to face each other across cold steel.

"Take the lass away," Monleigh said, never taking his eyes from Walter.

Evan turned me, holding my arms so tightly against my body that I could not have struggled even had I any such wish. We walked over the rise, down the slight slope to the level moor, continued to the very edge of the rugged precipice with its jumble of boulders marking the dangerous edge.

I looked below at the *Marie*. A punt was drawn up on the narrow wet shingle, a clansman standing guard over it. The ship was yet at anchor, but I noted that her decks were cleared and her crew stood ready for action at a single word from their captain. They were looking up, toward the summit of the cliff; and in the quiet air I heard a muttered impatient curse as plainly as if the man had stood beside me in Evan's place.

The harsh ring of steel against steel did not pause. It went on and on, with an inexorable steadiness of pace; the minutes dragged until they became separate endless years which stretched into eternity. Evan stirred uneasily, his hands tightened on my arms; but still the measured metallic beat never faltered but continued unabated, hastened, slowed carefully, scraped gratingly against my raw nerves until I longed to scream, to beat my hands against Evan's chest and destroy the tension rising to an unbearable intensity.

Then, abruptly, there was silence again, followed by an odd groaning sigh. More silence, threatening and ominous, and the sound of footsteps. And then nothing but silence.

His voice, quiet and oddly weary, came from behind me.

"Loose her, Evan. It is finished."

Evan took his hands from my arms. I turned, rubbing the blood back to life where he had held me in his tight grip; and Evan, looking at neither of us, began to climb down the twisting path to the shore.

I stared at Monleigh, at the sword still unsheathed in his hand; and one portion of my mind noted with a numbed impassivity that he had wiped it clean, while another clamoured with surging fear that I was once again to blame, I had forced him to this final irrevocable disaster.

At last he slipped his sword into its scabbard.

"You'll not be a bride this day," he said quietly.

"Is he dead?"

"Aye, he is dead."

I took a deep breath and discovered that I was trembling.

"Another moment or two," he said, "and it would have been you instead." Then, still in that cool level voice, "The bruises are beginning to show on your throat."

My hands moved involuntarily to my throat, felt the skin flinch from further hurtful pressure. I did not take them away immediately, however, as if by hiding the betraying marks from his view I might also keep hidden another shameful, if less tangible, blemish.

"Why did you come?" he asked then.

"The English know you intend to sail," I said. "Walter sent Robert for them last evening. He rode to meet them before dawn, but they must have been delayed." I added, attempting to steady the tremor in my voice, "He came back. He remembered I might try to warn you."

His eyes flickered over me, narrowed perceptibly. "It would seem," he said, "that the mischief we played the Clennons caused you more trouble than we reckoned for."

"It is done with," I said. "He is dead."

Our eyes met, and I saw the cold implacable gray of his as they had been when he came between Walter and me.

"Tell me what happened."

"No," I said, and repeated, "he is dead."

After a moment he said, his voice gone dangerously low, "I think I had more reason to kill him than I knew."

"He was mad. He must have been mad."

A muscle moved in his cheek, as if I had struck him; beyond that slight betraying sign, he was as inscrutable as always. But his eyes moved over me, came back to my face; and I knew that somehow my brief words had told him all that had happened during those dark hours preceding the dawn. Or perhaps, I thought with a weary despair, such dishonour showed on one's face like an ugly scar, forever disfiguring, marking one as odiously soiled and misused in the sight of those clear gray eyes.

"I had hoped to provoke him sufficiently to expose himself," he said, "but I did not imagine he would exact his revenge from you."

"You could not have known. He deceived me. He has deceived all of Scotland."

"He has never deceived me," Monleigh said flatly. "My error of judgment was to overlook his vicious habit of spending his rage on those least able to defend themselves. I had thought to take the brunt of his ill temper myself."

He had not moved, nor taken his eyes from my face; but his voice was edged with so cold and bitter an anger that I felt pause to wonder if he wished Walter Clennon alive again that he might deal the man a more ruthless and tormenting punishment than the swift finality of death.

"It doesn't matter. I am here, alive and whole."

"Small thanks to me. Was there no one in Clennon House to come to your aid?"

I shook my head. "No one knew. We were alone in Walter's chamber, and the door was latched." Then, because I was unutterably weary of thinking and speaking about it, I abruptly changed the subject. "So that was your reason for coming to Clennon House last evening. You still sought to show the foolish spinster the error of her ways."

"I fear I succeeded far too well."

"Did you never consider the simple expedient of telling me the truth about Walter?"

"Would you have believed me?" he countered.

I was obliged to say, quite honestly, "I don't know." I added ruefully, "Yet a warning might have saved me a certain amount of unpleasantness."

"No one," he said, "can save another from the consequences of wilful delusion."

"Wilful?" I repeated, taken aback. "You it was who advised me to marry him, who was pleased to rid yourself of my attentions by handing me to him with your blessing."

"I gave you no advice," he said curtly, "and no blessing. I only reminded you that the choice was your own."

The choice was mine? Only a choice between two evils, I thought miserably, a choice, with whatever unhappiness it might bring me, which might best fill the emptiness of the long years ahead, the frightening prospect of a lifetime without Simon Stewart.

"What choice was left me," I said, low, "once you had so bluntly refused me?"

"One would think," he said, "that recent circumstances would have better taught you the way of thinking with some measure of honesty and clarity. But apparently not; a pity for one so fair to be so muddleheaded in the bargain."

Confused, desperately unhappy, still stunned by all the shocking events leading to this moment, I stood there before him, feeling much like a chastened and tearful child, and said nothing.

For a long moment he looked down at me without speaking; then, putting his hands on his hips, he smiled faintly, his face taking on that amused and yet curiously compassionate expression I had come to know so well.

"So a poor hapless Anne Lindsay has had that taste of life once promised her," he said quietly, "and doubtless has not found it to her liking."

"No," I said, vastly grateful for his matter-of-factness, "I did not. And had I any say in the matter, I dare swear I'd have preferred a less harrowing introduction to the vagrancies of the world."

"But you are alive, as you pointed out. Alive and whole."

I lifted my chin. "Yes. Think what you will, I'll not be so easily bested by such as Walter Clennon."

"Then it was not a fate worse than death itself," Monleigh persisted softly. "He did not dishonour you as cruelly as he believed."

"Walter Clennon?" I said scornfully. "Indeed, it would take more of a man than he to so defeat me."

I met his eyes, saw the warm laughter flickering there, and suddenly I knew that the words I had just spoken, in defiance and self-defence, contained a greater portion of truth than I had imagined.

"I was mistaken," he said. "You have learned something about honest thinking, after all."

Another man, no doubt, would have behaved differently. He would have offered me a lavish sympathy, would have rubbed the soothing balm of masculine tenderness upon my bruised sensibilities, would be swift to comfort me with reassurances that never again would I be subjected to such infamous debasement. Another man, and perhaps quite properly, would expect me to swoon in his protective arms, would seek to dry my bitter tears, and all the while would attempt, with a great gallantry, to hide his conviction that I was, in truth, pitifully misused and maltreated beyond all hope of maidenly recovery.

But Monleigh was not such another man. He only smiled at me, and all at once there was no shame, no dishonour, no odious scar to mark and torment me forever. Walter Clennon might never have touched me, the hours of that dark night might never have happened, so surely did Monleigh erase the taint of them from my memory with his smile, his quiet pride in my faltering attempt to be as clear-thinking as he would have me.

"Did you know," he said, "that the English paid Walter Clennon to spy for them?"

"I am not surprised," I said. "He did not need the money, but he had sufficient purpose to spy on his neighbours. That, then, was why he was so furious at you for stealing the papers from his room. Had you suspected him before?"

"I have a suspicious nature," he said, "but I would not condemn a man without proof."

No, I thought, he would not; he had too much honest scruple to brand a man a villain before the world for no more reason than a personal dislike. And I would that a

few pious Covenanters of my acquaintance might know
him as I did, thereby learning a thing or two about fair
play and honour.

"Now you have the proof," I said, "and it is too late.
You cannot condemn a dead man."

"I am not so sure that it is too late."

I looked at him, waiting.

"The papers are aboard the *Marie* for safekeeping, but I
will gladly hand them to you."

"I've no use for them."

"Think carefully on't, lass."

I met his eyes steadily. Aye, I might find some small use
for such incriminating proof of Walter Clennon's perfidy; it
would not surprise me greatly if Margaret could be persuaded to pay highly to keep her brother's name pure and
unsullied before the world. There lay my security, my
safety, in a small packet of papers stolen from a careless
owner who now lay dead, finally foiled in his desperate
efforts to conceal the truth.

"I want no part of them," I said, "nor any further part
of Walter Clennon."

He looked, of a sudden, as if I had pleased him beyond
measure. And had I been given enough time, I thought with
a sigh, it was not beyond possibility that I could have given
him even better proof of my aptness as a pupil.

"When you came," he said, "did you think to escape with
me?"

"No," I said truthfully. "But perhaps I hoped you would
ask me."

"Did you?" he said. "Did you think it might be some
small comfort in your old age to remember that I had
finally come to ask you, and that you had the pleasure of
refusing me at last?"

I had lost all hope of understanding him and his reasons
for inflicting such endless pain.

"You seem quite certain that I would refuse."

He shrugged. "I know you better than you imagine."

"It is too late now, in any event," I said dully. "If I left,
they would know that you killed Walter."

"They will know," he replied calmly, "whether you leave
or stay."

"I will lie. Perhaps they will believe me."

Our voices went on and on against the possibility of silence, against the minutes moving inexorably toward the end. For it was the end; I had known, in that instant when he looked at me with his bared sword in hand, that there could be no other answer.

"You see, I have no sword." I looked down at my skirts, torn and muddy from my struggle with Walter. "I will tell them that we came to stop you, and were set upon by freebooters. Walter was killed as he tried to protect me. They may not believe me, but they can prove nothing."

His eyes were a cold gray once again. "Robert will know the truth, and Margaret. They are not fools."

"But they can only suspect, for they know only a part of the truth. Peter Finlay will help me."

"So you think to protect my good name. I dislike to think of your disappointment, lass, when you discover that the name of Monleigh is scarcely worthy of such sacrifice."

His scorn touched my nerves and sent them throbbing like small knives against my misery.

"There is Margaret," I said slowly, thinking of the barren and empty years before her now that her last bulwark against loneliness lay dead in the heather below Torra. "I cannot leave her alone."

"After all she has done to you," he said, "I am surprised you can yet think of her so gently." Then, with a twist of his mouth, "You've still a heart like warm butter, Anne Lindsay. One day, I fear, it may prove your ruin."

His eyes were not so sardonic as his voice, nor did they reproach me for my lamentable weak-mindedness. He merely looked as if he considered me very young and foolish and somewhat misguided.

"Did Walter tell you," he asked abruptly, "of his desire to avenge my wife's death?"

I nodded.

"Have you no curiosity? Would you not like to hear the whole of the truth before you see the last of me?"

"I am done with curiosity."

"Could it be that you are afraid of the truth?"

"You need not speak of it now," I said unevenly.

"You once said you loved me. Do you still, believing I murdered my wife?"

The terrible words, so long avoided and ignored, were no less frightening when spoken aloud between us.

"I don't care," I said, "it doesn't matter."

"Once before you saw me kill a man," he said slowly, "and you looked at me as if you thought the blood would never wash clean from my hands. Does it matter so little to you that I may have killed my wife?"

"I do not believe you murdered her."

Why do we not call her by name, I thought desperately? Lucy, the pretty child, the pitiful nagging wife. Lucy, the one who went before me, whose narrow grave is now encrusted with green lichen and knows only the lifeless quiet of a tomb, the quiet of white snow in winter, and the drifting thorn blossoms of spring. Lucy, Walter's betrothed, who had fallen in love with Monleigh.

"Why don't you believe it?" he asked relentlessly.

"You were kind to her. Evan said you were kind, even to the end."

"Does it turn your stomach?" he said softly. "Does your tight little conscience revolt at the thought of kindness and murder within the same heart?"

I thought of Walter and the black villainy disguised by his mask of kindness; and I said, with a trace of panic, "It has nothing to do with my conscience. I don't believe it, I will never believe it."

"Walter Clennon is dead, by my hands. My unwashed hands, if you like, and 'tis likely they'll kill again."

"But I am alive," I said. My hair caught in the freshening breeze and blew across my face. "I am alive because of you."

He regarded me silently for a long while. The wind whistled among the rocks and the sea toppled against the shore, so that the silence was uneasy and alive; and my ears strained for the sound of galloping hoofbeats that would be a troop of red-coated English soldiers.

"And if I said that the rumours are true? That I killed her?"

"I would hate it," I said at last. "Perhaps I would also grow to hate you."

"By all rights," he said, "you should already have come to hate me. You should have learned the folly of loving a man of such uncertain character."

"No," I whispered, "I cannot pluck it out whenever I wish, like a vagrant weed, and say good riddance to it. It will never be gone from me, no matter what you have done or will do."

And incredibly, something changed in his face as I spoke, something cold and harsh faded away, just as my own despair had so recently been vanished to oblivion.

"I did not kill her, Anne. She killed herself, with the aid of a dirty old woman she found somewhere in the hills."

I closed my eyes at last, hearing his words as if from a great distance. I must not look at him as he tells me, I thought, I must spare him as best I may.

"She did not want the bairn she carried, and she managed to rid herself of it. She gave me no chance to kill her; she was dying before I knew." His voice still level and quiet, he added, "But had I known, I would have strangled her to death and found great pleasure in it."

So he had told me at last, and I did not have to ask. But it did not matter, as I had told him; it was too late. Mayhap it had been too late for us from the start, and nothing mattered, nothing was important but the hours we had known together, and the words we had spoken or left unsaid, the aching fire between us which would not come again in a lifetime.

"You must go," I said, and opened my eyes.

If I still prayed that he would argue, or protest, or find the words to ask me to sail with him, after all, I was doomed to a more bitter disappointment than I had yet known.

"Aye," he said, "I must go."

He did not kiss me good-bye. He took a step and stood close above me; putting one hand under my chin, he lifted my face and looked into it, and for a moment the tiny flames in his eyes made me think he would smile again. But he did not. He only looked at my face, his eyes moving from my mouth to my eyes and hair, and back to my mouth, and his hand tightened momentarily before it dropped away.

Then he turned and descended the path to the shore and the punt, and Evan pushed it away from the shingle with a single mighty shove of his oar.

And so I stood and watched his ship put out past the headland, and somewhere behind me in the heather, I imagined that Walter Clennon lay with his face turned away from the sea, as if his staring eyes, even after death, could not bear to gaze upon the final and incredulous proof that Monleigh had triumphed once again.

The *Marie* bore due west, and the first rays of the morning sun stained her topsails the brilliant red of blood and shaded downward to shadows and the proud racing sheer of her dark hull.

It was the last time I saw him, nor did I look again upon that great gray mass of stone towering above the sands, Monleigh's stronghold of Torra, guarding the approach from the western sea.

⟬ 15 ⟭

BUT what use were memories, after all?

They did not ease the pain one jot, or the sick tears, or the frightening despair. They could not free Monleigh from his stone cell in Edinburgh Castle, nor blunt the sanctimonious wrath of the Kirk, nor give us a single precious hour like those we had once known.

I thought of Walter, who had died with such hatred in his heart. Had he known, I wondered, in that last moment when he faced Monleigh's ruthless sword and felt himself grow winded and helpless from the rage consuming him, that we would go unpunished for his death, and did the knowledge make the act of dying a more grimly frustrating one than men are normally called upon to bear?

For we had gone free, the two of us, and only Walter had known the final judgment, had been tried and convicted on the moors below Torra. Had there been a public trial, with all the testimony neatly arranged on either side, I cannot doubt the outcome. Walter would have had his due revenge. For who would have dared to give credence to our tale; who in all that hostile accusing world would have taken our word against that of the Kirk, Margaret, Robert, and all the powerful and godly host Walter had so carefully grouped around him to hide his sins? Who, except perhaps a few disreputable Stewarts, would have agreed with Monleigh that a miserable Anne Lindsay deserved another chance at that life Walter Clennon was so determined to wrest from her that day?

Oh, I did not wish Walter dead, nor had I ever; but he forced Monleigh to an urgent and inescapable choice, and I would be less than human were I to regret for a single moment that Monleigh had not hesitated, that he had con-

sidered my life a worthy and just trade for Walter's there
on the bleak moors above the sea.

So I lied for him, as best I could, and strangely enough
they believed my tale of robbers. Even Margaret, with her
endless lament and suspicious eyes, did not dare to call
me liar. There was about me those days, I think, an air
of remote and implacable aloofness, of emotions locked
so tightly within that I moved and breathed and lived in a
world apart, where no one could enter in or persuade me
to depart. They thought it grief for Walter, and in my
misery I cared little what they believed. It would serve to
protect and hide the truth, that much I realized, and if it
seemed strange that Walter, in dying, should give aid to
the man he hated most, I spent no time pondering that
final irony of an exceedingly ironic Fate.

Aye, we were freed of any blame, Monleigh and I.
Monleigh had been brought to grief, they had finally
snared him—but not because of Walter's death.

My position with Margaret was not clearly defined,
however, for I stood above the servants by virtue of my
brief betrothal to Walter, and yet could not be accorded
the exalted status of widow which would have been mine
but for a matter of a few short hours of havoc; but for
all practical purposes little had changed, and I fetched and
carried for Margaret, and prepared hot possets and delicacies for her, and listened, with a greater understanding
than before, to her bitter denunciation of that same Fate
who had treated me so shabbily.

Without Walter to be persuaded to her wishes, Margaret
soon ceased to suffer ill health, and within a few months
she forever abandoned the outmoded device of taking to
her bed with a sudden attack of some undefined malady.
If she still suspected behind her pale blue eyes, and if she
hated still, she was no more or less vindictive toward me
than before; and I had been unable to ascertain whether
she kept me with her for the comfort of my companionship or to assuage the world and its conventions which
dictated that I should not be turned away from her door
now that all succour in a cruel world had been snatched
away from me with Walter's death. What I thought of the
succour Walter might have offered me had he lived, or
what Margaret thought of the succour he had given me in

dying, would doubtless have created a curious sensation were the world to discover the truth; but neither Margaret nor I felt disposed to discussing the matter with the world or with each other.

But as I stood in my bedchamber that afternoon and looked out at the dying day, I wondered if Walter had been the final victor, after all. I had not been murdered at his hands, I still lived, but at so great a cost I perforce concluded that Fate was unduly angry that I had circumvented her plans for me.

Monleigh would hang, for they would make certain that he did not escape them again, and I would be truly alone in the world. Never again would I awake in the dawn to think of him watching the same crimson sky from the slanting decks of his ship, or hear a high gale out of the North Sea shaking our shutters and picture him standing at the wheel, his face running with rain as he watched the trim of his sails, his eyes laughing, in a way they had, because it pleased him to be riding out a stormy night together with his fair *Marie*. I could no longer content myself with the knowledge that somewhere he still walked proud and free, his dark head held high and his arrogance unhumbled, that because he lived and laughed, and went his turbulent reckless way somewhere in the same world, I might go my own way with a tolerable courage and peace.

"He will hang. At last he will pay for his sins."

A portion of the words repeated my own thoughts, but I had not spoken aloud. I stood quite still, startled and wary, and then with a stifled sigh turned to face Margaret.

"What do you want, Margaret?" I said quietly. "Your guests will think you uncivil to leave them."

"My guests have long since departed. It is almost night."

"So it is," I said. "I had not noticed."

"You never dreamed they would catch him, did you?" she said. "But I have always known that his sins would find him out. As will yours, Anne, when the day of reckoning comes."

"Do you deem my sins so heinous that I should hang beside him?"

"You will suffer enough," she said calmly. " 'Tis a more fitting retribution than the gallows."

She stood with her hands clasped before her, like a stern and avenging saint I had once seen carved in stone upon a tomb; and it seemed to me that her heart was no less cold and insensible than the one chiselled from marble for that passionless bit of statuary.

"Do you hate me so?" I asked very softly.

She said nothing. And that was answer enough.

But I tried again. "Is there no hope for us, Margaret? If we are to live together, we should strive to find some measure of harmony."

"It would be sacrilege," she said coolly, "to compromise with evil."

"Have you never sinned?" I asked, wonderingly. "Not even a small sin?"

"Time and again. But I have seen the errors of my ways, and have prayed for forgiveness."

"Yet you deny forgiveness to me."

"You have not sought it," she said. "You refuse to admit that you have sinned. You are diseased, in mind and flesh, and vaunt your immorality with an insolence that profanes the Kirk of Christ. There can be no forgiveness for such as you."

"Do you follow God's counsel," I asked, "or that of the Kirk?"

" 'Tis one and the same."

"No," I said, "I do not believe that God reserves Himself for presbyterians, nor that He turns His face away from all the unenlightened who do not follow the Covenant."

"His very name is blasphemous on your tongue."

"You may interpret Him as you wish," I said, "but He is not your own personal possession."

"You have become quite a scoffer, have you not? But one day, Anne, I will live to see you rue such heresies." Her thin mouth tightened in a semblance of a smile. "I think that day will be granted me soon. When Monleigh swings from a gibbet, you will be rewarded for your carnal behaviour."

For a moment I was sickened beyond speech; and then I knew only a vast and weary pity for all such women as

Margaret, who must spend their lives in barren loneliness, who had never known love in any form except it came to them in fearful shaming dreams to be despised next day and prayed away, who would indeed be horrified were they to meet love face to face.

She has never felt his words against her throat, I thought clearly, nor put her hands on his dark head to hold it close. She has not laughed with him, that rowdy laughter following so close upon the heels of passion, another side, warm and intimate, of the bright coin of love; she is ignorant of the high exhilaration of fencing with words, as one might bandy a sword, of taking to one's self the immense pleasure of being beloved and loving wholly in return. She knows nothing of such things, she will never know; and so I cannot blame her for her certainty that God has but one face, and that a sternly righteous mask of hatred, of fiery vengeance.

"Perhaps you are right," I said quietly. "Perhaps. And yet, somehow I think He weeps for Monleigh and me, and all those like us. Weeps, and puts out a hand to comfort us, and keeps aside a small portion of His heart for all such poor and miserable sinners."

Margaret frowned in exasperation. "It may be of some interest to you," she said, "that Robert and Jemmy Mac-Leish will shortly take up residence here with me. I would advise you to curb your wanton tongue henceforth; Robert will take it ill to hear a member of my household speak such wickedness."

I considered this newest development. I could not but see the advantages for Margaret in such a move, for now she could daily enjoy that communion of soul and mind which passed between those fortunate members of society whose convictions, both in theory and practice, were identical to the last fanatical degree.

"I am glad, Margaret," I said gently. "They will be a great pleasure and consolation to you."

And those two energetically pious persons would offer her a companionship, a bulwark against loneliness, that I could never hope to match; and even should Jemmy, of a certainty, refuse to fetch and carry for anyone but herself, it was still a wise and profitable move for Margaret Clennon.

"I should imagine," I went on, "that you will have little use for me in your household now, wickedness or no'."

Margaret regarded me stonily, her hands still folded before her.

"You will remove your possessions to your former chamber," she said. "It has been occupied by one of the maids, but I shall find another bed in some corner for her." She added coolly, "It would be quite remiss of you to think that Jemmy and I cannot find sufficient duties for you in the future."

So I was to be banished to that small room beneath the eaves; I was once again become the chambermaid, not only serving Margaret but a sharp-tongued Jemmy Mac-Leish as well.

"You need feel no further responsibility for me," I said. "But I must ask another night beneath your roof, since it will take me a few hours to make arrangements to move my possessions elsewhere."

For a curious moment I thought she intended to laugh in my face.

"Where do you think to go?" she asked. "A penniless wench, out of favour with the Kirk, leagued by gossip with a criminal who will soon be hung and quartered, a shameful heretic. Do you dream there will be any charity in Edinburgh for the likes of you?"

"I am not entirely helpless, Margaret," I reminded her. "I can still sew a fine seam, and I think I should make an excellent ladies' maid. You yourself have seen to my training."

"You forget," she said, "I know too much of your habits. No decent lady would countenance you in her household, even as a servant, once I made the facts plain to her."

"Then perhaps an indecent one," I said, "who would scarcely be likely to countenance you. I am not so particular about such matters as I might once have been."

There was a slight pause, but her pale eyes did not leave my face.

"I have a question to ask you," she said finally, "and I will have the truth."

I waited, not greatly curious, my mind still concerned with the meagre, and mayhap nonexistent, chance I might have of escaping her.

"Do you know aught of the papers that were stolen from Walter's chamber the night before his death?"

I stared at her, and my mind began a furious whirling, like that of a small ball sent spinning by a careless and impetuous hand.

"It was Simon Stewart and his ruffians who attacked Clennon House that night," she went on. "You need not deny it, I know the truth of that. But he is to die now, and the papers have not yet been found. Do you know if he kept them in his possession when he sailed from Scotland?"

I could not answer, I did not dare.

"Answer me," she demanded tautly, "and give me the truth. I can make your life most unpleasant, Anne, with no more than a word or two in the proper quarters, and I fully intend to do so should you attempt to lie to me now."

But she has not sought the truth before, a small clear voice cut through my confused thoughts; she has never hinted that she knew anything of the papers except that they were stolen on that long-ago night. And whatever she knows of me, she has known for some time past, yet she has never threatened me before. Why has she been silent until now?

"Walter told me that papers were stolen from his chamber," I said slowly, "as well as a certain amount of gold. I know no more than that."

"I warn you," she said, more coldly than before, "do not lie to me."

Was it because I had finally defied her, had betrayed my intention to leave her bondage at last? Or was it because Monleigh stood fair to die on the gallows and she must know if Walter's secret would die with him? My mind ceased to spin, paused incredulously at the possibility that Margaret, with her concern about the mislaid papers, had known the truth about Walter all the while.

I met her eyes as steadily as I could. Once again, I told myself, I must stand aghast and stunned because my judgment had proved me false; Margaret, like her brother, was not all she seemed, I had gone as wide of the mark in my estimation of her character as when I imagined I understood Walter so well. When would I learn, when would I cease to be astonished that I was, as Monleigh had once told me, a naïve innocent who knew nothing of the world and its peoples?

"Do you know," Margaret whispered, "what was written in those papers?"

I could not have lied with any semblance of poise, yet I still refused to divulge that certain truth; and so I remained silent.

"Yes, I believe you know," she said blankly. Then, "You could only have learned their contents from Simon Stewart, and you have not seen him since. When did he tell you? When?" Like a deadly spider, watching me, waiting to pounce, building her poisonous web with words that would entangle me the more even as I denied them. "It must have been that morning, you had no other chance."

I tried to defend myself. "The papers must have been vastly important," I said, "for you to show such concern."

"I have long suspected that you lied about that day," she said, "and now I know. You saw Monleigh that dawn, it was he who killed Walter."

"It was my life or Walter's," I said evenly. "Whatever Monleigh did, he is guilty of no crime but that of saving my life."

To my vast surprise, she did not dwell on Walter's death. Nor did she, at that moment, resemble a deadly spider. For the first time since I had known her, Margaret Clennon appeared confused, uncertain, almost distrait. A slight flush stained her thin white face, her hands moved together as if she must clasp them tightly to prevent an untoward trembling.

"You have known since then," she said, "and yet have kept the knowledge to yourself. Why?"

"I did not seek to cause you more pain," I said softly.

For a long while she did not answer, and we faced each other there in the cold chamber where the sun no longer warmed the air and the shadows grew chill and gray with the gloom of approaching dusk.

"He was enraged," she said at last. "I know his rages, you see, I have spent a lifetime teaching him to better restrain himself. But I could do nothing with him that evening." Then she added, low, "He told me what the papers contained immediately he discovered their loss. I tried to tell him he was insane to play so dangerous a game, but the harm had been done. There was nothing I could do, nothing at all."

I said nothing. Suddenly, as I looked at her, I knew that I had mistaken her. She was more a woman than I had thought; there was a weakness, a chink in her armour. She had loved a brother and I had loved Monleigh; but because the faces of love are so many and so varied, I had not given a proper consideration to that one which showed itself to Margaret Clennon.

Whatever Walter's crimes, she would forever hold him in her memory as a beloved brother, a paragon of virtue, the godliest man to ever sign the Covenant. His noble countenance would remain unblemished, his purity unsullied, his reputation damaged by no man living. Margaret would have it so, at whatever cost; and in the secret places of her heart she would not deem the cost too high.

Just so, I thought ruefully, did I regard a certain rogue and villain; we were foolish women, Margaret and I, swayed more by tender emotion than reason, and more alike than I would have deemed possible. And by virtue of that shared weakness, we had somehow gained a better understanding of each other than we had ever known before.

"I do not think it necessary, after all," she said slowly, "for you to change your chamber at Jemmy's convenience. Perhaps she would be better pleased with the apartment on the floor above."

I greatly admired Margaret at that moment, but I did not weaken. She did not need me, nor had she ever; and my time of penance, for so I had considered it, was no more than a farce, a foolish and unnecessary martyr's role which did not, when all was said, become me very well.

"I am leaving, Margaret," I said quietly. "I have no wish to stay, and I do not believe you will keep me against my will."

"Then," she said, "you must arrange proper accommodations for yourself. It is not safe for a young woman to live alone in Edinburgh." With no change of expression, no emphasis in her voice, "I will settle a certain amount of gold to your account. You will possibly do quite well for yourself as a seamstress, once my friends learn of your intentions, but I would not have you in any need."

"Never mind, Margaret," I said gently. "My need is not for bribery."

She did not believe me; it would seem a common failing of human nature to judge others by one's self.

"I will give you the gold, regardless," she said. "Do what you will with it."

I sighed and walked past her to the door, taking my cloak from a chair. But I realized at once, when I had slipped it around my shoulders, that it was Margaret's, and I took it off immediately and looked around the room for my own.

"You may have it," Margaret said quickly. "I have several, and you have long needed a better cloak. There is a purse of gold in a pocket of the lining; you may have that also."

I would not have dreamed myself still capable of feeling such pity for her.

"I do not want your cloak, Margaret, nor your gold."

"It is not bribery," she said, "whatever you may think."

"Then what would you name it?"

She brushed her hand across her forehead, as if to erase the puzzled frown that kept returning there.

"Perhaps a token of my thanks," she said. "I am grateful to you."

"I have not asked for thanks, or for gratitude." I added, more gently, "Margaret, you look quite ill. Please go and lie down until you are feeling better. And you needn't fret; I will not cause any trouble for you."

"Where are you going?"

"That is my affair," I said firmly. Then, because I would not leave her thinking that I would use my knowledge of Walter Clennon as a weapon over her head, I said, "You see why it would be impossible for us to remain under the same roof, Margaret. I am not the same person I was a few hours past, but it has naught to do with Walter or stolen papers. It is only that I have grown older, I think, and find myself come to a parting in the road ahead."

"You cannot mean to go to him."

"Would it matter so much if I did?"

"They will not allow you to see him. You will only make a fool of yourself, and arouse undue speculation."

"Never fear," I said, quite weary, "I'll not misuse your

reputation. I am merely going for a walk, and have no intention of trying to breach the walls of Edinburgh Castle."

I left her then, without a backward glance, and ran down the stairs. I was on the street before I realized I still carried Margaret's cloak, but I would not go back to that cold gloomy room; there would be time enough to return the cloak, and the gold purse, before I left Margaret's house that night.

The day was nearly ended; the sun had not yet dropped over the horizon, but had long since been hidden behind the grim leaning houses of Edinburgh town. The wind was cold and bitter with a taste of snow in it, and a damp chill ached in the very marrow of my bones. There was a weird yellow cast to the sunset, a jaundiced glow that glanced off the cobbled stones and staring windows with an alien hostility, making the familiar dirty streets appear unusually dismal and drab with winter.

The lamps were being lit, the curtains drawn, suppers put to cook on the fires of countless kitchens, the children had been called in from play. The stench of offal in the gutters was nauseating, and I had gone only a short way when the warning cry of "Gardey-loo!" forced me beneath a balcony to escape being drenched with a pail of refuse thrown from an upper window. A heavy coach passed me, and I dodged inside an open door to avoid being run down; the narrow street did not allow room enough for both, and I had no illusion that the coachman would swerve a single inch on my behalf.

Walking was not a pleasurable occupation in the streets of Edinburgh. But I was not searching for pleasure; and whatever I sought, I knew I would not find it. Despair and misery and heartbreak, once born and bred in the soul, are constant companions who never lag behind but go before one on all the streets of the world, and if I hoped to escape them I was sending myself on a fool's errand.

But I walked steadily on, careless of my direction or surroundings, ignoring the stares and curious comments that greeted me along the way. I must have gone some distance before I realized that someone was following me; perhaps I was first made aware of it by the continual thud of heavy boots, never pausing except as I paused, never deviating from the brisk pace I set down the streets and around corners and through narrow wynds and closes. They came on unceasingly like phantom footsteps, hard on my heels, but no phantom ever clomped with such a noisy clatter and heedlessness of discovery.

I was not so much frightened as puzzled, for if my pursuer was a thief or footpad, he would not attack without the concealment of night; I had only to scream and a passer-by or tradesman would come running to my rescue.

Finally I stopped in my tracks and turned abruptly to face whatever man dared to shadow my footsteps through the streets. He was so close behind me at that moment that he was forced to an equally abrupt halt to avoid stumbling over me.

It was Evan Stewart. He was dressed in dark town clothes and a heavy cloak to cut the bitter wind, and his face was as dark and sombre as his apparel.

"Evan," I whispered incredulously. "Evan Stewart."

We stared at each other there in the windy street with the cold unpleasant stench of Edinburgh thick in our nostrils and the dour inhabitants brushing by us with ill-concealed irritation that we would block the narrow way.

Finally he said bluntly, "We cannot speak here. Can you come wi' me?"

"Yes," I breathed. I did not ask how he came to be in Edinburgh, or where he meant to take me. There was but a single question I longed to ask, and it must wait.

He took my arm without further speech and turned into a dark twisting wynd which led at length to the still-crowded and bustling High Street. Here Evan waited a moment, his eyes searching the street in both directions, and as we stood there a coach-and-four, complete with groom and coachman, slowly came to a stop before us. The groom stepped down quietly, with no flourish, and handed me in; Evan nodded briefly to the coachman and was inside on the seat beside me, the door closed, at the same instant the horses began to move down the hill.

Then he moved, sitting across from me so that he might keep his eyes on the street behind us.

"Is there a chance we might be followed?"

"Not on my account. I often go for a walk, and Margaret will not expect me for some time yet."

"I've waited outside your house the day," he said, "hoping to see you. But I was beginning to doubt my luck."

I was shaken at how nearly I had missed him. "How long have you been here? Surely it is dangerous for you to be in Edinburgh at all."

"Since last evening when they lodged him in the Castle," he said shortly, "and he stands in far greater danger than I."

Then he lapsed into silence, and so I sat quietly and looked at him with much affection, seeing his ugly black-browed face and remembering when and under what circumstances I had seen it before and come to regard it so highly. I would not plague him with foolish questions; he would talk when he felt ready, and until then I was content merely to be with him.

I felt only a small curiosity as to our destination, but I knew enough of Edinburgh to realize that the coach was taking us down the road to the port of Leith, only a few miles from the city proper. It was wise of him to hide there; Leith was no safer than Edinburgh, mayhap, but it was like all seaports, crowded, unspeakably evil, and filled to the rafters with scoundrels and rough seafaring men who cared no more to meet the law face to face than did Evan.

Finally the coach turned into a courtyard and creaked to a halt beneath a swinging sign which proclaimed the dwelling to be an inn and tavern. The groom opened the door of the coach and Evan lifted me down, then turned to pay the coachman.

The inn appeared exceedingly small and crooked in the dusk, and not overly clean; but the light streamed from its windows to wet the cobbled courtyard with wide golden pools, and the voices within sounded very loud and gay and supremely unaware of long-nosed parsons and their laws against imbibing wine and good humours to excess.

"My rooms are above," said Evan, taking my arm. "We must go through the ordinary, but if you pull your hood about your face the men will not take exception to your presence."

And if they did, I thought, I would trust Evan to teach them better manners. I was amused by his plain-spoken

warning that women often went abovestairs in this sort of
public house, but that I must observe the proper rules if
I would arouse no curiosity.

We went inside and made our way through the hubbub
of the tavern; and I was grateful for both the strength of
Evan's hand on my arm and the shielding cover of my
hood. The loud shouts of laughter, the ribald humour
lacing the conversation, the curses, the thud of empty
tankards and the gurgling of the tap over full ones, all the
warmth and masculine vitality of the room swept over and
about me like a great wave; and I was thankful that we
reached the stairs and climbed them without mishap or
comment.

Evan's room was square and low, bare of any furniture
but a bed, a table, and a single chair; but it was very clean,
and boasted a bright counterpane on the bed as well as a
pair of curtains at the windows. A fire burned briskly on
the hearth of a small fireplace, and the candles looked to
be freshly lit.

It was not an unpleasant place to hide; and for a brief
moment of weakness I longed to remain there myself,
hidden from the world for as long as I chose. But the
moment passed, and Evan took my cloak and removed his
own, laying them across the bed.

"Would you like a bit of wine?" he asked.

He did not appear precisely ill at ease, but there was
an odd constraint about him now that we were finally
alone. It was not to be wondered at; the circumstances of
our meeting were in themselves too cheerless and melancholy to permit us any feeling but one of despondency,
and I well knew that Evan Stewart was not a man to
relish hiding away in a public inn while his kinsman and
master paced hopelessly in a prison cell a few miles away.

"Yes," I said softly, "I should like it very much."

"Then make yourself at ease," he said. "I'll be back
shortly."

He closed the door behind him, and I walked to the
window and pulled aside the curtain. The room overlooked
the harbour, but I could see little but the outlines of many
tall slender masts and the sparkle of riding lights across
the water. I tried to close my mind to all but the unfamiliar scene before me; and I succeeded well enough

for a moment or two. Then my thoughts began to push in upon me again, and I felt stifled and sick and wished very much that Evan would return with the wine.

I waited until the door had closed quietly behind him as he came back into the room, and then I could wait no longer.

"How goes it with him, Evan?" I asked, fighting a great lump lodged in my throat. My voice had a tremor, despite all I could do, and so I stared through the wavy panes of the window at the lights of the harbour below until I was more certain of myself. "You see my backbone is still made of jelly, and I've learned no more of courage. I've only my pride to keep me from weeping on your shoulder, and the fear of your ugly frown were I to so forget myself."

When he did not answer, I put my hands on the casement and held tightly to conquer my foolish unsteadiness.

"D'you think it will go ill with him? Will they truly . . ." I paused, unable to continue.

"Hang him? I think it most unlikely."

I whirled so quickly that my skirts made a rustling sound as loud as thunder in the silence, and my heart bid fair to outstrip them in noise, pounding in my temples like a troop of runaway horses.

Monleigh stood there, hands on his hips, surveying me with a faint inscrutable smile on his dark face.

He is no older, I thought erratically; he has changed not a jot since the last time I saw him. The price on that black head is death, how does he dare to linger here; and how did he manage to slip from their clutches, to escape his gaolers in the very shadow of the gallows? He is truly here, standing before me; the ghost has become warm flesh and blood, the memory has suddenly taken on life and urgency of its own.

"And how does it go with you, my sweet Anne?" he said quietly.

"I have never been better content," I murmured, my throat hurting with the words, "than I am at this moment."

"You are thinner than I remember you," he said, "and your green eyes are shadowed."

"I have spent a bad hour or so today."

A brow raised; his eyes laughed at me. "Were you concerned for me? You don't know me very well, after all."

"How came you here?" I said unsteadily. "What witchcraft did you employ to spirit yourself out of Edinburgh Castle?"

"I was spirited out by a troop of English soldiers," he said, sounding very amused, "who thought to take me south by General Monk's orders. It would seem the English do not trust the Scots, and the Scots have fair reason for distrusting the English; and so Monk decided to have the notorious Monleigh sent down to London to Old Noll."

"No doubt he thought you should be exhibited as a prime specimen of the barbaric and murdering Highlanders," I said faintly. "Think of it, all London would have thronged to see you in your cage."

"At the risk of wounding my vanity forever," he said, "I was obliged to decline the tempting offer." His grin widened, warmed his face incredibly. "It took no witchcraft to knock a few English heads together."

"You alone, against a troop of soldiers?"

"You flatter me, my sweet. I had the whole of my ship's crew to come to my aid."

I took a deep breath, and smiled back at him, and thought that I had never been so irrationally happy.

"Then they did not take the *Marie*."

"If you look behind you," he said, "perhaps you can see her from the window."

"In Leith harbour?" I said amazedly.

But why not? He had the nerve, the courage, the effrontery to do just such a thing. They would be scouring the coast for his ship, and all the while she was calmly riding to her anchors in Leith harbour.

"Why did you return to Scotland?" I asked. "Surely Charles Stuart did not send you back to tighten the noose about your neck."

"I had an errand or two to run," he said, "and a certain English general to see."

"Monk?" I asked thoughtfully. "I've heard it whispered that he'd have Royalist leanings were Charles' cause to show any signs of success. Was it Monk you came to see?"

"Affairs of state," Monleigh said lightly. "Don't let your curiosity lead you too far, lass."

But I had my suspicions. "And it was Monk who ordered them to take you to London. He must have known it'd be far easier for you to escape on the road south than if you'd been kept in the Castle."

Monleigh shrugged. "The ways of a general are difficult to fathom."

"Did you see to your errands?"

"With Evan's help," he said, and smiled at me.

He had not moved; he still stood across the room from me, wearing leather breeks and doublet and a white cambric shirt, looking as tanned and fit as if he had never left the deck of his ship, as unperturbed and coolly at his ease as if he had never been taken in chains through Edinburgh, or slept in a dank vermin-ridden cell, or suffered the endless diatribes of his captors.

"I am surprised," I said, "that you would risk the dangers of seeing me."

"Is it so great a danger, Anne Lindsay?"

"Once you said that you cared more for your King and your own neck than for any lass living."

His smile lingered. "Did I tell you that?"

"Near enough. We were speaking of survival, and you said you had developed quite a sharp nose for it."

"Since you've such a clever memory, you'll doubtless recall the day I warned you that it was a dull affair to preserve one's self to no avail."

"I've forgotten nothing you said to me," I retorted, "and I've had a lengthy time to ponder the whole."

"Then surely you have come to a better understanding of me."

"No," I admitted ruefully, "nor have I found the answers to your riddles."

"I suspect you are also inadequate at working simple sums," he said gravely, "and at spelling correctly. Your kinsmen, my sweet, have sadly neglected your training."

"Why did you distrust me?" I asked. "Why did you hint that I would bring you to ruin?"

"When I spoke to you of survival," he said calmly, "I was referring to a matter of vastly greater importance to me than my own neck."

The palms of my hands were damp; and so I unclasped them to wipe them against my skirt.

"The survival of your happiness, as well as my own. As for distrust," he went on, "the heart is an impetuous jade. One cannot always trust its affections to remain constant."

"You thought me fickle," I said incredulously, "and likely to be inconstant?"

It was past belief, he could not be serious.

"You had a habit of indecision," he said, "and wasted a great deal of time in futile quarrel with your conscience."

"Was that so reprehensible?"

"For a lass who would cast her lot with outlaws and join the crew of a smuggler's ship."

"Had you given me time," I said, "I dare swear I'd have rid myself of any lingering scruples."

"But there was no time," he said, quite gently.

After a long moment, I said unevenly, "I should have learned by now that you are not a man to force the pace."

"Aye," he agreed, "you should have, indeed." Then, quietly, "A wise man must learn patience, else he will be undone in the end. 'Tis much like riding a thoroughbred horse untrained to the bridle, or wearing a sword which has been hammered roughly into shape without the tempering art of the swordmaker."

"I do not relish the comparison," I said, "but I think I see your meaning."

"You might well consider yourself flattered to stand in the same company with a man's horse and sword," he said easily. "I can think of few things in life he values so highly."

"But only if they have proved their worth."

He shrugged. "He must be certain they will not fail him at a crucial moment."

"Did you think I would fail you?"

"I thought it too great a risk to put you to the test."

"You were wise to leave me on the shore," I said. "A foolish and deluded spinster such as I would be of less worth to a man than a faulty sword or an untrained horse."

"Foolish and confused," he amended, "and vastly uncertain of herself. I did not care to watch her face, a day or a month or a year later, when she weighed her hasty decision and found it lamentably wanting."

"So you took a course of patient forbearance," I said, "and allowed me to come to a decision. Quite farsighted of you, m'lord."

"Has it been a difficult time for you, lass?"

"A lonely time," I said, "but not unprofitable."

He raised a dark brow. "Indeed?"

"As of today," I said, "I am become a genteel seamstress with a comfortable balance of gold to my account. I've had no clients as yet, you understand, but Margaret Clennon has graciously offered to stand as my patron and recommend my skilful fingers to a select circle of her friends."

"I've heard it said," he remarked, "that a cat always lands on its feet."

"And I protest your insistence on likening me to a horse, or a sword, or yet a cat."

"I thought only to compliment you for being well-bred, finely tempered, and the possessor of a pair of eyes as green as emeralds." Then, lightly, "Do you anticipate a pleasant future as a genteel sewer of seams?"

"A proper one, in any case, were I to accept Margaret's kind offer."

"And quite safely dull."

"Quite," I agreed loftily.

"Do you intend to accept?"

"No," I said, "I think not."

"Then you can no longer count yourself among the foolish, confused, and deluded."

"But I suspect I shall always be a trifle muddleheaded."

His face was grave, but his eyes on mine were warm and bright with laughter. "A fault you must constantly strive to overcome, Anne Lindsay, else you will never snare yourself a man."

"What will you do now?" I asked suddenly.

"I have a plan or two."

"I am sorry," I said, remembering, "about the lass in Dundee. They told me she died; I was very sad to hear it."

His eyes darkened, but he said only, "I hope you said a prayer for her."

"I did," I said softly, "and for the child as well."

"The child is aboard the *Marie*. She is very tearful and

forlorn, and lonely for her mother; but one day, please God, I will persuade her to laugh and sing again."

I should have expected it; it was so like him that I could not understand why I had not thought of it at once.

"Then you will take her with you when you sail?"

"Aye," he said levelly. "I also have aboard a dour woman named Elizabeth, who cooks my food and minds my manners, and sees that my shirts are properly washed."

"Was she content to leave her peat fire and her hearth to go sailing over the world with you?"

"The world is a large place," he said, "and we've sailed over only a small portion of it. But we've been to France a time or two, and Italy, and one day we intend to see the new America."

"Then I imagine Elizabeth often longs for Scotland, and the hills of home."

"Doubtless," he said. "No one can have all his wishes granted at one and the same time; life is no' so perfectly arranged for our convenience. But she has her man, and she likes the life of a sailor, and mayhap one day she'll see her Scotland again."

I steadied my voice as best I could and said, "I should think she would like another woman to keep her company in the midst of that great horde of men."

"You are possibly quite right."

"And the wee lass from Dundee should have someone to teach her to laugh again."

His eyes were steady and dark on mine, and tiny flames flickered suddenly to life in them.

"I am sure of it," he said.

"And what of the Captain? Is he never lonely, does he need nothing but his crew and his ship and a dour woman to wash his shirts and cook his food?"

"The Captain does the work of ten men, hoping that he may be blessed with the dreamless sleep of exhaustion. But the dreams return, night after night, and will not be exorcised."

"Are his dreams so disturbing?"

"He is haunted by the memory of a lass with a sweet mouth and a way about her that stirs a man's blood to fire." He had not moved a muscle, yet I felt as if he had touched me. "She is like the ship he sails, as brave and

fair and winsome, and as easy to love. Do you blame him
for dreaming of her in the long watches of the night, for
holding her image in his heart through all the long days
of the year?"

We had bandied with words long enough. "But he has
only to ask," I said. "She is his for the asking."

His voice was low, suddenly hard and clipped. "No,
lass," he said, "I'll not ask."

I did not speak at once; I only stood and looked at him,
and thought many long thoughts, and felt the rapt silence
wrap me about.

I believed him. He would never ask me, or coerce me,
or force his will upon me. He did not possess me, he had
once said; he had wanted me to choose my happiness without pressure or temptation from him, he had determined
that I would know no regret because of him.

And now I understood that the choice had been mine,
that day in the glen when I thought he had refused me. I
loved him, but I had loved better the old dream, the
futile hope of peace and security. In my heart I wanted
both Monleigh and a safe placid future, I wanted him to
forego the perilous dangers of his life for the tranquil dullness of mine; and because he could not, because the two
could never be reconciled, I had traded Monleigh for a
dream that was no more substantial than a wish, a mere
whimsy, a bit of childish pretence.

And the day on the shore, when he left me behind,
when I fashioned so many foolish reasons for not sailing
with him, I had only strengthened his certainty that I was
unready for his love, too unsure of myself for him to be
sure of me.

I had thought him contradictory, as difficult to understand as his Highlands. But one may come to terms with
a land, however contradictory; and so had Monleigh come
to terms with himself. At his very core, the inviolable
center of his being, was a hard-won integrity which was
the true essence of the man. He had appraised himself
honestly, and in so doing had found the honesty of greater
value than the sum of the appraisal.

And in that steadfast integrity of his, I knew I had
found my strength, my salvation, my hope. For there was
only one certain peace, one security, one place for me in

all the world, and it was mine whenever I reached out for him and found him there. He had never failed me; he had always been there, he would ever be, and it had taken me a wretchedly long while to understand.

For me he was the clean yellow sun on a summer morn; he was the warmth of a leaping fire on a hard cold day, the ineffable joy of a snowflake caught in one's lashes to change the harsh world into a glittering prism of silver and white; he was the beauty of crimson roses in a copper bowl, of a heart-shaking sunset behind blue Highland hills; he was the fierce wild lilt in the blood that follows the skirl of pipes into battle, the blessed comfort of hot tears after a frozen moment of grief. All loveliness, all disquiet, all peace, all pain or happiness that I might know, all passions that might rule my heart, were mine because of him. He had given me the whole of life, a vital pulsing awareness, and he had given it without reservation or deceit, with a blunt masculine honesty untinged by the slightest guile; and if he had also taken, in the same manner, he had shown me in the taking that here was the man, however mortal and ungodly, that I would hitherto measure life by, and my world, to the end of my days.

"You are very grave," he said quietly. "Are you fighting another battle with your conscience?"

"My conscience has been sadly misplaced," I said, "and I think it past time. Twice over it has made me a coward, and I would not risk a third betrayal."

He stood quite still, not hurrying me.

"I am thinking of the proper way to ask you," I said, "for I dare not have you refuse me."

And suddenly I knew how it would be. They would conjecture, they would gossip, they would whisper all the evil tales and bring them alive again to prove their lies. But they would never know the truth.

They would not guess what I said when I asked him to take me with him, or how, instead of answering, he threw back his dark head and laughed, and took a long stride across the room, and closed his arms tightly around me. They, in their ignorance, would not imagine that we ran down the stairs of the tiny crooked inn, hand in hand like children, and laughed till the drunken sailors in the tavern raised their tankards and drank a toast to our mirth, and

neither of us looked back or cared that I had left behind
a sombre cloak and a purse of gold.

Perhaps someone will go to Torra, many years after,
and stand in the roofless keep, amidst the once-proud
stones which tumbled from the high walls only to surrender at last to the creeping lichen; and he will know
nothing of the passions which once touched the old gray
walls and the moors below, nothing of Simon, Earl of
Monleigh, and the girl, Anne Lindsay. He will wonder,
mayhap, why the castle stands deserted; and he will shiver,
and draw his cloak about him, and wish to be gone from
the desolate spot. He will not hear a thin gay thread of
sound, the faraway melody of a lute, nor heed the snatch
of laughter carried to him on the wind; he will turn his
back to the sea and never glimpse a dark-hulled ship
slipping past the headland to catch the morning wind in
its rakish sails.

We will be forgotten, no one will know how it happened
and no one will care.

But you who have read these words may, after all, see
him as I see him. You may nod your head and say, "Yes,
I understand why she loved him."

You will know, for I have told the truth of it all, what
happened at Torra in that dark year of Cromwell's rule,
and why we did as we did, and the strange passions ruling
the four of us, Walter Clennon, his sister Margaret, Monleigh, and myself. You will have decided for yourself, I
warrant, which of us was the sinner, after all.

And need you ask, now that the tale is done, what became of them, the two who loved so unwisely and so well?
Need you wonder, *How did it go with them, how was it
in the end?*

A PASSION
SO GREAT IT NEEDED
A NEW WORD TO DESCRIBE IT

LOVEFIRE
JULIA GRICE

*Afraid for her life, beautiful Brenna fled the lush emerald hills
of Ireland to seek the safety of the New World. For her marriage was a mockery that ended in one night—leaving her husband insane with thoughts of pursuit and revenge.*

*Ahead lay torment and untold adventure—among rogues and
pirates, on a slaveship bound for danger, and in the arms of
Kane Fairfield, the one man who could ever possess her spirit,
with a love only ecstasy could tame!*

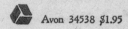 Avon 34538 $1.95

LF 10-77